THE
BRICKLAYER
OF ALBANY PARK

A NOVEL

TERRY JOHN MALIK

Blank Slate Press | St. Louis, Missouri

Blank Slate Press
Saint Louis, MO 63116

Blank Slate Press is an imprint of Amphorae Publishing Group, LLC
www.amphoraepublishing.com

For information, contact:
Blank Slate Press
4168 Hartford Street, Saint Louis, MO 63116
www.amphoraepublishing.com

Manufactured in the United States of America
Cover Design by Elena Makansi & Kristina Blank Makansi
Cover photography and graphics: Shutterstock
Set in Adobe Caslon Pro and Helvetica

Library of Congress Control Number: 2017947636

ISBN: 9781943075348

For Cathy, who gave me Michael.
For Michael, who gave us Amanda.
For Michael and Amanda, who gave us
Madeline Rose, Cecelia Grace, and Graham Michael,
and
for Maddie, CeCe, and the "Grammar"
who give us joy, day in and day out.

THE
BRICKLAYER
OF ALBANY PARK

A NOVEL

PROLOGUE
Detective Frank Vincenti

The local press dubbed him "The Bricklayer." When I first joined the violent crimes section of the Chicago PD, I played along and adopted the nicknames the press coined. That was four years ago, when I still had a wife and was able to sleep through the night.

But over time, I came to realize the callousness of it—naming a serial killer as if he were one of the boats at Belmont Harbor or a family pet. The man I was tracking was by all accounts a monster—a brutal killer who had bludgeoned and mutilated middle-aged men and then methodically buried them under piles of bricks in the peaceful Chicago neighborhood of Albany Park. I didn't know his real name, but for seven nightmare-filled months, I studied him.

When I wasn't interviewing construction workers and victims' families, I spent hours in the forensics lab. I stared at photos of his victims' empty chest cavities where he had left "mementos" for us. I wrapped myself in the blue polyethylene tarps he used as ritualistic shrouds, hoping their secrets would seep into my consciousness. Without donning evidence gloves, I sifted through construction debris and soil recovered from each crime scene, feeling what he felt as he scraped out shallow graves.

My partner, Sean Kelly, and I worked the streets and local bars until the odor of stale beer worked its way into our clothes. I spent exhausting coffee-fueled nights compiling and revising psychological profiles with my long-time friend and criminology mentor, Thomas Aquinas Foster. I traveled to Quantico to review FBI files, where I compared Foster's profiling with that of the Bureau's experts, looking for common denominators and patterns.

My leather sofa was littered with dog-eared psychology textbooks and psychiatric journals. Two red bricks from one of the crime scenes sat on my shower floor where every morning I took in the distinctive odor of wet clay and sand. My dining room walls were papered with crime scene photos, a matrix of common elements of victimology, the latest psych bureau profile, pictures of each victim retrieved from family photo albums, and a city map peppered with red and green pushpins.

During the day, I reconstructed the killings and the burials. At night, my dreams recreated the murders one by one until I jolted from my bed in a cold sweat. He was all I could think about. I knew him. I knew him, but not well enough to stop him.

PART ONE

CHAPTER 1
Detective Frank Vincenti

"Now look here, Detective Vincenti, I won't take no for an answer. You're spending Thanksgiving with us. We eat dinner at four, so you're expected here at noon."

Coming from Sean's mother, it had been more an order than an invitation and, if I'd learned anything from my four years as Sean Kelly's partner, South Side Irish mothers are to be obeyed. Besides, I didn't want to be alone for yet another holiday.

It would be the second Thanksgiving I'd spend with Sean's family. Last year, Beth had gone to Santa Barbara to be with her sickly mother, but I couldn't swing enough furlough days to make it anything more than an exhausting forty-eight hour turnaround. She knew I couldn't go, and I was pretty sure that's exactly what she intended. She repeated her little game again this year, and called just before I left for the Kellys'— not to wish me a happy Thanksgiving, but to issue an ultimatum. I told her we would deal with it when she returned and hung up. I refused to allow her to spoil my holiday.

During dinner, I enjoyed the Kelly family repartee: teenage cousins complaining about having to sit at the kids' table; Mr. Kelly, wearing an old gray checked vest and knit tie, recounting for his youngest daughter the days when the family was small enough to roast a single twelve-pound turkey; and Mrs. Kelly, still wearing a red-checked apron over her every-day house dress, insisting I eat more as she heaped mounds of dressing and mashed potatoes on my plate.

It was a far cry from my childhood Thanksgivings. After my mother was killed, my father continued to drink his way through holidays. More often than not, I ate Thanksgiving with the Protettore family who lived next door, and then returned home to find my father ranting in a drunken rage, spewing vulgar curses at my deceased mother and me. Eventually, I'd leave the Protettores' and wander the streets of Chicago's northwest side to avoid going home until I was sure he'd passed out.

I stood to help with the dishes, but Mrs. Kelly issued another one of her orders: "Sit. You men stay and swap lies about your golf games or whatever it is you lie about to each other these days."

Carrying a plate overflowing with pieces of pumpkin and mincemeat pie, one of Sean's brothers, Patrick, a Chicago Archdiocesan priest who had been studying in Rome for the last two years, pulled up a chair next to me. He was a tall, lanky fellow with red hair and a sea of freckles, and although he was probably twenty-five or twenty-six, he looked more like a high school senior.

"Mom says I'm supposed to talk to you." He repeated her words in a high-pitched tone and with just a touch of the brogue added for effect: "'Patrick William,' she said, 'go talk to Sean's partner—that Vincenti boy. It's your duty as a priest to fix what's ailing him.'"

"What's ailing me?"

"Don't worry." Patrick shrugged. "She's always trying to patch up troubled marriages. Oh, that's her diagnosis by the way."

Mrs. Kelly was no dummy. She already sensed what I refused to accept about my marriage. She wasn't buying the "sickly mother" excuse I'd used again this year to explain Beth's absence.

Before I could try to explain, Patrick continued, "Don't give it another thought." He paused as he studied his plate full of pie. "Most people get a little overwhelmed by the Kelly brood, but seems you handled us just fine. Jumped right into the debate about Mayor

Menendez's most recent run-in with the press. You probably didn't notice Sean glance at Dad who gave an approving nod."

"You've all made me feel at home. Your family is special."

"Sean used the same word to describe you—'special.' He claims you may be the best homicide investigator in Chicago."

Embarrassed, I looked down and twisted my water glass in my hand. I shook my head. "Sean tends to exaggerate."

He saw my dessert plate was empty, so he scraped his piece of mincemeat pie onto it. "Here, Mom knows I hate mincemeat. You eat it." He rearranged the pumpkin pie on his plate. "Oh, believe me, I know Sean is very capable of dishing out a load of B.S. with the best of 'em, but when I got home last week, all he could talk about was how you broke the Carlton case. I know my big brother—there's no bullshit coming out of that Mick cop's mouth when it comes to Detective Francis Vincenti."

"I do my job, just like every other cop."

Patrick reached across the table and retrieved a can of whipped cream. "Sean says you're not like other cops."

Not like other cops? Maybe.

It was by chance rather than design that I had come to wear a Chicago PD Detective's Star. Other kids in my neighborhood always seemed to know what they wanted to be when they grew up. My best friend, Tony Protettore, talked incessantly about becoming a Chicago cop. I'd listen to him, puzzled about how he could be so certain about a job and a career while he was still in junior high. Even in high school I had no idea about a career—any career—let alone one in law enforcement. I guess I lacked imagination. I just took life one day at a time, and my plans extended only to the end of the week. I figured a job was a job was a job. That's all. I had no goals, was totally without ambition, and didn't know why I needed either. That all changed when I met Thomas Aquinas Foster—a retired Chicago cop who possessed a troubled soul and his own brand of justice.

CHAPTER 2
Anthony

While I'm amused by what the press calls me—The Bricklayer—there's nothing amusing about what I do. And despite what the press and police say, I'm not insane. Not even close. The insane ones are the cowards who refuse to do what is necessary to protect the most innocent among us. I have the courage they lack. And the men I killed deserved to die. Every last one of them. No one should pity them or waste a moment on their knees praying for their wretched souls. But, you don't have to take my word for it. I'll tell you what I've achieved, and you can judge for yourself. I don't have enough time to tell you everything. For your own good, I won't tell you all of it. So, I'll start with Henry and the rainy night last November when I found him at a bar on the northwest side of Chicago, near Albany Park.

Standing across the street, just outside the reach of a streetlight, I watched the side door of Murph's Borderline Pub. The city's blue street cleaner moved slowly past me and down Damen Avenue, its stiff bristles whirling against the damp pavement. The Streets and Sanitation Department's temporary no parking posters affixed to light posts and parking meters forced Murph's patrons to park in the alley next to the neighborhood bar or in the parking lot of the church several store fronts down the street. Both areas were dimly lit, but the alley offered the privacy I would require. Ignoring the clank and screech of the overhead Brown Line 'L' cars, I glanced up to the night sky to gauge the cloud cover.

I watched, calmly and patiently. Sporting two days' worth of heavy, dark stubble, I was dressed for the night in paint-stained carpenter jeans, a gray hoodie, a dark colored ball cap and scuffed work boots. The evening's rain had turned the pavement from light gray to shiny black and brought with it a chill typical of a Chicago November night. But I welcomed it. People tend to mind their own business when it's cold and rainy.

I had chosen my target two hours earlier when I'd taken a seat on one of Murph's barstools, its vinyl seat cracked and duct-taped. Even before I ordered a drink, I had quickly become disgusted with the smell of stale beer and the banal chatter of an assortment of forklift drivers, mail carriers, and construction workers. Murph's was much like other Chicago bars I'd scouted, and the neighborhood was similar to other neighborhoods I'd visited in search of my next target. Its neon beer signs, glass block windows, and flagstone façade—once stylish in this neighborhood—were now outdated oddities. This part of the city was changing, too slowly for the young professionals flooding the area, too fast for the second-generation residents. The newcomers considered Murph's an anachronistic nuisance. The old timers sought refuge there. The bar offered cheap beer, old wooden floors that squeaked underfoot, and patrons who called each other by their first names. The regulars lived in the neighborhood and usually came straight from work— even today, the day after Thanksgiving. They carped about all things beyond their comprehension, voicing complaints in the vocabulary of the uneducated and misinformed. Murph's was the typical city dive bar where I could find yet another target.

Nursing cheap whiskey with too much ice, I'd watched the steady procession of work-weary men make their way to vacant seats, each greeting Murph with an almost imperceptible nod. I looked up from under the bill of my ball cap and studied the ruddy-faced regulars scattered around the bar and those ensconced in the worn booths squeezed together against the graffiti-scarred walls.

I first spotted the middle-aged man in the battered Irish gray tweed flat cap and dark green nylon jacket with "Henry" embroidered on a soiled patch under a company logo when he stepped through the front door. By the time Henry had tossed his cap on the table and slid into an already crowded booth, I had eliminated most of the other patrons. None looked as promising a target.

I glanced with feigned disinterest at Henry's reflection in the mirror. After downing a couple of shots and a few beers, he sat stone-faced as his companions shared a joke that seemed to be a mystery to him. He said little and drank a lot, his deep-set eyes focused only on the platoon of empty beer bottles on the table. His hands were dirty and heavily calloused, his hair gray and thinning on top. If there was a fire in the place, he looked like he'd be the last out, not as an act of heroism but more as a matter of indifference.

I tensed as Henry threw back another shot, said something to the other men in the booth, and started to stand. He'd walked in alone and looked like he was about to leave alone. He had the appearance and mannerisms of a man no one would miss, and although Henry looked like he was no stranger to bar fights, he was in no condition to offer resistance tonight. But when his legs wobbled beneath him, he sank back into his seat, and I let myself relax. There was plenty of time.

A stout, middle-aged man took a seat next to me, momentarily blocking my sight line to Henry. The stranger, a man who looked like he never missed a meal, wore a dark uniform with a badge peeking out of the zippered front of a dark blue jacket. I forced myself not to move away. The man signaled Murph for a drink, nodded up at the TV where Fox News was reporting on the president's trip to Europe, and then turned to me. "That son of a bitch ought to stay home and put all the goddamn Mexicans on buses. Send them all back is what I say."

The last thing I wanted to do that night was talk to a cop. I wasn't looking for conversation, especially with someone who could later identify me. If I moved to another barstool it might have called unwanted attention to me, so I looked away, pretending not to hear. I jiggled the ice in my glass and finished my drink, wincing at the taste of the house-brand whiskey. I'd seen all I needed. I stood, dug in my pants pocket for a handful of crumpled one-dollar bills, and tossed them on the bar. I eyed the bar's mirror one more time, checking to make sure Henry was still there, still drinking his boilermakers. As I headed for the door, I pulled my sweatshirt's hood up over my cap, and glanced back over my shoulder, taking one last look at Henry's booth next to the bar's side exit. Henry glanced over at me, our eyes met. I knew the look—I'd seen it before. I'd chosen well.

CHAPTER 3
Detective Frank Vincenti

I first encountered Foster (you don't meet Foster, you encounter him; he doesn't encounter you, he engages you) during my sophomore year at Northeastern Illinois University in the heart of the city near Pulaski and Brwn Mawr. I went to college for a single reason—to get out of my father's house. It was either that or join the Marines. College seemed safer and easier.

I was ill-prepared for college, partly because I was lazy and partly because I attended an over-crowded and under-staffed public high school where academic mediocrity flourished. Public school was my father's choice, not mine. Although most of my grade school classmates attended the smaller Jesuit college-prep school a few blocks from our house, my father insisted that I attend the local public school, claiming that because I was a "screw-up," the Jesuits would eventually expel me. His logic was simple: I might as well start where I'd wind up anyway.

Where I went to high school would not have mattered except that my only friend, Tony Protettore, was headed for the Catholic prep school. He and I had become friends even before first grade. I was shorter than most—still am—but back then it made me a target for the class bullies. Tony was always at my side on the playground, protecting me from their taunts. My jet-black hair and its stark contrast with my fair complexion—a combination that remains to this day—

somehow made me the butt of their jokes, but a quick glare from Tony silenced them. My father was already jealous of the time I spent at the Protettore house and wasn't about to provide another opportunity for me to increase my contact with Tony and his family, so he forced me into a cookie-cutter public school system where crowded hallways were patrolled by off-duty cops.

By sophomore year, Tony and his family had moved to Indiana. After he left, I had trouble making new friends. I didn't know what to say and usually wound up making some inappropriate remark that alienated everyone in earshot. It was just as well. I had no use for friendships in or out of school. I kept to myself. I preferred it that way.

I never was a good student. As if he was informing me that I was suffering from a terminal disease, my high school academic advisor cautioned me that the prospects of actually earning a degree were slim. I was barely in the top half of my class and had scored low on my ACT, but I met the minimum requirements for Northeastern, which many people derisively called 'Northeasy'. The tuition and room and board were manageable, and the size suited me. It was just big enough to allow me the anonymity I had become accustomed to. Whether or not I actually earned a degree wasn't important to me. I just wanted to get out of the house and be free of my father, free of his drunkenness, free of his beatings. That was all that mattered.

CHAPTER 4
Anthony

Murph's customers drifted out in twos and threes, having to get up early the next day to repeat the monotonous cycle that always led them back to the same old ratty booths and same old beat-up barstools. Many walked north toward the Damen 'L' station. Others headed toward the church lot down the block. A few stumbled toward their cars parked in the alley that ran alongside the building.

About fifteen yards from Murph's side door, the alley dead-ended at a chain link fence with green privacy slats. Topped by barbed wire, the fence surrounded a ComEd electrical substation housing transformers emitting a low-pitched buzzing hum that would act as concealing white noise. Where the rusted bottom of the chain link met crumbling pavement, an assortment of plastic garbage bags, grease-stained fast food wrappers, and empty beer cans were strewn about on a carpet of rain-slicked autumn leaves. It was there, at the end of the alley, where I had parked my camper and where I would guide Henry and lead him to a just punishment, as the apparition had demanded of me.

Adrenaline started to flow, I forced myself to be patient.

Finally, Henry staggered into the alley through Murph's side door. Alone. After a few wobbly steps, he steadied himself against one of the city's dumpsters lining the alleyway. When his weight caused the dumpster to slide away, he lost his balance and stumbled.

Time to move. I tugged my hood down so its edge hung over the bill of my baseball cap, shadowing my face. I surveyed the street and then crossed with deliberate strides, avoiding fresh rain puddles that looked like shiny black holes on the dark pavement. And then I stopped. The talkative, uniformed stranger emerged from Murph's front door. He paused, lit a cigarette, and headed toward the church parking lot. He caught sight of me and stopped, flicking his cigarette into the street.

"Hey you!"

Shit.

"Hold on a minute!" He walked straight toward me, but as he got closer, I breathed a sigh of relief. His uniform hat did not have the distinctive black and white checkerboard trim of the Chicago PD. He was nothing more than an aging, unarmed security guard—a rent-a-cop.

"Murph says you short-changed him."

Really? That's what this was about? I glared at him. Taking more crumpled singles out of my pants pocket, I threw them on the ground where they landed in a small puddle at his feet. "Here, now fuck off."

He froze. He peered at me and then slowly picked up the wet cash, wiped it on his pants and, without counting it, turned and walked toward the 'L' station instead of Murph's without another word. Asshole!

I resumed moving toward the alley and toward my prey, my pace still deliberate but more determined, faster. Again, I came to a sudden halt just outside the mouth of the alley. The side door had swung open, splashing light on the pavement where Henry was bent over, his hands on his knees. A tall, older man emerged from the doorway and approached Henry. I recognized him as one of Henry's drinking buddies from the crowded booth. He walked over to Henry and muttered what sounded like a question, but I couldn't make it out. Without looking up, Henry shook his head and shouted, "No! And, I don't give a fuck that it's raining!"

Henry's companion shrugged and went back inside, slamming the door behind him so hard that it bounced open leaving a sliver of light piercing the dark alley.

Relieved, I took a deep breath and slid into the darkness and isolation of the alley with its mixed odors of damp pavement, fresh vomit, and over-flowing dumpsters. The apparition had guided me here, guided me to Murph's. Guided me to Henry.

CHAPTER 5
Detective Frank Vincenti

I didn't have an easy time of it freshman year. I'd hoped college would provide a fresh start, that I could finally make a friend or two to replace Tony, and I thought I could handle the academics. Turned out, I was wrong. About everything.

After Christmas dinner at my aunt's in De Kalb, I casually mentioned I might drop out and get a job. Without looking away from the NBA game on television, my father said, "I'm not surprised; you've always been a quitter." He took his eyes off the game just long enough to look at me. "And, don't think for a minute that you're moving back in with me."

Move back in with him? Hell, that's the last thing I'd ever do. I'd live on the street before I set foot back in that house. Calling me a quitter? He was the walking, talking definition of the word. As a child I was eager to gain his approval; but at that moment, I was eager to prove him wrong. I decided then and there that I'd earn my degree just to spite the bastard.

I remained on campus during the summer between freshman and sophomore years, enrolling in two classes so I wouldn't be required to move out of the dorm, and worked in the university cafeteria to have beer money. I wasn't interested in much and was angry about everything. I drank a lot and often, something I had started in high school. For me, alcohol wasn't something to drink—it was a place to hide.

During the fall semester of my sophomore year I continued to just get by. I'd wake up some mornings with no memory of the night before, and was plagued by unrelenting headaches. Was I drinking too much? Probably. I didn't have trouble with drinking—it had trouble with me. I stumbled my way through the fall semester in a hazy dream state.

Back then, I was a habitual procrastinator. I waited until the last week of the fall semester to log in to the university's registration website to select classes for the spring semester. I chose classes based on what time they met—the later, the better—and how short the reading list was. I always looked for shortcuts and ways to avoid work. I was almost finished filling out my schedule, but I wanted to enroll in at least one more "A/B" class—one that required minimum work and in which the professor had a history of awarding a grade no less than a B.

My most reliable sources for academic counseling were the basketball players who lived in the dorm. At Northeastern, basketball was king, and its players were princes. I found a couple of them in the third-floor study hall where they were "studying" the latest edition of Madden NFL. I asked about an easy class that would guarantee a good grade. Without looking up from their controllers, and in almost a single voice, they recommended a criminal justice course taught by Thomas Aquinas Foster.

I returned to my room and brought up the course synopsis on my beat-up laptop. It was perfect! There was no reading list. The syllabus listed movies and "instructor-supplied materials," whatever that meant, and the final grade was to be determined by attendance and a take-home final exam. I really didn't care that I had no interest in the subject matter—just as long as it required minimum effort on my part and there was a B in my future. I registered for the last spot. Then I shut down my computer, grabbed a beer from my mini-fridge, and popped it open. I toasted myself, satisfied I could coast through another semester. I couldn't have foreseen that after taking Foster's class, I would never again take the easy way out or look for short cuts of any kind.

CHAPTER 6
Anthony

I leaned over Henry and put my outstretched hand on his shoulder. In a voice slightly louder than a whisper, I said, "Hey, mister, you don't look so good."

He had his back to the street, and was bent over at the waist. Wiping vomit from his chin with the back of his hand, he twisted slightly and looked up. "Huh? What do you want?"

Looking at his sallow features and then down at the puddle of vomit, I shook my head. "That piss Murph calls whiskey would make anyone sick."

Speaking slowly, apparently trying not to slur his words, Henry asked, "Do I know you?"

"Nah, I'm just tryin' to be a Good Samaritan."

"Be a Good Samaritan somewhere else."

"Look. I'm offering to lend some help, buddy—by the looks of you, you need it."

He ignored me. Obviously disoriented, he took a step toward the back of the alley but stopped suddenly and leaned over, readying himself to retch again. When he finished, he straightened up, removed his cap and tilted his head back, letting the light rain act as a cold shower against his face.

"Buddy, you're in bad shape. You need to get in out of the rain."

Without looking over at me, he growled, "I'm fine. Lemme be." He blinked several times as if clearing his vision then grabbed his crotch. "Gotta piss." He unzipped his pants and a trickle ran down his pant leg. "Damn it—gotta go, but can't!"

Don't worry my friend, I'm going to fix that for you. I surveyed the area again. Light spilled into the alley from Murph's partially opened side door, so I took a couple of steps back and eased it closed. A full recycling dumpster sat to the left of the door; I rolled it to block the door and locked its wheels in place. There was a single floodlight atop the boarded-up grocery store across the alley, but it illuminated only a small portion of the top of the brick wall where a billboard used to be. Otherwise the alley was dark, which suited me just fine. Darkness was my ally.

Earlier in the evening, I'd spotted two surveillance cameras that might later provide an incriminating image, and I'd seen a city traffic camera at the corner down the street, but it hung by a single cable and was clearly inoperable. Although there were cameras mounted on 180-degree swivels at the 'L' station, the entrance to the alley, like the storefront across the street where I'd stood waiting, was a blind spot.

Henry zipped up and steadied himself, one hand against the alley wall.

"Look, like it or not, you're going to need help gettin' home." Without waiting for a response, I placed a comforting hand on his shoulder.

Henry turned away and shrugged off my hand. "I told you, lemme be. I'm fine."

"Sure you are. That's why you got puke drippin' off your chin and you're headed for a ComEd station you think is the 'L'."

"What?" Henry peered down the alley and saw that I was right. "I just got turned 'round, that's all."

CHAPTER 7
Detective Frank Vincenti

It was rumored Foster was forced to take an early retirement from Chicago PD; in other words, he was a loser and, like others who could not make it in the "real world," had sought refuge in academia. At the time, I didn't know much about him, nor did I care to. Eventually, however, I came to know him like few others knew him, and over the years, I was allowed rare glimpses of his troubled soul.

Foster dispatched his graduate assistant the first day of class to explain the ground rules. She arrived late and explained that our grades would be determined by attendance and a one-question, take-home final exam, adding, "Unless you are a complete dolt, you will receive at least a B." She continued, "Foster has his own set of rules. Never ask questions in class; instead, send him an email and don't expect an answer unless your question interests him. And he doesn't hold regular office hours and doesn't generally make himself available to students outside of class, either." With a touch of sarcasm in her voice, she wished us luck and dismissed the class.

During the first two weeks of the semester, the entire fifty minutes of class were consumed with short clips from movies that Foster's GA projected against the beige cinder block wall of the classroom— scenes from *Deranged*, *Badlands*, and *In Cold Blood*. Foster provided no comments, shared no insights, and gave no lectures. While the movie clips ran, he positioned himself in the shadows near the front corner of the classroom. He stood rigid, his arms folded in front of him, and with a scowl on his face. It was difficult to gauge his age—late forties, perhaps. His full head of dark, thick hair was slightly graying at the temples. His brow was wrinkled, and he always seemed to have dark circles under his hazel eyes, but his tailored suits highlighted a youthful waist, a barrel for a chest, and wide shoulders on a six-foot frame. Occasionally, my eyes wandered from the movie images on the wall over to where he stood, and although he was perfectly still, his eyes were constantly searching the classroom—studying our faces.

On Monday morning of the third week, Foster's GA arrived early and set up a slide projector connected to a laptop, and then sat silently waiting for Foster. As he entered the classroom, Foster flipped the classroom lights off and nodded to the GA. Without explanation, she began to project crime scene and autopsy photos of bloodied, and sometimes mutilated, corpses on the front wall. Each time she pressed the Enter key on her laptop, the image on the wall faded to black and a new, equally horrific, photo splashed on the wall.

All the while, Foster continued his silent vigil in the front corner of the dark classroom, watching us from the shadows with an increased intensity, but never revealing his impression of our reactions to the grisly images. Foster and the GA repeated this show for the remainder of the week.

Then, Foster began telling his stories. He recounted violent crimes, explained the manner of death, and posed rhetorical questions regarding motive, pausing only to take a drink from his ever-present Starbucks paper cup. He entertained no questions, ignored raised hands, and glared with disdain at students foolish enough to offer an unsolicited comment. He alternated between his stories and a routine of teasing the class with more graphic crime scene photos, gauging our reactions. He explained the behavioral habits of sociopaths and psychopaths, putting the photographs in context.

I studied the photos that filled the front wall of the classroom and thought: This is what the killer saw, just before he turned and walked away, flush with the rush of adrenaline and indifferent to what the carnage would mean to others. What else did the killer think? What else did the killer feel? And if, as Foster claimed, every crime scene photo was like a jigsaw puzzle, then I saw in bold contrast the outlines of every tiny, oddly shaped, interlocking piece. I got an adrenaline rush with every new photo, every new story, every new killer.

As if he was speaking to me, and only to me, he told stories of both the victims and the killers, some of which were stories of torture and murder beyond what any human should have to bear. Foster reveled in relating tales of what he described as "monsters come to life, disguised as your neighbor who works in the mall or your cousin's friend who repaired your furnace late one night last winter." He tried to make his stories real for us by splashing gruesome crime scene photos on the front wall and, with a faraway look, asking how we would react if the victim was a loved one, maybe even a spouse.

By spring break, my odd fascination with the world of killers, their motives, and psychological afflictions had became addictive. The "why and how" of my fascination were lost on me. I couldn't explain it then, and I cannot fully explain it even now, but I knew that Foster was responsible for planting the seeds. Energized, my perspective on almost everything and everyone I encountered was different. I was different.

My fixation on my father's taunts and drunkenness faded, and by the time I started my senior year, I had changed my major to Justice Studies and had taken every course Foster taught. I enrolled in all of the criminal justice classes and seminars Northeastern offered. I even enrolled in psychology courses that focused on bio-physiological afflictions and abnormal psychology.

During the summer between my junior and senior years, I participated in a four-week extern program at the Cook County morgue, where I indulged my imagination as I witnessed autopsies of homicide victims. Classmates were puzzled, and asked what about the morgue intrigued me so much. I didn't have a good answer.

CHAPTER 8
Anthony

I'd parked my beat-up camper in the last spot in the alley, closest to the fence. It was a fifteen-year-old Toyota pickup that had been converted into a makeshift camper using a small homemade fiberglass slide-in topper. It had seen better days: cracks in the weather-worn fiberglass were mended with duct tape, rust stains wept from the two small painted-over windows, and its wheel covers were missing, victims of potholes. The pickup had been repainted a drab green that had faded and needed a touch-up—a project started but never finished, leaving the passenger door with a dark orange primer spot just below the window.

The camper stood only seven feet off the ground, which allowed me to park in most public multi-story lots and fit easily into a garage with a standard size door. There was a five-foot access door at the rear of the rig, and the bumper had been extended to provide a step up to the truck bed floor. I could hardly stand upright inside; it was cramped and always smelled of mildew and sweat. A five-foot long couch sat along one wall, and a bench with a full-length, pull-down cot above it sat opposite. The bench doubled as a storage bin for tools and gear. Dark, carmine-colored streaks had stained the mangy carpet.

The rain picked up. Lightning flashed silently over Lake Michigan. Henry tried to regain his bearings but slipped on the wet pavement, shooting a hand out to grab the now-stationary dumpster. His tweed cap landed in a puddle. When he reached down for it, he swayed, struggling to regain his balance. Without looking up, Henry surrendered. "OK. OK. Jus' help get me to the 'L'."

That was easier than I thought.

"Sure, but you should sit down for a few minutes. Clear your head. And we need to clean you up. You're a mess. Passengers on the 'L' will throw you back on the platform with that slop all over you and smellin' like you do. I have some towels in my truck." I nodded toward the back corner of the alley. "It's right over there."

Bleary-eyed, Henry looked back at the pickup. "OK. OK."

I moved to his side, lifted his arm, and placed it over my shoulder, then circled his waist with my other arm. I felt him shift his weight to lean against me as thunder rumbled in the distance followed by a silent burst of sheet lightning. A storm was coming. I knew better than to hurry though. Haste always led to a blunder, and the cops loved it when a guy like me made a mistake. I was too smart for that, too careful to make a mistake. I glanced back at the mouth of the alley. We were still alone. Walking slowly and almost in unison, we moved deeper into the darkness.

Startled by the sudden clink of bottles against pavement behind me, I paused and released my grip on Henry's waist, sliding my hand down into my pants pocket, ready to remove my folding knife and flip it open. I snickered when a large mutt appeared beside me, stopped, gave Henry a sniff, and then moved on. We made it to the back of the truck without another interruption.

"Here, sit for a second," I said, pushing him down gently on the bumper and opening the door to trap him between the camper, the door, the fence, and the alley wall. I'd backed the truck up to the fence so that when the camper door swung open, there wouldn't be enough space for a man to squeeze through.

"I'll grab some towels to clean you up."

Henry glared at me. "I don't wanna sit—I gotta get home." He looked back at the alley. "I'm feeling better. I can find my way." Henry pushed himself to his feet and tried to slip between the fence and the open door.

"I don't think so." I grabbed his right shoulder and hooked my right arm around his neck, forcing his head into the crook of my elbow. With my left hand over his left shoulder, I clasped my hands together, and began to squeeze, applying just enough pressure to the carotid arteries on both sides of his neck to cut off the oxygen-enriched blood from the heart to the brain. I knew what I was doing. I had done it before. Thirty seconds later, Henry went limp.

CHAPTER 9
Detective Frank Vincenti

I was anxious to engage Foster one-on-one. I had dozens of theories I wanted put to the test. But as Foster's GA had warned us that first day, he did not make himself available to students, and he didn't answer any of my emails. I often ran to catch up with him on his way out of class, pelting him with questions as he walked across campus. He ignored me. Undaunted, I tried to corner him when he was with other faculty members, hoping that he would be too embarrassed to be disdainful in front of his peers. Sometimes that worked and he spat one- or two-word answers looking both bored and irritated at the same time.

I finally got more than one-word grunts and dismissive scowls when, on the Monday after the fall break of my senior year, I followed him into NEIU's administrative building. I stood in the lobby at the foot of the main stairway and watched as he climbed the winding structural glass staircase to the third-floor faculty offices. He carried a black leather portfolio tucked under his right arm, his camel hair overcoat was folded over his left arm, and in his left hand he clutched his trademark hounds tooth bucket hat. He had ascended only four or five stairs when I called after him and, instead of a question, I issued a challenge: "He who fights with monsters should be careful lest he thereby become a monster!"

He stopped abruptly, turned, and sized me up. Squinting, he looked down to where I was standing. "I beg your pardon?"

"He who fights with monsters should—"

"Yes. And the rest of Nietzsche's Aphorism 146 reads: 'And when you gaze long into an abyss, the abyss also gazes into you.' A trite allusion, young man. What's your point?"

Refusing to be put off by him this time, I asked, "Does it take a monster to catch a monster?"

He stood silent for a moment, then moved down to the bottom step and, with a look on his face that revealed equal measures of distraction and inquisitiveness, asked, "What's your name?"

"Vincenti."

"I asked your name, not part of it."

"Francis Angelo Vincenti. Everyone calls me Frank." I never included the "Jr." part.

He stepped off the staircase, stood even with me, and said, "Interesting that you failed to include the suffix 'Junior'."

Startled that he knew who I was, I just nodded.

"Well, after all this time you finally figured out what to say that actually caught my attention. I am disappointed that it took so long."

Foster paused, presumably waiting to see if I appreciated the subtle quality of his statement. I did. "I have questions—"

"I know you do. I presume, however, that by now you have refined your questions—those you emailed me last year were interesting but quite sophomoric." He paused, no doubt to let his criticism sink in, and then he continued, "I might be able to make some time to listen, Francis."

I cringed at the sound of my first name—I hated it, but couldn't bring myself to correct him. I replied, "Yes, Professor."

"No one calls me Professor. The university pays me as an 'Instructor.' It's best that you simply address me as 'Foster,' as everyone else does." He paused, looking me over a second time, and, apparently having made a decision, he added, "We can meet from time to time at the Starbucks at the Student Union, and I will listen to your questions. Can you afford to buy me a cup of coffee at our meetings?"

"Yes."

"Then that will be the price of admission. No coffee, no meeting. Understood?"

"Got it."

"No. I asked if you understood. I am not interested in what you got."

"I understand."

He turned and resumed his ascent up the glass staircase and, looking back over his shoulder, he said, "Tomorrow, 8:00 a.m., at the Student Union. I'll have the Columbian blend—a venti, in a double cup. Have it waiting for me."

CHAPTER 10
Anthony

Henry wasn't dead. Not yet. Between the booze and the lack of blood to his brain, I figured I had at least forty minutes, plenty of time to drive to the safety of the garage where I stored the pickup and where Henry would pay for his sins. With my hands under his armpits, I positioned him so his back rested against the truck's bumper, and then dragged him up and into the camper. I flipped him onto his stomach, brought his hands behind his back, wrapped duct tape around his wrists and ankles, and then taped his mouth shut. That would hold him until I was ready to deal with him. I moved around Henry's limp body, down the steps to the alley, locking the door behind me.

I slipped between the truck's rear fender and the brick wall and opened the driver's door just wide enough to slide in. Large raindrops bounced onto the front seat of the truck cab as I pushed back my hood and took off my baseball cap. Shaking the rain off, I set my cap on the towel covering my .38 Special tucked into the cup holder, and then I stopped, staring at the cap.

"Shit."

I pictured Henry lying on the floor of the camper and realized his gray tweed cap was missing. I peered through the rain-spotted windshield, but couldn't see it. Should I go get it or risk leaving it there? What difference does it make? No, it's the small things that lead cops to killers. No, go get it.

I got out and slid between the front of my truck and the rear of the van parked in front of me. The alley was still empty. Walking briskly toward Murph's side door, I spotted the cap lying in a shallow puddle about ten feet ahead. Just then, the bar's door banged against the dumpster. I froze. It banged again and light snuck out into the alley. A man swore and tried to push the door open, but the dumpster didn't budge. One more time, the door banged against the dumpster's steel frame, sending the sound echoing off the opposite wall. Finally, the door closed, and the alley grew silent. I snatched Henry's cap from the dirty puddle and turned back toward the truck. Tempted to break into a run, I forced myself to walk casually, my slow pace belying my fear of being discovered, even though I knew my fear was unfounded. Stupid really. No one would suspect I had an unconscious man bound and gagged in my camper. I slipped back into the cab, started the engine, and flipped on the windshield wipers to their fastest setting. I sat in the dark and took several deep breaths trying to regain my composure. I closed my eyes and pictured what I had in store for Henry. The only noise was the pinging of heavy raindrops against the truck's roof and the swish and thump of the wipers. And Henry's screams. But they were only in my imagination.

CHAPTER 11
Detective Frank Vincenti

I met Foster the following morning. He had taken the chair facing out toward the dark tinted window. I sat opposite him. I had already placed his coffee on his side of the table, to his left, far from his bucket hat. I started to ask a question, but he stopped me. "I'll let you know when you may ask your questions."

He removed the coffee cup's plastic lid, placed it on the table, and pushed it aside. I waited. "Francis, a young man and woman are sitting at the table immediately behind me."

He was looking over my shoulder. I assumed he saw their reflection in the window behind me. "What are they talking about?"

"Well, I can't really hear them."

"Francis, what are they talking about?"

It took me a couple of seconds to comprehend the meaning of his question. Looking over Foster's shoulder, I took a moment longer to study the couple. "They're breaking up."

"And who is initiating the break-up?"

Trying to be inconspicuous, I took another look. "She is."

"The basis of that deduction?"

"He reached across the table. She didn't take his hand. She came without books. He has a laptop, a notebook, and a textbook. His coat is hanging on the back of his chair. She still has her coat on, although she has removed her hat and gloves. She seems to be all business. He is showing some stress."

"I don't see a hat. Nor do I see gloves."

"Her hair is matted down and there is a circular ridge or indentation in her hair."

"What about the gloves?"

"It's too cold for her not to have worn gloves."

Foster shook his head slightly. "Her hands would be red if she did not wear gloves. What do her hands look like?"

"I can't see her hands. She has them in her lap under the table."

"Then you have no basis to conclude that she wore gloves, true?"

"But it's freezing outside—can't I assume that?"

"No. There is a difference between assumptions and deductions. You make deductions based upon what you see or know, not what you assume." He took a drink and continued. "Otherwise, acceptable observations. Now, Francis, which one is capable of murder?"

"What?"

"You heard the question, did you not?"

I sneaked another look at the couple. Reluctantly, I shook my head. "I don't know—how can I tell?"

Foster took out a small slip of paper from his pocket on which he had scrawled his phone number and slid it over to me, saying, "When you determine which of them is capable of murder, call me, and we will schedule another session." He got up, slipped on his overcoat, and left, waiting until he was out of the shop to pull his houndstooth hat firmly down above his ears. The first session lasted less than ten minutes.

Two days later I called him, explained my theory that both were capable of murder, and described the circumstances under which each could resort to violence in the relationship. He seemed satisfied with my answer. "Tomorrow, 8:00 a.m.," and hung up.

For three days a week over the next month, he continued testing my powers of observation and deduction, assigning homework, and requiring a phone call to schedule the next session. In late January, at our first session of the week, he approached the table without removing his coat, hat in hand. He didn't sit down. He set a thick Redweld folder file on the table, pointed to it and said, "Read the file. Prepare a memorandum no longer than two pages, single-spaced. Summarize only the relevant evidence and list your conclusions. Call me when you are done." He picked up his coffee, took a sip, and headed for the door.

It took me a week. The organization of the file, the many technical terms, and the report's format were foreign to me. I felt like I had been thrown into a maze and wondered if I'd ever find my way out. I went through at least a dozen drafts before I produced a memo I thought Foster would find acceptable.

I called him and arranged a session for the following day. This time, he removed his coat, his bucket hat, and a pair of leather gloves, laying them all on the empty chair at the table. He eyed the cup of coffee I had placed on the table, sat down, and picked up my memo. About thirty seconds into his review, he looked up at me with a slight smirk, took a sip of his coffee, shook his head, and resumed reading. Using an expensive-looking pen, he wrote comments and questions in the margins. He pushed it back across the table. "Your writing skills need considerable work. Call me when you have addressed my substantive notations."

That type of session continued throughout the winter. Foster would stop at "our table" just long enough to pick up the previous week's Redweld file and my latest memo, hand me a new file, along with the previous week's memo full of corrections and questions, and collect his coffee. Slowly, my memos were returned with fewer edits, but with more questions scribbled in the margins. As winter turned to spring, his questions became increasingly disturbing.

CHAPTER 12
Anthony

"Dammit!" Still rattled, I'd put the truck in reverse and, without using my side view mirror, backed up too far, hitting the fence and scraping the rear fender against the brick wall. My mind raced. What if someone heard the scrape of metal against brick? It was loud enough. What if some nosy s.o.b. came to investigate? I could say no, of course. Unless it was a cop. What would I do then? I couldn't just pull away and make the cops chase me. The damn camper was too slow for that. I looked down at the towel covering the .38 in the cup holder. My last resort.

I shifted into drive and pulled out into the center of the alley. As I passed Murph's side door, I noticed that the dumpster was still where I'd left it. I eased the truck out toward the street, pausing just beyond the sidewalk to eye the foot traffic in both directions. To the left, the street was empty, and to my right, beyond Murph's, a few pedestrians, umbrellas up, were making their way to the 'L' station.

I pulled onto Damen, drove the mile or so to Irving Park Road, and headed west. At the first intersection on Irving I stopped as the traffic light changed from yellow to red, tapping my fingers on the steering wheel and picturing what Henry would look like in a few short hours. Lost in thought, I didn't notice the flashing blue light in my driver's side mirror.

The blue and white Chicago PD cruiser pulled up alongside me and stopped even with my truck. When I realized they were looking at me, I slid my right hand from the steering wheel and slipped it under the towel, wrapping my fingers around the grip of the .38. The police officer on the passenger side of the squad car lowered his window and signaled that I should do the same. I grasped the .38 tightly and complied.

"There a problem, officer?"

The officer called over, "You must be in a hurry, sir."

I shook my head. I had been watching my speed—that couldn't be it.

"No, officer. In this weather, I was bein' extra careful. I'm sure I was goin' the speed limit."

"Sir, your headlights aren't on. I'll give you the benefit of the doubt and assume that in your rush to get out of the rain, you forgot to turn them on. Are they operational?"

I looked down at the truck's panel. "Now that was stupid," I said to no one in particular. I flipped them on and looked over at the officer.

The officer gave a thumbs up and turned off the flashing light bar. As the cruiser pulled away, my thoughts returned to Henry and a long forgotten lesson from my childhood parish priest: "Vengeance is mine sayeth the Lord." He was wrong. It's mine.

CHAPTER 13
Detective Frank Vincenti

I waited for Foster outside Starbucks at a table on the brick patio that was crowded with students taking advantage of the first spring-like day of the season. Warm weather had surprised Chicagoans during the first week of March when the sun reappeared after another long winter of gray skies and mounds of snow. It was only a tease. I knew Chicago weather. Bone-chilling days would surely return, and we hadn't seen the last of the snow.

Foster arrived only a few minutes after I had placed his coffee on the opposite side of the table, where he had a view of the Student Union's courtyard. Surprisingly, he came empty-handed—no Redweld file, and no memo. He nodded but said nothing as he eased into the patio chair. He was in his usual attire: a blue blazer, a light blue pinstriped shirt with a red tie, and gray slacks with pressed creases that you could cut yourself on. For the longest time, Foster and I sat there in silence, each of us holding our coffee, taking an occasional sip, and enjoying the temporary respite from bone-chilling winds.

"Francis, tell me about your parents."

I didn't even try to hide my contempt for his question. "There's nothing to tell. Mom was killed in a car accident when I was four. I hardly remember her."

"And your father?"

"He lives on the northwest side near Grand and Oak Park Avenue, in the same cramped house where he was born."

"And you grew up in that house?"

I nodded.

Foster pursed his lips and squinted, looking down at his coffee cup. "That's a working-class neighborhood. Old houses—classic Chicago brick bungalows—originally populated by European immigrants in the years before World War I. Mostly Catholic, mostly Italian, Polish, and Irish, but changing now with a steady influx of Hispanics."

"I suppose so."

"You could take the CTA from there to campus, but you live in a dorm. Your father's choice or yours?"

"Mine."

"Did he approve?"

"Never asked. He was anxious to be rid of me, and I was just as anxious to leave." I was trying to find a way to move onto something else.

"It would be less expensive to live at home."

My attempt to deflect the questions with one- and two-word answers wasn't working. "The expense doesn't matter. My grandfather set aside money for a college fund. It was intended for my father, but Grandpa Angelo decided that my father had neither the aptitude nor the ambition for college. So Grandpa earmarked the college fund for his first-born male grandson. That's me."

"Like you, your father was an only child?"

Impatient, I sat back in my chair and pushed it about a foot away from the table. "Yeah."

"Did he remarry?"

I looked up, starting to show my aggravation. "No."

"Who raised you then?"

I wanted to blurt out, "None of your fucking business!" But I would never use that kind of language with Foster. "Aunt Anna, my mother's unmarried sister. She moved into our basement apartment, and then suddenly one day in the spring of my freshman year of high school, she packed her bag, wished me luck, and, without explanation, returned to her brother's farm in DeKalb."

"You never got along with your father, did you?"

It was more a statement than a question. I didn't respond. He must have taken my silence as an implicit "yes."

"What does your father do?"

"When he's sober? He does odd jobs for a local contractor and some auto repairs for a few extra bucks."

"I take it he is an alcoholic."

"He's a drunk. He used to be a Chicago fireman, an engineer—that's the guy who drives the fire truck. He showed up for duty once too often stinking of liquor, unable to drive his rig, and his buddies couldn't cover for him anymore. He was canned. He got what he deserved."

Foster showed no reaction and sat silent for a moment.

I finally summoned the courage to end the questioning. "Look, I'm flattered that you're curious about me, but none of this is relevant to our sessions."

Foster snapped back, "First, you're not flattered; you're annoyed. Second, I am not curious; curiosity lacks discipline. And I will determine what is necessary to advance your education." He placed his coffee cup down in front of him, slid it to the side, and asked, "What is your worst fear, Francis?"

I exhaled in frustration. Suddenly, one of those Chicago March gusts of wind kicked-up and blew my half-empty coffee cup off the table. It bounced and tumbled along the patio bricks. I looked over at it, but made no effort to retrieve it.

"Francis, what is your worst fear?"

I lied. "I suppose the same as everyone else—dying."

Foster wasted no time. "And yet your left wrist bears a two-inch scar, from the looks of it, self-inflicted. Too ragged to be a razor, so probably done with a dull box cutter. And from the way it's healed, I'd guess, it was done approximately four years ago."

So that's what this was about. The son of a bitch! Why play a game of twenty questions with me? Rather than look away embarrassed, I glared at him. But before I could speak, images of my father screaming at me when he found me on the bathroom floor filled my head, and his taunting in the emergency room for my cowardice in "not finishing the job" echoed in my memory. Memories I tried so hard to forget. Foster had gone too far. In one motion, I stood and, with the back of my legs, pushed my chair behind me, toppling it over. The chair clanged against the paver bricks, turning heads of those near us.

"That's enough. We're done!"

Without waiting for Foster to respond, I walked away and lost myself in the stream of students hustling to class.

CHAPTER 14
Anthony

I pulled into the alley, turned off the headlights, and dropped my speed to fifteen. Unlike the alley at Murph's, this one was well lit and relatively clean. It was lined with one- and two-car garages that sat at the rear of twenty-five-foot-wide city lots. I headed for a garage in the middle of the block where I intended to spend some quality time with Mr. Henry. The garage where I stored the camper was original to the 1920s-style brick bungalow that sat on the front of the lot, but the garage bore scars of modernization. A previous owner had altered it, adding fluorescent lighting, an electric overhead door opener, a five-thousand-watt space heater, an exhaust fan, and a drain. The drain, likely added to permit the owner to wash his car indoors in the winter, was located in the center of the garage floor.

The rain had stopped, leaving the windshield streaked with the blurred streaks of wiper blades long overdue for replacement. I squinted, eying the cars parked on garage aprons as I navigated around puddles and potholes. I watched for any activity, and gripped the steering wheel just a little tighter when I saw a neighbor, about thirty yards ahead on my right, lift the lid of a city-supplied refuse container. I tapped the brakes, but kept going as he dumped a couple of over-stuffed brown plastic bags into the container. I checked my side view mirror as I passed, but he never looked up, and soon disappeared behind the wooden gate to his yard.

Farther down the alley, I spotted what looked like a flash of fluorescent light creating a rectangular white sheet on the alley's pavement. I came to a stop ahead of the rectangle of light. At that moment, I heard the automatic garage door moan and close as the sheet of light slowly disappeared into the garage.

I drove past the empty lot next to my garage and pressed the door opener clipped to the driver's-side visor. The peeling and cracked wood paneled door haltingly responded to the signal and began its slow ascent. This time, I waited until it was fully opened before pulling in. The roof of the camper and the damn door frame bore reminders of the times I had been too anxious to spend time with a target.

I brought the truck to a stop just inches short of the window that faced the backyard. I depressed the remote control device again and waited until the door clanked closed with a groan and a thud against cracked cement. I stared straight ahead at the two painted-over windowpanes and could see the glow of a dim light from a window in my basement apartment. Had I left a light on?

I took a deep breath and reminded myself I was in no rush. I had rushed other times and made mistakes, mistakes that deprived me of the level of gratification I wanted. But they didn't ruin the whole experience. I could still hear the screams and see the look of terror in their eyes. I had to settle for that.

CHAPTER 15
Detective Frank Vincenti

I found myself sitting in the dark, on the floor in a corner of my dorm room, clutching my legs pulled up tight to my chest. The pounding of a crushing headache and the sound of rain pelting my window woke me. My rain-soaked jeans, sweatshirt, socks, and underwear were strewn on the floor around me. My desk clock read 10:00 p.m.

Confused, I struggled to recall what I had done after I ran from Foster and from the painful memories his questions had evoked. Nothing came to me. The sole image that lingered in my head was of a patio chair up-ended on the deep red-brown paver bricks of the Student Union courtyard. Exhausted, I pulled a blanket from my bed, curled up there on the floor, and had a fitful night's sleep.

For the rest of the week I skipped classes, stayed in my room and slept. The headaches continued, and I lost track of time. I had no appetite, but when I did get hungry, I ate from the vending machines in the first-floor lounge. My room was littered with discarded food wrappers and empty beer cans. I saw no reason to shower or shave. I spiraled into a deeper and deeper depression as I kept asking myself the same old questions. I had experienced episodes like this before, but this time it hit me with an increased intensity—it felt like a giant thumb pressing hard against my head and chest.

One day—I can't remember which—during my self-imposed

isolation, I sat at my desk composing a handwritten note to whoever might find it. I read and re-read what I had written. I didn't finish the note—it wouldn't matter. Instead, I looked down at the mini-fridge that sat next to my desk. I flipped it over, exposing its bottom panel where, three years earlier, I had taped one of my father's handguns that I had taken with me when I moved out. I stared at the gun and pictured putting it into my mouth and pulling the trigger. I imagined the taste of the steel barrel and could almost smell the dried oil used to clean it. I paused and stepped back from it, and from the temptation. I sat on the edge of my bed. I ran my finger over the scar on my left wrist and recalled that night in the emergency room when I was too embarrassed to even look at the doctor and nurse who tended to the wound. My world had changed since the night I tried to escape using a box cutter. Foster had changed it.

I needed to talk to someone. I was estranged from what little family remained, and I had made no friends. There was only Foster. Just Foster. Late on a Thursday night, I called him. "Can we—?"

"Tomorrow at eight, as usual."

CHAPTER 16
Anthony

I can't remember how long I sat in the truck, but when I finally felt composed, I grabbed my .38 from the cup holder, stuffed it in the muff pocket of my hoodie, and got out. Inhaling the familiar damp, musty odor of the old garage, I leaned against the truck's door, pressing my forehead against the cool, wet window.

I'd taken the flourescent tubes out of the overhead fixture so no light would leak into the alley or be seen by my neighbors from their back porches. I waited until my eyes adjusted to the darkness. I would work from the glow of the rusted Coleman kerosene camping lantern I kept for nights like this. It produced a dim yellow light that provided all the illumination I needed.

Listening to the comforting hum of the dented chest freezer that stood in the front corner of the garage, I moved around to the rear of the camper with the lantern in hand, reviewing my mental checklist with every step—the tarp was in place, bottles of bleach and plenty of towels were under the fold-away cot, and the wood-handled filet knife was cleaned and hanging on a hook above the camper's storage bin.

The solitude of the moment was interrupted by a scratch and rattle that seemed to come from the far corner of the garage. The teenagers next door? There it was again. No, not outside. It definitely came from inside the garage. I closed my eyes, listening for any hint of the source of the interruption. Damn, what is that? What's back there? I pictured the wall and floor on that side of the garage. Unlike the yard tools hanging on the driver's side, the far wall was bare, and although I couldn't picture it, I seemed to recall some debris on the floor near the door. Had to be some damn field mice—they always invaded the garage this time of year seeking its warmth. I was right—a gray mouse scampered past me, headed for the warmth of the underside of the freezer. The noise stopped. I didn't give it another thought. I had important work to do. I removed blue surgical gloves from my hoodie's pocket, patiently stretched the gloves over my knuckles, and pulled them up my wrists, tugging them tightly into place.

"No rush. No rush. Under control. Be patient. Stick to the plan."

I placed the lantern on the floor, out of the way of the camper's door. I removed the camper door key from my pants pocket, inserted it into the lock, and turned it slowly. It jammed. I tried again. It jammed again. What the fuck? I withdrew the key and examined it. I inserted it again, this time wiggling it as it slid into the lock. Success. I lifted the handle and the camper door burst open as Henry launched his full weight toward me. I fell backward as my body slammed against the garage door. He kept coming, ramming his shoulder against my chest until my head smacked hard onto the cold concrete floor.

CHAPTER 17
Detective Frank Vincenti

I didn't see Foster when I got in line for our coffee. But by the time the barista called, "Frank—venti, double cup, tall no-foam latte," he had walked in and claimed a table near the window. As I handed him his coffee, he looked up and said, "Good morning, Francis."

That was new—he had never said good morning before. Usually, he dove right into the discussion, positing theories, describing scenarios, and grilling me on my observations and deductions. Caught off guard, all I could say in return was a weak, "Hi."

For several minutes, we sat in silence with the whistling wind filling the coffee shop each time the door opened. The scene beyond the window confirmed my earlier suspicion that the so-called harbingers of spring that the city had enjoyed weren't harbingers at all, just pranks on the unsuspecting and uninitiated. Foster and I watched with shared subdued amusement as students unaccustomed to Chicago weather struggled against the strong, cold winds off the lake that were now accompanied by rain alternating with sleet.

I assumed his greeting was meant to put me at ease. It didn't. If he expected an apology, he was going to be disappointed. I did my best to control my emotions. My appearance—unshaven with dark bags under my eyes—may have given him concern, but he said nothing of it. I waited. I didn't care what we talked about. I just needed to be engaged.

"Francis, define the term, 'spree killer'."

Finally. Pleased that I didn't need to explain my appearance or rehash last week's questions and answers, I explained, "A spree killer is one who kills two or more persons in short succession at multiple locations. Some criminologists have coined a new phrase—'rampage killers'."

"An example please."

"Mark Barton, the Atlanta day trader. In July 1999 he shot and killed nine employees and wounded thirteen at two brokerage firms on the same day. Police later discovered that he had used a common carpenter's hammer to bludgeon his wife and two children to death."

Foster raised an eyebrow. I detected a slight grimace. He took a long, deliberate swallow of coffee. Looking past me, he said, "Your mother was a victim of a car accident—Barton's wife, a victim of her husband's rage. Mothers and wives shouldn't have to die that way." He studied his coffee cup and swirled what remained of his Columbian blend around the bottom of the cup. "But, yes, the Barton killings are a good example."

A group of giggling girls pulled open the shop's heavy glass door; a blast of cold air filled the coffee shop again. Foster sat silent for a moment, seemingly lost in thought, and then turned his attention back to me.

"Prepare a memorandum for me, no longer than two pages, single-spaced, explaining the manner in which you—or your 'subject'— would go on a rampage committing spree murders, starting in your dorm, with the final victim here in Starbucks. Create a profile of your subject. Identify your victims, not by name, but by characteristics or backgrounds. Call me when you have concluded the assignment."

He pushed his chair back away from the table and took a long last swallow of his coffee. Without looking at me, he swung his scarf around his neck and pulled on his leather gloves. He donned his houndstooth hat as he left the shop and casually strolled away, unfazed by the weather, and with no mention of our previous meeting.

CHAPTER 18
Anthony

With a knee to my chest and a hand at my throat, the son of a bitch had me pinned. He must've found the filet knife in the camper. His hands were free, and the tape on his mouth was gone. Even though he was still drunk and disoriented, Henry had apparently decided he wasn't going to go quietly. In an exaggerated movement, he raised the knife above his head, and plunged it down with a sudden, almost theatrical thrust. I twisted away at the last second, and he lost his balance and drove the blade into the garage floor instead. The tip snapped, flying up to nick him in the cheek while the knife bounced up against the garage door, clanged against the floor, and skidded across the pavement, landing under the truck and out of reach. Letting loose a torrent of curses, he kept me pinned with his body weight, pummeling me until my eyes started to lose focus. Then, with a primeval growl, he clamped his hands around my throat and squeezed.

Struggling to remain conscious, I tried to reach the gun in my pocket, but it was no use. I rolled to the right and left, trying to slip out of Henry's grip, but fear and adrenaline had transformed him into a killer. I tried in vain to throw punches in Henry's direction, but my fists failed to find their marks. I flailed and kicked and arched my back, but Henry tightened his grip. Finally, I was able to free one leg, and after several failed attempts, rammed my knee fast and hard into his groin. With a guttural moan and a stream of obscenities, he shifted his weight, but still didn't release my throat. Stars danced in a narrowing field of vision as my fingers groped for anything within reach. Anything I could use as a weapon—anything! Finally, my fingers closed around what felt like a chunk of a brick. I grabbed it and, in one quick and furious motion, swung it at Henry's head. He screamed as blood spurted from an ugly gash just above his left eye. Stunned, he reared back, blinking and loosening his grip. Searching through the darkness and the pain for the source of the blow, he turned toward the corner of the garage. This time the brick slammed into his left temple with such force and velocity that he surely never heard the crunch of his own skull shattering.

CHAPTER 19
Detective Frank Vincenti

I welcomed the diversion Foster's spree killer assignment provided. Three days later I called him to arrange another session. He was waiting for me at an outside table as spring teased the city yet again, and as he saw me approach the table, he pointed to the line for ordering coffee. I started to hand him the memo, but he just continued to point to the line.

"Coffee first, Francis."

I laid the memo facedown in front of him and got in line. When I returned, the memo was exactly where I had placed it, still face down. As he took a couple of drinks from his cup, he eyed my memo with a raised eyebrow. He flipped the piece of paper over and started to read. He frowned in places, grimaced once, and nodded as he finished. Then he slid it back across the table.

"Your first victim is your dorm's maintenance superintendent—then you move to the manager of the drug store that you pass on the way here. But your motivation for each kill represents nothing more than a shallow textbook analysis. It shows no feel for motivation. In fact, it shows no feeling whatsoever. Your inability to articulate a credible motive has rendered meaningless the sacrifice of your victims' lives."

"But I built motive on a foundation of underlying anger with society. The anger builds beyond a point the subject can control."

He shook his head. "Simple anger alone is a trite motivation for the killings you describe and simple anger would not push a rational person to surrender control. What's behind the anger? Where did it come from? Long brewing or spontaneous? When you understand a spree killer's motive as something more than a flash of anger at the world at large, your choice of victims will be sustainable. Forget who the victims are and consider what they are. Finally, your victim here at Starbucks is all wrong."

He stood to leave. "Try again. This time use your imagination, your gut, not your so-called 'book learning'."

We met again three days later. When I set my revised memo on the table, I noticed that he had placed a manila file folder off to the side. I said nothing about it and took my place in line. Upon my return with a coffee in each hand, I was surprised to find that he had just finished reading my memo. Before I could sit down, he took his coffee from my hand and took a sip. "As I anticipated, Francis, your analysis misses the mark again."

Dispirited and puzzled, I slowly sat opposite him. He slid the manila folder across the table. "Those are the Atlanta Police crime scene photos from Barton's rampage—photos of all twelve murder victims, including those of his children. Take them home. Study them, but don't write another word until you have used your imagination to experience Barton's feelings, thoughts and urges. And do not burden yourself with emotional attachment to the victims—it will add nothing."

When I returned to my room, I tossed the file on my bed intending to put aside Foster's assignment for a few hours and clear my head. I plopped myself onto my bed and reached for the TV remote, but one of the photos had slid out of the file. It immediately caught my attention, and without picking it up, I slid it across the bed sheet toward me. It was a close-up of Barton's eleven-year-old son—his head crushed. Deep indentations from the claw end of the hammer were clearly visible.

Stapled to the photo was a single sheet of paper at the top of which was a note in Foster's handwriting: "From Barton's suicide note." Below it was a news clipping quoting Barton's note:

I killed the children to exchange them for five minutes of pain for a lifetime of pain. I forced myself to do it to keep them from suffering so much later . . . The fears of the father are transferred to the son. It was from my father to me and from me to my son. My son already had it. And now for him to avoid my legacy, I had to take him with me.

One by one I tacked the two dozen photos to my wall, pushing each tack with increasing pressure—with each addition to my wall, my head throbbed. I sat Indian style on the floor leaning against the foot of my bed, and studied every detail of each photo. But I kept coming back to the photo of the young boy and to Barton's note. *Father and son. Son and father.* Foster had told me to use my imagination to understand Barton's motivation, but his admonition to stay emotionally detached was at odds with the horror of the image of the murdered young boy. After an hour of staring at the pictures, my headache became more than I could tolerate, and I resorted to hydrocodone that I had taken from my father's medicine cabinet. I became drowsy and must have fallen asleep there on the floor.

I heard muffled screams in my dream. I tried to make out the words, but I couldn't. It grew louder, and I jolted awake to discover it was my screaming. I looked around the darkened room not sure where I was or what time it was. I took a moment to clear my head. I stood and stared again at the picture of eleven-year-old Matthew Barton, tore it off the wall and re-read Barton's note.

I looked down at the scar on my wrist, closed my eyes, and saw the image of my father's handgun in my mouth. And I saw my father's face. Is that your legacy to me? "God damn you, you son of a bitch! You may have stolen my childhood, but that's all you're getting. You can burn in hell!"

If, at that moment, my father were there in my dorm room, I would have used the gun on him.

Then it struck me. "Jesus Christ! Foster, you baited me!" His little exercise wasn't intended to test my knowledge of spree killers or a simple lesson of motivation. The assignment was simply the second part of his game of twenty questions—a game that forced me to admit that I carried suppressed rage, uncontrollable rage, born of a mean-spirited alcoholic father, who could move me to violence. "Damn you, Foster!" But he was right—unless I confronted my anger, I could never understand the anger of others, and I would never understand the rage that causes a man to kill.

I called Foster and told him, "Tomorrow at 8:00 a.m."

CHAPTER 20
Anthony

Exhausted and light-headed, I struggled to push Henry's lifeless body off me until, with one final shove, I rolled him over to the side. His head hit the floor with a thud. Sprawled on my back on the cold concrete, I worked to control my breathing, the chunk of the jagged, bloody brick still clutched in my hand. I stared up at the rafters and listened to my heart pound, as loud as a hammer blow. Adrenaline still coursed through my veins, and time seemed to stand still. Finally, I struggled to my knees and braced myself against the garage floor, slippery with blood. The sight of Henry's battered face ignited the rage I tried so hard to control. He had ruined everything. The fucking bastard had fucking ruined everything!

I grabbed his head and turned it to face me. "Open your eyes, goddammit! Open 'em! I wanna see the terror in your eyes. I need to see you suffer!"

I let Henry's head flop back into the pool of blood. "You bastard. You fuckin' bastard." I shifted the chunk of brick to my left hand. "This is all your fault!" I slammed the brick down on Henry's head—again and again and again until my own face dripped with his blood and the garage door was splattered with gray brain matter.

Enough! I finally sat back against the bumper of the pickup and looked over to where the lantern stood. Spotted with blood, it threw distorted images against the garage door and the back of the truck. I inhaled. The smell of Henry's blood on my flesh was like nothing I'd ever smelled before. Oh, I knew the smell well enough—it was like copper, but this time . . . this time was different. The clay of the brick, the mix of copper and fear, salt, sweat and adrenaline combined to produce something like the dying sparks of a welder's acetylene torch. A single drop had settled on my upper lip, and for just a moment I thought of licking it to learn how bloodlust really tasted. But I couldn't. I was afraid Henry's evil would infect me. Instead, I wiped my sleeve across my mouth in disgust.

I still held the chunk of brick. I held it up to a narrow shaft of moonlight that seeped through a broken pane of a small decorative window that was three-quarters up the wall. The blood looked black in the moonlight. I turned the brick in my hand and considered the heft and shape of it. I studied it, admitting I had no idea why it was in the garage or how it got there. As I stared at the brick I sensed there was something familiar about it, and a painful image from deep within my memory flashed in my mind, disappearing as suddenly as it came. I strained to summon it again, but the only image I saw was the brick, in slow motion, crushing Henry's skull.

CHAPTER 21
Detective Frank Vincenti

I wasn't sure whether Foster was surprised that I had simply told him that we would meet instead of requesting a meeting. Either way, I didn't care. He had played a mind game with me, so I had decided that I would reverse the roles and play a game with him. I would become the game master.

I had our coffee waiting in place when Foster joined me at the outdoor table where he had started this little exercise ten days earlier. He sat down and took a drink from his coffee. Seeing the look on my face, he said, "I see you figured it out."

I nodded. "It's all about rage. Raw, unchecked rage. Rage born of being forced to feel worthless. Rage fed by being devalued as a human being. The rampage killer feels alienated and alone. He's not born feeling worthless. He is taught to feel that way, and his classroom is the home. His rage builds to a point at which, unlike other men, he can no longer control it.

"All my victims represent an oppressor or a transgressor in the mind of my subject. But none of them had actually wronged him. They are simply convenient surrogates for those who, in his eyes, had belittled him or deprived him of any shred of self-esteem. They represent people in his life who failed to see that he was special, failed to recognize that he was someone to be reckoned with.

"My subject isn't killing the maintenance man; he's killing everyone who ignored his pleas for help. And he isn't killing the drug store manager; he is killing every boss or teacher he ever had who, in his eyes, unfairly reprimanded or embarrassed him. Rage isn't rational or logical. And slowly—ever so slowly—the rage transforms your son's Boy Scout leader, or the person who sits in the cubicle next to you at work, into a psychopath capable of monstrous acts of savagery."

Foster sat silent for a moment. He sipped his coffee. "I trust you didn't come to that conclusion on an intellectual level. Did you rely on your intuition, your imagination?"

And now, the real game began. "No. I reflected on your little game of twenty questions and Barton's fear of the legacy he was passing on to his son." I paused and looked him in the eye to let him know I figured out his game and turned it into mine. "Then I summoned my rage."

He nodded with approval. "But it was not my questions that upset you, it was your answers that led you to discover and give voice to your own suppressed rage." He had taken the bait.

"True."

Foster looked down at his coffee cup as if it contained his next question. "And your rage grew out of being raised by an angry and bitter man and your fear of his legacy."

"There's no reason to get into that."

"I think there is."

"No." I was enjoying the game: Check.

Foster sat silent for a moment. "Another time then."

"Perhaps."

"And who is your final victim here at Starbucks?"

"You."

Checkmate.

Foster took a sip of his coffee and looked past me at the courtyard full of students. A smug smile slowly appeared as he nodded his head in approval. His eyes came back to meet mine. "Francis, may I buy you a croissant to go with that latte?"

CHAPTER 22
Anthony

After I calmed down and my head cleared, I realized that although Henry's attack had interrupted my plan, there was no reason not to finish what I'd started. My purpose had been served, if not its means. I still had work to do.

My latex gloves were covered in blood and had been torn during the struggle. I tugged them off, rolled them into a ball, and tossed them to the side of the garage near the freezer. I lifted the lantern from where I had so carefully placed it before Henry's attack, and held it at shoulder height, its dim light allowing me to inspect the scene behind the pickup. It was a grisly mess. I opened the door of the camper, stepped over Henry's body, and set the blood-spattered lantern inside on the floor. Grabbing a towel from the rear bench, I wiped my face, hands, and forearms, removing most of the blood, and then threw the towel toward the freezer.

I stood over Henry's body and stared at his crushed skull. Dammit to hell! Henry had denied me the pleasure of inflicting the pain he deserved while he was still alive. There was no satisfaction in this kill, no muffled screaming, no wide-eyed look of terror in his eyes. No desperate pleas for mercy. Henry had escaped the long and painful death he deserved, the death so many like him deserved. The death I had delivered so many times before.

My rage began to boil again. I grabbed the corpse by the feet and dragged it over to the front of the freezer, leaving a trail of smeared blood and gray brain matter. I walked back to the rear of the camper and grabbed the lantern. The heat of its glowing mantle had caused the spattered blood on its glass globe to dry, turning the bright red blood to dark carmine. Tilting my head, I stared at it momentarily with schoolboy curiosity, then regained focus and rotated the lantern's intake valve, leaving just enough light to see my way around the garage. I needed room to work. But first, I needed to back the camper out of the garage and park it on the alley apron.

I left the garage through the side door and surveyed the backyards and porches visible to the south. The neighborhood was dark. There was no activity. Staying close to the brick wall of the garage, I walked down the narrow sidewalk that ran along the side of the building and then swung open the rusty gate to the alley. Everything was quiet—I thought. At first I didn't notice it, but under the streetlight, no more than ten yards to my right, a man walked a German Shepherd. They were headed straight toward me. They hadn't spotted me yet, but I knew I'd attract attention if I rushed back into the garage. Instead, I eased the gate closed and stepped back into the shadows. I tugged up my hood, pressed my back against the cold and wet brick wall, and pulled my .38 from my pocket.

CHAPTER 23
Detective Frank Vincenti

Foster started to conduct our sessions at his home. When he suggested it, he told me that he lived in a basement apartment and scribbled the address on the back of a Starbucks napkin. I recognized the street name; it was located in Lincoln Park. I doubted very much that there were many basement apartments in Lincoln Park. It was an old area with a rich history and even richer residents.

On my first visit he greeted me at the door holding an unlit cigar and wearing a blue blazer and a light blue button-down shirt opened at the neck. He showed me around his one-bedroom basement apartment, explaining that the building, a 1900s-era brownstone, had been built by a displaced British aristocrat and that the ground floor had been designed to house his children's nanny. In the early '80s, the three-story brownstone had been converted into three luxury apartments, and the owner rehabbed the long-abandoned nanny's quarters to accommodate a fourth tenant. His apartment became a classroom for me then, and over time, it became a second home as well—a safe place where I knew I would never be turned away.

In his environment, the sessions changed—he changed. In soft, low lighting and with cigar in hand, he was more relaxed. Unlike our previous sessions, he encouraged discussion. He sought my opinions on files, psychological profiles and case rulings. He finally entertained my questions, although he had been right—I had answered most of them myself.

He freely discussed his cases, including the unsolved murders that still haunted him. He knew the name of every victim. He spoke of them as if they were members of his family—especially the children. "The most innocent of all victims."

Some nights, when it was late and he knew I was vulnerable, he returned to his game of twenty questions. The new questions were logical extensions of the first set, but questions I never gave much thought to: Why did Grandpa Angelo resent your father? Who else was in the car when your mother was killed? Sometimes, when I was caught off guard and too tired to resist, he would push back, refusing to accept my abrupt responses. He kept returning to Grandpa Angelo's dismissal of my father.

"Tell me about your grandfather. Obviously, to deny your father a chance at college and passing his money for tuition on to you has had consequences he may not have foreseen."

"My grandfather again, Foster?"

"Francis, some people are so afraid of the future that they cling desperately to the past, sharing it with no one."

"Not me."

"Really? But what about your father? The disdain he has for life, and you, started with your grandfather. So, tell me about him."

"My father never talked about Grandpa. But, I remember some of my grandmother's stories—they're not really informative. Grandma always acted like Grandpa's past was some kind of secret."

"Was it?"

"I'd rather not."

"And, I rather you would." Working on relighting his cigar and without looking at me, he didn't let up. "What about your grandmother? There's more about her that you're not telling me."

I looked over at him. Busy fumbling with matches, he didn't see my frustration. Grudgingly, I continued. "I won't bother you with fond childhood memories—I know what story you're fishing for. One

Christmas at my uncle's house in DeKalb, my father was being his usual obnoxious self, so Aunt Anna got me out of harm's way by asking me to help her in the kitchen. Without looking up from the sink full of soapsuds in front of her, she tried to explain my father's behavior. She told me that Grandma had become pregnant 'out of wedlock' and that Grandpa had refused to marry her. The unwanted baby was my father. After he was born, Grandma's family threatened to go to the immigration authorities and have Grandpa deported unless he married her. So he did, and according to Aunt Anna, entered a lifelong loveless marriage. Grandpa took out his shame and bitterness by beating Grandma, even repeatedly pushing her down flights of stairs. Grandpa, like my father, was a mean drunk, often taking a belt to my father's backside."

"So, your father was literally a bastard."

We both sat quietly. He succeeded in relighting the stub of his cigar, and examined it as if he had never seen it before. He looked up at me. "Francis, shame and bitterness, and the anger they engender, are not traits we inherit—we impose them upon ourselves. I had hoped you had come to that realization when you read Barton's suicide note. I suppose your aunt's story explains a lot—your grandfather's resentment of your father, for example—but it is not your shame, nor is it your father's. It is your grandfather's shame. It is too late for your father to understand he was a victim of your grandfather's bitterness; your father will go to his grave angry at the world and ignorant of the cause of his anger. But it is not too late for you to understand. That your father was a victim makes you no less a victim but, unlike Barton, you can reject your father's legacy."

Instead of going straight home that night, I headed toward the lake. I crossed Lake Shore Drive on the footbridge overpass at Fullerton and followed Lake Shore Trail north. I sat down on one of the Park District's benches and looked out over the water. It was churning, and waves pounded against the limestone revetment bulkheads put in place in the 1920s to contain the occasional fury of storm-stirred whitecaps.

The fears of the father are transferred to the son. Intellectually, I knew Foster was right, but I couldn't accept it emotionally—it was easier to hate my father than pity him. But Foster had forced me to realize that my father had sought approval from his father, and lost forever my approval. But that realization did me no good. It was from my father to me and from me to my son. I took no comfort in Foster's words. I refused to accept any excuse or explanation for the pain my father had caused. I spent the rest of the night walking along the shore, regretting the past and fearing the future.

CHAPTER 24
Anthony

I feared the damn German Shepherd would smell the fresh blood on my clothes and pull his owner up the sidewalk, directly to me. I tightened my grip on the .38. As the man and his dog neared the half-open gate, the dog stopped abruptly and raised his nose in the air, sniffing. The dog turned his head toward the gate, and started to bark wildly, breaking the silence of the night. He pulled his owner toward the garage, but his owner jerked the leash, tightening the dog's choke collar. "C'mon Rex. Let's go."

Rex pulled his owner toward the corner of the garage closest to the gate, only a few yards from where I hid in the darkness, his barking growing louder and more ferocious. I fingered the .38 and held my breath. Rex sniffed the gate and the corner of the garage and started to growl, but his owner tugged on the leash and choke collar. "Leave it!" The owner commanded and cajoled the whimpering dog as he dragged him down the alley. After several long minutes, I emerged from my hiding place, took a step toward the alley, and peered around the corner in the direction where Rex and his owner were headed. The alley was empty.

I went back inside, reopened the garage door, and backed the truck out to park it on the apron. I'd parked there before and was confident the truck wouldn't draw attention.

Slipping back under the garage door as it closed behind me, I got to work. With the valve opened as far is it would go, the lantern radiated a soothing glow, albeit shadowed with black spots from the dried blood on the globe. I grabbed Henry's feet and dragged him to the center of the garage where the floor sloped to the drain, then picked up the discarded gloves and towel and tossed them toward the drain.

Next, I pulled on a pair of nonporous latex-coated knit work gloves, picked up my Black & Decker mini electric saw with a reciprocating blade, and found the new shiny item hanging amidst the rusty tools on the crumbling pegboard. My thirty-six-inch long bolt cutters.

I pulled my hood over my head and tugged it down over my forehead, hiding my face from the blank gaze of the bloodied corpse. With a foot on either side of Henry's chest, I stared at him as if in a trance. The flickering light from the lantern cast eerie shadows on the angles and planes of his crushed skull. He barely looked human. He wasn't human. He was a monster. A monster who had died too soon. Died without suffering the same punishment the others had endured. Died without knowing real pain. My heart thudded in my chest. My hands twitched. I gripped the saw in one hand and the bolt cutter in the other.

"I am not quite done with you, Mr. Henry. I have a message to send, and email just won't do."

CHAPTER 25
Detective Frank Vincenti

I graduated that June, still not certain of a career. I took Foster's advice to continue my education under his tutelage, and to take some time away from school to plan my future. I still had money from Grandpa Angelo's college fund, so I sublet a third-floor walk-up studio apartment on the 3900 block of Fremont, near Byron, just on the outskirts of Wrigleyville. It was a little upscale, but it was only a one-year lease. It was close enough to Foster's apartment that I could walk to see him, albeit a healthy walk, or jump on the CTA if I wanted to get there in a hurry or avoid bad weather.

Our sessions had advanced to the point where I did most of the talking. Foster simply sat in his worn leather recliner, smoking his ever-present cigar, sipping on eighteen-year-old Bushmills, and posing an occasional question. To stimulate my inquisitiveness, he quizzed me on a variety of topics: sexual crimes, the psychological basis of dismemberment and mutilation, and methods of disposal of bodies. He tested his theories of the so-called perfect murder on what he called my "unpolluted" mind.

"Francis," he asked one day, "how far would you go to catch a killer, knowing he would kill again unless you stopped him?" I knew what he was getting at: my challenge to him on the steps of the administration building. I found my initial gut reaction disturbing, so I kept it to myself.

"I don't know."

"What if that killer had shot and killed your wife?"

I snickered. "I don't have a wife."

His raised eyebrow signaled his displeasure with my attempt to deflect his question. "You know what I mean. Tell me this, Francis, are you in favor of the death penalty?"

"There hasn't been an execution in Illinois since 1999 when Governor Ryan declared a moratorium."

"You know, Francis, you're not as good at deflecting my questions as you think. Yes or no—are you in favor of the death penalty?"

"No."

"You will be." He blew cigar smoke that formed a small cloud just above his head. "You might well change your mind if you lose a loved one to senseless violence."

One night in late November, Foster announced, "In December you will be sitting for the qualifying written exam for the Chicago Police Department. It is only offered every three to five years, depending on the department's employment needs. If you don't sit for the exam now, who knows how long you will have to wait. I had the application fee waived, and I have made what arrangements I can for now."

"What?"

"Obviously, Francis, this is how you start the process to become a Chicago police officer. You don't think I have been training you to become an office clerk or a lawyer?" He ignored the startled look on my face and continued. "Even after you pass the exam and are chosen 'randomly' by the departmental lottery, you'll have to get through the Police Officer Wellness Evaluation Report—that tests strength, endurance and flexibility—a personal background investigation, a polygraph, an interview with a panel of Department HR officers, a battery of psychological tests, a medical exam, and, oh yeah, they'll make you pee in a bottle for drug screening. You still have a good deal of work ahead of you."

Apparently, he had given more thought to my future than I had. I had become so immersed in Foster's world that I had done little about getting a job other than half-hearted visits to the university's placement office. I had considered graduate school and law school. I considered everything except what Foster seemed to have had in mind for me all along.

"If you successfully survive all that, you will get an acceptance letter for the Police Academy." He handed me a packet of incomplete forms. "You need to fill these out and mail them in. They'll need your fingerprints." As he handed me a one-inch-thick manuscript, clearly his work product, he added, "Here, you'll need this, too. Study it and you'll qualify. Call me when you get the acceptance letter from the Academy."

"And if I don't get an acceptance letter?"

"Then don't call. Ever again."

CHAPTER 26
Anthony

The secret to not being caught is organization and planning. I had removed Henry's clothing, shoes, wristwatch, and wallet, and placed it all in a five-gallon paint bucket, poured quick dry mortar over the contents, sealed it, and placed it in the front corner of the camper. I thoroughly cleaned Henry's body using the bleach and towels I kept in the camper. And then I took care of the souvenirs. I took two from Henry and added one before I wrapped him in a blue, plastic painters' tarp.

After loading him into the camper, I headed for the demolition site I'd scouted earlier in the week and had visited again the day before just to make sure nothing about it had been changed by the work crews. It was north, on Keeler near the intersection of Keeler and Grove, in Albany Park. The empty streets were washed clean by the night's rain, and the sky had cleared, but the early morning stars were hidden by the city's skyline and ambient light.

When I pulled up at the site, I flipped my headlights off. It was still quiet, and I figured the early birds probably wouldn't arrive for another three hours. The site was perfect. Only remnants of three exterior brick walls remained intact. The wall closest to the alley had been leveled, and a reinforced plywood ramp led into a shallow dirt-floor basement. I lifted Henry—still bundled in his shroud of blue—hoisted him over my shoulder, and headed for the gate.

I moved swiftly across a cement slab that had once been a garage floor, walked down the ramp, and dumped the body onto the middle of the dirt floor. I knelt down, not to pray for this asshole, but to scrape away debris and the recently excavated black dirt, creating a hollow in the floor the size and shape of the body. Still on my knees, I reached over and dragged the body into the space. Once I had Henry in place, I was able to perform a few housekeeping chores for the benefit of the detectives who would process the crime scene. As I got ready to leave, I noticed a makeshift wooden wheelbarrow full of salvaged bricks. They were the same brownish-red color as the broken piece of brick that saved my life and took Henry's. After a moment of reflection, I made my decision—one that would make me famous and give the press something new to talk about and the cops something new to worry about. I pushed the wheelbarrow toward the body and dumped the bricks. The bricks did not blanket the body, but were scattered on top and around it. The blue of the tarp was still visible.

I was halfway up the ramp on my way out of the basement when I stopped, turned back, and inspected my handiwork. The bricks were a nice touch, although the irony would be lost on everyone but me. I smiled, confident that the apparition would be pleased, and I would be able to sleep easy again.

CHAPTER 27
Detective Frank Vincenti

I spent long days and nights poring over Foster's exam preparation materials. On Monday of the second week of my preparation, I was finishing my breakfast when my phone rang. I was startled to see the caller ID: Chicago Police. I quickly answered. The voice at the other end asked curtly, "This Francis Vincenti?"

"Yeah . . ."

"I'm Eddie Dunbar, Captain Eddie Dunbar, Chicago PD. I'm the head of the CPD's North Area Violent Crimes Section, the VCS. I was on the job with Tommy Foster. I understand you know Tommy."

It took a minute to sink in. Tommy? I never knew him by any name other than just Foster.

"Yeah, but I—"

"Tommy says I should meet you. He says you guys used to meet over coffee. So let's have some coffee and a chat."

"Ah, OK. When?"

"Now. I'm out front in a patrol car."

I walked over to the apartment's only window, separated the blinds and saw the familiar blue and white squad car parked outside. Nervously, I responded, "I'll be right down."

A few minutes later I sat uncomfortably in the front passenger seat of Dunbar's car. He was a large black man who filled the driver's seat, which appeared to be pushed back as far as it would go. He had a thin, precision-trimmed moustache and was completely bald, so it was difficult to guess his age.

"Tommy says you have special talents—talents that could help track down this city's monsters before too many innocent people become statistics. He also says that you can identify with a killer and yet remain sufficiently emotionally detached."

That was something that had remained unspoken between Foster and me.

"If Tommy has taken you under his wing, then that's good enough for me. As far as I know, Tommy had room under that powerful wing of his for only one other recruit: me. He told me years ago that I had those same special talents."

He took a cup of coffee from the cardboard tray he had on the floor between his legs. "Oh, I almost forgot. Here's your coffee. McDonald's."

I took the small cup and lifted the plastic lid just enough to determine that it was black, no cream.

"Look kid. I have the idea that you may not appreciate what Tommy has done for you, and I don't mean your one-on-one private sessions with him, which, by the way, many of the guys in the Detectives Bureau would have gladly sacrificed a couple of years of their pension to have had that opportunity. No, I mean the qualifying exam and working your way through the process. You just don't fill out a job application, take a written test, and get handed a badge and a firearm."

"I never thought it would be easy."

"Remember your New Testament? 'Many are called, but few are chosen?' Well, thousands of people submit applications and become eligible to sit for the written qualifying exam. If you pass the exam, then your name is placed on a referral list. Where your name appears on the list is determined by a computer lottery. If the computer spits out your name, you get the privilege of undergoing more tests. Foster has made sure the lottery will randomly choose you."

If he was waiting for a reaction, I disappointed him.

Smiling, Dunbar shook his head and explained, "A lot of the guys in the department who worked with Tommy still hold him in high regard and think he got a raw deal when he left the force. He called in a lot of chits for you. You're probably going to be treated as if you actually qualify for some of the special preferences the Department is required to extend to eligible recruits. With those preferences added to your file, you'll be on the force."

"I guess I don't understand. How am I eligible for preferential treatment?"

"Because Tommy says you are. Forget all the hype about the city's so-called equal opportunity standards and transparency for hiring. It's all bullshit anyway. We take care of our own, and there are a helluva lot of guys in CPD Admin who continue to take care of Tommy Foster. This is still Chicago, and although the Daleys are long gone, it is business as usual when it comes to hiring."

"How can you get away with that?"

He looked at me as though I had just insulted him. I probably had.

"Because when it comes to tracking down monsters and putting them away before they kill someone's daughter or molest a five year old, I'd rather have the right guy on the job hired wrong, than the wrong guy hired right."

I looked over at Dunbar, "But why Foster?"

"Jesus Christ! You really don't know who Thomas Aquinas Foster is, do you?"

"No, I guess I got so absorbed in his case files—"

Dunbar jerked his head around toward me, startled. "He let you read his case files?"

"Well, yeah. He made me summarize the evidence, evaluate investigative strategies, challenge the psychological profiles he'd compiled. I must have looked at a couple dozen of his files last winter."

Dunbar grimaced and through clenched teeth muttered, "He never shares those files." He went silent. His radio crackled, and the screen of the Department laptop started flashing a newly issued BOLO. He ignored them. He turned to face me and looked me in the eye. "The day I was assigned to the VCS, I asked Foster if he would help me on my tough cases. He agreed, but cautioned, 'Through me you pass into the city of woe . . .' I had to look it up; it's from Dante's *Divine Comedy*. Go back to your studying—and kid, don't fuck it up!"

CHAPTER 28
Anthony

I had intended to return to the garage and dump the bucket containing Henry's personal effects in the north branch of the Chicago River while it was still dark, but on a last-minute whim, I headed west on Irving Park Road toward O'Hare. Although emotionally drained, I wasn't tired. The adrenaline high of the kill was slowly wearing off, and an inexplicable tinge of sadness and nostalgia had replaced it.

As I drove, I pieced together vague memories of high school when I'd head out to the airport on the same road. I used to spend hours parked on the grass roadside on Irving that ran along the southern edge of O'Hare, sitting on the hood of the family car and drinking beer from dark brown A&W bottles. The place was quiet between landings and takeoffs, and I'd close my eyes and wait for the roar and thunder of jet engines to shatter the peace. The sound and fury of the powerful turbines shook the car and rumbled through my veins, and I'd let myself fantasize about leaving, traveling to exotic destinations, going anywhere but back home.

It was almost dawn when I got to the familiar spot. Orange and pink rays seeped above the horizon, and the mystical pale blue that paints the sky as night turns to day hung over the runways. As I waited for the first flight to pass overhead, I pictured the scene that would soon unfold at the demolition site. I could see the workers begin to arrive, wearing their yellow hardhats and grungy, faded denim overalls, carrying over-sized thermoses of coffee and boxes of donuts from the neighborhood Dunkin' Donuts. They would sit on the tailgate of someone's truck and complain about having to work on Saturday to make up for lost time from the Thanksgiving holiday. Then a foreman would arrive, and the workers would scatter to their equipment, starting the engine of the crane or flicking the switch on an air compressor for their power tools. Then, from within the crumbling structure, a man's shout would ring out. Betraying his macho image, he would wave and yell until the other men joined him to view the grisly discovery. I figured it would be on the local news by six and perhaps the lead story at ten.

I leaned back against the windshield and let my thoughts wander as morning rush hour traffic picked up behind me. The lights of countless windows on Chicago's iconic skyscrapers faded to gray as the sun rose behind them, and I tugged my cap down over my eyes to protect them from the blinding rays illuminating the slowly awakening world. A familiar image flashed in my mind, and like a photographic negative, it instantly burned into my brain. I stared at the skyline, transfixed by the images as they played out like a muted movie, watching it all unfold again.

It was a spring night. I was seven years old. My best friend and I had been throwing an old tennis ball against the garage door when the streetlights came on. Time to go in. I said goodnight and watched my friend enter his yard from the alley and walk along the narrow sidewalk next to the garage. Then I saw the man. He appeared from the side door of the garage, lurched toward the boy, grabbed him by the back of his neck, and pushed him toward the side of the garage. The shadows were deepening, and it was difficult to see what was happening, but I couldn't look away. The man bent the boy over a pile of stacked firewood, pushed his face against the brick wall of the garage, and pulled his pants and underwear down around his ankles. Then the man leaned into him. I didn't understand what was happening, but I knew it was wrong. My whole body stiffened in fear when my friend cried out and struggled to get away. I couldn't move as the man slammed my friend's face into the wall with his right hand. His left hand was hidden in front of him. After pushing at him several times, the man stopped moving. Then he turned and zipped up his own pants and buckled his belt. He growled something at my friend, held his head against the brick wall, then let go and walked through the yard toward the house. And then the timer-controlled outdoor yard lights flashed on, and I saw the man plainly.

For years, that memory has floated in and out of my consciousness like an apparition without form. Sometimes I've wondered whether the memory was real or something someone described to me, but then I would remember the sound of my friend crying out and feel the rough brick as if it was pressed against my face. And now, each time the apparition comes to me, I renew my vow to wreak vengeance for my friend—vengeance I exacted on Henry and on the others like him rotting under sandy soil and rotting leaves along remote river banks. As I slid off the hood of the pickup, I knew the ghostly memory had been satisfied for now, but it would surely reappear. Maybe not tomorrow, maybe not for months or years, but I knew—oh yeah, I knew—that when it did reappear, I would protect my friend and exact revenge yet again.

PART TWO

CHAPTER 29
Detective Frank Vincenti

Sean and I had pulled the early morning shift on the Saturday after Thanksgiving when the first call came in. A construction worker had discovered a body wrapped in a blue tarp buried under a pile of bricks at a demolition site in the Albany Park neighborhood, near Keeler and Grove. The crime scene's supervising patrol officer had specifically requested us.

As we sped north on Pulaski, I was oblivious to the car's wailing siren and the dash-mounted blue strobe. Our wideband radio spewed reports from the scene, but they became indistinguishable and were background noise to my brooding. Beth had called from Santa Barbara Thursday morning and instead of wishing me a happy Thanksgiving, had abruptly issued an ultimatum: She wanted me out of Chicago PD within six months. If I stayed on the job, she would file for divorce.

I should have seen it coming. She had become increasingly ill-tempered and impatient, complaining that she was tired of sharing her breakfast table with grisly crime scene photos and case files, and claiming she could no longer live with my bouts of depression that came on the heels of every newly discovered murder victim. There was more to it than just that, but she didn't need to say it.

I stared out of the passenger side window, watching the storefronts whiz by in a blur. I thought back to when my life had been far less complicated, before I had met Beth, and before I had plunged head-first into Foster's real world of police work. I closed my eyes and recalled the naïve excitement of the day nine years ago when the Police Superintendent had handed me my Chicago Police Officer Star. And I thought about the photograph.

It was a black and white photo taken by the official department photographer at the swearing-in ceremony. There I stood at full attention in my crisp new Class A uniform snapping a sharp salute to the Superintendent of Police with Chicago's mayor in the background. I had just been sworn in along with fifty-eight other Probationary Police Officers at a ceremony in the ballroom of Chicago's Navy Pier.

Before I had received notice of the swearing-in ceremony, I didn't even know Navy Pier had a ballroom. I had arrived there while the maintenance workers were setting up chairs. I stood in the back of the cavernous room and watched it fill up with other PPOs' family and friends there to share in the pride and honor of the moment. Scores of parents, wives, children, siblings, and friends, all dressed in their best clothes, took their seats in white wooden folding chairs with official programs in their laps. They waited anxiously to hear their loved ones' names called and to see them ascend the stairs to the platform where they would be handed their Patrolman stars and where the upper echelon of the department and the mayor would shake the hands of the newly sworn officers. Only Foster attended on my behalf.

"On my honor ..."

As I raised my right hand and recited the oath, I reflected upon how my life had changed since that wintry day more than three and a half years earlier when Foster's graduate assistant had announced his ground rules.

"I will never betray my badge, my integrity, my character, or the public trust. . . ."

My life had changed for the better. I had direction. I had goals. I was proud of what I had accomplished.

"I will always have the courage to hold myself and others accountable for our actions...."

I still suffered bouts of depression, but less often and less severe.

"I will uphold the Constitution of the United States, the laws of the State of Illinois ..."

Nothing about my relationship with my father had changed, though. He remained a dark force who loomed larger than he was entitled to, and no amount of Foster's counsel eased that pain.

"And the core values and mission of the Chicago Police Department."

For more than four years after that photo was taken, I patrolled the streets of quiet neighborhoods in a blue and white cruiser emblazoned with the words, "We Serve and Protect." I spent long days and nights responding to emergency calls, burglaries, shoplifting, bar fights, domestic violence, and auto accidents. Then, when Foster pronounced me ready, I sat for the Detectives' exam. He had been right. I passed both the qualifying written exam and the police logic exam, and then survived the oral review boards. I did not know at the time that Foster had made some phone calls, and Eddie Dunbar expedited my actual promotion to Detective and my first assignment to the VCS. I wasn't too proud, nor was I embarrassed, to accept the special treatment. Foster assured me I was ready. And, according to Dunbar, I was needed.

I was assigned to the Violent Crimes Section, North Area of the Detectives Bureau, located in the lower level of the department's lock-up and station house on West Belmont in the 19th District. I got there early the first day and organized my desk—the first one I ever had. Using clear plastic pushpins, I pinned my ceremony photo to one of the partition walls on my half of my newly assigned cubicle. It was designed for two people; it was about sixteen feet wide with file cabinets at each end. My half of the twelve-foot desktop was separated from the other half by an eighteen-inch-tall partition; I assumed the other half belonged to my partner. I placed my favorite photo of Beth, taken during happier times, in one of the desk's corners. In the photo, she sat on a bench at the Fullerton Avenue Beach wearing a light blue pullover top that highlighted her freckled face, blue eyes, and auburn hair, and in her lap she held the small, seven-year-old, mixed-breed mutt we'd adopted that day from the Anti-Cruelty Society.

I was hunched over my desk trying to make sense of the instructions that accompanied the new telephone when someone placed his hand on my left shoulder. I turned around in my chair without getting up.

"You must be," looking down at a memo in his hand, "you must be Francis A. Vincenti, Jr."

"Most people just call me Frank."

He extended his right hand, and with a reassuring smile, said, "OK, Frank. I'm Sean—Sean Kelly."

I stood and shook his hand, not knowing what to expect.

"Well, Frank, I'm sorry to tell you that we are going to have a quiet and uninteresting time together. Normally, each of us would be paired with a salty veteran, but all the action is in the Woodlawn and Rosewood neighborhoods—that's where they sent all the veterans. The brass figures the North Side will be pretty quiet, perfect for guys like us."

Kelly stood about six foot and weighed about two hundred pounds. He had all the looks of an aspiring actor: chestnut brown hair, crystal clear blue-green eyes, and a bright smile. He looked like he was older than me—around thirty-nine or so. His chest and arms reflected hours in the gym working with free weights. His clothes were nothing special, but they looked clean and fresh and nothing was out of place.

I learned a lot about Sean William Kelly during the first year we were partners. I picked up some information from department summaries and some from detectives who had worked with him during his twelve-year stint on the job. When I wasn't sure whether what I learned was fact or rumor, I just asked. I knew he was divorced and had a son, but he never talked about it, and since he was so open about everything else, I thought it best not to ask. If he wanted me to know, he'd tell me.

Over time, he made every effort to teach me what it meant to be partners. Even before my inclusion in Kelly family Thanksgivings,

Sean had invited me to his family's Fourth of July picnics—the first time was the summer we started working together. By then, Beth had already become unhappy with the mood swings caused by my work in VCS. She refused to attend parties, dinners, or any other events that involved "that damn job." It had become evident that once her legal career was off to a successful start at a prestigious Chicago law firm, she was embarrassed to be married to "just a cop."

At the first July Fourth Kelly family picnic I attended, Sean's father led me to a corner of the yard, back by the garage, out of earshot of everyone else. We sat in old green- and white-weave lawn chairs. The smell of slow-burning charcoal and the sound of high-pitched bangs from cheap firecrackers filled the neighborhood. Holding a red Solo cup full of beer fresh from the keg that sat in a tub of ice, he told me about Sean's time in the army.

"You know Sean was awarded a Silver Star and a Purple Heart?"

"No. But I'm not surprised."

"He doesn't like me talking about it." He paused, scanned the yard to make sure Sean wasn't close by, took a long drink of his beer, and then started the story he was obviously anxious to tell. In January 2002, Sean had been deployed to Afghanistan during Operation Enduring Freedom as a part of the army's 10th, Mountain Division. In March of that year, in a valley known as "Hell's Halfpipe," his squad took heavy mortar fire. While engaging in a firefight with Al Qaeda fighters, he dragged three badly wounded members of his squad to the safety of a nearby creek bed, where he dressed their wounds. Sean was also wounded, catching shrapnel in both legs. He was sent home to mend and was awarded a Silver Star and Purple Heart.

While recuperating at Walter Reed Army Medical Center in D.C., he was offered the rare opportunity to transfer to the Army's Criminal Investigation Command, the CID. After three months of training, he redeployed to Afghanistan, where he undertook the thankless and dangerous assignment of investigating allegations that a small number of soldiers were responsible for the unlawful deaths of three villagers.

Six marines of the 26th Division pleaded guilty to the charges, and Kelly had made his bones as a top-notch investigator.

When he returned home in the winter of 2003, he decided to make law enforcement his life's work. Turning to the Internet for information about universities excelling in criminal justice studies, he discovered that Marquette University in Milwaukee offered a program that was ranked among the top ten in the country. It met all of his requirements: it was an excellent national university, it was close to home, and, between the G.I. Bill and a part-time job, he could afford the tuition.

Three years later, Sean graduated cum laude and set himself on a path that led him to another star, a CPD Detective Star, and a twelve-year career full of "righteous collars" and department commendations.

I watched the neighborhood Fourth of July fireworks that night from the park down the block from the Kelly home. I stole glimpses of Sean's family sitting together on old, threadbare blankets spread out on the park's lawn. Sean's dad sat in his green-and-white weave lawn chair, sitting on the rear edge of one of the blankets and holding court over the clan. Some of his younger grandchildren sat at his feet while Grandpa pointed to the explosions in the sky, making sure the little ones didn't miss a single burst of color. Sean's mother held the youngest Kelly grandchild in her arms, shielding the child's ears from the thunderous fireworks. One of the teenage grandchildren teased his cousin about a streak of purple coloring in her auburn hair. And on one of the blankets, Sean playfully wrestled with his young son, who I had met for the first time that day. I envied Sean—not for his wartime heroics or his career, but because of his family and especially his father. I wasn't sure if this family was special or this was the way a real family was supposed to be. Either way, I had found a home.

Suddenly, my memories of the fireworks' flashes of multi-colored light were replaced with the flashing blue light of the car's strobe. The siren wailed in my ears. Sean was looking over at me, struggling to get my attention. "Frank. Hey, Frank!" I turned away from the side window—and away from happier days.

We were approaching Pulaski and Lawrence. Sean looked over at me and asked for directions. "While you were off in your own little world there, the on-scene patrol bureau supervisor radioed to say that the demolition site where the body was found is completely fenced except for a gate that opens to the alley, so parking on Keeler isn't an option. He told me to enter the alley off Grove—the site's at the far north end of the alley. You used to work this neighborhood, so tell me where I can park, away from the scene."

CHAPTER 30
Detective Frank Vincenti

"The alley has to be part of the crime scene—we don't need another set of tire tracks and footprints there," I told Sean. "Take a left on Ainslie and then a right on Kedvale. There is a small warehouse on Kedvale near the end of the block where Kedvale dead-ends. It has an adjacent parking lot, which exits into the alley. Park in the lot, and we can walk across the alley to the Keeler demolition site from there."

As we approached Kedvale, Sean slowed and switched off the strobe and siren. We paused a moment to take a longer look. In the distance, we could see the flashing blue light bars of several patrol cars and a crowd that had formed on Keeler near Ainslie. Patrol officers had blocked off the entire block by placing crowd control barricades around the site. The press had beaten us to the scene. Reporters from WGN and the local affiliates of the three major national networks had arrived within thirty minutes of the first call.

Sean took a right onto Kedvale and headed for the end of the block, where we found the warehouse on our left. Abutting the warehouse was a parking lot, and just to the north of the lot was a 1950s-style ranch house partially obscured by overgrown bushes. I was right about the warehouse location, but it was boarded up and fenced off. Several City of Chicago notices were affixed to the chain link fence. The top line of the notices read "Off Limits—Do Not Enter" in letters large enough to read from the street. They were condemnation notices, faded by the sun and wrinkled by moisture. Sean drove past the warehouse to the parking lot and pulled into the driveway. He jammed on the brakes, sending both of us forward in our seats. The access to the lot was blocked by heavy rusted chains, padlocked across two fence posts.

We got out of the car and started walking toward the lot. I looked past it to the alley where I saw two more patrol cars parked. I was right about the backdoor short cut to the site. I walked a few steps ahead of Sean and stepped over the chain. Something caught Sean's eye. He stopped short, walked to the fence post where the padlock had been attached, and donned a pair of evidence gloves.

"Frank, hold on a minute."

I turned and walked back toward him. "What's up?"

"Take a look at this lock."

Without touching it, I looked at it from several angles. "Looks like fresh mud on the lock."

Sean wiped all the dirt off, revealing a shiny new brass surface. "This is a new lock."

Looking over to the condemnation notices, I asked, "Why would the city put a new lock on this lot—it's obviously been abandoned for months?"

"Even if someone from the city had put a new lock on this post, why is it covered in mud?"

I looked over my shoulder back to the lot's chained-off exit to the alley. As I strode toward the back of the lot, I pulled on a set of evidence gloves. I stood a couple of moments examining that lock, and then turned my head back toward him and shouted, "Same here."

As Sean approached, I said, "Well, we have two possibilities—"

Sean finished my sentence. "Either someone from the city installed new locks very recently and then rubbed fresh mud on them, which doesn't make sense, or the killer replaced the locks before he dumped the body."

Sean looked around the lot, beyond to the alley, and said, "The perp probably used bolt cutters to remove the old locks, replaced them with new ones, and rubbed dirt on them to make them less noticeable." Sean looked back to the alley and asked, "But why this way?"

I pointed to the end of the block. "Kedvale, deadends at an eight-foot-high wrought iron fence and behind the fence is a hedge just as tall."

"What's on the other side?"

"It's a park district property—Gompers Park."

Tilting my head toward the alley, I added, "The alley dead-ends at the park, too. Our guy had only one way in and out of this alley. He wanted a back-up exit in case the alley entrance at Grove was blocked."

I jerked my head back in the direction of the fence posts and chains. "Damn, by cleaning the locks we just contaminated fingerprints."

"I wouldn't worry about it." Sean shrugged. "This guy is too smart to have left prints. I mean, look at the thought it took to account for such a small detail of replacing the locks and rubbing dirt on them just to make sure he had an alternate escape route. He had scouted this site—it was neither random nor one of convenience."

"A lot of planning went into this. This guy is highly organized. I think we'll find more attention to detail when we examine the scene." I paused mid-sentence and looked back over my shoulder across the alley to the yellow tape. Without looking back at Sean, I said, "This wasn't his first kill. He's had practice."

CHAPTER 31
Detective Frank Vincenti

As we crossed the alley and approached the crime scene, I could see that everything had been done by the book. The first officer on the scene determined a homicide had occurred and notified the area's Bureau of Patrol Supervisor who, in turn, requested detectives and a forensic investigator be assigned. The patrol supervisor made sure that yellow barrier tape was used to create an outer perimeter.

Supervising Patrol Officer Fuentes saw us slip under the yellow tape and started toward us. Fuentes' greeting was usually laced with sarcasm, but not today. "When I saw the body, I had a feeling the case was in your wheelhouse—the scene looks staged, and the corpse—well see for yourself—it's why I asked for you two. I'm glad Dunbar had enough sense to honor my request."

Sean nodded to me and took Fuentes aside while I studied the overall scene from just inside the yellow tape. During our first two years as partners, Sean and I had broken several highly publicized multiple homicides, including the horrific Carlton family murders and one macabre cult killing. Sean attributed the collars to what he described as my ability to extract a "feeling" for the killer by immersing myself in the crime scene. He believed I did more than just inspect and analyze; he claimed I also "sensed" the killer's presence. He called it "getting in the killer's head." I suppose it was those special talents that Foster had first perceived years ago. Whatever it was, it seemed like we eventually drew mostly the bizarre and macabre cases—crime scenes that repulsed most detectives. I was glad to take them. Sean came along for the ride, trusting my instincts. As a result, we had established a routine that gave me the first crack at examining a crime scene.

I took only a few steps beyond the yellow tape. At that point I wasn't looking for anything specific. I just wanted to stand in the spot where the killer stood when he first entered the site, and picture what the killer saw. Near the front of the thirty-foot wide lot, I observed what little remained of three exterior brick walls and what I assumed to be a shallow basement or crawl space surrounded by a cement foundation. The demolition crew must have removed the wall facing the garage and created a ramp leading down into the basement.

Sean stepped up beside me. "I told Fuentes about the locks and advised him that we've assumed custody of the scene and instructed him to enlarge it to include the parking lot. A three-man forensics unit is here. I sent one of them to scour the parking lot and mark and bag the locks. And I have two standing by in the alley waiting for you to tell them where to start."

Looking down at his notes, he continued, "Fuentes told me that only the first-on-the-scene patrol officer had entered the basement and that he didn't disturb the crime scene, although one or more of the workers may have moved some bricks off the body. Now this is interesting— he also told me that the site foreman said that the place is well lit at night with portable floodlights on a timer. We checked the timer, and it had been reset to turn off at 2:00 a.m. I've got a couple of patrolmen canvassing neighbors, but so far no one saw anything."

"Tampering with the timer confirms that our guy was on the site before the gate was locked. Somehow he gained access."

"Yeah. The entry to the site was locked with what the foreman described as a Master Lock Pro model, but he said its shackle could have been snapped off with a set of long-handle bolt cutters."

Sean flipped his small notebook closed, stuffed his mechanical pencil in his shirt pocket, and looked up at me. "OK, Detective Vincenti, I'll step back and let you do your thing. Signal when you're ready for me."

I stood at the top of the wooden ramp that led into the basement and surveyed the scene. From where I stood, I could see salvaged, reddish-brown bricks spilled over what I presumed to be the body. The bricks were scattered, and a blue tarp was visible. The body lay perpendicular to the far wall opposite the ramp.

I walked down the ramp, stepping only on the outer edge, and then over to where the bottom edge of the ramp met the dirt floor. I stood still, visualizing the killer at work scraping out a shallow grave. I walked the perimeter of the basement, careful of where I stepped, staying as close to the cement foundation as I could. Oddly, I found a clear space between the far wall and the corpse; it showed no footprints or other disturbance. It looked liked it had been purposely cleared, almost like a path. I considered the possibility: he wanted the police to approach the body from this angle. OK, I'll play your game. What do you want me to see? I stepped gingerly along the makeshift path and approached the body. As I did I could see what the killer had intended. The body's head, covered by the tarp except for the eyes, was propped up as if looking at me—and its eyes were wide open. I was pretty sure our guy wanted us to first see the body from this perspective and wanted us to look into the victim's eyes. The obviously staged scene didn't startle me. There was no terror in the dead man's eyes.

"You forced those eyes open for my benefit, didn't you?"

I tiptoed through the bricks surrounding the body, then squatted and removed the one brick that remained near the top of the victim's head. I placed my hand on his head. It was soft and mushy. I looked down the entire length of the body and then placed both hands on the corpse's chest. It felt inflated or bloated on the left side, and I felt the sharp edges of what had to be his ribs, picturing them separated from the sternum. I closed my eyes trying to imagine if there was something extra under the tarp there. The image that came to mind was startling, and I drew my hand back as if I had touched a hot stove. I'm not sure how long I stared at the body, opening my imagination to the killer's mind. Finally, I heard Sean shouting to me: "Frank! Frank! You finished? Can I come down?"

I waved him down.

"What do you see on this one, Frank?"

"Fuentes was right to have us assigned to the case. This was a calculated, ritualistic kill. Our guy is killing with a purpose. He didn't know the victim, but it wasn't a random choice either."

"You're probably right. He's definitely a planner."

"I think he chose this site long before he entered with the body. Hell, he probably chose the site before he chose his victim. He knew ahead of time exactly where and how he was going to place the body. Placing the body was part of a ritual for him—shroud and all."

"Shroud?"

"Yeah. The blue tarp."

I looked over to where the killer had cleared a path and continued. "He sent a message to his victim. And he's sending us a message, too."

"You mean like 'stop me before I kill again' shit?" Sean asked.

"No." I pointed to the path. "He wanted us to walk around the body and approach it feet-first—that's why he faced the body toward the far inside wall and cleared a path for our approach. He knew that we would walk the perimeter before we started to examine the body."

I turned and looked at Sean. "Posing the head and forcing open the eyes could have been intended to shock and maybe even horrify us."

Sean nodded and finished the thought. "Or he was saying, 'Look at me!'"

"Yeah. That might be an even better explanation. I'm anxious to see what's under that tarp."

An assistant Cook County medical examiner appeared at the top of the ramp and called down, "Guys, time to let me and the evidence techs down there."

Sean was about to protest, but I waved them down, instructing them where to walk. With my assistance, one of the evidence techs removed each brick, bagged it, and labeled it. When the bricks were removed, the M.E. retrieved surgical scissors from his bag, and as the evidence tech and I held the body in place, he began to cut into the tarp, starting near the chin and working his way down toward the torso. As he cut, it became apparent that the body was unclothed. When the M.E. got as far as the abdomen, he stopped and looked up at us. "Well, this is a new one. Seems your perp cracked open the victim's rib cage and dislodged each of the ribs on the left side. Appears to be some foreign object slipped just under—" Startled, he stood up like he had just been poked in the ass with a stick.

"Jesus Christ!"

CHAPTER 32
Detective Frank Vincenti

Two days later, we still didn't have even a preliminary autopsy report. I checked my email one more time before I called. I was on the phone listening to the assigned assistant M.E.'s preliminary report when Sean placed a cup of coffee on my desk and sank down into his chair. We had been working virtually around-the-clock and needed to refuel.

"Anything yet?"

I held up my index finger, indicating just a minute. Then I hung up and quickly scribbled some notes. Picking up my coffee, I said, "The M.E. isn't done writing up the final report. He claims that they have a three-day back-up, but I've got the basics." I took a sip of my coffee and read from my notes: "Time of death was about 11:00 p.m. the night before the body was found. The victim died from blunt force trauma. His genitals were severed with some sort of thick-blade snipping tool, probably a bolt cutter, and his right hand was cut off with a reciprocating saw blade—both postmortem."

Sean interrupted. "Probably used the bolt cutter to crack open the victim's chest—probably the same one he used on the locks, and the—"

I nodded. "Yeah, and he knew what he was doing—he opened the chest cavity just enough to stuff his little 'memento' under the ribs."

"That's why the torso was such a mess when we saw it at the morgue."

I continued reading from my scribbled notes. "The M.E. found writing scrawled in blood on the right side of the victim's chest. He couldn't make it out, so he photographed it and is emailing it to me to see if we can decipher it. That's all he has for now." I stood and stretched out my back. The catnaps at my desk provided little real rest and left me stiff. "What did you find out about our victim?"

Sean shook his head. "Forensics still hasn't identified him. Nothing turned up in the fingerprint identification databanks, IAFIS, so far, and it will take a week to run the DNA."

"How about missing persons?"

"None that fit the victim's description."

"And that, Detective Kelly, tells us a lot about our killer, doesn't it? He chose someone who would not be missed."

"Yeah, but it's early. One still might come in."

"If you're right, it won't be for awhile and it won't be from a family member."

Sean looked up and shook his head, knowing better than to ask me how I knew that. "When you get the photograph from the M.E., would you print it for me?"

Sean preferred to work with paper and photographs that he could hold in his hands. I preferred to be as paperless as possible. I usually read reports and viewed crime scene photos on my computer screen or on the newly issued departmental iPads. "I'll leave it on your desk," I told him.

Sean was busy taking notes. He actually used an old yellow legal pad like those Foster was fond of, and they were the only two I knew who still used them. Without looking up, he asked, "What about the tarp and trace evidence?"

"The tarp's been sent to Forensics. The M.E. scraped under the fingernails, but they were clean. He sent samples of dried blood from the rib cage where our guy had severed the ribs from the sternum and some from the facial laceration on the hunch that it might not be the blood of our victim. No trace evidence. The body had been purged with oxygenated bleach."

"I'll call my buddy in Forensics in the morning to put a rush on the blood samples." Sean replied.

"Oh, and he found red particles of what appear to be fragments of a brick."

Sean stopped taking notes and looked up at me. "Bricks from the crime scene?"

"I don't think so. He found them under the portion of the tarp covering the victim's head." I was tired. Looking down at the cup of coffee on my desk, I said, "Sean, I think I'll skip the caffeine jolt and take a quick nap." My head ached, but there was no reason to tell Sean. Every time I complained of a headache, he told me to see a doctor. I didn't need a doctor. I needed a good night's sleep.

"Go ahead. While you take your nap, I'll ask the M.E. to get me a photo of the victim's face. I know it's pretty beaten up, but I've had good luck with our sketch artists over the years. One of them may be able to put together a sketch of what our victim looked like before his skull was crushed. If it's any good, I'll circulate it as a BOLO."

"Yeah, but 'Be on the Lookout' is hardly going to be an effective means for identification. Give it a try though. Come get me if something comes up."

I popped two Advil, washed them down with day-old Coke, and headed for the lower level bunkroom, a room with bunk beds and lockers intended for those occasions when a case kept us at the Belmont station past our shift. I kicked off my shoes, and placed my cell phone, weapon, and star in the small locker welded into each of the steel bed frames. As tired as I was, I still had trouble falling asleep. Details about the mutilation kept running through my head—it all seemed strangely familiar. Did I see it in Foster's files or was it something Foster had described to me? I wasn't sure. I'd have to ask him, but not yet. I finally succumbed to exhaustion and fell into a restless sleep.

I woke after about ninety minutes. I was in that twilight state, somewhere between being asleep and being fully awake, just lying there. Suddenly, the face of a man wearing a hoodie flashed in my head, and then, just as suddenly, it was gone. This had happened to me twice before: the face of a killer we pursued appearing in my dreams and, strangely, the face I saw turned out to match the killer's, but I never told anyone about it. Who would have believed me? I suppose it was a part of those "special talents" that Foster and Dunbar had spoken of years ago. I sat up, clearing my head. I tried to recall the details of what I had just seen, but the face under the hoodie was expressionless and unremarkable. Still . . . I sat on the edge of the bunk with an uneasiness in my gut.

CHAPTER 33
Detective Frank Vincenti

Finally, after a few more long days, we received more details from the M.E.'s office. Some of it made sense—some of it didn't. It was time for a chat with Foster.

Even after more than fourteen years, the man remained somewhat of a mystery to me. He spoke little of himself or family and never mentioned friends, although I knew of his relationship with Eddie Dunbar. I had done some research on my own about him. I learned that his mother had been the sole heir of the wealthy Chicago Galt family who had made their fortune in the stockyards of Chicago's South Side and had risen to notoriety when they financed some of David Burnham's early skyscrapers. His mother had died while Foster was a student at the University of Washington where he had some tangential involvement with the search for the Green River Killer. I asked him about that, but like so many other things about his life, he refused to talk about it. As an only child, he must have shared in his mother's wealth—there was no other way I could explain his lifestyle. He seldom spoke of his father. I got the sense that he was both proud of him and yet intimidated. His father was the longest sitting chief judge for the Northern District of Illinois, and during his tenure he had gained a reputation for meting out harsh sentences to felons who had a history of violence. And, although Foster had spent a year in law school in Seattle, he had little regard for lawyers and judges. He had been married, but he never spoke of his wife—over the years I had learned bits and pieces about her from Dunbar: she had been killed, and twenty years later, Foster was still no closer to tracking the killer down than he was when he was forced to resign. Foster had never spoken a single word about her to me, but I had sensed from my very first visit to his home that he was searching for something—or someone.

It was a little after 11:00 p.m. when I visited him that night. His so-called office hours started around 10:30, after the evening news. I ignored the faded "Out of Order" handwritten note he had taped over the 1960s-style doorbell. He had placed it there years ago to discourage uninvited visitors, preferring his solitary existence, uninterrupted by distractions. Only visitors who could bring insight to a cold case or a new conundrum for him to ponder were welcome. These days, if the bell actually rang, he knew it was me.

As usual, Foster yelled from somewhere deep in his apartment, "It's open, Detective."

I pushed hard against the door that was slightly swollen in the door jam and entered his small hallway. There were no lights—not unusual for Foster. He had told me that it was easier for him to visualize and recreate his cold cases when sitting alone in the dark. The short hallway opened to a large room that he used as a combination living and dining room. As I turned the corner and peered into the darkness, I yelled back, "Where the hell are you?"

Two clicks and then a splash of light from a table lamp silhouetted Foster in his beat-up leather recliner. "Here," he said, and with a faint smile, he looked up at me.

The apartment was filled with the odor of cigar smoke. Foster had hardly aged since I first saw him stride into the NEIU classroom almost fourteen years earlier. He was still trim and fit, but now his salt-and-pepper hair was more salt than pepper, and he had taken to wearing reading glasses. Classical music filled the apartment. I didn't recognize the score that was about to serve as background music to a discussion of murder and mutilation.

"You got some time?" I asked.

"Yes, but you don't."

"What?"

"You have a killer on your hands who mutilates his victims." He saw that I was surprised. "Come now, Francis, I still have plenty of friends on the job. They keep me pretty well informed, but they couldn't—or wouldn't—tell me all the details. I've been waiting for you to show up." He pointed to the upholstered wingback chair opposite his. "Now, take a seat and tell me what you've got."

I dumped myself into the only other comfortable chair in his apartment and leaned back. "Well, I can tell you what we don't have—we haven't been able to identify the victim."

"Anonymity of the victim makes it harder to trace the murder back to the killer. That was intentional and typical of a serial killer."

"What makes you think it's a serial killer?"

"You know damn well it is, Francis. Otherwise you wouldn't be here. He took a souvenir, didn't he?"

"Two."

Foster nodded. "Body parts?"

"A hand—the right one—and the genitals."

He didn't seem surprised. "Do you know how he removed them?'"

"Crudely. It looks like the hand was severed by some kind of power saw. He used bolt cutters on the genitals. And our victim was sodomized with a length of wood. The M.E. speculates it was some kind of old tool handle."

"Torture."

"That seems right, but all of that occurred postmortem."

"Then something must have gone wrong. What else?"

"What else?"

Foster sat forward in his chair. "Yes. There's more. A guy like this always leaves something behind—a memento to impress the police or to send a message. What did he leave behind?"

I surrendered the information that only four other people knew, including the killer. "He cracked open the victim's rib cage on the left side and stuffed a set of genitals under the ribs, but the genitals didn't belong to the victim."

Foster leaned back in his chair and momentarily stared past me into the darkness of a corner of his apartment. Without looking at me, he explained, "Some rape victims gain symbolic revenge by killing their attacker and stuffing the attacker's genitals in his mouth. But, that's not what your guy did. Francis, don't focus on stuffing them under the ribs. He placed them on top of the heart, didn't he? Your killer is telling you that he has internalized the pain of a homosexual rape."

"But why not just use the genitals of the victim? Why leave behind the genitals of an earlier victim?"

"Oh, he's just playing a game with you. He's letting you know that this isn't his first kill and that he is smarter than you. He's saying, 'I've done this before, but you stupid cops didn't find the body, did you?' He wants you to find the other bodies. What about the hand? Did he leave behind a severed hand?"

"No. He must be taking them with him."

"Trophies. Your killer is a confused and complicated person." He looked back over to me asking, "What are you holding back?"

Now he was pushing me for more than I wanted to disclose, but to get his help, I had to tell him one more detail. "He wrote a message on the victim's chest using the victim's own blood. It took us some time to decipher it. It was written in a child-like printing style, and it smeared against the tarp."

I started to explain about the blue tarp, but he cut me off, "Yes, I know about the shroud—we'll come back to that later. The message . . ."

"We're pretty sure it reads: 'h-e-i-m.4.'"

Foster raised his thick graying eyebrows, lifted his chin ever so slightly and, in a measured tone, said, "The word 'heim' is the German and Norwegian equivalent for the English word, 'home,' but I suppose you already figured that out."

Actually, I hadn't figured that out. I was focused on the severed body parts.

"The dumpsite—did it reflect any remorse?"

"That's a tough one. The way the body was wrapped suggests remorse, but I don't think this guy is capable."

"Nor do I."

For a moment or two he lowered his head and closed his eyes. To anyone else, he may have appeared to be dozing off, but I had seen it before—he was visualizing the murder. He opened his eyes and reached over to his Dunhill crystal ashtray, retrieved a half-finished cigar, and relit it. He sat back in his chair, took a long draw on his cigar, and let a cloud of smoke slowly escape from his mouth. Finally, leaning forward and pointing his cigar toward me, accentuating each word, he said, "You do realize that he isn't finished killing?"

"You mean because he wouldn't have taken the genitals from this victim unless he was going to—"

"Yes—make a gift of them to someone else. Like I said when you walked in, you don't have time. This guy is going to kill again—and soon. You have to think of this as if you walked into the middle of a movie. You're viewing just a few scenes. You didn't see the beginning, and you don't know how the movie will end, but you can anticipate the ending. Visualize, Francis, visualize."

I stood to leave. Foster reached out and put his hand on my arm. "Francis, you knew all this before you got here."

"Yes. Except for the significance of the placement of the genitals. I missed that. I failed to recognize that he placed them on top of the heart. And, I need to look closer at the message on the torso. About your movie—I have visualized the ending and I don't like what I see."

CHAPTER 34
Detective Frank Vincenti

I buried my father two weeks before Christmas. With three inches of snow on the ground, the day was bright and sunny, albeit bitterly cold. I stared at traces of steam that rose from the hole into which my father was about to be lowered. There was no priest. The funeral home provided an assistant director who hurried through a reading of the Twenty-third Psalm and quickly mumbled an Our Father, Hail Mary, and Glory Be.

Three days before, I had been awakened by an early morning call from the desk sergeant at the 25th District. "Detective Vincenti, I'm sorry that I have to advise you of this, but a patrolman has found your father deceased. The officer is still on the scene and hasn't disturbed anything pending your notification and instructions."

I later learned that one of my father's neighbors, a middle-aged woman who apparently had befriended him, had alerted the police. The neighbor's phone had rung around midnight. The caller ID displayed 'F. Vincenti' and my father's phone number. She answered, heard incoherent mumbling, then nothing. She called back several times, but the line was busy each time, and after several failed attempts at the front door, she finally called 911. The police found him dead on his bathroom floor wearing only his stained boxer shorts. The first-on-the-scene patrolman recognized his name and realized that he was my father. He then went through channels to make sure notification was courteous. He'd thoughtfully covered the body with a sheet he found in the linen closet.

I pulled the sheet back and stood over him. He appeared to have lost a lot of weight, and his face was drawn and sunken. His eyes were still open, staring at the ceiling. I bent over to close his eyes. I was about to place my out-stretched fingers on his eyelids, but changed my mind. Let him enter eternity with his eyes wide open so he could see what awaits him. I felt neither remorse nor satisfaction that he was out of my life. What was it Foster taught me about emotional detachment?

On the kitchen table, I found an empty pill bottle of Avinza, a prescription-only form of morphine used for severe pain. Out of curiosity more than anything else, I called the doctor whose name and phone number appeared on the pharmacy label. He told me with a degree of distress in his voice that in May my father had been diagnosed with stage IV pancreatic cancer. It was untreatable, and much to the doctor's disappointment, my father had refused palliative treatments until this past October when the pain had become debilitating and caused him to be confined to his home.

I did not arrange for a wake. Nor could I muster the hypocrisy of asking the local parish priest at St. William's to say a funeral Mass for him. Sean's brother, Father Patrick William, offered to perform the ceremony, but I was too embarrassed to accept. No, I ushered my father from the nearby funeral home's embalmer's table straight to the St. Joseph Cemetery plot next to my mother. As the assistant funeral director concluded the service with the usual "May perpetual light shine upon him" drivel, I looked at her gravestone and then back to my father's coffin suspended above the freshly dug hole. I hadn't known my mother, and wished I had never known my father. I realized I'd been an orphan all along.

Although Beth initially resisted attending the funeral, she finally acquiesced. She understood the anguish I suffered because of my father and questioned why I even bothered with a graveside ceremony. She was right. I had no good answer. Beth carried her large Prada handbag, and under her quilted winter coat, wore a St. John black knit dress—signals to me that she intended to go directly to the office at the conclusion of the ceremony. Foster and Sean attended the funeral, but no one else. I preferred it that way.

As the four of us walked back to our cars, Foster looked over to me and said, "Francis, let your pain be buried with him."

I stopped. Foster took a few more steps before he realized I wasn't beside him. He stopped and turned to face me. The sun was bright behind him, just over his left shoulder. I was looking almost directly into it and was forced to squint. My eyes didn't quickly adjust, and darkness covered Foster's face. I stepped closer to him, gently placed my hand on his shoulder and said, "Many years ago, you told me that my father never understood that he was a victim of his father's shame and bitterness and that he would carry both to his grave. I'm sure you were right, but you may have been wrong about my father's legacy of anger and bitterness. I fear his legacy is mine after all."

Foster looked down at the snow, now trampled with footprints. His shadow reached across the snow to me, and, after a long moment, he looked up at me with a sadness I had not seen on his face before. For the first time in years, I let my guard down: "I don't know how I'll ever let go of all of the pain he caused—I've tried, believe me, I've tried. His death changes nothing for me."

Foster stepped forward, embraced me, and whispered in my ear: "God is just. He will pay back trouble to those who trouble you." He stepped back and looked me in the eye. "I'm counting on it Francis, and so should you." Without waiting for me to react, he turned and walked away.

CHAPTER 35
Detective Frank Vincenti

The snow crunched under our feet as we walked from the gravesite to our cars. Sean stopped and walked over to me. "Frank, in my neighborhood, after we put a family member in the ground, we have a final drink while we sit and reminisce. Let's head over to Annie's Bar and have a Bushmills or two and drink to the future instead."

I glanced back at Foster. Sean added, "He's agreed to come." I wasn't sure I wanted his company.

I looked to Beth for a reaction. She was reading emails on her iPhone. Without looking up, she muttered, "You go with Sean. I'm taking the car to the office." Then she turned and walked away without saying another word.

Once we were ensconced in a booth at Annie's, Foster asked me about Beth. He waited until Sean had stepped outside to take a call. As was Foster's custom, he questioned me about deeply personal issues when I was most vulnerable—and after I had a couple of Bushmills.

"Beth's attitude today had more to do with you than with the death of your father, and Sean tells me that ever since Thanksgiving you've been withdrawn and distracted—your head is not in the game. What's going on?"

Like me, Foster loathed sports bars and always insisted on sitting at a booth or table, never at the bar. We took a small booth away from the crowd and out of earshot of cheesy Christmas carols. I looked down at my drink. "You're about to give me some unsolicited advice, aren't you?"

"The only advice worth listening to is unsolicited."

Foster had never been in favor of the marriage. When I had visited him late one night six years ago to tell him that Beth and I were to be married, he puffed away on his cigar and poured drinks for the two of us.

"Don't be confused, Francis," he'd said then, "this isn't a congratulatory drink. It will help me digest your news and perhaps help bring you to your senses."

"Foster, she said that she loves me and I—"

"You don't love her. Sometimes I'm not sure you even know what love is."

I'd taken a long drink from his Lismore tumbler, tired of his amateurish psychoanalysis and meddling.

"I'll take your silence as agreement. You're making a mistake, Francis. This won't end well."

And now, years later, he was at it again. I tried to deflect his question about Beth's latest slight.

"She's just having a tough time at the firm. She's under a lot of pressure, works all hours, and is frustrated. She hates being relegated to mundane assignments, craves recognition, and gets upset when I get immersed in these macabre cases. I'm sure she's depressed, but it's situational. She'll feel better when she's assured she's on the firm's partner track."

Foster stared down at his glass momentarily, shook his head, and in a tone reminiscent of a reprimand from my father said, "No, she'll remain depressed, Francis. Lawyers as a group suffer from depression at a rate three times the national average and have a drug addiction twice as high. There's a lot going on with her that you refuse to acknowledge. Don't kid yourself about her problem."

He was right, but I wasn't ready to admit it. I took a long, slow swallow, draining the glass except for a few half-melted ice cubes. I was in no rush to explain. Foster sensed I was stalling.

"I warned you. You came from two different cultures and two vastly different economic backgrounds. Blue bloods don't marry cops. You married the first woman who told you that she loved you."

I stared down at the melting ice. I knew now he had been right all along. I just didn't want to face facts. I surrendered the information he was fishing for. "Thanksgiving morning she called me from Santa Barbara and issued an ultimatum: either I get off the force or she'll leave me." There was no sense hiding it from him any longer.

Foster finished his drink and pushed the empty glass to the side. "Well, she finally got around to it. I knew she would. It was just a matter of time before she made you choose between her and me."

"What?"

"It has little to do with your job or with you. She resents me—sees me as competition."

"I don't buy that for a second. She's forcing me to make a career choice I don't want to make. That's all."

"You're wrong. She's the one making a choice—actually, she's already made it. So let her live with it and move on."

Jealously? Was that it? Was she jealous of the time I spent with Foster or was Foster jealous of her? Was he, after everything, a clinging father who wouldn't let go of his only child?

I signaled the waitress for another round.

Sean got me home safe, but late. I cracked our bedroom door and saw that Beth was already asleep. She had been working fourteen-hour days at the firm and was likely exhausted again. I had trouble understanding how she could complain about the shifts I worked and my late nights when her hours at the firm were usually longer and just as unpredictable. I stood quietly and stared at her. She appeared content and peaceful, but I knew she was filled with contempt for my world. I hoped it was fleeting and that, when she was confident that she was on the track to partnership at the firm, she would return to being the woman I had married.

I closed the door, made a bed on the couch, and thought about how much I missed the warm comfort of a dog curled up at my feet. We'd said goodbye to our mutt at the beginning of December. We both knew it was coming. The good folks at the Anti-Cruelty Society had warned us when we adopted him that he had a heart defect. It's probably why I convinced Beth to take him home with us. I used to believe in lost causes. I reached up to flip out the light. My dad and my dog had died within weeks of each other. I'd only cried once.

CHAPTER 36
Detective Frank Vincenti

"We got a hit," Sean announced from his end of the cubicle.

"A hit on what?"

"Our friend in the morgue. His name is Henry S. Edwards. His landlord recognized the artist's rough sketch that went out on the BOLO. He rents an apartment in a rooming house at 8213 North Summerdale. The landlord said that on the Tuesday after Thanksgiving he got a call from Edwards's boss at an auto repair shop in the city. Apparently, Edwards gave the landlord's phone number as his emergency contact information."

I interrupted. "No family."

"Right. Anyway, Edwards's boss told the landlord that Edwards hadn't shown up for work or called for three days. The landlord pleaded ignorance and hung up. Then he let himself into Edwards's flat. Everything looked normal, so he left and didn't give it another thought. A week later, the landlord found a post office notice taped to the outside of Edwards's mailbox; the post office had suspended delivery because his mailbox was full. So the officious proprietor reported a missing person. The desk sergeant was sharp enough to show the guy BOLOs from the past few weeks, and the landlord ID'd him."

I shut down my computer and slipped on my jacket. "Let's go!"

As we walked to the station's parking lot, Sean asked, "Are you up for this? I was surprised to see you this morning. You are entitled to a few furlough days for a death of a family member, you know."

"No, I'm fine. I don't feel any differently today than I did last week or last month." It was pretty much the truth, except for Foster's unsuccessful attempt to comfort me at the cemetery and his lecture at Annie's.

The building was a large four-floor structure built in the 1920s. The landlord, a bald elderly shriveled-looking little man, met us at the ground-floor front entrance in a small alcove with plastic holiday garland hung over the interior doorway. As he led us up the three flights of worn wooden stairs, he explained that there were thirty-two one-room apartments in the building, eight to a floor, and a shared-bath for every four units. Edwards's flat was on the top floor.

The fourth-floor lobby smelled of disinfectant and stale cigar smoke. Light from an old-fashioned sky light with several cracked panes filled the hallway. Cold air leaked from it into the lobby where some of the doors were decorated with cheap artificial Christmas wreaths. Others still displayed cardboard cutouts of Thanksgiving turkeys. With a master key in his hand, the landlord stepped toward the only door without any kind of decoration. Sean gently placed his hand on the landlord's arm and said, "Please. Let me open it." The landlord handed the key over to Sean who then unlocked the door, carefully swung it open, glanced inside, and then stepped out of the way. Sean looked back at me and said, "Let me know when I can come in."

I stood in the doorway for a few moments and surveyed the room. It was no more than twenty by twenty-five with an unmade twin bed, a mahogany chest of drawers, an old blue vinyl LazyBoy recliner across from a small television sitting on a cheaply made pressed-board cabinet, a kitchen table with just one chair, and a kitchenette with relatively new appliances. It had a wooden floor, and in the middle Edwards had added an old dark green throw rug. The room was very cold. I looked for and found a radiator just to the right of the door. I placed my hand on it—no heat.

I sat on his unmade bed. I pictured Edwards going about his day in this small flat. I got up and looked in the refrigerator. I was surprised to see that he ate a balanced diet: milk, cheese, a partial head of lettuce, eggs, packaged lunchmeat, and the remnants of a case of Budweiser. His freezer was empty except for a package of frozen broccoli, a carton of chocolate ice cream and some frosted-over ice cube trays. The sink contained a dirty knife and fork, a small frying pan, a crumpled ball of aluminum foil, and a dinner plate crusted with egg yolk.

Next to the recliner was a stack of newspapers and under them, magazines. I moved the papers aside and took a quick look at the magazines. They were hardcore porn. Instinctively, I looked over to the television. I noticed wires leading from the back of the TV through a hole in the top of the cabinet. I walked to the cabinet and opened the doors. Inside was a small, inexpensive looking DVD player and next to it sat a pile of unmarked DVDs. I found the remote, turned on the TV and DVD player and slid in one of the discs. I saw just enough to recognize that the boys pictured were no more than ten years old and were engaged in sex acts with older men. Child porn.

I recalled Foster's outrage about the abuse of "the most innocent among us." His anger became my anger. I snapped it off as quickly as I could and threw the remote hard against the wall behind the TV, smashing it into a dozen small pieces—I had to dodge what remained of the remote as it careened back at me. If it had evidentiary value, I just ruined it. Without looking at Sean, I bolted out of the room, and as I crossed the threshold, I said, "Let's get evidence techs here. We need to know a lot more about this guy and why our killer chose him."

CHAPTER 37
Anthony

It didn't take months or years for the apparition to return. This time, it was only a few weeks. This time, I knew it was coming—I felt it in my bones. Because the message that was to give meaning to Henry's death had gone no farther than the dirt floor on Keeler, the apparition hadn't been satisfied.

It wasn't my fault. The press gave only superficial coverage to the discovery of Henry's body and made no mention of its condition. Instead, Chicago media continued to be preoccupied with the mounting number of gang-related murders in pockets of the city's south and west sides. With each new shooting, the press gauged the number of murders against historic levels, month-by-month, year-by-year, as if it were some kind of contest to set a new record—deaths without meaning, deaths without a message. And the police . . . well, the police were just too damn stupid to appreciate the subtlety of my handiwork.

While the city prepared for Christmas, I prepared to kill again. I had no choice. I returned to scouting potential dumpsites, visiting neighborhood bars, and watching for my next target. I stayed true to my routine.

A few days before Christmas, I headed to O'Hare to take a look at a new construction project on the northeastern edge of the airport's property where a back-up communications center was being built. Its construction was controversial, over budget, and behind schedule. And the project was already in the public eye. As a dumpsite for a mutilated body, it could immediately garner the kind of attention demanded by the apparition.

I had stopped at the corner of Montrose and Karlov, waiting for the traffic light to change when I spotted a cement mixer turning onto Karlov, white exhaust smoke billowing from its tailpipe. New construction in this neighborhood? Curious, instead of continuing west on Montrose, I took a quick right onto Karlov and spotted the cement mixer where it had taken its place in a line of trucks loaded with building materials waiting to enter a construction site. I drove slowly past the line of trucks, keeping my eyes on the street in front of me and throwing glances at the site that stretched from mid-block all the way south to the next intersection at Kelso. I turned right onto Kelso and circled the block. As I approached the entrance on Karlov for a second time, I tapped the brakes, paused momentarily, and spotted a partially complete walled structure where workers were unloading cinder blocks. It was worth a closer look.

I parked on a side street three blocks away, and walked back to the site, cutting through alleys and backyards. A stainless steel step-up van selling coffee from its side counter was parked on Karlov, just down the street from the work site. I zipped up my black fleece vest, pulled down my ball cap just above my eyes, and headed for the cover of the food truck.

"Lemme have a coffee, black,"

"I'm getting ready to shut down, pal. What's left isn't fresh."

"Don't matter. I'll take whatever ya got, as long as it's hot." I didn't look back at the counterman; instead, I studied the site across the street. It looked promising.

"Doesn't your union have rules about working in the cold?"

"Huh?" I didn't turn around.

"Your union. Shouldn't it be out here shutting down the site? Seems to me you shouldn't have to work when the temperature is in the teens."

"Suppose so."

The counterman poured a full cup and slid it across the counter toward me. Steam rose in delicate swirls, then disappeared. "And that emptied the pot, so it's on the house."

I nodded and blew on the coffee as if it were too hot to drink while slowly surveying the scene across the street. I was already familiar with the area—it was primarily residential with a mix of blue-collar workers, office staff, and latchkey kids. The kind of place people looked out for their next-door neighbor, but no one else.

An old three-story brown brick building sat mid-block; immediately to its south was the construction site. It appeared to be a school to which a gym or auditorium was being added. The main building looked like countless other aging Chicago schools: depression-era stonework, light brown bricks, tall windows. A sign naming the architects and the construction company stood in front of the building's entrance. It blocked my view of the full name of the school, but I could make out the words "High School" on the building just beyond the right edge of the sign. I glanced back to the line of trucks unloading construction material. That can't be the only entrance to the site. Scanning the fence line I confirmed my hunch. There was a second entrance just off Kelso and, just beyond that, across the street, there was a large blacktop parking lot, presumably for the students and staff.

It had potential. It was closer than the O'Hare site, there was an area near the entrance off of Kelso where four cinder block walls had been constructed, and the Kelso entrance would allow quick access and the privacy I would require. I could dump the body at night and be assured the construction crew would find it the following morning.

A school—how could the press give short shrift to the discovery of a mutilated body left in a schoolyard? Dumping a body there would shock this peaceful neighborhood and provide the press a basis for the sensationalized headlines they always chased. The accompanying story would have to fully describe the condition of the body and finally, finally, spread the message. And it would be a message that would survive the passage of time as students would repeat the details of the murder, pointing to the very spot in the gym where I had left the mutilated corpse. My handiwork and message would become school legend. I liked that idea. I liked it a lot.

CHAPTER 38
Detective Frank Vincenti

It had taken more than ten days since Edwards's body had been found for the M.E. to send us a final written autopsy report. He emailed it to us on the morning after our visit to Edwards's apartment with a note to let us know that the M.E. staff had been overwhelmed by the five bodies that had hit their tables over the past ten days. Gang-related shootings didn't slow down because of bad weather or the Christmas season. I had no reason to doubt him. He assured us that the autopsy was completed the day after the body was delivered to the Cook County Morgue, only the paperwork had been delayed.

As was our custom, Sean and I read it separately, and we each made our own set of notes and lists of questions. Regardless of how long or short the report, we always waited an hour or so to confer after we concluded our separate reviews to ensure that we had developed independent analyses; that way, we avoided feeding into each other's observations and conclusions. We advanced the process by disagreeing, not agreeing.

After an intense hour, I looked over to him. "Coffee?"

"Yep." He nodded.

A string of frigid days gripped the city. Even for Chicago, it was unusually cold for mid-December, and there was still a layer of snow on the ground, although the main thoroughfares and sidewalks were clear and dry. I put on my scuffed and worn black leather waist-length jacket that I bought while still in college, wrapped my wool scarf around my neck, and pulled my Bears stocking cap down over my ears. "I'm good to go."

Sean had his cell phone pressed to his ear while he put on his sport coat. I could tell it was a personal call, so I took a few steps toward the stairway. I waited only a few minutes, and as he pulled on his overcoat and navy wool ball cap, he said, "Sorry. I had to take that—it was Mom."

We headed out to the closest good cup of coffee—a Dunkin' Donuts shop three blocks away. As we walked against the cold gusts blowing off the lake, Sean broached the topic of Christmas dinner. It was the last thing on my mind. I was completely preoccupied with some of the more disturbing details of the autopsy report.

"Mom called to say that she wants you and Beth to come for dinner Christmas Day."

I looked over at him, puzzled. I was both pleased that his mother had thought of me, but annoyed knowing, as he did, that Beth would likely decline. Again. "Tell her thanks," was all I was able to muster.

"Maybe you can convince Beth to come this time."

"What? You think that Beth would suddenly become sympathetic because my father died? That has nothing to do with it." I snapped back in a tone harsher than I intended.

"I know better, but Mom doesn't, and you should know by now that she never gives up."

"I'll bring it up with Beth, but she's probably already made reservations at the Four Seasons for Christmas brunch."

As Sean swung open the door to Dunkin' Donuts, he warned me, "Well, don't be surprised if you get a call from Mom."

Apparently, the subzero temps had won out over the need for caffeine. The line for coffee usually snaked through a roped queue around the front of the shop this time of day. But today there were only three other customers in the shop. They appeared to be students, each with a laptop open; parkas piled high in the corner of their booth.

Motioning to the counter, Sean said, "I got it. Get us a table."

I chose a small table in a corner far out of earshot of the other customers, grabbed a napkin, and wiped the table clean. Before I could get my jacket off, Sean put our two large coffees on the table. He removed his ball cap and overcoat, tossing both of them on the bench seat opposite me, and sat down.

"Well?" asked Sean.

"This guy worries me."

"He has a working knowledge of forensics."

"You mean his use of oxygenated bleach?"

Blowing on his coffee to cool it, Sean nodded. "Yeah, he knew to purge the body of trace evidence. Regular bleach would have left something behind."

I lifted the plastic lid off my cup. "The post-mortem mutilation had a very specific purpose. The mutilation was motivated by this guy's conflicted aggressive emotional state of mind."

Sean hesitated, but then asked, "Are you in his head yet?"

"No," I replied, irritated with the question. No sense telling him about the hooded image I'd seen.

Sean let it go. "His methods were crude and brutal."

"I don't know what to make of that—he chose this victim for a reason. Did he want to punish or torture him and then changed his mind? Is the mutilation a part of the message that he's sending us? It can't be a message to his victim since the mutilation occurred after his victim could no longer feel pain."

Sean used a napkin to blot spilled coffee off of the right sleeve of his sport coat. "The mutilation here seems to have a control element to it, though. Maybe he had intended something more but was interrupted. There's a lot here, Frank. If you're right that this guy is just getting started, we don't have a lot of time to speculate." Then he glanced over at me with a quizzical look. "Time to talk to Foster again?"

I didn't answer. I was still conflicted over my reaction to Foster's unexpected show of emotion at the cemetery. I turned my head to the street and looked out the window, watching a few flakes of new snow blow and swirl. Another two inches had been forecast, but it wasn't supposed to start this early. Without looking back at Sean, I sighed. "Yeah. Let's talk to Foster."

As we left the shop, someone called to me from across the street. Although I didn't recognize him, he obviously recognized me. It was my only friend from the old neighborhood, Tony Protettore. I hadn't seen or talked to him since our sophomore year in high school when his family moved away. Sean headed back to the station as Tony and I talked briefly. He told me that he had never realized his dream of becoming a Chicago cop, but had become a high school teacher and wrestling coach and was now "between assignments" as he phrased it. He said he'd been the director of the Racine County Park District wrestling program, but had just returned to Chicago and was staying at a friend's place in the old neighborhood. Sensing I was anxious to go, he handed me a scrap of paper with a phone number and asked me to call him when I had more time to talk. As we parted, I recalled how twenty years earlier he had looked after me on the school playground.

Sean wasn't too far ahead of me, so I jogged to catch up. "Who was that?" he asked.

"Just someone—and something—I thought I'd left behind in the old neighborhood."

At the corner, we waited for the light to change. I looked down at the piece of paper Tony had handed me, then wadded it up, and tossed it into a city trash bin. I didn't give it another thought.

CHAPTER 39
Anthony

Heavy cloud cover blocked the morning sun on yet another bitterly cold day. More snow had fallen overnight, leaving a fresh coat on the lawns and sidewalks still undisturbed by foot traffic. The snow gave the raw ground of the site a look of purity that would soon be trampled into gray mud to match the morning's slate gray sky.

The truck's heater blew intermittent blasts of hot air, shutting down every ten minutes or so like it had a mind of its own. I circled the block at the Karlov site, scouting the area again, watching the comings and goings and getting a feel for the construction crew's routine. After two trips around the block, I parked down the street in a spot that still had an hour on the meter. I pulled my hood over my ball cap, slipped on my black fleece vest, and jammed a pair of Atlas work gloves into one of the vest's pockets before heading toward a mom and pop diner a few blocks north on Pulaski. It was packed with blue-collar guys, most dressed in winter gear for outside work. Carpenters, bricklayers, and material men filling up on greasy hash browns and runny eggs before heading to the school. I wasn't there for breakfast, though. I was there for information, to learn what I could from listening to and watching the men who spent the day in the cold, grinding out a living at a school construction site I intended to make famous.

I opened the steamed-up glass door and slid past three bulky guys on their way out. I didn't bother removing my cap or hood. I found a small, unoccupied booth in the back corner, slid across a cracked vinyl seat, and pretended to be interested in the menu. After my order came, I ate slowly and studied the faces of the workers. Dressed as I was, I would blend right in once I got to the site. I paid the bill at the front of the restaurant, and asked for a large coffee in a to-go cup as the other workers had done, and then walked back to the booth I had just occupied and tossed down a tip that was neither too generous nor too little. As I headed toward the front door, I spotted a battered and scuffed yellow hard hat sitting on a chair where, a few minutes earlier, one of the workers had eaten alone. I snatched it up as if it was mine and hurried out the door.

I took my time walking to the site, lagging behind other workers as I tried to get the lay of the land. Although I knew the neighborhood, I now viewed the alleys, the narrow side streets lined with parked cars, and "one-way" signs with a strategic eye. Once at the site, I stopped between parked cars and sipped my coffee. I could see that the crews gained entry to the site off Kelso through a single gate. It appeared that the wide gate on Karlov was clearly for access by large trucks like the cement mixer that had first drawn my attention to the site. Even now, trucks were lined up again, waiting to deliver pre-fab steel window frames and doorways, roofing materials, cinder block, and what appeared to be decorative façade bricks. I could use the Kelso entrance when the time came, and use the Karlov gate as a backup if Kelso was blocked. Identifying two ways in and out of the dumpsite was always a part of my preparation.

Time for a closer look. I tossed the half-empty coffee cup under one of the parked cars, stuck my cap in my back pocket, and put on the hard hat, angling it forward to cover as much of my face as I could. As I approached the gate on Kelso, I was pleased with what I saw: no temporary floodlights, and the gate appeared to have been secured with a heavy duty, but otherwise common, lock—a duplicate of which

I could buy at any discount home supply store. I stopped about twenty feet short of the gate to study the cinder block walls, making sure they would screen my placement of a body. Good enough.

As I walked back along Kelso, I spotted a short, middle-aged man wearing black pants, an old black cloth overcoat, and a black and white checked wool scarf. There was something about him that immediately didn't sit well with me. As I drew closer, I could see in his eyes that he had something to hide. The eyes. It was always the eyes that revealed a man's sins. I had seen the same look in other men—the same look on Henry's face—it was a look that shielded dark secrets. He stood on the sidewalk at the corner, yelling and gesturing at someone down the block. I took a few more steps toward the corner and saw that the target of the man's ire was two small boys trying to sneak through an opening in the chain link fence.

"You two again! I've told you kids a dozen times to stay away from this site. Now get the hell out of here! Is there something wrong with you that you don't understand? I don't want to see you around here again!"

I choked down the urge to lash out, to tell him in no uncertain words to leave the kids alone, that there's nothing wrong with them. Just a mix of curiosity and innocent mischief.

The small man turned and started to walk toward the Kelso entrance and toward me. Wanting to take a measure of the man, I kept my head down, nodded slightly and, in a low voice, said, "Mornin'." With a blank stare, the son of a bitch ignored me, walked quickly past, and approached two men in suits wearing white hard hats and holding what appeared to be rolled-up site plans and blueprints. I stopped, turned, and casually moved closer, trying to overhear their conversation.

"You guys are behind schedule. You're not getting another damn penny until you catch up with the project schedule and get back on budget."

The back-up alarm of a diesel dump truck, dropping its load of gravel, drowned out most of what they were saying, but I heard the older suit call the small man something-or-other Anders and, between the beeps of the truck's alarm, I was able to overhear the younger suit explaining that the contract required regular installment payments.

"I don't give a damn what it says. I'm getting heat so you get heat. Get it done!" He started to walk away, stopped abruptly, and turned back to the suits. "Oh, and one more thing. Check your fencing. I don't want any more damn kids poking around the site."

So, Mister Anders, you're a first-class bully, huh? What else are you?

CHAPTER 40
Detective Frank Vincenti

"What took the M.E. so long to get this report done? And why didn't you come sooner?"

Foster bellowed his greeting as we took off our coats and shoes, careful not to track in any snow. I knew the cold weather routine at Foster's. We left our shoes on the large rough-hewn fiber mat at the front door and hung our coats on the hooks of an old oak coat rack that had stood guard in his hallway for as long as I had known the man. Instead of the usual odor of full-bodied cigar smoke, the faint aroma of fresh pine greeted us as we entered his combination living and dining room. As was his tradition, Foster's sole Christmas decoration was a fresh Douglas fir tree wedged in the far corner of the living room and decorated with old fashion bubble lights and his Grandmother Galt's antique ornaments. Wagner's *Siegfried* played in the background.

Sean walked over to the tree and studied each ornament as if it were a work of art—which, in fact, they were. Foster had told me the story before; in fact, he told me the same story every Christmas. His deceased maternal grandmother, Violet Ann Galt, had made it a family tradition to collect handcrafted ornaments from all over Europe as the family traveled abroad. The Galt family had a lot of old world traditions and a lot of old money. Sean had seen the tree and its ornaments over the years, but it was his way of paying respect to Foster's traditions.

Dressed for the chill of his basement apartment, Foster wore a wheat-colored Irish cable knit sweater and was hunched over the dining room table, reading glasses perched on the tip of his nose, with his yellow highlighter in hand. I had emailed the report to Foster to give him a chance to review it before we arrived. He had printed it and yellow Post-it notes already decorated the pages. I could see his yellow highlighting from across the room.

"Where the hell have you been, and why didn't you get this to me sooner?"

I ignored both questions. I was too embarrassed to tell him that I had signed out right after I called him about the report and that I'd taken an unplanned furlough day. I just couldn't get out of bed. Maybe my father's death had taken a toll on me after all. Sean had covered for me both days and said nothing about it now. I changed the subject.

"Here, I picked up a toasted onion bagel with cream cheese for you from Jake's."

Without looking up, Foster shot back, "No time for that." His brusque reply was out of character. I figured his tone was a form of reprimand for not coming to see him sooner. He looked up, saw that Sean was with me, and nodded toward my partner. "Detective Kelly, as always, you're welcome here. I trust your father is well?"

Over the past few months, Sean and Foster had developed a friendship of sorts. I'd told Sean that Foster was struggling with his father's mental deterioration as the first signs of Alzheimer's took hold. It was difficult for Foster to see his father, a widely respected jurist and legal scholar, unable to recall his own name. Sean had reached out when his own father's faculties begin to wane, and now they occasionally met for lunch.

"The bagel was Sean's idea," I interjected.

"No time to eat right now. It's been three weeks since this guy's last kill. I am certain he is out there hunting even now."

"Or he has already killed again," I added.

Sean pulled up a dining room chair next to Foster and looked down at Foster's marked-up copy of the report. "No, Frank," he said in a low voice, "I think Foster here will tell you that if he had killed again, we would know it."

Foster looked up from the report and stared at Sean, obviously impressed with the observation. "Detective Kelly is right. This guy wants the world to sit up and take notice. I imagine you have some questions though, Sean. About the mutilation."

"I've seen a lot over the years, but nothing like this. What do you make of the severing of the genitals—what's the sexual connection?"

"I told Francis that your killer may have internalized a homosexual rape—or at least that's my theory. May or may not be a direct sexual connection to the mutilation. There are several other psychological basis for mutilation of this nature: destruction of the victim's identity, abhorrence for the victim, or disregard for the victim's value as a human being."

"Or a combination of motives?"

"Absolutely. Although this guy is well organized and focused, he shows flashes of emotional confusion. But he isn't confused about his mission. Figure out his mission and you can predict his next move."

"And if we can predict his next move, we can be there," I added.

As Sean was looking over Foster's shoulder to see what he had highlighted, I looked at the two of them and thought back to the funeral and our drinks at Annie's. I wasn't sure what bothered me more—Foster's dismissal of Beth's ultimatum or his whispered New Testament verse. What did he expect of me? Just then, I heard the faint and familiar ding of my cell phone. I returned to the entryway, retrieved the phone from my coat pocket, and opened my email.

As I walked back toward the dining room table, I announced, "I have more for us to look at. I just received an email from Forensics. I haven't opened the attachment yet, but the attached PDF is titled "Preliminary Report—"

Before I could finish, Foster was up out of his chair and walking toward his laptop and printer. "Forward the email to me. I'll print the report."

"Three copies." Sean added.

Foster grumbled. "Yes, three copies, plus one for my journal."

CHAPTER 41
Anthony

If my instincts were right—and my instincts about guys like Anders were always right—I could skip hanging out in neighborhood bars, searching for my next target. I had seldom stumbled across a target so easily. I usually spent weeks going from bar to bar, sizing up men like Henry, watching for the telltale signs of a coward who took pleasure in exploiting small children. Based on my brief encounter, Anders seemed to be that kind of man, but I had to be sure that he was the right man to carry the message. After all, it was all about the message.

Confident Anders would monitor the work at the Karlov site on a daily basis, I returned there the next day and parked among the workers' pickups in the school's parking lot across from the Kelso entrance. Slouching low in the front seat, I adjusted my side view mirror on a right angle, allowing an indirect view of the entrance, and waited. Around three o'clock, Anders returned and was once again barking orders to the crews. When he was finished, he got into an older model black Ford Crown Victoria and pulled away in a hurry. "OK, Mr. Anders, let's see where you're going."

I followed the Crown Vic for about twenty minutes east on Montrose, staying well behind, but keeping a keen eye on the black sedan. Anders took a right on Broadway and headed south. Five minutes later, he turned right on Hutchinson and then took a quick left up the alley.

"What are you up to, little man?" I stopped the pickup at the mouth of the alley just in time to see the Crown Vic pull into a small parking lot no more than fifty yards into the alley. I drove around the block looking for a convenient and discreet place to park, and spotted a grocery store lot at the end of the block. Speeding up, I headed for it. Rather than parking in the main lot, I drove around to the rear of the store, where the lot emptied into the alley, seemingly out of range of security cameras. I shut off the engine and hurriedly pulled on a wool knit stocking cap, zipped my fleece vest, and tugged on winter gloves. Trying to get a feel for the neighborhood, I walked back north along Broadway. The street was lined with specialty shops, clothing boutiques, chic restaurants, and bars, all expensive places to shop and eat, and all colorfully decorated for the Christmas holiday. I sensed I was out of place here, and based on my initial read of Anders, it didn't seem to be his kind of neighborhood, either. Did I misjudge this guy?

As I approached Hutchinson, I tried to figure out which building was adjacent to the parking lot where Anders had parked. Finally, I just guessed it was either the restaurant a couple of storefronts from the corner or what appeared to be a bar next to it. There was a sign on the restaurant door: "Closed for Remodeling." That left the bar as the logical destination for Anders.

Trying to be inconspicuous, I crossed the street, stood in front of a row of newspaper vending machines at the corner, looked past the newspaper racks, and observed the comings and goings at the bar. It had an unusual appearance, not at all like the neighborhood bars I had scouted. Vertical wood plank siding painted a light shade of gray had been added to the surface of the front exterior wall. The bar's large bay window was painted over with a deep purple tint and framed by over-sized white shutters. In large white script letters across the window's purple background were the words, "White Shutters Lounge." The door was also painted the same shade of purple, with tall, narrow white shutters on either side. On the door hung a large Christmas wreath decorated in white and gold with multi-colored ribbon.

As I watched customers come and go, a pattern began to emerge. They were mostly well-dressed young and middle-aged men; these were not the blue-collar working stiffs I'd found at other bars. Some left carrying white bags, presumably carryout sandwiches or burgers. I was tempted to go in and order a sandwich to go, hoping that while I waited, I would be in a better position to observe Anders. But clearly the White Shutters was a high-end bar and grill—I would look out of place. It was too big of a risk.

Instead, I walked to the mouth of the alley. The Crown Vic was still there. Two other cars, both dark BMWs, were also parked in the small lot that led to the rear entrance of the bar. Just then, two well-dressed young men exited the rear entrance of the bar. The shorter of the two wore a brown leather jacket, and his hair seemed to be unnaturally blonde. The other wore a navy double-breasted overcoat and a fashionable fedora. They stood just outside the door talking. They were too far away for me to hear what they were saying, but judging from the tone of their voices and their gesturing, they were arguing. The argument ended apparently without resolution as they headed to their cars. Just before they got into their cars, the taller of the two yelled over to the blond-haired man, who then hung his head, looked up at the other, and nodded in agreement. Both walked around to the front of the cars, exchanged what seemed to be friendlier words, and then embraced.

The embrace lasted a little too long for my liking. "There's something wrong here," I whispered to myself. I was trying to make sense of it when the two men kissed—a long passionate kiss on the lips. "Goddammit! It's a gay bar. Anders is a fag!"

I was suddenly blinded with rage. Gay men fuck small boys! Those liberal intellectuals on TV who claimed otherwise were either idiots or queers covering for their own disgusting impulses. I had been right about Anders—he did have something to hide. Standing motionless, I struggled to control myself while my mind was flooded with images of new ways to inflict pain on this "chester."

I returned to the camper and sat staring at nothing in particular as the windows frosted up. Anders was definitely the guy. Now, only the questions of "how and when" remained.

CHAPTER 42
Detective Frank Vincenti

When we left Foster's apartment, we were both too tired to think clearly enough to piece together what we had gleaned from the reports. But Sean was anxious to sketch out his own rough profile of the killer. He suggested we start early in the morning, and when he saw me hesitate, he offered to pick me up at the apartment.

As I got into Sean's car the next morning, he skipped his customary small talk and jumped right in. "OK, let's go through it again."

"You want to go over it now? It can't wait until we get to the station house and have our morning coffee?"

"No," Sean said with some irritation. "Yesterday, Foster was coming up with theories, some of which I didn't understand. So I want to make sure I have all the pieces straight in my head, even if we have to go over them a dozen times."

Sean was a great detective. I still had a lot to learn from him, especially his interrogation techniques. It had been his idea to withhold from the press the details of the mutilation and the message scrawled in blood on Henry's chest. Usually he was very good at putting the pieces of the puzzle together, but he hadn't been trained in the "Foster method" of autopsy and forensic report analysis. It was an acquired taste.

I started the summary. "Cause of death: blunt force trauma. Superficial bruises on either side of his neck, and slight damage to brain tissue not related to the blunt force trauma, suggesting brain ischemia. Also a lack of any significant petechia in the eyes. The M.E. says that adds up to Edwards being rendered temporarily unconscious, probably by a chokehold and, based on his stomach contents and his blood alcohol level, he was probably snatched or attacked at a restaurant or a bar. Our guy needed privacy for the kill and mutilation, so Edwards was probably transported to another location. Clearly there was a struggle, but there's no way of knowing if it occurred during the abduction or at the kill site."

"You're concluding that there was a struggle because the first blow to his head was not the kill blow?"

"Yeah, the first and second blows were on the left side of the head, but the rest were on the right and delivered postmortem. That suggests he was left-handed. The abrasions on Edwards's back plus the laceration on his cheek also suggest a struggle; the laceration was clearly made with a particularly sharp blade, we just don't know what kind."

"And all of the head blows were inflicted with a brick?" Sean asked.

"Right. According to Forensics' analysis of the reddish-brown particles they removed from Edwards's skull and brain tissue, the brick is known as a 'Chicago Common Brick,' manufactured in the early 1900s. It's easily identifiable by its high organic clay content. That particular clay was a by-product from the construction of the Illinois-Michigan Canal, and that type of brick was most commonly used to build Chicago bungalows."

"That's a starting point."

"C'mon Sean. There are thousands of those bungalows in Chicago."

"Yeah, but at least we will be able to match the particles to the kill brick, if and when we find it."

I nodded in agreement, although I knew it would be a long shot. I continued. "Tissue samples from the genitals he left behind indicate that the genitals had been frozen, maybe for as long as a year, so we know the prior kill was not all that recent. The M.E. confirmed that a small electric reciprocating saw was used to sever the hand, and he speculates that bolt cutters were used to remove the genitals."

"What do you think happened to the severed hand?"

"Foster thinks he's collecting trophies."

Without taking his eyes off the road, he asked, "I understand Foster's explanation of possible motivation for the mutilation, but does this guy get off on the mutilation or not?"

"The report says that no semen was present anywhere on the body—that could have been as a result of the bleach. But that doesn't mean the killing wasn't sexually motivated. The removal of the genitals and the postmortem anal penetration with a wooden object certainly point to some sexual connection."

We were stopped at a traffic light, and I could see that Sean was piecing it all together.

"The tarp was no help: mass manufactured and available at thousands of home improvement stores. And it was clean except for the smeared blood message."

Sean looked over to me and said, "The M.E.'s hunch about a third person's dried blood being on the bolt cutter and transferring to the sheered ends of the rib cage was right on. The DNA from those samples didn't match Edwards's or that of the severed genitals stuffed in Edwards's chest."

Sean continued trying to get a fix on the complicated blood sample analysis that was yet to come: "So, we have four DNA samples."

"Right. One from Edwards; that's easy and the least complicated of the four. Forensics will run the other three samples against the FBI's CODIS DNA database and let us know if they get any hits."

Sean finished the thought. "But only if these guys have a record."

He was right, of course. Only convicted felons were required by law to provide DNA samples that were then added to CODIS. There is an exception under both federal and Illinois law: A suspect arrested and arraigned on a short list of specific felonies could be ordered to provide a DNA sample that would be fed into CODIS. That list included murder, aggravated sexual assault, and predatory criminal sexual assault of a child.

Sean continued. "Right now we don't know much about the other three samples: one from the dried blood on the rib cage, one from the genitals, and one from the dried blood in the facial laceration. All we know for sure at this point is that none of them match." As he pulled into a parking space at the station house lot, he looked over at me. "The question is, which of the unidentified DNA samples belongs to our killer."

"We'll get all the DNA results in the next few days. The DNA Unit is running what they have against CODIS."

"Hopefully, we'll have something to go on."

"It would be great if either the dried blood from the rib cage or from the facial laceration was the killer's, but I doubt it. I agree with the M.E.'s hunch that the dried blood that he took from the rib cage came from the bolt cutters and probably was left on the cutter's blades from a prior victim."

As Sean turned off the engine, he looked straight ahead at the traffic on Belmont. With frustration in his voice, he said, "If that's the case, then you and Foster are right. There's at least one other body out there somewhere. And more on the way."

CHAPTER 43
Anthony

It was 3:00 a.m. on a night when the city braced for more frigid weather. The garage's electric space heater couldn't generate enough heat to keep up with the plunging temperature—the orange glow of its single coil element had faded to black around two o'clock. I had rooted through the camper's storage bin, found a heavy red plaid wool blanket stinking of mildew and musk, and had draped it over my head and shoulders. The yellow light from the kerosene lantern atop the freezer threw my shadow across the side of the camper so that it rippled as I paced, cursing the night, the cold, and the apparition's unrelenting demands.

I'd scoured the area around Broadway and Hutchinson searching for a secluded spot to subdue and abduct Anders. I even considered grabbing him at the school, but I couldn't risk the possibility of being seen in daylight by curious neighbors, late-working laborers, or students in no rush to go home. My head throbbed. The pain kept me from thinking straight, kept me from planning the how and when, kept me from the peace of a single night's sleep. Tonight, the apparition had called to me in anger, displeased with my delay, displeased I had not yet exacted retribution for the attack on my friend. There was no escape from it, no refuge from its demands.

My knees suddenly gave way and I staggered, reaching out with one hand, leaning on the freezer to steady myself. Blinding pain, as if my skull had been cleaved in two by lightning, shot through my head. I dug knuckles into my temples and tried to blink away the vision before me, the replay of that spring night more than thirty years ago—an erratic black and white slide show projected on the garage wall.

My friend entered the yard from the alley and walked along the narrow sidewalk next to the garage.

"No! Stay away from the garage! Stop!"

The man appeared from the side door of the garage.

"Run, dammit, run away!"

The man grabbed my friend by the back of the neck.

"Yell! Scream. Do something!"

He pushed the boy's face against the brick wall of the garage and pulled his pants and underwear down around his ankles.

"You fucking weakling! Fight back! Kick, bite—whatever it takes!"

The lights flashed on, and I could see the man's face.

"You bastard! You'll pay for this—you and your like will pay. And I'll make sure that the whole world knows what you did!"

I slammed both hands on top of the freezer. The lantern tumbled to the floor and rolled under the camper, its flame extinguished. My brain pulsed and throbbed as if trying to burst through my skull. The memory of the pain of skin and bone against the bricks became real, digging deeper and deeper. Sweat trickled down my back and beaded up on my brow as the pressure of the man's body pushing against the boy hammered into my psyche—bile soured my mouth. I clutched my head in both hands and dared to scream at the apparition. "Stop! I'll make them pay. I swear. I'll make them all pay. Just leave me alone for now. For God's sake, leave me alone."

I threw off the blanket as if it were a shroud I refused to accept, and then, one by one, the faces of the men I'd killed looked back at me from the darkness. My vision narrowed, and I felt myself sway, stagger, steady myself, and sway again until I toppled backward and lay sprawled on the freezing floor, in a garage where the muffled screams of horror escaped from even the tiniest cracks in the blood-stained concrete slab—screams that filled the garage and echoed in the rafters. The screams grew louder and louder, until I realized they did not come from the lips of dead men, but from my own gaping, gasping mouth.

CHAPTER 44
Detective Frank Vincenti

We didn't have to wait long for the DNA results after all. The report was emailed to Sean and me three days before Christmas. I was at my desk that morning before Sean arrived.

"You're in early."

Disconnecting my iPad from its charger, I explained, "I had trouble sleeping. I finally gave up, went to Jake's for an early breakfast, and decided to catch up on our overdue incident reports."

"What's the problem with the sleep? Our guy in your head?"

I couldn't help but glare at Sean. He knew better than to keep asking me. "No. Beth is."

Beth and I had argued again last night over Christmas at the Kellys'. She had made reservations for Christmas brunch at the Four Seasons, and when I suggested we could just stop in at the Kellys' afterwards, the best I could get from her was a muttered, "maybe." I doubted she meant it. No point in telling Sean until I had a definite answer.

"You two going to be OK?"

"Normal husband-wife stuff, that's all."

"There's been nothing normal about you and Beth for a while, buddy."

Without looking up, I changed the subject. "The DNA Unit sent over its report late last night. It's on your desk."

Sean glanced at his desk. "Anything interesting?"

"Take a look for yourself."

Sean threw his coat over the cubicle's partition wall, eased himself into his desk chair, and began to read. He wasted no time reacting. "Christ! The foreign DNA from the rib cage is different from the DNA of the genitals found in Edwards's chest cavity."

"Yeah, and the DNA sample from the severed genitals didn't get a hit. And you'll see on page two that the blood sample from the rib cage can't be the killer's. It's from someone named Joseph Druski of Melrose Park. He was reported missing more than a year ago."

"Why was he in the database?"

"Convicted pedophile. Served six years at Danville." I made the connection to Edwards, but I wasn't sure if Sean did.

Sean looked over at me. "That makes him the second victim—although we can't be sure of the timing. The severed genitals could have been victim number one, and the blood from the rib cage victim number two, or visa versa."

I looked up from my iPad. "It's the second victim we know of. Either way, Foster was right. There are more bodies out there. The DNA from the facial laceration was fish DNA. I'd say the blade was likely a filet knife like the one my father used when we went fishing in Wisconsin." I immediately regretted mentioning my father or the damn fishing trips.

Sean looked up at me. He knew better than to pursue it. Instead, he simply said, "Fishing wasn't a Kelly family thing."

I changed the subject again. "Looks like Henry Edwards doesn't have a criminal record; no hits in CODIS. But that only confirms the AFIS fingerprint search."

Sean leaned back in his chair. "OK, so there may be two other victims we haven't found, but Foster confirmed my theory that our guy wants the bodies to be found. He wants us or the press to deliver his message—whatever the hell it is. Have we missed something?"

"I'll go online and check the felony databases of the Indiana and Wisconsin state police. If our guy has killed before and we haven't

TERRY JOHN MALIK

found the bodies, maybe he started out of state. If they don't have anything, I'll widen the search."

"I'll make some phone calls. Some details don't always get into those databases. There's an unassigned detective in VCS who just transferred over from Property Crimes. I'll see if she can help out by checking incident reports that haven't made their way into the Department databases."

Just then, Sean's phone rang. He looked at the caller ID. "It's Mom. She's probably calling about Christmas. She's going to want to talk to you."

My morning was already going downhill, and I had run out of excuses for Beth's intransigence. I had also run out of patience with Sean's mom. I got up to get coffee. "Tell her I'm not here."

CHAPTER 45
Anthony

Guessing Anders was the kind of guy who hung around a bar until "last call," I returned to the White Shutters shortly before closing time, a couple of days before Christmas. The winter sky cloud cover had moved out during the afternoon and it was a clear night with a full moon—too cold for snow. As I turned into the alley off Hutchinson, I was pleased to find the Crown Vic again parked in the bar's lot, this time next to a white Cadillac. I touched the brakes slightly, paused momentarily, and then continued down the alley, returning to the grocery store parking lot.

Satisfied the camper was out of the line of sight of security cameras, I started toward the other end of the alley, trying not to be seen by walking on the far side of the alley where the piled slush had frozen over and crunched underfoot. Although there was a city streetlight perched on an old wooden pole near the mouth of the alley, the stretch of alley immediately behind the closed restaurant and the gay bar was dark except for an intermittent splash of light from a large electric sign over the back door of the bar. The illuminated words on the sign, White Shutters, flickered and blinked and made a clicking noise as if there was a loose connection or a short in the circuit.

The bar's lot was only about thirty yards ahead of me when I heard a car door slam and a car engine start. I could see only the entry to the lot, not the car. A red glow splashed on the pavement followed immediately by small white shafts. Taillights and back up lights! Damn. If that's the Crown Vic, I've lost him before I've even started.

Careful to stay in the shadows, I waited. The Cadillac backed out, turned toward the mouth of the alley at Hutchinson, and drove away. After five minutes, there was no new sound from the bar's lot, only the occasional crackling of the electric sign. Anders was still there.

When I was within ten yards or so of Anders's car, my observations from the other night were confirmed: the only security camera in sight was located on a metal pole behind the restaurant, pointed toward its rear entrance. There was no traffic on Hutchinson, but there was still the chance that a car could turn into the alley and make a quick entry into the White Shutters lot. If a car approached from the opposite end of the alley, I'd have plenty of lead time to move behind the dumpster sitting next to the restaurant's fence.

Walking briskly across the alley and into the lot, I dug into my pocket for my car keys. If anyone had seen me at this point, I would've looked like just another customer hurrying to get a beer before closing time. As I came to the rear fender of Anders's car, I released my grip on my keys and let them fall to the ground, where they landed near the left rear tire as I'd intended. In case I was being watched, I shook my head in feigned disgust as if surprised by my clumsiness. I got down on one knee, swooped up the keys, unscrewed the cap on the tire's valve stem, and pressed the tip of one of the keys against the top of the tire's valve. Just as I started to release the air, the distinct bright light from LED headlights illuminated the fence on the other side of the alley.

"Shit."

I paused, then quickly unlaced my work boot, and started retying it, keeping my head down the entire time. A black Audi turned into the alley but didn't stop; it sped down the alley and out of sight. It took two minutes to completely flatten the tire. Crossing back to the other side of the alley, I took up a position just behind a large blue residential recycling bin. I waited calmly, unafraid. Impatience and fear breed mistakes.

It was a long twenty-five minutes before the bar's back door opened and Anders stepped out. He held it open as he turned and said something to someone still in the bar. Anders laughed, waved, and headed to his car. He turned up his coat collar and adjusted his scarf. As he dug in his pocket for his key fob, he spotted the flat tire, stood still momentarily, shook his head, and pointed his fob at the car, popping open the trunk. He stared into the trunk with a look of bewilderment. He bent over and retrieved the hydraulic jack from the trunk, and stood reading the instructions for more than a minute, and then walked to the side of the car, squatted down on one knee, and fumbled with the jack.

Just as I thought. The faggot doesn't even know how to change a tire. Watching him closely, I left the shadows, and walked back across the alley toward Anders.

"Hey, buddy, ya got a flat tire."

Without looking up, Anders grumbled, "Yeah. Tell me something I don't know."

"Ya ever change a tire on a Crown Vic before?"

Anders glanced up and replied, "I'm learning on the job."

"Lemme help."

Anders turned away and resumed fumbling with the jack. "I've got it."

I bent over and wrapped my right arm tightly around his neck, and whispered in his ear. "No. I've got it, you little fag!" Anders gasped for air and tried to scream for help, but no sound came out as my chokehold closed his windpipe and put pressure on his larynx. He struggled, trying to reach over his head to grab my face. In one last desperate attempt to break free, he twisted and turned and then kicked his feet up against the rear fender trying to push backward against me, but his attempts were futile.

I didn't release my grip for almost forty seconds. I didn't want this one to regain consciousness as quickly as Henry had. Finally, his body went limp, having put up more of a fight than I had expected.

I took a quick look around the alley and back at the bar door. No one. Bending low, I lifted Anders under the arms and, walking backward, dragged him to the rear of his car. I lifted his body, hoisted it over my shoulder, and quickly flipped it into the trunk. The bully's limp body hit the padded floor of the trunk with a muffled thud. I removed the car fob from the pocket of his overcoat and slammed the trunk shut.

I stopped for a second to catch my breath. Another set of headlights suddenly turned into the alley. I waited, hoping whoever it was would be in a hurry and just drive past. Shit! A Chicago PD cruiser came to a stop in the alley no more than a few yards from where I leaned against the trunk. The driver's door swung open and a tall, thin African-American cop got out of the car and walked toward me. "Sir, may I help you?"

"Help me?"

"Yeah. You have a flat tire there and looks like you're having trouble with the jack," the uniformed officer said as he pointed to the side of the Crown Vic where the hydraulic jack lay on its side. "It's late. I'll be glad to help change the tire."

Shit! "No. I got it covered."

"Sir, I do this all the time. It's easier if the two of us tackle it together." He walked closer and squatted near the wheel well. "Nothing to it." He walked back toward me, slapped the trunk saying, "Pop it open. I'll help you with the spare."

"I'm good, Officer. Really."

"We'll get the spare on in a jiffy and get you on your way on this frigid night. Go ahead. Open the trunk."

I had to come up with something—quick. "You know officer, I already called AAA. Their truck is supposed to be here in ten minutes. But, thanks anyway."

I wasn't sure if he heard me. He seemed to be distracted and focused on the trunk as he rapped his knuckles on the trunk lid a couple of times. "Open the trunk, sir."

Jesus Christ, I thought. "Really Officer, I pay good money for my AAA membership. Might as well use it once in a while."

I had regained his attention. He shook his head and with a knowing smirk, explained, "Sir, at this time of night and in freezing temperatures, it could be hours before they get here. Just open the trunk—"

I quickly scanned the alley. It was empty—just the meddling cop and me. Dammit! I had left the .38 in the glove compartment of the camper. What if—

At that moment his radio came alive, squawking out, "Car 211, a 10-10, fight in progress, two blocks north of your 20."

He looked at the trunk again and then turned his attention to me. No doubt, he was sizing me up. His radio repeated the call.

"Sorry, sir, but I've got to take that. Looks like you'll have to wait for AAA after all."

He returned to his cruiser, slamming the door and speeding away, his blue strobe light piercing the darkness of the night and bouncing off the buildings lining the alley.

I wasted no time. I slid behind the wheel of Anders's car, quickly pulled the door closed, started the car's engine and eased out of the lot.

OK, faggot, I thought. We're going for a short trip just to the other end of the alley and then to my garage. I've answered the questions of "how and when." Now the question for you, Mr. Anders, is how much pain can you endure before you beg me to put you out of your misery—and misery it will be, Mr. Anders. Misery it will be.

CHAPTER 46
Detective Frank Vincenti

Sean and I hadn't said much to each other since the morning I refused to take the call from his mother. He wasn't upset with me. He was just letting me work through it, knowing anything he might say would only make it more complicated. We each had leads to run down and calls to make about Edwards's whereabouts the night he was killed, and there was always the paperwork. I was ashamed that I had avoided talking to his mother, but I was too embarrassed to explain we wouldn't be coming for Christmas dinner. Mrs. Kelly would be too polite to ask why. She wouldn't need to, of course. She would know it was all about Beth.

Beth and I had been fighting more and more lately. She claimed it was always about my job, but I knew it was more than that. According to Beth, I had a job while she had a career. Our fighting started in earnest about two years earlier with the Carlton family murders. My constant "brooding" as she called it, had pushed her over the edge.

On a bright spring Sunday afternoon, Mr. Carlton's sister had paid a visit to drop off a birthday present for the Carltons' youngest daughter, Daniella. When no one answered the door, she let herself in, and to her horror, found the partially clothed body of Mrs. Elaine Carlton in a pool of blood on the living room floor.

Sean and I arrived at the scene about fifteen minutes after an assistant Cook County medical examiner had begun his preliminary assessment. As we walked in and pulled on our evidence gloves, the M.E. called to us, "Guys, you better come see this."

Sean asked, "What d'ya got?"

"This is the wife, Elaine Carlton. She was accorded special treatment, different from the other victims." Pulling back what was left of her blouse, the M.E. asked, "Did you ever see this before?"

Carved into her chest just above her bra were the bloody letters, "N-I-G-G-E-R."

"I saw something like it when I was in the Army, stationed in Camp Shelby in Hattiesburg, but that victim survived—the word was etched into his forehead. Was it made post-mortem?"

"Not sure. There's sign of a non-fatal blunt force trauma on the back of her head. Hopefully, she was unconscious. There appears to be a bullet exit wound about four inches below her right breast. I'll tell you the cause of death for sure when I complete the autopsy."

Elaine Carlton's husband, Daniel, and their two daughters had been shot multiple times at close range in the dining room while they ate their Sunday dinner. They were all pronounced dead at the scene except for the oldest daughter, Daniella, a twelve year old. The first-on-the-scene patrolman detected a slight pulse, plugged the bleeding, and administered CPR until the EMTs arrived. Perhaps unmercifully, she survived.

I had to look past the horror of the mutilation, and although I could probably have conjured up empathy for the girl's pain, it would serve no purpose—it would only cloud my feel for the scene and the killer.

The Carltons had lived in their house for only two years. They were the first black family in a mostly white, middle-class neighborhood, but they were well liked and had made friends quickly. It wasn't enough that the killer had carved the word "nigger" on Mrs. Carlton's chest, he had also spray-painted the word "niggers" on the dining room wall. Sean figured it to be a hate crime. I didn't. It seemed contrived, too obvious. Sean spent long hours interviewing the neighbors, several of them three or four times. He got nothing.

I returned to the crime scene several times on my own. Daniella's birthday cake was still in the refrigerator. Candles lay on the kitchen counter. I sat in each of the dining room chairs where the family members sat when they were gunned down. Because they were shot at close range, the killer had to be someone they knew. I removed my evidence gloves and pressed my hand against the spray-painted epithet and studied each letter, picturing the killer stopping after each letter to shake the can and start the next letter. I sensed the writing lacked the passion that spawned racial hatred. I felt the same way about the carvings on Mrs. Carlton. When I had examined Mrs. Carlton's body in the morgue, I ran my finger over the letters, tracing each and imagining the killer kneeling over her, knife in hand. The cuts weren't deep and appeared to be made with a hesitant hand. Like the epithet on the dining room wall, I believed it was a contrivance to deflect the investigation in the wrong direction.

Daniella spent six weeks at Lurie Children's Hospital undergoing seven different surgical procedures. At first, she refused to speak to anyone except her favorite aunt, who had driven straight through from Georgia and was at her bedside when Daniella regained consciousness four days after the shootings. It took her aunt more than a week, but she finally succeeded in convincing Daniella to see me. I spent two days with her, talking about her school, her friends, and whatever else I could think of before I eased into the topic of "that afternoon." She turned away from me and claimed that she must have fainted when the first shots were fired and couldn't otherwise remember a thing. The doctors ascribed the loss of memory to PTSD-induced temporary dissociative amnesia. I wasn't so sure. There was terror and fear in her eyes that belied a lost memory.

I re-read statements from neighbors and community leaders and reviewed post-incident surveillance reports. I studied the crime scene photos; they were no worse than what I had seen before, but I couldn't reconcile the terror in the girl's eyes with memory loss. It just didn't feel right to me. I knew that Daniella was the key, but I just couldn't break through the girl's barriers.

I tossed and turned so badly at night that Beth exiled me to the living room couch. I stopped eating. I paced. Beth grew impatient with my blank stares as she related her frustration with new assignments at the firm. I became sullen and moody—even more than usual. She became angrier and angrier. Losing track of time, I went for long walks trying to piece it together. I was a good cop. I was trained for this work—why couldn't I get through to Daniella? I went to see Foster. He told me I was both too close and too far from the girl's experience to see past the obvious.

"What the hell does that mean?"

"Draw on who you are, not what you are."

For several days, I sat at her bedside while she slept. I stopped asking her questions and started telling her about where I grew up, where I went to school, and about my first love. I talked for hours about Beth. And then I told her about my father. Finally, sitting up in bed and looking out the hospital room window, she described months of sexual abuse suffered by her eight-year-old sister at the hands of their next-door neighbor, Herbert R. Straus. She had been forced to watch.

I sat and listened. When she finished her story, she cried uncontrollably until exhausted, laid back, rolled over, and slept. I wanted to hug her and tell her everything would be alright. I couldn't do either. I sensed she carried the guilt of failing to run to her parents and tell them of the abuse. I was sure she blamed herself for the death of her family.

We made the collar the next morning. The first time Sean had interrogated Straus, he had put on a convincing act. With Daniella's statement in hand, it didn't take Sean long to break him. Straus admitted it all. Daniella had threatened to tell the entire story to her father, and Straus couldn't let that happen. He showed us where he had tossed the gun, knife, and paint can into the south branch of the Chicago River. He had won the girls' trust because he was a high school teacher who helped them with their homework.

When I got home that night, I found Beth sitting up in bed wearing her Northwestern sweats that doubled as pajamas, her reading glasses balanced on the tip of her nose, her laptop propped up against her knees, and surrounded by legal pads. As I undressed, I began to tell her about the breakthrough. She took off her glasses, pointed them at me, and said she didn't want to hear another word about the Carlton family, the shootings, or the girl.

"Ever since you joined the VCS, I have had to listen to stories of death and mutilation, stories of abuse, and stories of cruelty that I never thought possible. I'm tired of you planting those images in my head! I've had enough."

"But, Beth, there's a happy ending—"

"Are you fucking kidding me? How is there any kind of happy ending in anything you do? The girl's entire family is dead, and she's left with memories of the brutality of that afternoon, abject guilt, and she'll never get over her sister's abuse!"

I started to explain that, with counseling and the love of her aunt, she could recover. I thought Beth would understand, but she screamed, "Stop!"

She tossed her glasses on the floor, pushed her laptop aside, threw off her covers, then marched toward her closet. "Enough already! I'm going back to the office. End of discussion."

Blurting out "end of discussion" and retreating to her office had become a habit. Whenever we argued, it was her way of shutting down. It had happened again last night when I insisted that we spend Christmas afternoon at the Kellys'. But last night it had been me who stormed out. I woke up the next morning in one of the beds in the station's bunkroom.

CHAPTER 47
Anthony

Chicago woke Christmas Eve morning to temperatures hovering around six below zero. The wind chill factor rendered the weather dangerous. Some businesses had issued blast emails the night before advising employees that nonessential personnel need not report to work. Metra commuter trains were delayed while the blue and yellow flames of gas-fired switch heaters danced in the blistering wind as weary, bundled-up railroad workers struggled to keep the trains running at all. Chicagoans who relied on public transportation crammed into CTA bus shelters equipped with electric heaters. IDOT closed Lake Shore Drive from North Avenue to Division as spray from the crest of Lake Michigan's waves had covered the road with a sheet of ice.

At one time, Christmas Eve had been special for me, but not anymore. Now I took perverse pleasure watching mindless last-minute shoppers jam into crowded stores. It was always the same. Suburban shopping mall parking lots would fill up quickly; suburban shoppers would drive their salt-stained cars up and down the aisles looking for the last best parking spot. Walmart stores would offer valet parking for senior citizens, and Macy's would run closeout sales on Christmas decorations. O'Hare and Midway airports would be jammed with holiday travelers carting carry-on luggage stuffed with unwrapped Christmas presents. Stylishly dressed young women from Gold Coast high-rise apartment buildings, wearing full-length mink and sable coats, would scurry between exclusive men's boutiques along the Magnificent Mile, swearing they would never again wait until Christmas Eve to finish their shopping. Carefully wrapped presents would be placed under Christmas trees already shedding dried-out pine needles. But this year was different. This year—as a gift to all Chicagoans—a special present, artfully wrapped in a blue tarp, lay under a pile of bricks near Karlov and Kelso.

CHAPTER 48
Detective Frank Vincenti

On the Monday morning after the four-day Christmas weekend, I again found myself in one of the bunks in the station's bunkroom. I was curled on my side with my eyes half-open, facing a wall where other detectives had scrawled their star numbers, a tradition by which they announced they had sought refuge in the bunkroom after their wives had kicked them out for good. I had no intention of adding my star number to that wall. After I spent another late night at my cubicle, sorting through FBI databases looking for similar signatures and patterns, I crashed in the bunkroom around 4:00 a.m. I tried to convince myself it had nothing to do with Beth.

By pure happenstance, I had avoided another confrontation about Christmas with the Kellys'. Two days before Christmas, the unit sargent had stopped at my desk and informed me that one of our detectives had been involved in a civilian shooting and that the "dicks" in Internal Affairs had directed he be placed on administrative leave.

"I need someone to cover his Christmas Day shift. I've been making the requests by reverse seniority, consistent with department directives, and haven't got any volunteers yet. I'd hate to order someone—"

"I'll take it. No problem."

"You sure? Don't you want to check with your wife first? I hate to disrupt family Christmas plans, especially on such short notice."

With just a slight smile, I replied, "Trust me. I'm glad to do it."

Beth wasn't happy that I had taken the extra shift. She curtly advised me she would go to the Four Seasons brunch anyway and would invite a friend to take my place. Although I was on duty Christmas Day, I tried to placate her by showing up and joining her and another associate from the firm for a sweet roll and a quick cup of coffee. She seemed embarrassed that I showed up and tried to make excuses to her fellow associate for my appearance. I politely excused myself, pleased with the brevity of my stay, and thankful, for the first time, for the guys in Internal Affairs.

As I stared at the scribbled star numbers, I heard metallic rattling. I thought it had been part of a dream from which I was slowly waking. I usually couldn't remember dreams anyway, so I put it out of my mind. The rattling started again. I jerked my head off the pillow to listen more closely. "Damn, that's my phone!"

Before I had crawled into the bunk I had absentmindedly turned off my cell phone's ringer, and placed it into the small metal locker attached to the bunk's frame. I must have left it set on vibrate. Instinctively, I checked my watch. It was 9:10 a.m. already!

By the time I retrieved the phone, it had stopped vibrating. I scrolled down through the log where I found a string of calls from Sean starting at 7:40 a.m. I listened to the last couple of messages. Another body wrapped in a blue tarp and buried under a pile of bricks had been found at Sacred Cross High School, near Karlov and Kelso—again in the Albany Park neighborhood.

Showered, shaved, and wearing my cold-weather gear, I sped toward the school. As the flashing blue strobe and wailing siren cleared my way, I recalled Foster's warning of ten days earlier that our guy would kill again. This second body confirmed we had a serial killer on the loose in Chicago, and my problems with Beth shrunk in relative importance.

Patrol cars with their light bars flashing were parked at both ends of Kelso, blocking all vehicular and foot traffic. I entered the school's parking lot from an alley entrance at the southeast end of the lot. The on-scene patrol bureau supervisor had seen to it that his officers had placed blue wooden "Police Line" barricades along the northern edge of the school's parking lot immediately across the street from the school property. Despite the bitter cold, the lot had already filled up with reporters, police-scanner groupies, and curious neighbors.

Two patrolmen helped me push through the crowd, past reporters and television camera crews, and around one of the parking lot barriers. As a third officer lifted the yellow crime scene tape, I spotted Sean and Dunbar just outside a doorway of a partially completed cinder block building.

I was surprised to see Dunbar. He was now Area North Commander. His career had advanced by leaps and bounds since the days when he headed the North Area's VCS. The last time I had seen him was at the ceremony at which Sean and I were awarded commendations for breaking the Carlton case. Unlike Foster, Dunbar was showing his age. There was gray in his eyebrows and moustache, plus a paunch above his belt.

With some trepidation, I approached Sean and Dunbar and asked, "Same guy?"

"Where the hell have you been?" Sean snapped. "I've been calling you for hours."

I pulled out a pair of evidence gloves. "I want to examine the area around the body and then I need to—"

Dunbar put his hand on my shoulder. "Detective, slow down."

Sean explained. "I've already walked the exterior perimeter. I entered the building where the body was found, conducted a preliminary survey, and established a second perimeter around the body."

"OK, but I can still get a read on the killer. You know the routine."

"The M.E. and evidence techs are already working the inner perimeter," Sean said. "So far, everything is the same as the Keeler site. And we caught a break. The tarp wasn't well secured this time. It tore away from the head, and we were able to make a preliminary identification."

"Huh? So soon?"

"When I couldn't reach you, I tried Beth but got her voicemail. Per department directives, I was required to have a second detective on the scene, so I called Commander Dunbar to assign a temporary substitute. When I told him where we found the body, he insisted on meeting me here."

Dunbar explained, "I got a call at home yesterday morning from the superintendent's office about an archdiocesan priest that had gone missing. The Chancery's Office was reluctant to file a missing persons report, and I was asked to make some discreet inquiries. The priest's name is Jack Anderson—he's a monsignor. The Chancery sent Superintendent Di Santo a photo of Anderson, and Di Santo sent it to me. So when Sean called me and told me the location of the body, my gut told me it was Anderson."

Sean finished Dunbar's explanation. "We identified the body as the missing priest using the photo that the dommander had been given."

Dunbar took his hands out of the pockets of his down jacket and blew on them. "I'm told Anderson was recently appointed head of a School Buildings Task Force to get control of cost over-runs, and reduce construction delays. He'd probably been to this site overseeing the construction of the school's new gym."

"But that doesn't explain why our guy dumped his body here."

"Yeah, well, you guys will have to figure that out, but more on point, I made some initial inquiries about the monsignor. The Task Force assignment was intended to deflect him from an unpopular ministry. It seems the monsignor was the self-appointed minister to Lakeview's gay community. Apparently, some Catholics believe priests should not be seen saving souls in gay bars."

Dunbar looked back over his shoulder at the row of news vans. "The press is going to love this. They'll spin the incident to describe Anderson as a rogue priest who wandered off course and will try to make this into a homophobic hate crime."

I stepped forward. "This is the second body deposited in Albany Park. We need to determine if our guy lives in the neighborhood, or there's something that's drawing him here."

Dunbar nodded and without saying another word, headed back toward the warmth of his car. After a few steps, he stopped and turned. "Keep me in the loop, boys. Foster, too."

As soon as the M.E. had removed Anderson's body, we headed to the Town Hall station, headquarters for Chief of Detectives Thomas for a briefing. Sean always took the lead on dealing with command officers. He was polished and more articulate, and far more patient with the politics involved in the chain of command. I spoke only when asked a direct question. He provided a sitrep that was brief and succinct.

The chief paused, looked back and forth between Sean and me, and then settled his gaze back on Sean. "Kelly, I spoke to Dunbar. I think it's time to assemble a task force."

Sean demurred. "Please hold off, Chief. Give us a few days to sort things out."

"Dunbar predicted that would be your reply. Look, I'll get pressure from Di Santo on this, especially if the press reports that we have a serial killer on our hands. We aren't really sure how many more bodies are out there, are we?" He turned to me. "Frank, have you involved Foster in this?"

With some hesitation, Sean responded, "Foster is helping us work up a profile. He has his own theory of the case."

There was silence in the room before the chief let out an exasperated sigh. "Nothing ever changes with Tommy."

Sean glanced at me, then broke the awkwardness of the moment. "If that's all, we'd like to get over to the morgue." With a wave of his hand, the dismissed us, and we beat a hasty retreat from his office and made it to the morgue just as the M.E. finished.

"Exsanguination," the M.E. said as we walked in. "Your victim bled out from the severing of the genitals."

"Was he was alive when the killer sliced off his testicles and penis?" Sean asked with a shudder.

"Yes, but he may have been rendered unconscious by shock. The removal of the hand was certainly postmortem."

I pointed at the man's neck. "Was he strangled?"

"Well, the bruises on either side of his neck are very similar to those we found on the body of Henry Edwards, so our thinking at this point is that, like Edwards, he was strangled to the point of unconscious prior to any other wounds being inflicted."

"Anything that would suggest he made an attempt to resist the torture?"

"Not sure. He may have been very subdued. The autopsy revealed inflamed bronchial tubes. The victim had asthma, and from the looks of it, he seems to have had a severe case. Your victim could have been passing in and out of consciousness from narrowed and inflamed bronchial tubes exacerbated by the strangulation. And, just to correct your thinking, the genitals were not sliced off. I'm pretty sure he used his bolt cutters again."

"Time of death?" Sean asked.

"The freezing ambient temperatures during the last week makes determining time of death difficult. The body could have been at the scene as early as four days before it was discovered."

"What about a foreign item on the body?"

"You mean genitals stuffed in the victim's chest? Yes, they were placed under the left rib cage. I removed tissue samples and sent them to Forensics. I can tell you this: Those tissues had been frozen for some time. Not just from the recent cold spell."

"Otherwise, is there anything different from the prior victim?"

"Not really. Not my job to speculate, but I'd say the person who killed Mr. Edwards killed the good monsignor and, except for the removal of the genitals while he was alive, your guy hasn't altered his M.O."

Once in the elevator, Sean leaned back against the wall, exhaling in frustration. "OK. Same method of rendering the victim unconscious, same mutilation, same message on the torso, different cause of death."

"But except for their ages, these are two very different victims."

"Yeah. Sit down with Foster and chart it out."

"Sure. But listen, I need to spend time with the body, preferably alone."

The elevator doors opened at the first floor, and as Sean stepped out, he turned back to me. "Yeah, well, you blew that opportunity, buddy, when you turned off your phone."

CHAPTER 49
Anthony

I woke confused. I squinted, trying to focus on the cheap electric clock that I had balanced on top of an outdated but still operational Sony TV. The clock's small red numerals read 9:58, but I wasn't sure if it was morning or night. I threw off the two layers of blankets and sat up on the couch where I usually crashed. I searched for the TV remote but couldn't find it among the mess of empty pizza boxes, paper plates, and empty fast food bags and wrappers. The basement apartment had only a single window, placed high above the painted cement foundation. It was frosted over. The basement was always damp and cold, and the original owner had done little to mitigate either.

I gave up looking for the remote. In stocking feet, I walked across the cold linoleum floor and turned the TV on using the set's manual control. The local ten o'clock evening news was just starting. I returned to the couch and draped one of the blankets over my shoulders to ward off the chill. As I had hoped, it was the lead story. I watched and listened closely, intending to savor every detail.

Now they'll understand. Now, the loathsome press will describe the nature of what I had done to Anders while he was still alive. Now, the message that the apparition had demanded would be delivered as a warning to the likes of Anders, Henry, and all the others.

But the details reported weren't what I had expected. I sat

hunched over, stunned by what I heard: Anders wasn't his name. It was Anderson. Monsignor Anderson. He was a well-known Catholic priest who counseled gay men and was described as an advocate for abused children. The report on the murder and discovery of the body featured twelve-year-old file footage of Anderson when he first became an outspoken and fiery critic of the Church's cover-up of pedophile charges against archdiocesan priests. The report included a clip of a ten-year-old PBS interview in which he accused the Vatican of "reckless ignorance" when it had announced in the late '90s that gay men should not be ordained in order to prevent sexual abuse of children by the clergy. He had condemned the Vatican's announcement, claiming that it perpetuated the myth that gay men are more likely than heterosexuals to engage in child sexual molestation.

At the conclusion of the two-minute segment, I sat perfectly still staring beyond the television at the frosted-over window, only half-listening to reports of fatalities from the bitter cold. In the darkness beyond the window, I replayed my encounters with the man I thought was named Anders. A fucking priest? A priest at war with his church over protection of innocent children? Damn, I should have known. With the revelation that he was a priest who had challenged the church over its cover-up of pedophile clergy, my encounters with him took on a new meaning. And, Jesus Christ, I tortured and killed a man who, like me, in his own way, fought to protect the innocents among us. Worse yet, by killing a priest who spoke out against abusive clergy, trying to protect children, I had sent the wrong message. How was I so wrong about this one?

The bolt-of-lightning pain in my head suddenly returned. I stood, letting the blanket fall to the floor, and began to pace, clutching my head in both hands, knowing that the haunting nightmares would soon return and fearing that the apparition would make more demands.

CHAPTER 50
Detective Frank Vincenti

I had no reason to celebrate the arrival of the New Year. I'd dropped Beth off at O'Hare, where she caught a 6:45 a.m. flight to Santa Barbara to be with her brother and his family for the holiday weekend. It was a last-minute invitation, and Beth had jumped at the chance to escape the Chicago winter. I was invited too, but I wasn't about to sit on the side of a mountain dotted with over-priced houses and peer out through layers of fog trying to enjoy the so-called vistas of the Pacific Ocean while a serial killer prowled the streets of Chicago. Beth wasn't disappointed—nor was I. Sean had been right, she was getting under my skin; worse, her moodiness was beginning to interfere with my ability to get into our killer's head.

The lower level of the station house was quiet as I sat alone at my desk, hours before the next shift of detectives would start arriving. I looked over to the corner of my desk, where I had accumulated several handwritten notes from the desk sergeant letting me know that Tony Protettore had been trying to reach me since Christmas Day. I had no interest in renewing that relationship and hoped he would finally understand that. I truly felt sorry for him, but some relationships are better left behind.

Besides, there was a killer to catch. I thought back to the call I'd received the previous day from the Deputy M.E. "There's something you should know," she'd said. "One of my pathology techs, a guy named Allison, became very upset when he showed up to work today—he was virtually hysterical about the Anderson murder. He had taken off the week after Christmas so he wasn't here when we performed the Anderson's autopsy. He claimed that Monsignor Anderson had been his parish priest, but I have no way of knowing if he's telling the truth. He not only cursed the killer, he also cursed you guys for not preventing the priest's murder."

"Not the first time that kind of thing has happened. What do you know about him?"

"Allison seemed alright when we hired him a couple of years ago. I got a reference on him from the Hines County Medical Examiner in Jackson, Mississippi. Very sound from a technical point of view, but lately his reports have been sloppy. He doesn't interact well with his co-workers, either leaves early or calls in sick, claiming to suffer from migraines, and seems to spend way too much time alone with the bodies he works on. Candidly, I would like to fire him."

"Can I talk to him?"

"If you can find him. He stormed out, swearing he'd get even with Anderson's killer. I've called him on his cell, but he's not answering. Maybe he went home to his ex in Jackson. If he fails to report for five consecutive days, I can fire him. It would save me a lot of paperwork if I could can him for unexcused absence."

I'd made a few notes after I hung up and emailed them to Sean. Out of an abundance of caution, he replied letting me know he'd call the M.E.'s office in Jackson to see who knew him in there. If this guy was telling the truth—that he had a connection to the priest—I could understand his reaction. If not … no word yet from Sean on that front.

I picked up the piece of creased, dog-eared paper on the desk in front of me. I'd retrieved it from my file cabinet, and now stared at the handwritten list. The craziness had started when the details of the Sacred Cross killing were leaked. The Chicago press had learned that Monsignor Anderson's body was found under a pile of bricks, just like

Edwards's at the Keeler demolition site. The reporters put two and two together and reported that Chicago had a serial killer who has "a thing" for bricks.

The name had first appeared in social media: crime groupies tweeted a whole host of names, each Twitter user trying to be more clever and more colorful than the one before, but the press picked up on just one and made it stick: "The Bricklayer." I had grown tired of giving names to killers. In fact, I was disgusted by it. It glamorized the killers and gave them undeserved attention that served no useful purpose.

At first, I had played the game and adopted the nicknames the press had coined for serial killers. Over time, that changed. I grew to shun nicknames and labels. I cringed when I heard a fellow detective refer to a victim as the "vic." Try using that term when you have to inform a mother that her son has just been murdered. Detectives and FBI agents used terms like, "perp," or "subject," or "unsub." I didn't like any of those either. For me, the murder of an innocent person was always personal. I made it personal, and, for better or worse, I always called the killer "our guy." Foster had taught me that, but it took a couple of years staring at autopsied corpses for it to sink in.

Early in his career, Foster had expressed his disdain for the press generally, but especially when they sensationalized a murderer. Foster lectured: "Thanks to the morally bankrupt press, ten years from now the public will still remember the catchy nickname given to a serial killer, but, after the trial, no one will recall the names of the victims."

Now I was thinking of another piece of Foster's advice. He had once told me that people shouldn't make lists of things to remember, they should make lists of things to forget. He said, "If there is something you would like to forget, put it out of your head by writing it on a piece of paper and stick the paper in a cabinet drawer."

It was good advice, and I had done just that several times since I joined the Violent Crimes Section. I desperately wanted to forget the callousness of naming serial killers like they were boats in Belmont Harbor or a family pet, so I made a list:

The Cleveland Torso Murderer
Lipstick Killer
The Zodiac Killer
Moors Murderer
Co-ed Killer
The Trash Bag Killer
The Freeway Killer
The Scorecard Killer
Killer Clown
Casanova Killers
Green River Killer
BTK - Bind, Torture, Kill
Houston Candy Man
Riverside Prostitute Killer
Genesee River Killer
Hillside Strangler
Son of Sam
The Baltimore Cannibal
The Kindly Killer
The Milwaukee Cannibal
The Tool Box Killer
Coast-to-Coast Killer
Bike Path Rapist
Sunset Strip Killers
Night Stalker
The Happy Face Killer
The Psycho Sailor

This morning I had retrieved the folded and dog-eared sheet of paper, and, after a few minutes of reflection, added The Bricklayer to the list. Then I refolded the sheet of paper in half, and half again, and returned it into an unmarked envelope and shoved it back into a seldom-used cabinet drawer.

CHAPTER 51
Anthony

For days, the TV remained on the floor where it finally came to rest on its side, unplugged, with its screen shattered and dark. It had betrayed me. Everything and everyone had betrayed me. Even Anders, or rather Monsignor Anderson. He'd looked the part. He'd been at that gay bar. He'd yelled at those kids. Surely he was just as much to blame for my mistake as I was.

Asleep or awake, it didn't matter. I was tormented by images of the priest. They materialized on the blank television screen as if seeing the killing on a replay loop: the terror in his eyes as he laid on the garage floor, his trembling lips as he cried for mercy, his blood swirling around and down the drain. I couldn't remain in the same room with a television that had become a cruel instrument of the apparition, so despite the freezing temperatures, I moved out to the camper and slept on the pull-down cot.

Monsignor Anderson did not deserve his fate, the fate I forced on him. I couldn't allow the city to believe that he had been punished for his sins; of course, I did punish him, punished him without mercy, but for sins he hadn't committed. I had been wrong, and now I had to make amends. From the freezer, I removed the clear plastic bag that contained the priest's severed body parts, tenderly placed them in a purple velvet bag with gold ribbing that I had taken from a bottle of

Canadian whiskey, and placed the bag in the snow on the steps of Holy Name Cathedral.

It was my sacrificial offering. The body and blood of a man who had dedicated his life to helping others just as I had dedicated mine to avenging others. Regret took the place of guilt. I asked for no forgiveness, knowing none would be given.

But my offering and repentance did not rid me of the unceasing torment of the apparition. I struggled to clear my head. In lucid periods, I planned more carefully and devised a new approach. I had to be certain that my targets were guilty of sexually molesting small children. I discovered that state law required communities to maintain a public registry of convicted sexual offenders. The official list for Chicago, accessible on its website, identified the offender by name. And although it did not provide an exact address, it reported the residence of the offender by block level. The report included race, age, and whether the victim was a minor, all conveniently arranged in columns and rows that reminded me of a baseball box score.

I obtained a printout of the first fifty names and taped it on the inside of the camper's door. Sitting on the edge of the cot that reeked with my own body odor, I studied the list. I had circled three names: white males, between the ages of fifty and fifty-five, whose victims had been minors, and who lived no more than thirty minutes from the garage. I started with the first name on the list: Harold Mathias of Sunnyside Avenue. On a scrap of yellow-lined paper, I scrawled his street and block, and, early on a dreary Sunday morning, weary from another sleepless night and in desperate need of a shower and shave, I set out on yet another scouting expedition.

Using the list of registered offenders proved more difficult than I had anticipated. Without a specific address, I had to park on the 3100 block of Sunnyside near Kedzie, and wait and watch. On my first try, I parked at the end of the block and scanned both sides of the street. My next target could live in any of nineteen residences, nine of which were three-flats. That meant forty-six homes in all. I had rejected the notion of surreptitiously looking at mailboxes for the Mathias name—a registered sex offender was hardly going to announce his presence with a label above the mail slot.

Although the temperatures had moderated, it was starting to snow again, heavily. I started the engine and flipped on the wipers for just two full swipes when I heard it. The voice on the radio said the psychopath now known as "The Bricklayer" had brutally mutilated the beloved priest who would now never get to see the school expansion project he championed through to completion. From the men with HIV he counseled to the youngest students and oldest parishioners, the whole city mourned the senseless slaying. Hundreds were expected at the funeral to be held that afternoon.

I slammed my hand on the dashboard. "I'm not a fucking psychopath! I'm just doing as I'm told, trying to relieve my friend of his pain. I'm just his messenger."

This time, I vowed I wouldn't make a mistake. This time, I'd pick the right man. I sighed and checked my watch. I had been parked in the same spot too long. I drove to the end of the block and turned into the alley to determine if it gave me a better vantage point to observe the comings and goings of the residents. I drove through both alleys several times. Frustrated, I decided to return to the garage before the snow began to accumulate. I'd return later and try to mark the man who the City of Chicago had already marked as a sexual predator of children.

CHAPTER 52
Detective Frank Vincenti

Beth called from LAX. She had flown there from Santa Barbara earlier in the day after saying her goodbyes to her brother. Her flight was due at O'Hare around 4:00 p.m., and she asked me to pick her up. She was waiting at the passenger pickup island on the arrival level at Terminal 3 when I finally pulled up just after five. Her cheeks were red from the cold, and she was stomping her feet to stay warm. I was prepared for her explosion—she hated waiting. And she would probably throw a fit that I was picking her up in an unmarked department car. As I got out of the car and looked across the roof of the black Interceptor, I saw her stare at the car with a look of disbelief. Oh shit. Now it starts. I walked over to where she stood and reached out to take her bag, expecting a sarcastic comment meant as a reprimand. Instead, she said nothing and got in the car.

I pulled out and merged into I-294, expecting the worst from the traffic and from Beth. The National Weather Service had issued a winter storm warning; another six inches of snow were predicted to fall overnight.

"Did you spend New Year's Eve with your mother at the club?"

"No. I barely saw her. I stayed with Ted in Monticello. I needed brotherly advice."

"Oh? Since when do you ask anyone for advice?"

"You know that's not true when it comes to Ted." Beth looked over at me, "I told him I wanted you off the force. He really laid into me for that—told me I was being selfish."

Ted was older than his sister and was a successful Santa Barbara psychiatrist. She'd always looked up to him and respected his opinion, whether or not she asked for it. Their father had died unexpectedly when she was a freshman in high school. She had become deeply depressed after his death and turned for comfort to "Aunt Nora"—a pseudonym for cocaine used by rich kids to give themselves "street cred" among their WASP friends. Aunt Nora was readily available in the wealthy areas of Santa Barbara County, and trust-fund teenagers had the cash to pay the inflated prices. When her mother discovered Beth's addiction, she was more embarrassed than alarmed, and insisted that Beth be admitted to an out-of-state rehab clinic. Beth refused and defiantly flaunted her drug use. Finally, her brother gave her the attention and understanding she craved and convinced her to enter a program in one of the two-dozen rehab centers located near home. To make sure his little sister stayed sober, he transferred from Yale to attend a local college. He'd earned the right to criticize her life choices many times over.

"He asked me about The Bricklayer case even before he asked about how I was doing at the firm. I told him I was sick of hearing about the goddamn Bricklayer."

Without taking my eyes off the road, I said, "The case isn't really the issue, is it?"

"No, probably not. Frank, don't you see what your job is doing to you—what it's doing to us? You sulk, and you walk around in a fog of depression for weeks at a time. And your hours are worse than mine. Sometimes when I leave in the morning I find you asleep on the couch, fully dressed, like you just dropped there. And when was the last time—"

"The last time we slept together? That's it, isn't it?"

She didn't answer.

"Beth, there are plenty of nights I come home to an empty apartment.

I understood the demands on a young lawyer in a big firm, and I always figured that's what I signed up for."

"Yes, and that's what my brother said."

"A cop is who I am."

"I get it. Honestly, I do. That doesn't mean I like it, but I get it. I know that I haven't been supportive—it's just that so much of the horror that you deal with winds up in our private life."

"You mean it winds up in our bedroom, don't you?"

She turned away abruptly and looked out the window without responding. We sat in silence watching the first few snow flurries of a coming storm whirl past the windshield as traffic inched along.

The next morning I woke to five inches of snow and an empty bed. Beth had left early to beat the rush hour traffic that was going to be even more snarled than usual. She'd invited me to share her bed, like usual, looking for instant solutions to long-simmering problems. She was wrong to invite me. I was stupid to accept.

I called her at the office to make sure she had arrived safely. Initially, I thought that was another mistake. She said matter-of-factly that she had been very early, but wasn't the first in the office. I listened, not wanting to broach the disaster of last night's sex and hoping she'd let it go for now too.

Picturing her in one of her expensive black and white pantsuits pacing around a cluttered desk as she talked, I replayed yesterday's conversation during the ride from O'Hare. I tried to pick up the thread. "What else did your brother say?"

"He said I was acting like a spoiled, condescending bitch. Is that what you wanted to hear?"

"No, Beth, not at all."

Finally, she got to it. "Last night was nothing new and you know damn well why!"

"It was too soon."

"And that's supposed to be your latest excuse? That's not it, and you know it!"

I stopped listening as a rush of images suddenly reappeared from last night. I watched, unwillingly transfixed.

In the darkness of her room, my head was filled with images of shiny bolt cutters tearing away at Edwards's and Anderson's soft flesh.

"I know Foster says you have a unique talent for getting into a killer's head, but Foster and the rest of them don't crawl into bed with you."

As her breathing became heavy and warm upon the side of my neck, I saw Anderson's blood seeping into the dark cracks of a garage floor.

"Whenever you get a new case, you become obsessed. It's like the monster you're chasing gets into your head and then worms his way into mine."

When she rolled over on top of me, I pictured freezer shelves crammed with frosted-over plastic bags containing colorless hands, fingers splayed wide as if reaching for help.

"Like I said in the car coming back from O'Hare, I get it, but this can't go on."

When I placed my hand against her breastbone to steady her atop me, I saw gray brain matter and shards of a shattered skull spray into the air.

"I can't take it any longer, Frank!"

As she moaned, screams of terror echoed in my head.

"It has to stop, Frank. It has to stop."

As she cursed—a field of blue tarps stretched to the horizon.

"You just don't get it, do you?"

And there was always a hooded face covered in darkness lurking behind those images, but I still couldn't make out who it was.

"Frank! Have you heard anything I've said?"

Suddenly, a woman's face appeared and then disappeared just as suddenly. I didn't recognize her.

"Yeah. Of course."

The images faded, and although I wasn't sure what Beth was saying, I knew what I wanted to say. "Beth, I'm a cop. I don't know anything else, and frankly, I don't want to know anything else."

I said nothing and we sat in silence for almost a full minute. I was finally getting into his head, getting an instinctive feel for the killer. It had started last night as I lifted the sheet and slid across the bed toward her. I felt his rage—and his fear. He was on a mission. But I couldn't make the connection between Edwards and Anderson. Not yet. I needed more time, a breakthrough, something.

But then Beth regained my attention. "When I called you Thanksgiving morning I told you that I'd give you six months to make a change. But, how about this? You remain on the job until you get this Bricklayer guy off the streets and then you can see a career counselor about a career change—a career that's related somehow to law enforcement."

"Sounds like another ultimatum."

"You can take it however you like, but will you at least think about it? Can you do that much? For us?"

I'm sure she meant for *her*.

An hour later, I leaned against the smooth marble tile wall of our glass-enclosed shower. I had adjusted the electric temperature control to a level that produced a heavy steam. After several minutes of deep breaths, inhaling the steam's moisture, I stood directly under a cold spray of the shower's rain head. I watched the clear water swirl into and down the drain. I could now summon at will the images that had flooded my mind last night and that had reappeared this morning. All I could think about was the rage stoked by a sense of revenge that must be driving him, amazed that he had held his rage in check long enough to carefully select his victims and dumpsites, but I was sure of two things as I toweled myself dry. He was out there planning even now and eventually his rage would consume him. And destroy him.

CHAPTER 53
Anthony

After two early morning vigils on Sunnyside and more passes through its alleys, I had narrowed it down to two men. Both were white and appeared to be in their mid-fifties. I had followed one to a west side automobile paint shop. I called the shop, asked for an appointment to obtain an estimate to paint a pickup truck, and then asked to speak to Harold Mathias. They never heard of the guy. By the simple process of elimination, the other man had to be Mathias.

I returned to Sunnyside late the next evening. As I slowly cruised the alley behind Mathias's house for the second time, I saw him walk down the back stairs of his house, toward the garage. I sped up and pulled into an empty lot farther down the alley. I watched my rearview mirror and waited. A few minutes later, an old silver Chevy passed slowly with Mathias at the wheel. I backed out into the alley and followed him.

Following Mathias wasn't as easy as following Anderson. He didn't use his turn signals, traffic was heavy and slow, and the roads were snowpacked and treacherous. He drove south on Kedzie, turned west on Irving Park and then turned onto the Kennedy Expressway. I almost lost him on the Kennedy when a semi pulled in front of me and blocked my view. As Mathias approached the North Avenue exit, he cut in front of a slow moving van, regained control of his car after it fishtailed on a patch of ice, and headed up the exit ramp. With some difficulty, I was able to change lanes and followed him up the ramp, maintaining a safe distance. He proceeded left on North Avenue and, after crossing over the expressway, drove one more block before he pulled into a 7-Eleven parking lot. As I drove past the lot, I saw him sitting in the Chevy with the engine running. I drove to the next stoplight, made a quick U-turn, pulled over, and watched for the Chevy to exit the lot. Five minutes later, Mathias was on the move again, returning to the Kennedy and heading into the city.

"What's this son of a bitch up to?"

He exited at Ohio, turned south on LaSalle Street, and drove to Lake Street and Dearborn where he entered a twelve-story self-park garage. I followed close behind to avoid being cut off by traffic.

"Now where's he going?"

As the electronic gate rose at the entrance, I looked around the immediate vicinity—office buildings, high-end restaurants, and the Goodman Theatre. "Hell, there's nothing here for this guy, especially at this time of night."

I wasn't sure where the Chevy was parked, so I pulled into a spot on the eleventh floor assuming he wouldn't have parked on the roofless top floor unprotected from the weather. I hurried to the elevator and impatiently pushed the down button three or four times. Finally the door opened. There in the elevator stood Mathias with a tire iron in his hand.

"What the fuck do you think you're doing?"

Mathias rushed me and pushed me hard against the cinder block wall opposite the elevator, pressing the rusted tire iron across my throat. "You think you're the first self-appointed vigilante to find me on the goddamn Internet?"

With his free hand, he pushed my head against the cinder block and brought his face close to mine. His breath stunk of onions and garlic.

"I've seen that shitty little homemade camper of yours drive by my house, and I saw you late one night poking around my garage. Yeah, I'm awake at three in the morning, motherfucker!"

Pinned against the wall, I struggled to breathe and fought to get free, but when I pushed back, he applied even more pressure, almost cutting off my windpipe altogether. "Look, asshole, I've done my time and I've paid a price, but you wouldn't know about that would you? You wouldn't know about the beatings, you wouldn't know about prison scum lining up to stick their cocks up my ass. I've had enough. I don't need pathetic little do-gooders like you watching my every move, trying to find a reason to send me back to Danville!"

I couldn't breathe and feared I was about to pass out. Mathias paused suddenly and eyed a security camera hanging from the top of the wall just to the left of where he had cornered me. He put his head down, turned away from the camera, and delivered a solid swift blow to my gut, causing me to double over. Then Mathias rammed home a knee to my groin. I collapsed, writhing in pain.

"Stay away from me, goddammit!"

CHAPTER 54
Detective Frank Vincenti

I had just returned to my desk with a vending machine ham sandwich as Sean hung up his phone. "Ditch the sandwich, pal. We've been invited to lunch." Sean announced with some mischief in his voice.

"By whom?"

"None other than your old buddy, North Area Commander Edward Dunbar," he replied as he opened a cabinet drawer.

"He's not my buddy." I was still living down the four-year-old, whispered rumor in the Detective Bureau that Dunbar had done a favor for Foster, his former mentor, by intervening and fast-tracking my promotion and assignment.

"Well, buddy or not, he wants us to meet him at Jake's in thirty minutes."

"Did he say what it was about?"

"Come on, Frank, it has to be about The Bricklayer," Sean replied as he rooted around a cabinet drawer.

He pulled a red tie from the bottom of the cabinet, looked over at me and saw my scowl. "Frank, get over it. I don't like nicknames for serial killers, either, but like it or not, it has become a part of the street vernacular now."

"Just don't use it around me, OK?"

He had turned his shirt collar up and was tying his tie when he stopped and looked at me with a wrinkled brow. "Frank, you look like crap!"

"What's wrong with the way I look?"

"When was the last time you got a decent night's sleep?"

I ignored him, pulled out my bottom drawer, and dug around for a tie.

Jake's was a ten-minute walk, and on our way I told Sean I'd received two threatening phone messages in my voice mail. "It's the same guy. He keeps talking about Anderson and his body parts."

"Have you tracked down the number?"

"No luck."

"Are you worried about it?"

"Not really. I checked with the M.E.'s office. I thought it might be their tech who claimed Anderson was his parish priest. You know, that guy, Allison. He never showed up again after he stormed out that morning. He was living with his mother since he moved here, but she claims he moved out right before Thanksgiving and hasn't heard from him since. I've got some uniforms tracking him down. I'm sure this guy's just some nut job. You know how it is when a case like this goes public; all the attention seekers crawl out from under their rocks."

Dunbar was waiting for us in a booth near the kitchen with a half-empty cup of coffee on the table in front of him. He had his cell phone pressed against his ear and signaled us to wait. We stood with our backs to the booth, keeping a respectful distance, but I could hear snippets of the conversation. "They're not going to like it . . . let me talk to them . . . Yeah, that works for me, but . . ."

Thirty seconds later, Dunbar snapped shut his flip phone, stood, and called to us, "Guys, good to see you." He extended his hand and greeted us with his usual strong handshake. "Sit. Sit."

Dunbar took a long drink of his coffee, eyeing Sean and me. "Frank, you getting enough sleep?"

Sean kicked me under the table. I didn't answer. Instead I pre-empted Dunbar's next question.

"I've kept Foster in the loop like you asked. But you should know that I've been getting his advice since we found Edwards, and I've shared our file with him."

Looking over at Sean, he asked, "You good with that? You'll get some push-back from Superintendent Di Santo if Foster's involvement goes too deep."

Sean picked up the menu as he shook his head. "We need him, although I sense he is holding something back."

"Foster never shows his hand before he has to. It's probably nothing more than that. Be smart about how you use him, though."

Dunbar signaled the waiter, and we placed our orders. He knew, as did both Sean and I, that Foster would insert himself irrespective of Di Santo's objections. "Di Santo has suggested that I bring in the FBI's Behavioral Analysis Unit. It's more than a suggestion; he's getting pressure, and you know the saying: 'Shit flows downhill.'"

"They'll only get in my way. I'm in our guy's head now," I shot back.

Sean snapped his head in my direction, startled. "Since when?"

"Since last night, and I have to stay in it. I've had brief glimpses of what he saw, but I don't need anyone getting in my way." No need to tell them about the hooded figure or the image of a woman I couldn't identify; those would only raise questions for which I didn't have answers.

"I just need time alone. Outsiders will be a distraction."

Dunbar took another drink. He looked over at Sean. "Where are you on the investigation?"

"We still don't know where Edwards was abducted. His landlord named three or four bars in the neighborhood that Edwards frequented, but we haven't had time to talk to customers from the night Edwards was killed. We know Anderson was grabbed behind a gay bar on North Broadway. We found his car in a grocery store parking lot at the end of the block. It had a flat tire that was shredded as if someone had driven on the flat. Forensics has the car and is reviewing the store's exterior security camera footage."

"Anything on the video?"

"So far all they have is a blurred image of a 'possible' walking out from behind one of the store's delivery trucks. Looks like he's white, about 5'8" wearing a thermal vest of some kind over a hoodie with the hood drawn up over a dark-color ball cap. Anderson's car was parked behind the truck, too."

"Why is the image blurred?" Dunbar asked.

"It was pretty damn cold that night and moisture got on the lens. He knew where the camera was though, because it seems he purposely parked behind a delivery truck that acted as a shield from the security camera. I took a still of the guy and showed it to a couple of bartenders. One of them recalled seeing someone like that, but he couldn't be sure."

Dunbar stared at his half-empty coffee cup and then finished it. "OK. No FBI for now, and I'll deal with Di Santo. I may not be able to hold him off much longer. Frank, go talk to Foster first chance you get. Tell him what you're seeing."

Reluctantly, I nodded. Foster hadn't really been cooperative as of late and his questions about the murders seemed to go beyond professional curiosity.

"Sean, was Captain Lewis able to free up someone to help you canvass the area and interview witnesses?"

"Yeah, but I don't know her well. She just transferred over from Property." With a chuckle, he added, "Skuttlebutt says she was bored over there."

"Well, get her unbored and in a hurry."

"Yes sir."

"What's her name?"

"M'Bala. Keisha M'Bala."

Dunbar broke into a big smile as his phone rang. He answered, grunted into it a few times, and then stood to leave. "Another shooting. Gotta go." He dug into his pocket and tossed two twenties on the table, and then put a hand on my shoulder. "Frank, don't let my lunch go to waste. You look like you need it."

CHAPTER 55
Anthony

I wasn't about to let Mathias's little game of cat and mouse and his ambush scare me off. If anything, it only confirmed that he had to be taught a painful lesson before I killed him. That night I had trouble sleeping. It was a combination of throbbing pain in my groin and imagining what the six years at the Danville Correctional Center had brought Mathias—hopefully nothing but suffering and misery. If what I heard on the street about how child molesters are treated in prison was accurate, what he yelled in my face in the elevator lobby was probably true. When he entered Danville, word would have quickly spread among fellow inmates that he was a "chester," a prison term for a pedophile. Having been marked by his fellow inmates, he would have taken the beatings—resisting would have only provoked attacks more brutal than those that would leave him bruised and bloody. And then there would have been the rapes. Straight and gay men alike would visit his cell in the dark of night and sodomize him over and over again until he bled. When he had finished serving his six-year sentence, he must have naively believed that he had left his tormentors behind and could slip into anonymity. He'd admitted he'd been up at three in the morning, and I bet his sleepless nights were accompanied by vivid memories of each and every attack.

Good. But it wasn't enough.

So, at 3:00 a.m. the next morning, I watched him. I watched from his garage, from his backyard, and then, from a dark corner of his back porch. He stood at his kitchen sink finishing off a second bottle of water, looking like he'd just finished working out. He seemed to be staring into the yard without really seeing. Then his back stiffened and he leaned forward toward the window, squinting at a light coming from the garage, a light I'd turned on.

The brick was wrapped in a chamois. I'd retrieved it from the corner of the storage bin in the rear of the camper, where I had placed it after I used it to kill Henry. Earlier in the day, I had laid the soft lambskin chamois open on the pull-down cot and examined the brick. I turned it over in my hand, considered its heft, and wondered how it got into the garage that night. I then placed the brick in the center of the chamois and brought each of the four corners together, twisted them, and tied them in a knot.

Now my duffle bag was at my feet and my hand gripped the chamois knot as I waited. My breathing quickened. My blood pulsed at my temples as Mathias slammed down the bottle of water and pulled on the peacoat that hung on a coat rack next to the door. He grabbed the baseball bat leaning in the corner by the back door. He struggled with the deadbolts and finally flung open the door to the screened-in porch. He was angry, just as angry as he'd been the day before in the elevator lobby. I counted on him to storm out toward the garage without any thought about what might await him before he even made it that far.

He cleared the back door, strode across the porch, and stopped to fumble with the handle on the door that opened to stairs down to the yard. I stepped out of the shadows and swung the chamois-covered brick fast and hard against the back of his head. Mathias's hand instinctively flew to the back of his head. The bat fell from his hand and rolled toward me. I kicked it aside. His knees buckled. He wobbled forward. I smashed the brick into the back of his head a second time—this time the force of the blow produced a spray of blood that spattered my face and blurred my vision. He twisted to the left, went limp, and fell flat on his back, his eyes wide open with a stunned look on his face.

I wiped the blood from my eyes, stood over him, and watched as his breathing became more labored. Although I was tempted to let my rage boil over and kill him with a third blow, I remained in control and loyal to my plan. I intended to spend a long night with Mathias, inflicting pain the likes of which I was sure he hadn't suffered in prison.

Using the sleeve of my already blood-stained hoodie, I wiped my face and glanced out to the yard where snow fell in heavy wet flakes. Drops of blood splattered against the porch screen were frozen in place like pink snowflakes. The night was quiet. Satisfied rage makes no noise.

I regained my focus, retrieved my duffle bag, and placed the brick back inside. With the door propped open, I slung the duffle over my shoulder, grabbed Mathias by his feet, and dragged him over the threshold, through the kitchen, and into the first-floor bathroom, leaving a trial of smeared blood. I eyed with approval the stained and chipped porcelain clawfoot bathtub—cramped quarters for what I had in mind, but nonetheless suitable for my purposes. I dug into my duffel for the bolt cutters, saw, and a roll of duct tape. First things first. I peeled back the leading edge of the roll of tape and secured several long strips over Mathias's mouth. No need to wake the neighbors.

CHAPTER 56
Detective Frank Vincenti

"Sean, you're not going to like what the out-of-state searches turned up."

Sean had his phone wedged between his shoulder and ear trying to reach M'Bala. "There's nothing about this case that I like. What did you find?"

"Something in Indiana. The Lake County Sheriff's Office in Crown Point has a six-year-old cold case. The victim was missing his genitals and wrapped in a wool blanket in East Chicago."

Sean hung up his phone and scooted his chair over to my side of the cubicle. "Where did they find the body?"

"Buried along the banks of the Calumet River. But there's more; they have two missing persons reports, both from Merrillville."

"Connection?"

"All three are described as Caucasian males, ages fifty to fifty-five, all single. The two that are missing lived alone in trailer parks. The murder victim was never identified."

"Pretty thin."

"Maybe, but I had them send over photos of the three men."

I brought the three photos up on my computer screen, one at a time. "Look at these guys, Sean." I scrolled through the photos several times.

"I suppose you think they resemble each other?"

"You don't see it?"

"Coincidence maybe. Pull up the photos of Edwards and Anderson."

I displayed all five photos on one screen; for all intents and purposes, the five could have been cousins their features were so similar.

"Damn. OK, I'm convinced. Does the sheriff's office have a DNA sample from the cold case?"

"I called and asked for it as soon as I saw these photos, and I've alerted Forensics that a sample may be on its way to see if it matches any of our extra body parts. I'm still waiting for the Wisconsin State Patrol in Madison to get back to me."

Sean's phone rang. It was M'Bala. They chatted briefly, and as Sean put on his coat, he looked over at me and explained. "I'm meeting M'Bala for lunch to bring her up to speed. I assume you'd rather not join us."

"No, you can handle it. She's your problem."

"Look, Frank, she's not a problem. And face it—we could use the help. Besides, the way I heard it from Dunbar, it was her or the FBI."

Sean was right. If we had resisted taking her on, we'd be babysitting a team of FBI agents, and that was the last thing I needed. But M'Bala and I clashed from the outset. On the morning she reported to our team, I found her sitting in my chair with her feet on my desk, reading through my handwritten notes on Edwards's forensics report.

"Hey, what are you doing?"

She looked back over her shoulder. "Going over Bricklayer case notes. Let me ask you something—"

"Get out of my chair and put the notes back where you found them."

"I'm Kay M'Bala. I've been assigned to help you guys. I was waiting for Kelly."

"I know who you are. Get your feet off my desk."

She spun around in my chair and stood. Keisha's looks were striking. She was a tall African-American woman with short-cropped black hair and green eyes; she was dark-complexioned and her features were soft. She wore a loose-fitting pullover and practical jeans.

"Damn, you're Vincenti, the guy with a murderer's imagination."

"I'm Detective Vincenti, and I have no imagination."

I stepped between her and my chair, waiting for her to move. "Do you mind?"

She stepped back out of my way.

Without looking at her, I asked, "Why 'Kay' if your name is Keisha?"

"Keisha is Swahili. My grandparents were part of the 1960s 'Black is Beautiful' movement and they changed their last name to M'Bala to reclaim their African heritage. When I was born, they insisted that their only son name me Keisha."

"So?"

"Some guy in Property Googled 'Keisha' and found that it means 'great joy.' I took a lot of crap for it. Rather than fight it, I go by Kay now."

As I grabbed my notes from her hand, I said, "You shouldn't have done that."

"I'd put everything back."

"No. I mean you should not have abandoned who you are. If you go by another name, you become a different person."

CHAPTER 57
Anthony

This time, I got it right, and this time the press took notice.

Chicago Tribune [online edition]

Chicago IL—January 11. A body was found early this morning in the alley on the 3100 block of Sunnyside in Albany Park. Members of the Chicago PD Violent Crimes Section have identified the body as that of Harold T. Mathias, 38. A search of the city's registry of sex offenders shows that Mathias was convicted of sexual assault on a minor and released from the Danville Correctional Center two years ago after serving a sentence of six years.

It appears that Mathias had been tortured and then killed in the bathroom of his house. The apparent cause of death and mutilation of the body suggests that Mathias is another victim of the so-called Bricklayer, according to a police department source who spoke on condition of anonymity because he was not authorized to release information to the media about the deceased.

The body was found by a retired Illinois State Trooper, Joseph Nowacki, who lives across the alley from Mathias. In a telephone interview with WGN News, Mr. Nowicki described the discovery:

"I go to 6:00 a.m. Mass every day. I'm usually ready to go at five-thirty sharp, while it is still dark. As I was pulling out of my garage I flipped on my headlights, throwing a beam of light across the alley. That's when I saw it—when I saw the body. It was in a five-foot mound of snow, wrapped in a blue tarp, and tied to a utility pole with duct tape. His face was as white as the snow, and his eyes were opened wide and staring at nothing at all."

PART THREE

CHAPTER 58
Detective Frank Vincenti

After one of the coldest winters on record, Chicago was blessed with moderate temperatures, clear skies, and bright sunshine. The paths along the lakeshore from North Avenue to Belmont Harbor were once again full of joggers, walkers, and young couples pushing strollers, all having been freed from months of confinement imposed by sub-zero temperatures and mountains of snow. A few optimistic souls spread out blankets on Oak Street beach under cloudless blue skies even though the traditional opening of the beaches was still six weeks away, during the Memorial Day weekend.

After the Mathias murder, our killer had gone quiet, and our leads had dried up. The file from the Indiana State Police on their cold case was sparse; no trace evidence had been found, and the DNA sample they supplied didn't match any of the body parts recovered from the three known victims. No one had claimed the body, and it had been buried in an unmarked grave in the Luther Burying Ground in Crown Point along with other John Does. That cemetery had been closed, and in the transfer of remains to other cemeteries, the victim's remains had been misplaced.

The Wisconsin State Patrol didn't immediately respond to my initial inquiry about homicides with similarities to our three known murders, but they finally advised us that they had a four-year-old cold case: the body of a white male, mid-fifties, showing signs of mutilation and wrapped in a paint tarp, had been found along the banks of the Des Plaines River about a mile east of Route 31 in Kenosha County, about eleven miles south of Racine. They sent me their file, and although I was convinced this was our guy in his developmental stages, the file added little to our investigation other than to confirm my belief that the body count might exceed our earlier speculation. The county had cremated the body and the ashes were stored in an evidence warehouse.

With the help of the Cook County Medical Examiner, the Forensics Division, and gallons of Foster's Columbian blend, Foster and I had worked up a profile that the FBI pronounced reliable. From footprints in the snow at the White Shutters abduction site, we determined that the killer was about 5'8", weighed about one-eighty, and wore a size nine work boot that was common among construction workers. We were convinced that the killer was a white male, twenty-eight to thirty-five years old, physically fit, most likely left handed, an avoidant loner who drove a van, and worked in the construction industry; he was of average intelligence, but smart enough to leave no trace evidence on the bodies or at the dump sites. For the most part, he was calculating and careful; although he didn't know his victims, he selected them for specific reasons. To have time alone with his victims and complete the torture and mutilation, he had to have a private place, perhaps a workshop, garage, or abandoned house.

Sean and Keisha visited bars in Edwards's neighborhood and the northwest area where Edwards had worked. Finally, a bartender at a place called Murph's Borderline Pub identified Henry Edwards, explaining that Edwards was a regular who largely kept to himself, but had little else to offer. They made several trips to the White Shutters Lounge in search of witnesses to Anderson's abduction, but it was a neighborhood where residents kept to themselves and avoided involvement. They canvassed Mathias's neighbors on Sunnyside hoping someone might have seen any activity the night he had been killed. A few of the neighbors had been shocked to learn that a pedophile lived among them; others expressed support for the killer of a child molester. Commander Dunbar dispatched patrol officers to go door-to-door in the entire Albany Park neighborhood trying to find a connection, but other than being our guy's preferred dumping grounds, they found none.

Although I had made brief excursions into our killer's state of mind, I couldn't get past the images I'd seen that night in Beth's bed. Living with the case files, crime scene photos, autopsy reports, forensics reports, and interviewing construction workers got us no closer to a suspect. I stared at autopsy photos of his victims' empty chest cavities, where he had stuffed severed body parts from yet unidentified victims. I wrapped myself in the blue plastic tarps he had used as ritualistic shrouds, hoping their secrets would seep into my consciousness. Without donning evidence gloves, I sifted through construction debris and soil recovered from each crime scene, feeling what he felt as he scraped out shallow graves. I pored over the materials and revisited the crime scenes and the Anderson abduction site. And although I was starting to know him, it wasn't enough to take us anywhere.

I tried to get Foster's help, but for a time he was simply unavailable to me. I went to his apartment several nights—leaning on his doorbell without an answer. I knew better than to call him; he generally ignored his phone. He was probably consumed again by his futile search for a killer from twenty-five years ago.

Beth worked longer hours, continuing to be ill-tempered and critical when she finally made it home. I turned to working longer hours, too, just like her—the more I wasn't home, the less chiding I had to endure. And, she wouldn't stop prodding me to leave the department. She had asked me to think about it, and I did, readily dismissing the prospect but not telling her of my true intentions to remain in VCS. In any event, she had tacitly agreed that I remain a detective until we apprehended Chicago's first serial killer since Gacy—the infamous Killer Clown.

By mid-April, I was exhausted. Sean suggested that Beth and I take a long weekend, saying I needed a change of scenery and a chance to clear my head. He also thought that it might help salvage the marriage. Beth jumped at the idea, not so much for my benefit, but she had come under ever increasing pressure at the firm and needed a break. Demand for billable hours, a lack of control over her workload, and a couple of losses at trial had started to take its toll. She hadn't taken a real vacation in more than eighteen months. I assumed that she would tolerate my company in exchange for sleeping late, sunning poolside, and afternoon martinis.

She made the travel arrangements, sparing no expense for the trip now that she was making real money. We upgraded to first class and had a suite reserved at the Ritz-Carlton South Beach. She planned our arrival on a Thursday night with a return to Chicago Monday night.

As Beth checked us in at the front desk, I stood off in a corner out of Beth's line of sight and checked my cell phone for messages. Sean had called several times, each time asking me to call him immediately upon arrival.

When I called, Sean was short and to the point: "We have a suspect in custody. He looks good for it, but he won't talk."

"He's waiting for his lawyer?"

"No, Frank, he's waiting for you."

"Huh?"

"Claims he'll tell the whole story, but only to Detective Francis Vincenti."

CHAPTER 59
Detective Frank Vincenti

The next morning, Keisha picked me up at O'Hare and had a sandwich and bottle of water waiting for me in the car. "Sean's idea?" I asked as I unwrapped the sandwich, still unwilling to give her credit for much of anything.

"Mine."

Without taking her eyes off the road, she said, "Eat your lunch. You're going to need it. I think you're going to have a long day." Before I could thank her, she sped onto I-294 with the siren blaring.

"You can turn off the strobe and siren, Keisha. The guy's not going anywhere."

"Commander Dunbar's instructions."

I didn't show it, but I was bothered by Dunbar's involvement at this early stage. The suspect had been in custody less than twenty-four hours and he wasn't talking.

"What's Dunbar up to?"

"Right now? Mostly managing the press—and pacing."

I was anxious to know more, and I was sure Keisha was anxious to tell me more, but I still viewed her as an inexperienced and over-confident rookie, and I wasn't about to give her a sense of importance by engaging her in discussion about the circumstances that led to me being summoned home. I resented her involvement in the case, especially the expanded role that Sean had permitted. I should be chasing down leads with Sean, not her.

As we approached the Belmont Avenue exit, she said, "You were right, you know."

"About what?"

"About my name. My parents named me Keisha, not Kay. I should've ignored the teasing I got from the assholes in Property and refused to let them intimidate me."

I gave her an appraising look. That earned her some respect, but I said nothing.

To avoid the press gathered in front of the station house, Keisha pulled around to the back of the building and made a sharp, fast turn into a fenced parking lot where the department's surplus motor pool vehicles were stored. Sean was waiting for me at the rear entrance. "We need to talk before you go in. We picked this guy up based on an anonymous tip on The Bricklayer hotline."

"So?"

"So Dunbar doesn't like it. He hasn't fully inserted himself into the investigation yet, but I sense he wants to. That this guy won't talk to anyone but you has been a double-edged sword. It's held Dunbar at bay, but he's suspicious."

I followed Sean down the narrow corridor that led to a string of interview rooms. Dunbar stood alone in front of the two-way mirror outside the room where our suspect sat, patiently waiting for my arrival. Dunbar simply nodded at me and grunted, "Let's go. I haven't told the chief about this guy refusing to talk to anyone but you. I can't put him off much longer."

I understood the nuance of his message. Looking at Dunbar, Sean said, "I'll take the lead."

I agreed. "Sean is better at this than I am. This guy will just have to accept that."

Dunbar nodded. "Kelly, tell Frank what we know."

"Two days ago, just after we left for the day, the hotline received a call from a pay phone in the Loop. The caller refused to identify himself. He said that Joey Stella, a registered sex offender living on the West Side, was being stalked by The Bricklayer and then hung up. We informed Stella and that night we staked out his house. We picked this guy up in front of Stella's house around midnight. He refused to give his name or say anything else all night. Then early yesterday morning he finally said something: 'I'll only talk to Detective Francis Vincenti.' His name is Frederick 'Ricky' La Pointe."

"Does he have a record?"

"Yeah. A sealed juvy file and a string of residential B&Es. Served three years of a five-year sentence in Danville; released fourteen months ago. He turned twenty-five last week."

Dunbar interrupted, nodding his head toward the interrogation room, and without explanation added, "Don't bother with the juvy file. Stay focused on what's in front of us."

I looked to Sean. "Any connection to Indiana or Wisconsin?"

Dunbar raised an eyebrow. We hadn't told him of the possible interstate nature of the murders. We were already wary of FBI involvement. Because a forced abduction, which was part of The Bricklayer's M.O., made it a federal matter, we weren't anxious to let Dunbar know of the interstate implication.

"La Pointe claims he's from Hobart, Indiana, but his driver's license contains an address in Forest Park, just off the Ike near First Avenue. His van has Indiana plates. In his van we found a pile of blue tarps, surgical gloves, a set of bolt cutters, and bleach. He also—"

"No saw?"

"No."

"Was the bleach oxygenated?"

"Yes, but when I asked him about the items in the van, he clammed up and insisted on talking only to you."

"Look Frank, I do not like that he knew to ask for you," Dunbar nervously interjected.

CHAPTER 60
Detective Frank Vincenti

Before we entered the cramped interview room, I had La Pointe's cuffs removed and had the guard supply him with a Coke. He stood when we entered. He was 5'9", slender build, seemed physically fit, and drank his Coke using his left hand. Sean asked most of the questions, but La Pointe looked only at me as he told his story and occasionally at the two-way mirror, as if he was addressing whoever stood on the other side. He knew virtually all of the details of the killings, but he never admitted that he killed any of the victims.

Finally, Sean asked, "What did you do with the hands?"

La Pointe hesitated and looked past us at the two-way mirror. For the first time he appeared to be searching for an answer. Ricky La Pointe's hesitation and blank stare answered the question.

Sean told him that it was time for a break, but I knew we were done.

Dunbar and Keisha were waiting for us as we left the interrogation room. Looking at me, he said, "Well?"

"Not our guy—just a small time thief, looking for a little attention. After the first five minutes of Sean's questioning, I sensed he wasn't capable of torture and mutilation. Hell, if you showed him the autopsy photos, he'd probably piss his pants. I loved it when Sean asked about the severed hands—Ricky wasn't thinking fast enough to come up with a plausible explanation."

THE BRICKLAYER OF ALBANY PARK

"He knew a lot. Although he knew where Edwards was abducted, he couldn't tell us what kind of car Anderson was driving. I agree with Frank, this guy is a petty thief, but he's not a killer," Sean added.

"But, he knew details we haven't released to the press." I looked back into the room through the two-way mirror. "You know, even though he's not our guy, he fits the profile—"

Sean interrupted. "So, where did he come from and who made the call to the hotline and the press?"

"Couldn't he have made the call?" Keisha asked. Although she asked a good question, none of us responded.

"Do we have a leak in the department?" Sean wondered aloud.

"Or in the M.E.'s office?"

Dunbar looked back over his shoulder down the long corridor that led to the lobby at the front entrance where the press was waiting to report that The Bricklayer was in custody. Finally, he looked back at us and said, "You're right about him. I had a bad feeling about the situation from the outset. Keep him in custody for now. Let Keisha ask him some follow-ups. He might let his guard down."

I shook my head, but before I could protest, Sean cut in. "Good idea. I'll brief her before she goes in."

Dunbar stared at me momentarily, making me feel uneasy. "Frank, let's take a walk."

Curious, I followed him to the rear door of the station house and to the middle of the motor pool lot. Dunbar leaned up against one of the SWAT wagons. "Frank, my instincts tell me we've been played. Every once in a while we'll get some nut who turns himself in and confesses just to get attention, and yeah, we get copycats, too. But this guy knows too much—way too much. There may well be a leak somewhere."

"OK, say there's a leak. Why does this guy show up now?"

Dunbar shook his head. "I don't know. He may just want to get his name in the papers or become a trending topic in social media."

I was surprised that Dunbar knew anything about social media. "What do you tell the press?"

"Nothing for now." He paused, and looking back toward the rear entrance asked, "You're supposed to be on a four-day furlough, right?"

"Yeah, but Beth—"

"Stay on furlough, but instead of going back to Florida, spend some time with Foster. No need for you to tell Sean what you're doing. Make up some bullshit excuse."

"What do I tell Foster?"

"Anything you want, but get him talking about the case. Suggest dinner. He won't go out, but he'll fix you a nice meal, probably his pot roast. Tell him about La Pointe in a casual 'Oh, by the way' manner. Suggest a walk around the North Pond or up to the zoo."

"Won't he sense I have an agenda?"

"No, he'll know that it's my agenda. Can you do that without feeling you're betraying him?"

"If he doesn't like it, he'll tell me and change the subject."

Dunbar turned and started to walk away. He stopped suddenly, and looked back at me. "Frank, did you ever get around to asking him why he took an early retirement?"

"No. I always figured that if he wanted me to know, he'd tell me."

CHAPTER 61
Anthony

The apparition had been satisfied—for now. Mathias had been the ideal target, and the press had not only given a complete report of the mutilation, but had also disclosed he was a convicted child molester. Although there was still no mention of the dedication to my friend that I had scrawled on his chest and on the chests of my other targets, the press coverage was starting to report that the motive for the killings was related to sexual abuse.

For more than three months, I had no haunting memories or flashes of unwanted scenes of my friend's childhood pain. I had returned to sleeping in my basement apartment, although I had left the broken television where it fell, now covered with one of my tarps. I wanted to maintain my truce with the apparition, but I knew all too well that I couldn't control it. It controlled me, pulling strings like a puppet master.

And then I heard reports that The Bricklayer was in custody. I walked over to a sports bar not far from the basement apartment and watched the news as reporters dissected and analyzed Ricky La Pointe's psyche and his supposed motives. It was beyond belief! I had to do something to dispel the idea that this little nobody was capable of the planning necessary to carry out my kills. My head pounded, and I feared the headaches and nightmares would return unless I could be sure that the right message was being delivered and received. Neither La Point nor anyone else was worthy to deliver the message. I was worthy—no one else. As I finished off my second beer and picked at my late dinner, I noticed that the girl at the next booth was conducting some kind of Internet research. I smiled, paid my bill, and headed down the block to a Starbucks.

As I walked into the coffeehouse, I was glad to see a long line as it would gave me the opportunity to watch the customers working on their laptops or talking on their phones. After I ordered my coffee, I spotted what I was looking for: A teenage girl had spilled her coffee and was on her way to get some napkins to clean the mess, leaving her cell phone unattended on the corner of the table. Walking briskly past the table, I inconspiculously grabbed the cell phone, slipped it into my pocket, and continued out of the shop. I walked to the street corner and ducked into the alley. I checked the phone; it was still connected to Starbucks' Wi-Fi. I quickly found the website I was looking for and spent a few minutes typing. Satisfied, I turned off the phone, wiped it clean, and tossed it in a recycling bin. Pleased with my ingenuity, I took my time walking home.

CHAPTER 62
Detective Frank Vincenti

It wasn't pot roast. Foster grilled a pair of thick veal chops on the apartment building's gas grill in the backyard. I sat on an old wooden bench opposite the grill drinking a beer from one of Foster's fancy pilsner glasses. He always insisted that his guests drink beer from a glass, never from the bottle. He called it a "house rule." I didn't see the difference. The beer tasted the same.

As he stood at the grill, white smoke leaking out of its sides, he told me about his mother's reluctance to eat veal because of the cruel methods by which male calves are raised and force-fed to produce the tender white meat. He claimed it didn't bother him, and explained that he had seen so much of the brutality man inflicts on his fellow man that he could hardly care what happened to baby cows. He served the chops with grilled asparagus, a potato au gratin dish he claimed was his own concoction, and a Napa Valley cabernet. We made small talk over dinner. I was certain that he knew why I was there, but I said nothing of it.

"Neither of us needs dessert," he declared as he got up from the table and headed for his cigar humidor. He offered me a glass of Croft Ruby port. I declined. He poured himself a generous amount in a small spirits glass. He sat back down at the dining room table, and after lighting his cigar, turned his chair toward me and asked, "Am I correct to presume that Eddie Dunbar sent you on this little errand?"

My smile was all the answer he needed.

"He suggested we take a walk."

"A walk?" Foster burst out laughing, not a chuckle or a chortle, but a deep-throated hearty laugh. "Eddie always thought he could soften me up and solicit advice by taking little walks around the North Pond or sitting in front of the gorilla exhibit at the zoo. I played along with him; it made him feel clever. I don't think we need to take a walk; you're clever enough."

With his glass in one hand and cigar in the other, he got up and motioned me over to the couch. It was his way of controlling the conversation. As he eased into his leather chair, he asked, "What did you think of Ricky La Pointe?"

He saw the stunned look on my face.

"So, you're not so clever," he quipped.

I recovered quickly. "He's not our killer. He knows a lot, but not enough to maintain our interest in him as a suspect. We'll probably kick him tomorrow."

Foster leaned back in his chair with a hint of a devious smile. "Did he tell a convincing story?"

"Not really, but he described details common to all three murders that haven't been released to the press, which means he had to learn it from an inside source. There may be a leak in the M.E.'s office or Forensics."

"Did you believe any part of his story?" he asked, exhaling smoke in my direction, with a knowing look on his face that I hadn't seen since the days I was his student.

I ignored the question. "Is there a leak?"

"Certainly."

"Who?"

He leaned forward in my direction, exhaled another thick cloud of smoke, and shot back, "Come on Francis, you know damn well who."

Then it hit me. "Sean and me. We're the leaks."

"Precisely."

"Dunbar was right. It was a set-up, and obviously he had a hunch it was you. That's why he sent me here. Dammit! But why? Why would you—"

Foster cut me off mid-sentence. "So, Eddie had his suspicions?"

"Did you call the hotline?"

"Yes, Francis. I made the call from the pay phone in the lobby of City Hall. Nice touch don't you think? Actually, had I known you were out of town, I would have waited for your return to place the call. I suppose Beth is mad as hell."

"Yeah, but that doesn't matter. And you called the press too?"

Foster took a sip of his drink and replied, "I still have some friends at the *Sun Times*." Looking for a reaction from me, he asked, "Maybe you will take that drink now?"

I nodded.

As Foster poured me a Bushmills, I ran the entire scenario through my head. He was right. Sean and I had told him everything. Hell, Foster had seen confidential files and reports; he knew about the torso scribbling; he had helped me build the profile.

He handed me the tumbler of Irish. "Have you figured it out, Francis?"

"I'd rather hear it from you."

"If you prefer. Our guy has stopped killing, but it's only temporary. He killed Mathias only days after he dumped the good monsignor's body at the high school. I am certain that he wrongly assumed Anderson was a pedophile and then regretted his mistake, thus, the placement of Anderson's hand and genitals at Holy Name. After Anderson, he refined his selection process by choosing Mathias, a registered sex offender."

He paused to take a sip of the port, probably for dramatic effect. "He's punishing and killing off society's scum, Francis—pedophiles."

"Mathias was his perfect target; not only did he fit the physical characteristics, but our guy knew for sure that he was a convicted child molester. He must have found him on the CPD website of registered sex offenders."

"Correct. I think that's why he has stopped for now. Whatever is driving him has been appeased for the time being with the Mathias kill, and there have been no triggers for another kill."

"You fabricated a trigger, didn't you?"

"Something triggers this guy. Something sends him out to find his next victim. The news stories that claim The Bricklayer is in custody have probably pissed him off. By now, he'll be boiling over with indignation that a nobody like Ricky is getting media attention that rightfully belongs to him. He is quite the narcissist, and he is not about to let someone else take credit for ridding Chicago of child molesters. I believe he sees that as his mission."

"But how did you enlist La Pointe?"

"He owed me a favor, a big favor. I presume that you wanted to get Ricky's juvy records unsealed, but Dunbar said it wasn't necessary?"

"Yes. But why?"

"Dunbar probably suspected that my name might show up in Ricky's file as the investigating detective. When Ricky was twelve, he drove the family car over his teenage brother, maiming him. As far as I was concerned, his violence was justified. He did it to stop his brother from beating his mother. The state's attorney wanted to try him as an adult. I made it go away."

"You're trying to smoke out our killer. But he may well kill again."

"He will kill again regardless of what I have done or what I do. I have merely expedited the process to force him into a mistake. If he takes a life next week and makes a mistake—and he will make a mistake, they all do eventually—then we have prevented a murder next month and the month after that and . . ."

I stopped listening. I was seeing Foster in a whole new light, and I didn't like it. Didn't like it at all. But he was right. Our guy had been dormant for more than a couple of months. I feared that he had moved out of state and was dropping bodies in somebody else's jurisdiction. We had no leads, and we'd exhausted the search for evidence and related cases or patterns. And if Foster's profile was correct, we could now anticipate his next victim. He killed his last victim likely using the Registered Sex Offender publication, so he would probably rely on it again.

"Study the city's list of sex offenders. You should be able to anticipate his next victim. He seems attracted to Albany Park for some reason. Correlate the sex offender registry with that neighborhood."

"You've done this before." It wasn't a question, but an accusation on my part.

Foster put his cigar out in his ashtray and finished off his port. He stared down at his empty glass. "Francis, I trust you recall the day you stopped me on campus on my way up to the faculty offices, the day you finally caught my attention. You asked, 'Does it take a monster to catch a monster?'"

I sat silent, as did Foster.

I realized then the importance of Dunbar's question about Foster's so-called early retirement. I had always dismissed the rumors that he'd been forced out of the department. Now I knew they were true. I saw it in his eyes.

CHAPTER 63
Detective Frank Vincenti

Although it was clear by late Friday that La Pointe was not the killer, we kept him in custody as long as we could without charging him: seventy-two hours. Keisha had continued to interview him with Sean's supervision, and La Pointe's story hardly varied by a few words each time he told it. I observed Keisha's interrogation and admitted to Sean that he had taught her well. I didn't tell Sean or Keisha about Foster's ploy, and knowing that Dunbar would be the first to be called on the carpet for Foster's gambit, I didn't say anything to him either. I wanted to give him cover in the form of plausible deniability, but I'm sure he believed my silence confirmed his hunch.

While Beth remained in Miami, I had a couple of sleepless nights struggling to find a justification for Foster's gamble. It was difficult to reconcile his willingness to sacrifice a life at the hands of our killer with his view about the sanctity of life. Perhaps he thought our guy was performing a service to the city by imposing the ultimate punishment on child molesters. At first I thought it out of character for him to have planted La Pointe and exploited the press, but then decided I was wrong. It was perfectly consistent with the sense of self-righteous indignation that fueled his pursuit of monsters, whether killers or pedophiles. He was a master manipulator. I knew that—after all, he'd been manipulating me since our first meeting outside of class—but I'd allowed myself to forget it. Now he'd had manipulated me again. And I didn't like it.

Dunbar briefed the chief of detectives: He explained that La Pointe was merely seeking attention from authority figures and the press. Hearing the level of detail that La Pointe recited, the chief ordered Dunbar to investigate the source of the leak, asking him to focus on the Medical Examiner's office. Dunbar never mentioned Foster.

Dunbar had played along with Foster's game, holding a press conference at which he reported the interrogation team's progress. He had climbed far out on the limb Foster created and had told the press that he believed that The Bricklayer was in custody. The local press had run with the story and included summaries of the killings, photos, and videos of each of the dumpsites. If Foster's plan and Dunbar's complicity were effective, we would hear from the real killer—hopefully, by means of something short of another murder.

Beth returned from Miami angry and distant. She took a cab from O'Hare—no limo, no telephone call for me to pick her up. I had made two mistakes by leaving Miami when I did. First, I basically abandoned her for the sake of the job she despised; second, I had allowed her three days alone with her thoughts and with her unabated anger. She hardly said a word to me the night she returned. I decided that it would be another mistake to explain the importance of my participation in the La Pointe interrogation, and a mistake to attempt an apology.

Finally, she confronted me at breakfast three days after her return. She was sitting at the breakfast bar reading *The Wall Street Journal* with a cup of coffee in her hand. I stood opposite her, eating over the sink. After a long silence, she pushed the paper aside and looked up at me. "You have no intention of leaving the department, do you?"

Without looking up from my bagel and coffee, I said, "You told me to think about it. I'm thinking about it."

"Bullshit!" I put my bagel down and shot back. "Beth, you said I didn't have to make a decision until The Bricklayer was apprehended, and he hasn't been apprehended. I still have time to make a decision."

"Sure, and you're taking advantage of that. You're stalling."

"I am not. Perhaps you've noticed—there's a lot of activity in this case right now, and I'm right in the middle of it."

"I want a decision, and I want it now. I want to know where I stand."

"I don't think it wise to try to manipulate me. Don't push me for an answer you might not like."

"Leaving before we were even unpacked was the last straw, Frank. Do you understand what I went through just to get a few lousy days off? I can't take it anymore."

"I really thought you would have preferred to go alone, but I needed a vacation, too."

"You ruined it for me, anyway!"

"It's always about you, Beth, isn't it?"

"God damn you!" she yelled and retreated to the bedroom. I didn't follow. Thirty minutes later, dressed in another one of her black pant-suits, she headed for the door. As she passed me, she blurted out, "I wish that damn Bricklayer of yours would cut off your dick for all the good it does me!" She stormed out of the apartment without saying another word, no doubt proud of the cleverness of her parting shot.

Her sexual frustration was her fault, not mine. I wasn't always the reason that she fell asleep unsatisfied. Yeah, there were times when I was too tired to perform to her expectations. When I did, she always wanted more. Occasionally, she dropped her demands, which caused me to fear that she was having an affair with someone at the firm. Sometimes when she had to work until two or three in the morning, she checked into the hotel next to the firm's offices. I suspected she didn't check in alone. I guess I just didn't want to face that possibility. Ultimately, I didn't care.

The hell with it. Beth would have to stew. I was going to hold her to her self-imposed deadline. I went to work still preoccupied with doubts about Foster's little game with La Pointe and his implicit admission regarding his so-called early retirement. I spent another full day reviewing the forensics reports of the known victims trying to determine if there was anything I missed. I studied the department's list of registered sex offenders trying to identify his next victim.

As I left the station house for the day, a process server was waiting for me in the lobby. I expected it to be a subpoena from a La Salle Street lawyer, a scumbag named Allan Goldberg, who was representing a suspect from another case. They accused us of using excessive force when we brought him in for questioning. It was bullshit. We had been cleared by Internal Affairs months ago. It was a shakedown suit against the city and the department.

I was wrong about the papers he handed me. They were a Divorce Petition and an Ex Parte Restraining Order requiring me to vacate our apartment in twenty-four hours.

CHAPTER 64
Detective Frank Vincenti

I sat in my car in the station's lot staring at the divorce petition. My head pounded, but I felt no emotion. I was neither bitter nor relieved that Beth had finally decided to officially end the marriage. It had been over for some time; I just refused to accept it. She must have had the petition and motion for the TRO prepared right after she returned from Florida. Maybe she had her lover at the firm prepare the papers—whoever he was probably took great pleasure in it, as the petition contained an extraordinary amount of venom and outright lies. As I drove home, I was uncertain of what awaited me in our apartment. I had twenty-four hours to move out, and I was in no rush to have a confrontation with Beth.

Instead, I found a note in Beth's stylish handwriting waiting for me. She had taken an afternoon flight to Santa Barbara to be with her brother, and she expected my belongings and me to be gone when she returned three days hence. I poured myself an Irish whiskey, plopped down on the couch, and looked around the living and dining rooms, conducting a mental inventory of my "belongings" as Beth called them. I'd never really had much. She'd bought all the furniture, and there were no souvenirs, no childhood mementos, no photographs, and no plaques or trophies—oh, there were several medals and commendations I had collected during my time on the job, but Beth was always too embarrassed to have those on display when we had visitors, so I kept them in a cabinet drawer at the station house. Other than my clothes, there simply was very little else I could claim as my own. After a second drink, I fell asleep on the couch. It was a restless sleep.

By 9:00 a.m. the next day, I had called the divorce lawyer that Sean recommended. I was on hold listening to canned music when a recording interrupted: "Your call is important to us. Please remain on the line as we help other clients." After a couple more minutes of the annoying music, a live person answered. I explained to her that I was a cop and gave her my name and asked to speak to her boss.

"I'm sorry, but he is participating in an emergency telephonic hearing. May I take a message please?"

"No. I'll hold, but please slip him a note."

"I'll take him a note, but I'm quite sure he won't be able to take your call."

"Fine. Give him a note anyway, but I'll stay on hold. Tell him it's Detective Vincenti of Area North—"

Before I could tell her that I couldn't wait much longer, she said, "Please hold."

I looked over to Sean at the other end of our cubicle. "I've been on hold for twenty minutes, Sean. I hope you're right about this guy."

Just then, Sean's phone rang.

The divorce lawyer's secretary came back on my line. "Detective, I gave him the note and he wrote 'ten more minutes' on it."

"Fine."

Sean hurried over to my desk. "Hang up. That was Dunbar on the phone. Kids playing in an abandoned house a few blocks from United Center found a body wrapped in a blue tarp. Dunbar said the detectives from the 1st District are already at the scene. Let's go!"

"Get the car. I'll meet you out front."

I was bothered by the location of this new dumpsite. As we sped south on Ashland, I let Sean know my concern. "Sean, this is a long way from his other dumpsites."

Sean glanced over at me. "Maybe this was a secondary site. Maybe he was interrupted or his primary site became unavailable. You've said it before: Without being sure of a killer's motivation, predicting behavior is mostly unreliable speculation."

When we pulled up to the scene, the Supervisor of Patrol for the 1st District, Captain Joseph McArthur, was waiting for us at the curb in front of a boarded-up house. "Detectives Kelly and Vincenti—The Bricklayer boys! I was warned you were on your way."

Sean didn't like it, and neither did I.

"Can't believe they don't have you shackled to a desk at the State Street station, Mac," Sean shot back.

"Be a smart-ass if you want, Kelly, but we've got this one covered. You and your psychic sidekick are going to have to take a back seat."

I wasn't going to take his crap either. "I'm not psychic, just smarter than you, and—"

Sean cut in, "The Bricklayer is our case."

"And a helluva job you're doing! Area Central detectives have this one. I already cleared it with Area Commander Nagle."

"Fine. I'll talk to them. Who has it?"

"Ortiz and Miller. Go ahead, talk to them all you want."

As Sean sought out our counterparts, I stepped aside and called Dunbar on my cell.

"Commander, we're at the crime scene across from the United Center. Area Central has taken control of the crime scene and is claiming it as their case."

"Frank, settle down. I know. I just got off the phone with the chief of detectives. He said he doesn't see the harm in a fresh set of eyes looking at it."

"That's bullshit and you know it."

"I don't like it either. Let them play it out, though. You know as well as I do that this kill is out of our guy's comfort zone."

"That's what I told Sean on our way over."

"OK then. Sit back and see what they come up with. If it's not our guy, they'll have wasted their time, and not yours, and they'll look foolish. If it looks like our guy, then I'll get the chief to order them to turn it over to you. Good enough?"

I didn't answer right away. I wanted to examine the body, but Dunbar was a sly old fox and I couldn't argue with his logic.

"Yeah. Good enough."

Sean walked briskly back toward McArthur and me, removed his evidence gloves, and without breaking stride, said, "Always a pleasure to see you, Mac."

McArthur yelled back to him, "And the horse you rode in on, Kelly!"

I ran to catch up with Sean. "So?"

"Wrong side of the rib cage, and the body smells of rubbing alcohol, not bleach. We'll let these clowns chase a copycat. We have better things to do."

As we pulled away, news vans started to arrive.

CHAPTER 65
Detective Frank Vincenti

I spent a second night at our apartment, again sleeping on the couch, but with a better night's sleep than the night before. When I woke, my first thoughts were of the body found on the west side. As I showered and shaved, I recalled Captain McArthur's sarcastic remark—"a helluva job you're doing"—and thought that it wasn't far from the truth.

I filled a suitcase and a large duffle bag with most of my clothes and dumped everything else into two large garbage bags. I left behind the lonely nights, Beth's harangues, and a bed I shared only with images of bloodied and mutilated bodies.

I finally got a call back from my newly retained divorce lawyer. I told him that we couldn't let stand the allegations in Beth's motion for the restraining order. The allegations claimed that I "was mentally unstable and capable of violence." It also asserted that Beth feared for her safety because I carried a firearm. It was more of Beth's venom coming to the surface. I wanted the allegations and the corresponding findings in the TRO struck from the record.

"Other than your clothes looking a little wrinkled, I'd say you're handling this well," Sean observed as he threw his jacket on his desk and came over to talk to me.

"Yeah—good enough," I replied without looking up from my computer monitor.

"Had your breakfast yet?"

"Just about to."

We headed to the row of vending machines. While I tried to decide which flavor granola bar would go best with an energy drink, Sean asked, "Now what?"

"I have all my stuff in the trunk of my car. After work I'll probably look for one of those cheap extended-stay hotels," I said as I tore the wrapper off my breakfast.

"You're staying with me until you find something better."

I didn't even try to resist. "Thank you, but I'll stay only until I can find something more permanent."

"Nothing is permanent, my friend."

Although I had been to Sean's apartment before, I never had reason to see his second bedroom. The door was always closed, and I never thought anything of it. He opened it now and flipped on the light. "You can stay in here."

The door opened to a room decorated for a child. I stood at the threshold not quite comprehending the décor or the furniture.

He saw the puzzled look on my face. "Well, I guess I have some explaining to do."

Confused, I replied, "Yeah, I guess so!"

"Drop your stuff, use the head, and I'll explain over a Bushmills or two."

I knew that Sean had a son, but I assumed that he lived with his mother. I naively wondered who would give custody to a cop.

After a couple of Bushmills and almost an hour of Sean doing all the talking, I learned that nine years earlier he had married a girl from a wealthy suburban family but divorced her four years ago when she failed to finish her third drug rehab program, after which she abandoned Sean and his son.

"Usually, the wife gets custody, but because of her history of drug abuse, you got custody?"

"Sort of."

Sean explained that his son lived with his in-laws during the week, but with him on the weekends. Staring into his empty glass, Sean said, "When she took James for three days to live with her and her supplier, well, that was the last straw. I wasn't about to expose my son to the potential for abuse."

"Where is she now?"

"She and her supplier moved somewhere in southern California."

"And you get along with her parents?"

"Oh yeah. They've always considered me to be another one of their sons. Besides, they've got a lot of guilt about their daughter and are determined that their grandson never have contact with her."

"Where do they live?"

"River Forest. James is enrolled in a Catholic grade school there. He lives with his maternal grandparents in an affluent suburb that gives him opportunities I could never have afforded."

"James, huh? Not Jim?"

"We named him after her dad. James Lehan, and no one calls Mr. Lehan anything but James."

"What does his grandfather do?"

As Sean walked to the kitchen to get more ice, he replied, "He has his own business, mostly construction, some demolition work—that kind of thing."

When he returned with more ice and a refill of Bushmills he asked a favor: "Look, you're welcome to stay here as long as you need to, but I have to ask you: When James is here on weekends, can you find another place to bunk?"

"Sure."

"But you're good for this weekend. His grandparents are taking him sailing. Mr. Lehan owns a Hylas 63 and moors it in Racine Harbor, in Wisconsin."

"What the hell is a Hylast 63?"

"It's Hylas, no "t" at the end. A Hylas 63 is a big-ass sailboat that sleeps six. It has a price tag that would make your head spin. Sometimes, I go up to Racine and spend a night on the boat alone to unwind. I can't sail the damn thing—I just use it as a floating hotel room."

He turned one of the stools from the breakfast counter toward me and perched himself there. Looking down into his refilled glass of Irish, he asked, "Frank, your father's house has been sitting empty since he died last winter. Have you considered moving in there?"

CHAPTER 66
Detective Frank Vincenti

My daily routine returned to normal. Although my divorce lawyer was still arm wrestling with Beth's lawyer over striking the allegations that I was mentally unstable and accusing me of being a danger to his client, he assured me that negotiating a favorable divorce decree would be easy since Beth's income was a multiple of a detective's pay and there were no children involved. The sooner it was over, the better.

My father's house was the last place I ever wanted to set foot in again, but Sean was right—it had been empty since Christmas. I had paid one of my father's neighbor's to check on it from time to time but never heard from her. As a teenager, I couldn't wait to move out. That my father no longer lived there didn't matter, the memories still did.

I spent the second weekend as Sean's temporary roommate at a suburban hotel. The hotel was Foster's idea. When I was about to explain to Foster the situation about Sean and his son, Foster admitted that he had known about James and Sean's dilemma for some time. In fact, he confided, he was the one who had tracked down Sean's ex in California and had provided a full report to the family.

"Candidly, Francis," he told me, "I have been very concerned about Sean for some time. His ex discovered that she was being investigated and threatened to return and take James back to California with her. Sean may never have shown it, but he was going through hell. It's a wonder he didn't snap under the strain. He would do anything to protect James—anything."

I resented the fact that Sean had shared his secret with Foster and not with me. I was also displeased that Foster had never let on about what appears to be a growing relationship with Sean. There was really no reason for Sean and Foster to have left me in the dark, but no useful purpose would be served by questioning either of them about it. It was petty jealousy, nothing more. It was beneath me, but still it rankled.

The following Monday morning, I arrived at the station's lower level and found Dunbar sitting at my desk drinking from a McDonald's paper coffee cup. He turned to look at me when he heard me approach.

"Where's Kelly?" he asked.

I looked at my watch and stumbled for words. "Maybe in another twenty minutes."

Dunbar glanced at his watch and looked as if he hadn't realized what time it was. "There's been a development."

"Another body?"

He deflected my question. "Let's wait for Kelly in the parking lot."

After Dunbar paced for ten minutes at the rear entrance, Sean pulled into the lot. Dunbar motioned him over to where we were standing. He grabbed the passenger door handle and quickly pulled the door open while Sean's car was slowing to a stop.

"Don't bother parking, Kelly, we're taking a ride. Frank, get in the back."

Confused, Sean asked, "Where are we going?"

While Dunbar secured his seat belt, he explained, "We're headed to the Town Hall Station to meet with Chief of Detectives Thomas."

Twenty minutes later, the three of us sat with Chief Thomas at a round table in his private conference room. "Ok, Eddie, it's your show."

Dunbar pulled four folded sheets of paper from his coat pocket, handed one to each of us, and placed the last one directly in front of him on the table. His copy had handwritten notes.

"Approximately ten days ago, someone posted a note on the message board of a blog that serves as an anonymous Internet hotline for pedophiles trying to get help. It took more than a week for the blog administrator to figure out the message was intended for us—actually, intended for Frank."

The room went silent, the only noise coming from the vibration of Dunbar's cell phone, which he chose to ignore.

"The message has been reproduced on the sheet of paper I just handed you. As you can see, it is barely decipherable."

*cpd vincenti. I'm the rael 1. look in despalesn rievr—
near the palens froget beth. hiem.4*

Finally, Sean spoke, "If this is from The Bricklayer—and I think it is—then he's dyslexic."

The chief looked up, and after eying me, he looked over at Sean. "I'm listening."

"One of my younger brothers is dyslexic. I used to help him with his homework—this is what his written homework assignments looked like before I helped rewrite them."

"That makes sense," I added. "Some psychiatric studies have found that dyslexics have a tendency to be aggressive and violent." I had my suspicions about the note—it seemed too easy. The killer may have purposely adopted a dyslexic style to mislead us, but I didn't voice my concern.

The chief nodded. "OK, assuming that's true, what does it mean?"

Sean studied the typed message, his brow furrowing slightly. "Well, the easy part is that he knows Frank is on the case. And, he's trying to prove that he is The Bricklayer."

"Signing it with the same message that appears on each torso confirms it's our guy," I added. "We never released that detail."

The chief's leather seat creaked as he leaned forward. "And the rest?"

Still staring at the message, Sean answered, "He's telling us there are more bodies and where they are. He's presenting his bona fides."

"OK, but where are the bodies?"

I recalled reports that Gacy and Dahmer had dumped bodies in the Des Plaines River. Sounding out the misspellings, I was quick to answer. "The Des Plaines River."

"Near the airport," Sean explained. "I think that's the meaning of the second use of the word, 'palens.'"

Dunbar didn't react. Instead he said, "That he posted it on a pedophile help blog, confirms Frank's suspicion that a childhood sexual assault provides the motivation for his killings."

Addressing Dunbar, the chief said, "I still don't like that he's trying for the second time to communicate with Detective Vincenti." Looking at me, he asked, "Detective, is there something we should know?"

Knowing that Dunbar hadn't told him of Foster's ploy, I shook my head. "No."

Dunbar tried to wrap it up. "Chief, there are two things to do: First, let's get help from the Cook County Sheriff's office to coordinate a search of the Des Plaines River—"

I interrupted. "He wants the bodies found. They won't need to drag the river. They should be able to find them buried on a river bank virtually in plain view."

Dunbar continued, "Second, Vincenti needs to review his case files to see if he's run across this guy before. I want Sean to help him."

Then the chief asked the question the rest of us had been avoiding. "What's the reference 'froget beth'?"

"Beth is my wife's name."

The room went silent again. Finally, the chief spat out, "Now how the fuck does he know that?"

He ran his hand over his thinning hair. After a few moments of silence, he looked over to Sean and me. "Detectives, you're dismissed. I want a few minutes alone with Commander Dunbar."

CHAPTER 67
Detective Frank Vincenti

When we returned to the station house, we entered through the rear door and followed Dunbar down the narrow corridor lined with three interview rooms. He stopped in front of the first room on the right, checked to be sure that it was empty, and motioned us in. He pulled up a chair with his back to the two-way mirror. Pointing to the two chairs opposite him, he said, "Detectives, take a seat."

He paused, rubbing his brow. "Frank, the chief is concerned that The Bricklayer is sending you messages directly. I don't like it, either."

"But really, the first time was Foster."

That got Sean's attention; he immediately jerked his head in my direction.

Dunbar tried to downplay it. "Sean, you're in good company. I haven't told the chief about that yet, either."

Turning to Sean, I explained, "Foster was behind La Pointe—he was a plant. It's a long story, one that I am not particularly happy with. And in case you're wondering, neither the commander nor I knew about it ahead of time."

Looking back at Dunbar, Sean asked, "Did Foster send this blog message?"

I leaned back in my chair. "I wouldn't put it past him."

Dunbar looked at me with a smirk. "I called him as soon as the message hit my desk. He denied sending it. He didn't seem surprised by it though. In fact, he correctly guessed what it said. Frank, has a killer ever tried to communicate with you before?"

"No, but the press has used my name in its coverage."

Dunbar replied sharply, "Yeah, Sean's and mine, too, but The Bricklayer addressed the message to you, and not either of us. Besides, the chief is right—how does he know your wife's name?"

I didn't answer. Dunbar paused, checked his watch, and fidgeted with his tie.

"Look, Frank, the chief wanted to put you on administrative leave."

"That's bullshit!"

Dunbar frowned. "Of course it is. I talked him out of it. I convinced him that the more The Bricklayer communicates with you, the more we'll learn about him."

I didn't push it, but I voiced my objections. "We don't need the Sheriff's Office to help with the search—"

"Commander, I have a pretty good idea where to look," Sean said. He's telling us to look in the Des Plaines River near the planes, near O'Hare. Frank and I could take half-dozen uniforms and start the search in Schiller Woods. The Des Plaines River runs through it and it's a stone's throw from O'Hare."

"I do not want you two wasting your time looking for bodies. Let the sheriff's office help. I'll make M'Bala the liaison with their office. I want you looking at old cases for connections to Frank." Dunbar looked at me. "I want to know why he's chosen to communicate with you, and why he's now implicated Beth."

Sean reluctantly agreed.

"Oh, and by the way, I got a call from the M.E.'s office yesterday. Why didn't you guys tell me about the M.E. tech named Allison?"

I looked up, surprised. I hadn't heard that name since after the Anderson murder. "That's old news. There's nothing to tell. He's just some whack-job who claimed he knew Monsignor Anderson. He overreacted to the killing, that's all."

"That's all? I learned yesterday for the first time that he threatened you guys."

I shook my head and replied, "Commander, you know that shit happens all the time. Nothing ever comes of it."

Sean interrupted. "Allison made a couple of calls to us at the station and left incoherent messages. We had patrol officers try to pick him up, but he seems to have moved or something. Frank got a threatening call—we weren't sure if it was from Allison—but like Frank said, we get those all the time."

Dunbar nodded. "OK, but be alert. The M.E. said he got a threatening call from him, too."

Dunbar removed his suit coat, and, looking at Sean, said, "Kelly, will you excuse us? I need a few moments alone with Frank."

After a minute or so of silent pacing, he stopped on the other side of the table directly across from me, placed both palms on the table, and leaned in.

"How deep into this guy's head are you?"

He and I seldom discussed those so-called special talents that years ago Foster had claimed Dunbar and I shared, but the fact that the blog message was addressed to me and that he was sending a secondary message about Beth apparently unnerved Dunbar, as it did me.

"Deep enough to understand your admonition about entering Dante's 'City of Woe.'"

"That was Foster's admonition, not mine. I merely repeated it. Cut the crap. How far?"

"I first saw images of the Edwards and Anderson murders in January, but the images were fragmented." I didn't tell Dunbar that the images came to me during bad sex with Beth. Of course, I was never sure if images like those made the sex bad or bad sex evoked the images.

"At the time, I speculated he was able to control his rage while he selected his victim and dumpsite but he unleashed it savagely when he was alone with the victim—extraordinary characteristics for a run-of-the-mill psychopath or sociopath. I tried to piece together Edwards's and Anderson's murders by looking for attributes they shared, but got nowhere. Obviously, the removal of the genitals confirms the sexual element, and the fact that our guy sodomized his victims with a wooden object suggests that the killer had been sodomized."

"Go on."

"Mathias opened a new door completely. When we found the body tied to the utility pole, I saw a flash of a chunk of brick, although Mathias wasn't buried under a pile of bricks like the other two. And then, while I watched the M.E. empty his rib cage, an image of a small child flashed in my head, but I didn't recognize him, and I felt our killer's pain and anger. Foster is pretty certain our guy has been stalking and killing pedophiles and that Anderson was a mistake. I agree with him. But in view of Sean's interpretation of 'heim.4' as 'for him,' my original hunch about seeking revenge for a sexual assault on him is wrong. The assault was on someone else, someone he was close to— maybe a brother, a son, or a friend."

"What about his attempt to communicate directly with you through this last message?"

"This guy is all about messages. His kills themselves are messages. As Sean once observed, he wants the world to sit up and take notice. I think our suppression of his torso message has frustrated him. To the extent that he sent a message to someone on the case justifies Foster's little game, but unless we deal with his message in a fashion he's satisfied with, he'll up the ante and kill again. And, one other thing. I haven't told anyone because I don't want to make a big deal of it, and besides the image lacks detail."

"OK, what is it?"

"An image of a man wearing a gray hoodie, but his face is covered in darkness, so I haven't been able to make out any features." I didn't bother to tell him that the image had appeared to me more than once.

Dunbar knew not to pursue it. He knew that when I could identify the face, I'd tell him.

"What about the reference to Beth?"

I paused, reluctant to answer. Dunbar repeated the question just as Foster used to do when I tried to deflect his questions.

"It scares me."

"Do you want to get Foster's opinion on this?"

"No."

"Why not?"

"He's starting to scare me, too."

CHAPTER 68
Anthony

My post on the so-called pedophile hotline blog didn't look much different from what other people had posted. I'd always had trouble reading and writing. I never thought it serious, nor did I really care. Somebody at school, I don't recall who—it may have been a fourth-grade teacher—concluded I had some kind of reading disorder. The teacher gave me a note to take home that recommended the name of a specialist I should see for treatment, whatever that meant. I was tired of people always saying that there was something wrong with me, so on my way home from school that day, I crumbled the note into a ball, and, imitating a Michael Jordan jump shot, threw it in a neighbor's trash bin. Now, I figured my reading problem was shared by many of the other people posting on the hotline blog. Maybe we all had the same problem or maybe none of us had a problem.

If the note was received by the police and understood, then they would be searching for bodies in Schiller Woods, but after a week of daily vigils in the woods waiting for the police to show up and search the river banks, I became worried the note hadn't been found or my spelling and grammar were not deciphered. I mean, if someone did find it, would they have comprehended enough of it to bring it to the attention of someone at Chicago PD? And, even then, would the cops have been smart enough to understand it was intended for one cop in particular—Detective Francis A. Vincenti? Did I need to take some additional action to draw them to the spot along the banks of the Des Plaines River where I had buried two bodies?

I waited and watched as jetliners roared overhead. The Schiller Woods Forest Preserve was no more than a mile from O'Hare. The airport was busier now than those nights when I'd spent time on the hood of my father's car watching takeoffs and landings. Now, every minute or so, an airliner took off or touched down at O'Hare, some flying so low and the sound of their engines so loud, that windows rattled in the nearby neighborhoods. On the planes' landing approach from the east, the aircraft flew directly above the Des Plaines River where it bends and turns through the Schiller Woods Forest Preserve. That was where I had buried the bodies, less than a mile from O'Hare's main runway, along the east bank of the river. At the time, I had carefully placed them in shallow graves and concealed them under leaves and loose brush. Now I wanted them to be found.

It was ten days since I posted a note on the blog when a search team finally showed up. After two days of combing the forest preserve at Schiller Woods, they found the site. As jets thundered overhead casting shadows on the woods, I watched from across the river, behind a clump of short evergreen trees. A group of officers and others in civvies gathered around two large mounds only a few feet from the river's edge, while two techs wearing green neoprene waders stood in the river guiding the removal of surface debris from around the site. When I had dumped the bodies three summers ago, the river had been shallow and its banks wide. The heavy snow of this past winter had melted and swelled the river, slowing the work of the evidence technicians.

I watched, gratified, as the evidence techs dug up and removed one set of remains, and then started digging near the second mound where a patch of a dirty blue tarp had been spotted. I had hoped that the search team would be startled, excited even, and would call out to each other. I had counted on the Woods's parking lot overflowing with press and crime groupies. I was disappointed on both counts. I didn't know it then, but I would be even more disappointed later when there was no press coverage of the discovery.

CHAPTER 69
Detective Frank Vincenti

I called the M.E.'s office to get a report on the newly discovered bodies. The pathologist assigned to the case estimated that the remains of the two white males wrapped in blue tarps removed from the riverbank had been placed there almost three years earlier. Placement in the moist soil and three years of exposure to the elements had accelerated decomposition, and the tarps had done little to preserve the bodies. Although the victims' right hands were missing, the M.E. couldn't determine whether the victims' genitals had been removed.

I was certain the killer would know we'd uncovered his victims, and warned M'Bala that he might take obscene pleasure in having his handiwork discovered and receiving inordinate publicity of the find. I had instructed her and the search team to keep the search and discovery low-key. Dunbar and I agreed with Foster's recommendation that the discovery of the bodies be kept out of the press for now. We had intentionally delivered a mixed message to the killer: *Yeah, we received and deciphered the message you left on the pedophile blog, but we're not going to let you enjoy any publicity*. Even without the publicity, I was certain he'd know we'd found the bodies. Yet a week after the discovery, we still hadn't heard anything more from our killer.

"I don't like it," Sean declared, shaking his head.

"I don't like it either, but Foster thinks it will force the killer's hand."

"But the lack of press coverage may trigger another kill."

"That's Foster's point."

"That's a dangerous game." Sean leaned against the cubicle partition between our desks and fiddled with a pen, flipping it end over end in his hand. "I would have preferred sending him a message back on the pedophile blog. You know something like, 'We feel your pain. We can help you.'"

"Yeah. In fact, I suggested just that to Dunbar. Foster nixed it. Said that if we mollify his rage, he might go quiet for an extended period of time, maybe years, and we may never catch him."

"You believe that?"

"I don't know. If we're right about the bodies in Indiana and Wisconsin being his early kills, that means that he's moved around—maybe for a job or he got married or something. If we don't force his hand here and now, he may wind up killing in California or New York or who knows where."

"And Dunbar bought into this?"

I nodded.

"What does Foster say about The Bricklayer mentioning Beth in the message?"

"I haven't asked."

"Why not?"

"He doesn't need to know everything we do, Sean."

"Since when?"

"He's enjoying the chase and gamesmanship a little too much lately, and continues to be consumed by a twenty-year manhunt. I still don't like that he deceived me planning the La Pointe setup. Besides, Beth isn't his problem."

"Have you told her?"

"She won't take my calls, and the one time she did answer, she told me to go to hell and hung up. Sometimes I think she'd like to have my balls in a plastic bag in her freezer."

"Jesus, Frank!"

"Never mind. Anyway, my lawyer sent her lawyer a letter advising him of the possibility that she may be stalked. Although she refused police protection, they've retained a security service at the office for her, but I don't know about the rest of the time. She's on her own now and can figure out what to do. She's a big girl."

CHAPTER 70
Anthony

The police weren't following my breadcrumbs. It was clear Detective Vincenti had received and understood my message. I'd watched the deputies from the sheriff's office and their evidence techs find the bodies at the river. I watched the news for more than two weeks waiting patiently for some mention of what I had hoped the press would tritely describe as "grisly discoveries," but there was no mention of it. That had to be at the direction of the CPD, but surely not Vincenti.

I was also confused by the failure of the press to give adequate coverage of La Pointe's release and the reasons for it. And, although I had been flattered temporarily by the copycat's efforts, he had gotten more press coverage than the discovery of the riverbank bodies. I was frustrated and angry, and the disjointed scenes of the attack on my friend reappeared more frequently, always followed by headaches and repeated episodes of blacking out from the pain. Everything was getting confused, scrambled in my mind as the pain became too much to bear. I could wait no longer.

The widely reported fact that Mathias was a convicted pedophile proved my reliance on the CPD list of sex offenders to be sound. I turned to the list again where I found Luis Cervantes of the 4900 block of Lawrence Avenue. This time, I was determined to go undetected as I surveyed the block that was harboring a child molester. This time, it took me only one long afternoon to single out Cervantes from the rest of the residents of Lawrence Avenue, and I pledged I would do more homework and spend more time observing his habits. And, this time, I would make sure the CPD would receive my message, understand it, and spread the word. This time, I would leave no doubt about its meaning.

CHAPTER 71
Detective Frank Vincenti

After three weeks at Sean's apartment, I decided that being with Sean at work and at home didn't give me the time I needed to be alone, and living at a hotel on the weekends was becoming cost-prohibitive. It was time to face the only viable, affordable alternative: moving back to my father's house.

I stopped by the house on Newland that weekend. It had sat empty for almost five months, and as I parked on the street and killed the engine, I thought back to the day I claimed my father's body. I hadn't stepped foot in the place since and hadn't paid attention to its condition. I approached the concrete stairs leading to the entrance with more than a little trepidation, and paused momentarily at the front door, knowing that painful memories lurked on the other side. I put my hand on the doorknob and squared my shoulders. I feared that only regret would greet me.

The house was dank, the air stale. The furnishings were just about the same as I remembered them and located in the same places as when I had left fourteen years earlier, but I noticed the television was missing and empty beer bottles and fast food wrappers littered the floor. Damn! Had the place been taken over by a squatter? The kitchen was also a mess. There was food in the refrigerator and a pile of unwashed dishes in the sink. I checked the back door. The lock had been jimmied and duct tape had been placed over the lock's faceplate holding the latch in the open position. I was right. Someone had broken in and made himself at home. I was tempted to call the desk sergeant at the 21st District and have them send over a forensics team, but decided against it. It would serve no useful purpose at this point.

I was able to convince a neighborhood locksmith to come to the house later in the day and had him change the locks while I checked all the windows on the first floor to make sure they were closed and secured. Layers of paint and swollen sashes apparently served better than any window locks. If my squatter returned, he would take the hint that he had been discovered when he tried to gain entry, and, if not, then he'd find an armed Chicago PD detective waiting for him. I hired a neighborhood cleaning lady to make the house minimally livable. It took her and another person two days of hard work. I told them not to bother with the bedrooms. Even then, she apologized that they couldn't do a better job. I paid them, thanked them, and made arrangements for them to clean every two weeks.

I refused to sleep in my old bedroom. The day I moved in, I opened the door just to see what my father had done with it and discovered that he had turned it into a junk room. It appeared as if every time he had an old or broken piece of furniture or a pile of old clothes, he just opened the door and threw the unwanted items into the room. I closed the door and decided to leave it closed. I didn't even bother with my father's bedroom. The door was closed, and it would remain closed. I replaced all the furniture in the living and dining rooms with inexpensive furniture from a neighborhood superstore that promised next-day delivery. I solved the sleeping arrangement by ordering a leather sofa bed for the living room.

I fell into a regular routine. Get to work early and stay late. In between, I pored over old case files, trying to find a suspect or collar that might be carrying a grudge, or, more likely, someone I had helped convict who wanted to show me that he was more clever than me. All of it seemed so familiar. I had gotten to know this guy. I thought I knew him well, but every time I tried to visualize him or anticipate his next move, I got lost in my own analysis. This had become far more than a serial killer case. Our guy had made it personal.

At night, I reviewed all the crime scene photos on my iPad. In addition to the photos that forensics techs had taken, I had taken many myself, including photos I took as I witnessed the autopsies. I had also downloaded autopsy photographs of the Indiana and Wisconsin victims. I had obtained photos of the known victims from family albums, and in the case of the monsignor, old newspaper articles, and posted them on my dining room wall with pushpins. Next to their photos, I had taped four maps: one each of Illinois, Iowa, Indiana, and southeastern Wisconsin, placing red push pins where we had found his five confirmed kills in Illinois, and green push pins for the suspected killings in Kenosha County, Wisconsin, and East Chicago, Indiana, near the Calumet River. When I was too tired or too lazy to make my own meals, I walked across the street and down the block to the Grand Grill, a little neighborhood diner on Grand Avenue that had been there since I was a kid. It became my regular breakfast spot.

On a late spring Friday morning, my breakfast routine at the Grand Grill was interrupted. I immediately called Sean on my cell.

"Hey, we may have a problem. I think I'm being stalked."

"Are you in danger?"

"I don't think so."

"Is it that Allison nut from the morgue?"

"No, it's not him. It's a long story. I'll explain when I get there."

Sean was waiting for me at the rear entrance to the station. "Were you followed here?"

"No. Let's go in and I'll brief you, and you'd better get Keisha."

Five minutes later I briefed Sean and Keisha. Sean leaned against my desk with his arms folded in front of him. Keisha pulled Sean's desk chair next to mine. I sat at my desk and turned my chair to face them.

"OK. Start from the beginning," Sean directed as if I were a witness.

"Remember last winter when I ran into someone from the old neighborhood?"

"Yeah, he was someone you wanted to forget."

"That's right. His name is Tony Protettore. He lived next door to us when we were kids. He called me several times after that, but I never returned the calls. It isn't a relationship I want to renew. This morning I saw him outside the restaurant where I usually have breakfast. He stood on the sidewalk across the street on Grand staring into the diner."

"Are you certain he saw you?" asked Keisha.

Replaying the scene in my head, I answered, "Yeah, he was looking directly at me. When he saw that I had recognized him, he seemed startled, quickly looked away, hurried down the street, and then ducked into a backyard in the middle of the block."

"OK, so maybe he's just visiting the old neighborhood."

"No. It's got to be more than that. Last week while I was eating a sandwich over the kitchen sink, I looked out the window and saw someone standing in my backyard. When he realized I had spotted him, he turned and ran into the alley. I saw the guy's face just momentarily, but now I'm sure it was Tony. I didn't think much of it then because I couldn't have imagined it was him."

"Again, harmless coincidences, Frank?"

"And then I found this note stuffed in my mail slot. I found it this morning when I went back to the house after I called you. It may have been there for a couple of days. I don't always check my mail." I handed Sean a crumpled-up piece of yellow paper with child-like block printing that read, 'how do I get yu atentoin?'

"You think it's a note from Tony?" Sean turned it over in his hand, then gave it to Keisha.

"I really don't know."

Keisha examined it, and held it up to the light. "It sure looks like the handwriting from the victims' torsos and the spelling is similar to the note left on the pedophile blog. Was Tony dyslexic?"

"I don't remember. That's not something you talk about when you're a kid."

Sean turned to Keisha. "Run it over to Forensics and see what they come up with. Of course, we just added two more sets of fingerprints to it."

Sean studied my face. "I don't like it, Frank. The note puts his visits to the neighborhood in a different light. I think we need to do a little homework on this guy. See what he's been up to."

CHAPTER 72
Detective Frank Vincenti

Two days later, Sean called me at home right after the ten o'clock news. "Frank, stay put. Keisha and I are on our way."

"Is there a problem?"

"Yes and no. We'll be right there."

"But—"

"Damn it, Frank, we'll be right there!"

A light drizzle had just begun when they walked through my front door. Sean headed for the kitchen and helped himself to a beer and then joined Keisha and me around my dining room table that was littered with case files and spiral notebooks.

Sean got right to it. "First, the guys in Forensics say that the handwriting on the note is a close match to that scrawled on the bodies—not an exact match, but pretty damn close. And your friend must have wiped down the piece of paper because the only set of prints on the note were yours, Keisha's, and mine."

"Sean, we don't know that the note came from Tony! We don't even know what it means."

"True, but listen to what Keisha dug up on Protettore and then do the math."

Keisha began her report, reading from a small notebook: "When he was fifteen, he and his family moved from here to Gary, Indiana, where his father worked in the steel mills until the plant closed five years later. Your friend had just transferred from a junior college to Ball State in Muncie when his father was laid off. His father took on several odd jobs, including painting houses to support the family, but Tony was left to fend for himself to pay tuition. He worked several jobs while at Ball State and relied heavily on student loans. He double majored in History and Physical Education, and, get this, he qualified for the NCAA wrestling championships when he was a senior."

"Yeah, I remember that he wrestled freshman year."

Keisha continued. "After graduation, he took a job in a Crown Point high school where he taught history and coached wrestling for four years before he was arrested for assaulting the parent of one of his wrestlers. The arrest record shows that he struck a parent when, after a wrestling meet, he saw the father slap the son in the school parking lot after the boy had lost his match. He got a year's probation, but was fired by the school."

"I have already called to have his booking prints sent to us," Sean explained.

"Isn't that rushing things a bit?"

"Frank, he was working in Crown Point! Hell, Crown Point is only twenty-five miles from where the Indiana State Police found a John Doe wrapped in a blanket along the Calumet River—around the same time he was fired."

I didn't even try to respond. I turned back to Keisha. "Go on."

"A year later Tony followed his parents to Racine, Wisconsin, where his father landed a job on the assembly line of J.I. Case. Tony took a job in the local park district, coaching wrestling and doing maintenance work at the rec center."

Looking over to Sean, I interrupted Keisha. "I suppose that you're going to try to tie his job in Racine to the body in Kenosha County?"

"It's less than an hour's drive away—"

"Yeah, but your father-in-law docks his sail boat in Racine and sometimes you stay on his boat there for long weekends—neither of which makes you or your father-in-law suspects." I looked back to Keisha. "Keep going."

"After two years he was fired for public intoxication and lewd behavior." Keisha turned the page of her notebook and continued. "He got drunk and took a piss in front of the rec center. The incident was witnessed by families leaving a grade school basketball game."

Sean added, "Then he falls off the radar until he shows up and stops you on the street. We haven't been able to run down a current address for him. We have no idea where he's living."

"Yeah, I couldn't find anything that might tell us where he might be—nothing." Keisha flipped her notebook closed.

Sean took a long drink of his beer, stood, and looked into the kitchen, "You know, Frank, it just occurred to me. You saw Tony in your neighborhood twice: once in front of the diner and once in your backyard. He could've been your squatter. Hell, when he stopped you on the street last winter, didn't he tell you he was staying with a friend in the old neighborhood. Maybe you were that friend. Could be that he stayed in the basement until your father died and moved upstairs when—"

"Pretty far fetched, Sean." I got up from my chair, walked around to the other side of the table, and studied the maps with their red and green pushpins. Sean and Keisha said nothing.

"Even if he was the squatter, that doesn't make him a murderer. Just a tresspasser."

"Look at the geography and time frames. It adds up."

Sean was too quick to conclude that my old friend was our killer and was building a case against him without any tangible evidence to tie Tony to the murders and without any explanation of motive. Foster had taught me that when you focus on only one possible scenario, you start to discredit other viable evidence that doesn't fit your theory of a case. Sean was falling into that trap.

Keisha must have sensed the growing tension. "Guys, we don't have any other leads, do we?"

"Sean, is there anything new on Allison? You know, we have written him off as a nut job who made idle threats, but we've never seriously looked at him as a suspect in the killings. Did the uniforms ever locate him?"

Sean replied with uncharacteristic sarcasm: "Hey, he's from the south—Jackson, Mississippi—I think. Maybe he couldn't handle Chicago winters and returned to Jackson."

I glared at him. He got the message. "Fine, Frank. I'll have a couple of uniforms try again to locate Allison, but our main focus ought to be your buddy."

"Tony was never my 'buddy'. His showing up now could be no more than a series of coincidences."

"Bullshit. I want to put out a BOLO on him first thing in the morning."

Still staring at my wall of maps and photos, I ran my finger over the photographs of each of the victims and took my time answering, finally saying, "No."

Sean snapped. "Holy shit, Frank, don't you—"

"Let me finish. First of all, I'm not convinced Tony's our guy. I'm telling you, it just doesn't feel right. You've trusted my instincts before, so hear me out." I turned away from the victims' photos, leaned against one of the dining room chairs, and gathered my thoughts.

"So?" Keisha said.

"So, no BOLO on Tony; not yet, anyway. I don't want to alert him to the fact that we're on to him. We'll lose him if he's our guy. He's been in the neighborhood twice now. He'll be back. I want to see what he's up to. He may have a totally innocent reason for being back here. Maybe you're right, Sean. Maybe he was staying in my father's house. Maybe he had nowhere else to go."

"And I suppose that you're going to simply engage him in conversation."

"Maybe." Looking over at Keisha, I asked, "Can you handle some surveillance work?"

Surprised that I had asked her for help, she jumped at the chance. "Sure."

Sean immediately understood. "OK, Frank, now that makes sense. Keisha can put a team together and discreetly hang around the neighborhood. If they spot Tony, they can follow him to where he's living and then get a warrant."

I nodded. "One step at a time, Sean. One step at a time."

CHAPTER 73
Detective Frank Vincenti

There was no shortage of volunteers among Area North's detectives to work the surveillance team headed by Keisha. Everyone wanted in on the apprehension of the killer called The Bricklayer. Sean and I screened the volunteers and settled on two veterans: Mike Johnson and Ricardo Alvarez. Johnson and Sean had been at the academy at the same time and came up through the ranks together. Sean assured me that Johnson could be trusted to follow instructions. I didn't know Alvarez, but Sean had worked with him before I was assigned to VCS and assured me that he "has a good nose for trouble." Both had a record of impressive collars, and already held a number of department commendations. Sean assured me they wouldn't be inclined to show-boat or try to draw attention to themselves by making a hasty arrest if it came to that.

Keisha developed a strategy for surveillance and deployment. She would provide coverage at and around the station house and wherever I went on a call. Johnson would begin taking his meals at the Grand Grill, acting as if he was new to the neighborhood and trying to establish himself as a regular. He would also frequent the two neighborhood bars located within six blocks of my house. Alvarez would park several blocks away from the Grill and respond to sightings radioed to him by Keisha and Johnson. Keisha called me at home every night reporting on their progress—or the lack thereof. On the fourth day of surveillance, she didn't wait to provide her report.

It took four mornings for Tony to show up outside the Grill. He made an initial pass around eight-thirty a.m., walking quickly, presumably to determine if I was there having breakfast. When he saw I wasn't, he entered and ordered a black coffee to go, keeping a watchful eye on the front door. As he walked out the door with his cup of coffee in hand, Johnson radioed Alvarez. A few minutes later, Alvarez spotted him walking leisurely west on Grand Avenue. Johnson caught up, and the two experienced cops alternated as tails to avoid detection.

Grand Avenue between Newland and Harlem Avenue is a wide, busy street lined with large franchise stores, auto repair shops, several ethnic restaurants, and a few neighborhood mom-and-pop shops—remnants of a different era. As Tony proceeded west on Grand, he occasionally stopped to look into store windows, and, after a short pause at each window, simply moved on, in no particular hurry. He finally entered a bookstore just west of Harlem Avenue in a new strip mall, where he sat at a table next to the front window and spent time reading newspapers and drinking coffee. He reappeared around 11:00 a.m., when he walked to the corner, waited briefly at the bus stop, and boarded the CTA #43 bus headed north on Harlem.

Johnson kept up with the bus while Alvarez purposely lagged behind. At the intersection of Harlem and Belmont, Tony exited the bus through the rear door, crossed the street, and stood on the north side of Belmont, joining a group of young people presumably waiting for the eastbound #77 Belmont bus.

Johnson radioed Keisha. "He just got on the CTA at Belmont headed east. I think he's heading toward the station house. Alvarez is moving ahead of me now and will tail the bus. I'll fall back."

"Got it. In case that's where he's headed, I'll go over to Campbell Avenue and Belmont. I'm pretty sure that's the bus stop closest to the station." Keisha watched several buses pass before she radioed Alvarez. "He hasn't shown."

"His bus just passed you, and he didn't get off."

"Ok. Stay with him. Is Johnson a safe distance behind you?"

"He should be." He checked his rearview mirror. "Shit! I don't see him."

"Did he get caught at a light?"

"Maybe, but he's too good at this to let that happen. What do you want me to do?"

"Stick with the bus." Keisha shouted into her mic, "Johnson! Johnson! This is M'Bala. Come in. What's your 20? Repeat. What's your 20?"

Silence.

"Johnson. Do you read?"

Silence.

"I can't raise Johnson."

"I still don't see him."

"Stay with the bus. If Johnson is having trouble, he'll catch up."

Five minutes later, Alvarez alerted Keisha. "Protettore got off at Clark and is on foot along with twenty or so young people headed north."

"Where the hell is he going?"

"Maybe he's going to the Cubs game," Alvarez joked.

Keisha didn't treat it as a joke. "Damn it, we could lose him in those crowds! Johnson's still not responding. Do you see him?"

"Nope. Could be that his radio isn't working."

"Forget it. Just stick with Protettore."

"10-4."

Keisha sped the short distance from Belmont and Campbell to Wrigley Field at Addison and Clark, where as she feared the place was already full of anxious fans. She parked in a no-parking zone and took to foot, making it easier to work through the throng of people standing shoulder to shoulder in long lines at the entry turnstiles. She took a position across the street on Addison in front of an auto repair shop in the middle of the block where she could observe both streets that intersected Addison—Clark on the west and Sheffield on the east. Finally, she spotted him.

He was walking east on the north side of Addison toward the outdoor beer garden at Sheffield. Keisha strained to keep him in sight among the crowd at Gate D waiting to take their seats along the right field foul line. Tony looked over his shoulder as he approached the beer stand just outside the gate. He casually ordered a beer and sat at one of the street-side tables. Either he was oblivious to the fact that he was being followed or was testing the surveillance team. Keisha watched and waited for his next move.

Out of the corner of her eye she suddenly caught site of flashing blue strobes on an unmarked squad car speeding on Addison toward Sheffield. It stopped abruptly at the curb near the street-side table where Tony was sitting. The car's door swung open. It was Johnson.

"What the hell? What's Johnson doing?"

Tony appeared to panic. He knocked the beer off the table in the direction of the charging Johnson, darted to the other end of the bar, and jumped over the four-foot aluminum fencing. He ran north on Sheffield immediately behind the right field bleachers. Johnson hesitated, appearing to decide whether to go around the beer garden or through it. Buses unloading high school students blocking Sheffield made the decision for him. Johnson had trouble clearing the fence, stumbled and fell into the beer garden, upending a table and knocking over two middle-aged women. The women screamed and several men in the crowd converged on Johnson knocking him to the ground. He showed his Chicago PD star, and the crowd finally gave way. He rushed past the bar and out onto the plaza where he stopped and scanned the crowd, his head on a swivel, desperately searching for Tony.

Tony had blended in with the large crowd on Sheffield. Mid-block, he stopped suddenly, looked behind him, worked his way through the press of fans, and crossed Sheffield. He headed for the rooftop bleacher buildings that lined the east side of Sheffield. For years, the four-story gray stone apartment buildings that lined the east side of Sheffield directly across from Wrigley had simply been convenient places to live if you wanted easy access to the Red Line of the 'L' to downtown or watch the Cubs from a lawn chair perched on the roofs, but in the early 1980s the owners abandoned their lawn chairs, erected bleachers on their roofs, and converted residential apartments into luxury party rooms. Tony slowly melted into the crowd streaming into these renovated vintage buildings.

As soon as Keisha spotted Johnson jump the fence, she took off after Tony, bypassing the beer garden, slipping between two of the high school buses. She searched the crowd for any sign of him. All she could see was Johnson still fighting the push and pull of the crowd on its way to the turnstiles. Then she spotted Tony. He had slowed his pace, making his way toward one of the roof-top buildings. She caught up with him just as he walked past the first apartment building, but she stayed ten yards behind using the crowd as cover. Tony suddenly turned into the main floor of one of the rooftop bleacher buildings. She followed him, but there was no sign of him in the lobby. She worked her way up the stairs, eyeing the corporate party rooms on the first two floors, ending up on the roof, where fans had already filled the seats. He wasn't among them.

Looking down at the street where Tony had entered the building, she spotted him—he was back on Sheffield. He shouldered his way through the throng, turned into an alley, and cut through a back yard. He was out of sight in a matter of seconds.

CHAPTER 74
Detective Frank Vincenti

"Dammit, Sean! I thought you said Johnson could be trusted. What were your words? 'Johnson won't showboat'. For Chrissake, that's exactly what he did. Now Tony knows we're on to him. Thanks to Johnson's foolhardy attempt to make the collar, Tony will go to ground and it may take months to track him down again."

I was fuming. I sat across from Sean in an interrogation room. A fluorescent light flickered overhead. We sat in silence. I glared at Sean as I waited for an explanation. He got up and started pacing, his hands plunged deep into his pockets.

I finally lost my patience with him. "Well?"

"We'll still get Protettore, Frank. We'll get him."

"You know damn well we need to 'get him' with evidence. The whole idea of the tail was to follow him to where, according to you, he was torturing and killing his victims. I'm going to ask Dunbar to put a letter of reprimand in Johnson's file. That was blatant insubordination—"

"He was following orders, Frank."

"Whose?"

"Mine." Sean stopped pacing. "Look Frank, I gave him instructions that at the first chance he got, he was to apprehend Tony and bring him in for questioning."

"What the fuck, Sean?"

"Frank, since Tony first showed up, you've been turning a blind eye to him for no reason other than he's an old friend. I'm convinced he's our guy. Hell, a few hours with him I could've gotten an airtight confession."

"You're a better partner than that! You should have given me a heads up on your little plan."

"And what would you have done?"

"I would've called it off!"

"Exactly! Like it or not, Tony is The Bricklayer. The pieces fit: He lived and held jobs in Crown Point and Racine where the locals found bodies wrapped in tarps, and by God, the timelines match." Sean paused, ran his fingers through his mussed hair, and kneaded the back of his neck like there was a stain there he was trying to rub off. "I'm convinced, too, that he was your squatter! I can picture him sitting on your Dad's sofa, drinking beer, and planning his next kill. You refuse to face facts!"

Maybe Sean was right. Maybe I had refused to face the facts, or at least I failed to analyze them objectively. But my gut and those damn so-called special gifts of mine continued to nag me: It's not Tony. It's not him.

CHAPTER 75
Anthony

The headaches had started again. This time, they retuned with a merciless vengeance. No amount of drugstore meds relieved the recurring and incessant pain. And, then the whispering began—an ever-so-soft whispering in my ear that repeated, "Another one. Another one." It was the last thing I heard at night and the first thing I heard in the morning. As the whispers grew louder, I would cover my head with a pillow to block the sound, but it was still there. It wouldn't leave me alone. "Another one. Another one." It kept me from eating and forced me to the neighborhood sports bar, hoping that a few beers would numb my senses and help me to resist the apparition's seduction. It didn't work.

"I will, dammit! I will. Cervantes will be your next one, but I need time to set things up. Need to plan," I whispered.

No. Today! Now!

"Enough! OK, godammit. OK." I gave a quick glance around the bar to see if anyone had heard that. No one reacted or looked my way. Maybe I shouted it only in my head. I finished off my beer, pulled my hood up over my head, and searched the bar for "another one." I felt the weight of my .38 in my hoodie's pocket.

I spotted him. He looked like all the others I had punished—middle aged, sloppily dressed, with slicked-back black hair. But it was his eyes that revealed himself to me. There I saw what set men like him apart from the rest of us—a combination of perverse lust and unfettered cruelty—just like the others. Yeah, I knew the look. A perfect target, ripe for the picking.

This one was eyeing a small boy in the next booth who seemed to be pestering his father for another Coke. The boy's father nodded, got up, and set out for the bar, leaving the boy alone. I wanted to shout, *No, you fool!* Trying to get the bartender's attention, he shouldered his way through the crowd of raucous Black Hawks fans who created a din each time a Hawk player checked an opponent hard into the boards. Forget the goddamn Coke!

I couldn't let harm come to this boy. Without pulling my gun from the pocket of my hoodie, I gripped the .38 tight and rushed toward the small boy's booth, intercepting his would-be captor just as he approached the boy. I thrust the .38 in his side.

"There's a back door just past the restrooms in the rear. Head for it."

He hesitated and without taking his eyes off the boy, he answered. "Go fuck yourself!"

"I could kill you where you stand. A gunshot won't be heard over the roar of the drunks at the bar and the blaring TVs. I'll be out the door before you hit the floor. Now move!"

He turned, looked me in the eye, and must have realized I was serious. He nervously picked his way through the crowd toward the back door. I followed closely behind.

A full moon spilled light into the narrow alley. I made sure we walked to the side in the shadows. The stench of rotting food from overflowing dumpsters filled my nostrils, adding to the throb of my headache. The only noise came from the clatter of a large kitchen exhaust fan with a bent blade and an occasional muffled roar from behind the heavy metal door that I had shut behind us. After a few steps, I spun the bastard around and stuck my gun in his gut. "You're done, asshole. No more snatchin' little boys. No more pleasurin' youself at their expense."

The idiot looked up and down the alley. There was panic in his eyes. I knew what he was doing. He was trying to figure a way out of this.

"Oh no! Don't even think about it," I said. I pressed the barrel of my gun hard against his ribs and leaned into him until I could smell the whiskey on his breath.

With a sudden and careless move he pushed me backward. I lost my balance. He started to run, but stumbled after only a couple of steps. I regained my footing and grabbed him by the shirt collar, spinning him around to face me. Now his eyes burned with fear. Instinctively, I hit him full force on the side of his head with the butt of my gun. He collapsed.

"Hey you! Stop right where you are!"

I twisted to my left, holding my gun at my side, out of sight of the tall figure standing just outside the bar's door, no more than twenty feet away. He looked strangely familiar, but I couldn't place him. He held a gun pointed at me.

"Don't move!"

"What da'ya want?"

"Last couple of days I've been following you. Waiting for you to make a mistake. I figured out what you were doing. Deep down, I believed in your mission. But now I want to be the one who brings you in. It wasn't easy tracking you. This is my first real opportunity to get you alone."

"You think this is your opportunity?"

"Yeah, and when I turn you in, I'll be a fucking hero."

"You got the wrong guy. Go back in the bar and spy on someone else."

"Oh, no! You're the one."

"And who are ya? Some kind of vigilante?"

He reached into his sport coat and was distracted momentarily as he fumbled with what looked like a wallet. Seeing an opening, I went to one knee and fired. I got off a clean shot. He staggered and fell to his knees, moaning in pain. As he struggled to get up, he shot wildly over my head. My second shot finished him off.

"Fuck!"

This had gone bad, very bad. With all the others I always followed a well-planned routine, even down to logistics—obviously, for good reason. I turned and looked at the creep from the bar. He wasn't moving. Now what? I had to think fast in case someone heard the shots. I wiped down my gun and placed it in the child molester's hand, making sure that his prints were on the grip and trigger. I raced to the man I had just killed, grabbed his gun, and fired a shot that blew a gaping hole in the neck of the molester who lay no more than ten feet from him. I watched a slow stream of his blood ooze onto the pavement. It would look like a bar fight that had gotten out of control when it moved to the alley. They had shot each other. Yeah. That's right—in a mean twist of fate they had shot each other. I left them there, crossed the alley, and cut through a narrow gangway between a liquor store and a boarded up old three-flat and then out to the next street. I calmly headed for the camper, confident that no one saw what happened, and hoping that the scene would fool the police.

I scoured the papers the next morning looking for a mention of the shooting. It was a short article in the *Trib's* Metro section below the fold. I was proud of my little scheme—it had worked. The article reported that it was a shoot-out between a bar patron whose drivers license identified him as Samuel Thayer and a Chicago cop—Detective Michael I. Johnson.

CHAPTER 76
Anthony

Several days after the shooting in the alley, the press reported that the police had concluded that Thayer, who had a record of small-time drug arrests, had opened fire on Johnson and the cop returned fire, killing Thayer but not before suffering a gunshot wound just below the heart that proved lethal. The police found twelve dime bags of coke on Thayer and had surmised that Johnson, who was off-duty that night, must have seen a drug buy and was trying to make an arrest.

I had been lucky. Nonetheless, I had made a stupid mistake that I couldn't repeat if the message was to be delivered. Early on I had learned the lesson to shun spontaneity. Never again would I deviate from my routine.

The apparition resumed its seemingly never-ending demands, this time denying me any rest. For the solace of a night's dreamless sleep, I had to comply. The headaches had grown worse and had become debilitating. I returned to the hunt and my careful planning.

Posing as someone who was interested in renting an apartment on Lawrence Avenue next door to where Cervantes lived, I stopped his landlord early one morning as he was leaving for work. I asked about the neighborhood, and told him I was considering renting a two-bedroom apartment in his neighbor's three flat. He was an older obese man who looked like his oversized gut reached his destination a full five seconds before the rest of him, but he proved to be friendly—and talkative. He told me it was a quiet area, a lot of young people moving into the neighborhood, renovating houses. "We got no spics, no gays, and no blacks. Just mostly Polish and German and a few dagos."

"I saw ya got a little attic apartment. Is it for rent? I don't need two bedrooms. I could better afford something small like that."

"No mister. It was originally intended for my son when he got out of the service, but he got wounded in Iraq—a real hero, don't you know. He got a Purple Heart. He's disabled and living in the Hines veterans' facilities in Melrose Park."

"A real hero. Does that mean it's available or not?"

"Aren't you listening? I just told you, mister. It's not for rent. See, a good friend of mine asked if I'd put his father up there. I did it only as a favor, conditioned on his father finding another place within ninety days."

"Why ninety days? It'll be available after that?"

"Well, at the risk of being nosey, let me ask you: Do you have kids?"

"Just a son. He lives with his mother during the week. I get him every other weekend. Is that a problem?"

"I'm not supposed to say anything, but my border, well, he just got released from Menard, you know the prison, where he did time for trying to screw a little girl. I didn't want to have someone like him any where near this neighborhood, but I owed a favor to his son who's been a friend to my boy."

"Jesus! I mean, how do ya put up with that?"

"The guy's a loner. He's got a job at the senior living facility just a couple of blocks away. He usually takes his meals with his son—"

He stopped abruptly, mid-sentence, and checked his watch. I wasn't sure if he was on to me, afraid he had given out too much information, or if he just lost track of time and didn't want to be late for work. "Got to go."

Didn't matter. I had what I needed.

I began monitoring Cervantes and discovered that Cervantes was a creature of habit, probably some kind of prison conditioning. Each night at precisely 9:30 p.m., Wednesday through Sunday, he haltingly navigated the old steep, rickety, wooden staircase down two flights from his apartment, followed the uneven sidewalk that led to the alley, and seemingly painfully walked north three blocks to the urgent care center to work his 10:00 p.m. to 5:00 a.m. shift. He never deviated from his routine. His regimen would betray him.

At 9:35 p.m. on a cool spring Saturday night, Luis Cervantes closed the small chain-link gate at the end of the back yard's sidewalk and stepped into the empty alley. I'm certain he didn't notice the small camper parked on a garage apron one door south. And equally certain he never saw me charge toward him from behind, wielding a chunk of brick wrapped in a blood-stained chamois.

CHAPTER 77
Detective Frank Vincenti

I found myself back at my father's house just before midnight. Although my instincts led me to suspect that Tony's reappearance in my life was somehow connected to the string of mutilated bodies that had begun to haunt me, I still wasn't convinced that Sean was right about Tony. I was penetrating deeper and deeper into the killer's consciousness, but it didn't lead to Tony. It may have been that my imagination was being blocked by my past friendship with Tony. I wasn't sure.

I didn't even try to sleep. Sitting at my dining room table and staring past the clutter at the red and green pushpins on the maps, I pictured the dumpsites and saw the faces of each victim. Around 1:00 a.m., I decided I needed to talk to Foster, and it couldn't wait until morning. I headed out the front door to where I had parked my car on the street in front of my father's house. Before I pulled away, I scanned the street's shadows for any indication that Tony was lurking about, or that nut job Allison was stalking me.

About thirty minutes later, I leaned on Foster's doorbell, knowing that he wouldn't turn me away regardless of the hour. I figured I would be waking him, but he quickly answered the door. I must have interrupted him, because, oddly, he wore old work clothes and held a dirty towel in his hand. He stood in the doorway momentarily and then said, "Francis, you look terrible."

"I haven't been sleeping."

"It's more than that. Come in. Come in."

He tossed the dirty towel on the dinning room table and pointed to his couch. "Francis, this is the first time in years you have visited in the middle of the night. I assume Protettore's emergence as a suspect is not sitting well with you."

He caught me off guard and saw that I was surprised that he knew about Tony. He dragged over a dining room chair and sat directly opposite me. "Oh, don't look so surprised. Eddie called and briefed me. He's concerned you've lost your objectivity because this Protettore fellow was a friend—"

"That was a long time ago."

"Still . . . Eddie says Sean is convinced that your old friend is our serial killer. Tell me about Protettore, and I do not mean the information that M'Bala dug up. What do you remember about him?"

"He always looked out for me, and growing up, I ate more dinners at his house than I did at my own."

"No. No. No, Francis. That tells me nothing about the person. What was it about him that does not allow you to believe he is a killer?"

I struggled to explain. "The Protettores had four children: three girls and Tony. They said grace before every meal, and I remember his Papà—that's what they called him—always ended his prayer thanking God for his children."

I hesitated, and Foster jumped in. "A contrast to your household, is that it? You don't believe good families can produce monsters?"

"Studies show—"

"I do not care about studies, tendencies, or propensities. I care about a man's soul."

Distracted, I looked past Foster to the dining room table behind him where he had thrown his towel. Next to it was his laptop, several notebooks, and a set of car keys. Turning back to Foster, I continued. "Tony was a bully—the worst kind of bully. He only felt important when he was protecting me; otherwise, he was a misfit and failed at everything he tried. These killings are well organized by a person with imagination. Tony isn't capable of either."

"Few people are, Francis. But there is more, isn't there?"

I was reluctant to tell the entire story. "I was, and maybe still am, ashamed that I had to rely on a bully for protection. I never really liked him, but I couldn't risk alienating him. By the time his family moved, I was glad to be rid of him."

"He carried with him all your secrets—he still carries them."

"I never told him any."

"All the same, he knows."

CHAPTER 78
Anthony

Mr. Luis Cervantes, convicted child molester, suffered a painful death. I had perfected my methods and routine. Looking back, too many of my early targets had died too quickly—before I had figured out how to make them pay for their crimes. But now I smiled as I recalled Cervantes's pleas for mercy. Like so many of the others, he claimed he never touched the child—it had been a misunderstanding. Each time Cervantes claimed to be innocent, I tore at another piece of soft tissue. As I told the others, admit your sin and the pain will end. Only a few understood how the pain would end.

As I hosed down the garage floor with a strong stream of water and watched his blood and other residue swirl into and down the drain, I reconsidered the dumpsite I had identified earlier in the week. Because of Vincenti's failure to acknowledge the note I had left for him on the blog's message board, I decided to abandon the site—a condo conversion near Elston and Montose—but hadn't yet identified a more effective substitute.

I needed a site that could no longer be ignored. The kill itself was not enough. The message was paramount. The world had to know that victims of child abuse would be avenged.

After I added my souvenirs to the freezer's inventory, I left a memento with the body, and wrapped Cervantes in his blue shroud. Then the two of us set out in the camper in search of a location that would draw the attention of the press and public to my mission.

After hours of driving through the side streets and alleys of my old neighborhood, my headache returned, and I decided I needed to clear my head. I'd hoped that spending time there would rid me of my headache. It didn't. In fact, it made it worse. So, as I had done countless times as a teenager, I headed toward O'Hare. This time, on a whim, I parked in the middle of a sea of cars in one of the airport's massive long-term parking lots. I knew I risked showing up on security camera footage later, but was sure that the camper would appear as just a blur in the thousands of cars in and out of O'Hare on the holiday weekend.

My three-hour retreat to the airport provided the inspiration I had hoped for. Instead of dumping Cervantes's body, I would deliver it to a "friend"—on an altar of concrete.

CHAPTER 79
Detective Frank Vincenti

The Area North detectives' rolling duty schedule broke my way for a change. A holiday weekend away from the station provided a welcomed respite. During the week I relied heavily on the Internet for timely news and watched both the early morning and the 10:00 o'clock local television stations' coverage. But Sunday morning brought me a half-day's reading of the Sunday edition of *The New York Times*.

I slept in. I had stayed too late at Foster's. I thought he would have insisted I crash on his couch, but this morning I woke on my couch without even opening it into a bed. Still bothered by Foster's questions about Tony, I made my way to my cluttered kitchen, filled a white paper filter with a Dunkin' Donuts dark roast, turned on the machine, and headed to the front door and the cement stoop where my *Times* waited for me. I unlocked the new deadbolt and swung open the heavy, weather-stained oak front door. I froze. A pair of wide-open brown eyes stared up at me from a corpse wrapped in a bright blue polyethylene tarp.

An hour later, I sat on the edge of my sofa drinking my third cup of coffee as the M.E. and evidence techs huddled around the body, speaking in hushed tones. Keisha stood at the door, supervising the processing of the scene. Dunbar had pulled up a dining room chair next to me.

"You OK?"

Without looking up from my coffee mug, I replied, "Yeah. I've seen our guy's handiwork before, Commander."

"Not on your front stoop. I want to post a blue and white in front of your house 24/7 until we catch this guy."

"That's a waste of manpower. He knows who I am. He knows my wife's name, and obviously he knows where I live. If he wished me harm, he'd already have done it by now."

"So, you still think this is about messaging?"

"Yeah, and he's pissed that we haven't disclosed his messages, especially the blog post and finding the John Does at the river. It seems he's now chosen me to spread his message."

Just then, Sean entered the room. "Well, if he wanted attention, he's getting it now. There are CNN and FOX mobile camera units out there in addition to the locals."

Foster arrived behind Sean. Dunbar nodded at Foster and turned to me. "I thought it best to get Foster over here as soon as—"

Foster interrupted, "Francis, did you see this coming?"

"Hell, no!"

Keisha excitedly joined my already crowded living room announcing, "Our guy finally made a mistake. Forensics lifted a full set of prints from the tarp just below the head!"

"Commander you know I like Protettore for these murders," Sean quickly interjected. "I mean, look, he knows where Frank lives, and he was stalking Frank. We already have Protettore's prints—the Crown Point police sent them to us a couple of weeks ago. I'll go back to the station with the forensics techs and run the prints they found against Protettore's set on file. It could save us a lot of time."

I answered for Dunbar. "OK. OK, but I doubt you'll get a match. Tony may think that he's still a tough guy, but he's not smart or calculating enough to pull this off. Just doesn't feel right." Almost as an afterthought, I added, "And don't call off the search for Allison."

Sean looked to Dunbar for approval and Dunbar replied, "Do it."

Foster sat down next to me and said, "Francis, the killer is sending messages to you, and, whether you like it or not, we have to conclude that he has some kind of connection to you."

I knew what he was driving at. His subtlety was not lost on me, and I began to question myself. Was I wrong about Tony?

CHAPTER 80
Detective Frank Vincenti

By noon, the forensics team had finished its work and the M.E.'s van was on its way back to Harrison with the body of the killer's latest victim. Convinced that the prints on the tarp were Tony's, Sean had left in a hurry to pull the prints we had on file from his arrest in Crown Point. I still thought it was a waste of time, but I didn't try to stop him. I was glad he'd gone. I was tired of him spinning his bullshit theories of why Tony was The Bricklayer.

"Frank, sure you're OK?"

"Yeah, Commander, I'm fine. Go ahead. Get out of here. You gotta have better things to do on a Sunday afternoon." Eddie subtlety motioned to Keisha to leave, and he closely followed.

Only Foster stayed behind. Claiming to be hungry, he coaxed me into the kitchen, poking around in the fridge he called back to me. "My God, your refrigerator is practically empty except for a partially eaten pizza and a six-pack of beer!"

"Yeah. Just grab me a beer, will ya?"

"You need to eat." His tone was almost like that of my father's endless scolding.

"What I need is a beer. OK?"

"Where are your beer glasses?"

"This isn't your house. My house—my rules. I drink out of the bottle."

Foster sat at the card table I used in the kitchen, drinking my last can of tomato juice—out of a juice glass, of course. God only knows how long the can had been sitting in the back of the pantry. There was only one chair, so I leaned against the sink, nursing a second beer.

"Sean may be right about Tony. The pieces fit. And like I said, this killer has some connection to you. It makes sense that the connection is your old friend Tony."

I didn't have a good answer. I turned and looked out the window. Although the grass needed mowing, there was no color in the yard—it had always looked like this. My father never planted flowers or even a vegetable garden like the neighbors, and I could still see him pushing the lawn mower with one hand and a beer in the other. Without looking back at Foster, I tried to explain. "My gut just says he isn't our guy—I don't completely understand it, and don't ask me to explain it. I can't."

"Francis, you've used those special gifts of yours over the years—"

I angrily spun around almost losing my grip on my beer. "Look, stop with the damn 'special gifts' or 'special talents' crap. I've had enough of them! They keep me up at night. Sometimes I see things I don't want to see. It's a curse, not a gift, and there's nothing special about it!"

Foster sat silently for almost a full minute swirling the last of the tomato juice in the bottom of the glass. "Have you considered the possibility that you may be wrong this time?"

"Wrong? No . . . maybe . . . hell, I dunno!"

"On the most important matter of my career, perhaps the most important matter of my life, I was wrong. Terribly wrong, and I refused to admit it. I've paid the price for it. Take my advice. Consider that you might be wrong about Tony."

He stood and began to leave, stopped suddenly and returned to stand next to me. He pulled out his wallet, fumbled with it, and retrieved a small dog-eared black and white photograph. With a glassy-eyed stare, he said, "Ellen."

He hesitated. His hand trembled. Without looking at me, he explained, "When she was murdered, I lost everything—even my respect for the law. I stubbornly insisted that we had her killer in custody. Because of my refusal to admit I was wrong about the guy, her killer is still out there. I'm still searching . . ."

He handed me the photo. A shiver ran down my spine and I lost my breath. It was the same woman I had seen last winter when images of The Bricklayer's work had popped into my head while having sex with Beth. Frightened of what it meant, I handed it back to him without saying another word, resolved that I would never tell him of the vision.

Again that night, sleep was hard to come by. The image of Foster's wife flashed in and out of my consciousness. Just as I would fall asleep, there she was, staring at me with a plaintive sadness in her eyes. An unwanted distraction.

I watched old black and white movies until two in the morning, all the while troubled by the prospect that I could be wrong about Tony, just as Foster had warned. Finally, I gave up. OK, dammit, I'll give Sean the benefit of the doubt. I'll let him play out the string and see where it leads. I fell asleep just as Bogart handed a bundle wrapped in newspaper to Sidney Greenstreet.

CHAPTER 81
Anthony

Late on an unexpectedly warm Sunday night I was back at the sports bar for dinner. While the rest of the crowd at the bar watched a Cubs game or ESPN splashed on the two dozen TV screens strung around the restaurant's dark gray walls, I kept my eye on the one that was turned to WGN News. After drinking two beers and jostling with other customers at the bar for the seat closest to the TV broadcasting news, I waited for the news conference to begin. Finally, the picture on the screen switched to a shot of the City of Chicago Press Room. At the front of the room stood the mayor, the superintendent of police as well as others who appeared to be senior law enforcement officers. A handsome black woman stepped forward, introducing herself as the CPD spokesperson. As she read off a list of the law enforcement agencies that were aiding in the investigation and thanked them for their support, I studied the faces of the police officers who stood silently behind her. I recognized some of the grim-faced officers. Detective Vincenti was not there.

She concluded her perfunctory opening remarks, and then, with a firm grip on each side of a lectern adorned with the city's official seal, she read from a prepared statement, addressing the recent discovery of the body of a person she referred to as "The Bricklayer's latest victim."

Damn it, they weren't victims! The victims were the children. Get it right. What else are you going to screw up?

"The mutilated body wrapped in a distinctive blue polyethylene tarp found this morning is that of Luis P. Cervantes, a registered sex offender. Mr. Cervantes was convicted in 2009 of sexual molestation of a six-year-old girl, for which he served a seven-year sentence at Menard Correctional Center. We believe this to be yet another revenge killing by the person who the press is calling The Bricklayer, and who we believe was himself the victim of childhood sexual molestation."

No. Not me. It was my friend!

"Mr. Cervantes's body was left on the stoop of the home of a CPD Violent Crime Section detective, Francis A. Vincenti, who has been one of the lead investigators of these grisly murders. He has no other connection to Mr. Cervantes or his killer."

Not yet.

Looking down at her notes, she added, "Like all Chicagoans, we are always outraged when we learn that children have been abused, and, although we may understand The Bricklayer's motivation and empathize with his pain, we can never condone vigilante actions."

The police were mistaken. Although my basic message had been received, understood, and now shared with the world, they apparently still didn't understand the word I scrawled on each target's chest. I wasn't avenging an attack on me. I did it for my friend. I did it for all the innocent children among us. If only I could talk to Vincenti. I knew he'd understand. All I needed was a few minutes.

The spokesperson concluded by saying, "Anyone with information about The Bricklayer should call the Department's non-emergency hot line, 3-1-1."

"Three one one." I repeated the number out loud. That was easy enough to remember.

CHAPTER 82
Detective Frank Vincenti

Dunbar insisted I stay home on Memorial Day and gather my thoughts. For a change, I welcomed the opportunity for another day away from work. Over my objection, Dunbar stationed a blue and white in front of my house, and a second patrolling the neighborhood. I'd intended to spend the day reading psychiatric journals and reviewing my case notes trying to prove to myself that Tony couldn't possibly fit any of the known subcategories of a psychopath, but an early morning call from Sean changed my plans.

"Frank, the prints match! They're Protettore's. Dunbar has authorized a citywide BOLO."

I didn't react.

"Frank, you still there? Frank?"

"I'll come in."

"There's no need for you to be here right now. Nothing will happen today anyway. I was about to call Foster."

Recalling his odd appearance and behavior when I visited him last, I said, "No, damnit, leave him out of it." As I made my morning coffee, I wondered if I was starting to believe that Tony was the killer. Hell, how did his prints get on Cervantes's tarp? Maybe Sean was right after all. I couldn't make heads or tails of it at this point. I took a long, hot shower, and was toweling myself off when my cell phone rang. It was Sean again.

"He called!"

"Who called?"

"Protettore. He called on the 311 hotline. He saw the press conference and wants to come in and talk, but only to you."

"When? Where?"

"Don't know yet. He told us to call you. Before he sets a time and place for the meet, he wants your agreement that you'll come get him— alone. He's calling back in twenty minutes."

"Tell him yes."

"You're not going alone."

"The hell I'm not!"

We were back in Chief of Detectives Thomas' private conference room at the Town Hall station. Sean, Keisha, and Alvarez joined Dunbar and me around the table waiting for the chief to conclude a call with the superintendent. We had waited ten minutes when Thomas pulled up a chair. He didn't seem happy to be there on a holiday.

"Di Santo says it's up to Commander Dunbar how to play this. I agree."

Dunbar and I had already met privately and planned the logistics for the meet with Tony. He looked over at me and nodded. I laid it out for the team. "I'm going alone. I'll wear an earwig to communicate with Sean. Alvarez and M'Bala will be in an unmarked car no farther than two blocks from the meet site."

I looked over at Keisha. "He made you the other day. If he sees you anywhere near the location of the meeting, he'll be gone. So, don't move in until Sean radios you." Looking at Sean, I continued, "Sean, if he poses a threat, I'll say a distress word and you can move in."

"Got it, but I still think I should go with you. This guy is a stone-cold killer, old friends or not."

"Look, I'm buying into your theory, but I've got to handle it my way."

"I'm going along with Frank on this one, Sean. So drop it," Dunbar shot back.

TERRY JOHN MALIK

"I want to make sure everyone understands—nothing happens unless I use the distress word. I don't mean to speak ill of the dead, but I don't want a repeat of the Johnson fiasco."

"What word will you use?" Sean asked.

I thought for a moment. "Tony's mom fed me a lot of pasta growing up. Sean, if you hear me use the word 'pasta', it's time to move."

Tony was clever and cautious if nothing else. The Cubs were playing a night game at Wrigley. He wanted me to meet him twenty minutes before game time in front of Gate D near Addison and Sheffield, almost the same spot he'd been sitting when Keisha had followed him earlier. It's the busiest gate, at the busiest time. He said that he'd find me in the crowd. I arrived early. He arrived late.

He had a week's worth of beard, his clothes were crumpled, and he had the odor of someone who hadn't bathed in several days. "It's not me. I'm not your Bricklayer." The way he said it, the look in his eyes . . . I desperately wanted to believe him.

"What makes you think you're a suspect?"

"You found my prints on the tarp, didn't you?"

"How did your prints get there, Tony?"

He deflected my question. "Frank, I lost the only good jobs I ever had and—"

"You mean in Crown Point and Racine?"

"So you've done your homework. Then you know I'm telling the truth. I screwed up at those jobs and now that I have a criminal record, I can never teach again. I came back right before Thanksgiving hoping to land some kind of job, but I wasn't having any luck. I tried to get your attention. I thought you could help. That's why I approached you last December on Belmont."

"Why didn't you say something then?"

"That day in December I was too embarrassed to look you in the eye and beg for help. I figured it might be easier if I spoke to you on the phone. But when I watched you walk away, I saw you throw my phone number in the trash."

"I had a sense that you were looking for me to help you, but I simply couldn't re-engage. I had my own problems."

"You mean your wife?"

"Among other things. But, I regret that I didn't give you a chance to explain. Believe me, I regret it now."

The crowd was getting thicker. We were being jostled by fans working their way to the entrance. "But, Tony, you didn't answer my question. How the hell did your prints show up on the tarp?"

"I was getting desperate, you wouldn't take my calls, and so I hung around the old neighborhood looking for the right moment to approach you. But then I realized I was being followed. That's when I decided I'd just ring your doorbell and try to face you, but when I started up your stairs, I saw the blue tarp. I didn't know what to do. When I turned it over and saw the face, I panicked."

It was getting close to game time. The national anthem had just concluded. Anxious to get through the turnstiles, fans began pushing and shoving. The crowd swelled and a woman fell back against Tony, who then fell against me. I lost my footing momentarily. Tony reached out suddenly and grabbed me to keep me from falling.

Out of the corner of my eye, I saw Sean running toward us, yelling at the crowd to get out of his way. He had his weapon drawn. Tony saw it, too, and, with a woeful look on his face, he asked in a barely audible voice, "Frank, why?" Then he took off running through the crowd, shoving people out of his way.

"Sean, no!"

He ignored me as he raced past.

Tony ran to the middle of the block, waited for a bus to pass, then crossed the street, sprinting toward an alley off Sheffield, the same alley where Keisha had lost him a few days before.

With M'Bala in the passenger seat clutching her two-way radio, Alvarez navigated his way through traffic on Sheffield the best he could as the crowd overflowed into the street. Sean was out ahead of all of us. I took off, trying to stop Sean, but by now the crowd was mad and wasn't going to let another person manhandle them. I pulled my detective's star out and held it above my head as I shouldered my way through the crowd. Just before another string of buses passed and blocked my view, I saw Sean running at full speed into the alley. Over the crowd noise and the deep-throated acceleration of the last bus, I heard two gunshots from the alley. Alvarez and M'Bala had abandoned their car, and the three of us converged simultaneously at the mouth of the alley.

Keisha had drawn her weapon. "Did you fire those shots?" I demanded.

She shook her head as she looked down the alley where the stream of fans using the alley as a shortcut had stopped and gathered. They were looking back up the alley where the gunshots originated. The three of us waded through the crowd and came to a sudden halt. Fifty feet into the alley, Sean stood looking down at Tony lying on the ground, both highlighted by an overhanging streetlight. Keisha holstered her weapon. Alvarez came up behind us and said under his breath but loud enough for us to hear, "Que chingados?!"

I ran to Tony and knelt down on one knee next to him. I felt for a pulse—nothing. "Sean, he's dead! What were you doing? I never used the distress word! What the hell were you thinking?"

"He went for a gun. Your innocent, little, harmless friend, Frank, was carrying a gun."

I turned back to Tony. Clutched in his right hand was a .38 revolver. Numbed and confused, I stood with my back to Sean, and, without saying another word, walked away, and lost myself in the crowd.

PART FOUR

ABOUT MY JOURNAL
Thomas Aquinas Foster

The story of the killer, who the press infamously named The Bricklayer, ended as all true stories must—in death. But not the death I expected, nor its manner. During my many years of police work, I have recorded my observations and analysis of events and developments concerning serial killers whenever any new such individual is discovered. I have done so in the hope that my observations would some day help unlock the mystery of why some men mature to be morally grounded and contributing members of society, and some grow into homicidal monsters. It is the study and pursuit of these monsters that has dominated my adult life on and off the job. But my limited observations and sometimes flawed analysis serve as only small parts of unlocking the mystery. As I once told Francis in the early days of his personal education and journey into the dark side of men's souls, too often you have to crawl into the cage with the monsters. Murderers aren't to be studied, they're to be experienced.

When the body of Henry Edwards was found at the Keeler Avenue demolition site shortly after Thanksgiving just past, I began this journal. The circumstances of the killer's mutilation of Mr. Edwards and the staging of the crime scene was a portend of more torture and murders. In its original form, my journal was little more than a series of notes, some of which were in my own shorthand developed over the years as I learned to take notes at crime scenes and while interviewing witnesses. Some of the entries were more complex as I attempted to trace cause and effect. My journal in its original form often served as the basis for a more complete narrative, as is the case here.

As was my custom with cases in which my protégé, Detective Francis A. Vincenti, was involved, my notes included observations and analysis of Francis's investigations, and, this time, his mental state, which had become increasingly fragile as Beth pulled him into a spiral of depression and despair. Francis had been blessed—or cursed—with certain gifts, or special talents, that allowed his imagination to experience the feelings, urges, and motivations of killers without the burden of emotional attachment. And because nothing good in life comes without a price, I discovered that as a child, Francis had paid a heavy price for those so-called gifts.

When I first began to observe Francis as a student during his sophomore year at Northeastern, I sensed there was something special about him, something extraordinary. I saw it in his eyes as I studied his reactions to the gruesome crime scene photos I forced students to view. His interest in my recounting of horrific murder scenarios was real, and his questions frighteningly insightful. As our one-on-one sessions progressed during his senior year, I realized three things about him: He'd had a troubled childhood that scarred him for life and caused him to always live on the edge of depression and suicide; the special talents he possessed for identifying with the minds of killers would make him an exceptional homicide detective and be helpful to me as I continued the twenty-year search for the killer of my Ellen; and he had the potential to become a tragic figure if I did not befriend him. And when he asked me whether it takes a monster to catch a monster that day on the admin building's staircase, I was convinced he already knew the answer—as did I.

The investigation of Detectives Kelly and Vincenti into the murders of Henry Edwards, Monsignor Jack Anderson, George Mathias, and Luis Cervantes has already been well documented and, therefore, there is no need for me to repeat here the journal entries I made contemporaneously with those investigations.

Rather, I have produced this narrative, beginning with the shooting of Francis's childhood friend, Tony Protettore, and documenting how that shooting plunged Francis into an episode of debilitating despair that overshadowed his pursuit of the killer the press had infamously dubbed "The Bricklayer."

My Post-Shooting Summary

The morning after the shooting, an elderly homeless man, who simply gave his name as John, wondered into the 19th District station on Addison just three blocks east of Wrigley Field and claimed to have information about the shooting. He said that Tony had been his friend and had been living on the streets. Detectives Alvarez and M'Bala were called in to interview John, who identified Tony from a photo that Keisha carried with her. He took the detectives to Tony's "home" among cardboard boxes, crates, and tents under the Red Line elevated tracks, no more than two hundred yards east of where Tony had died. A small community of homeless men used the shelter of the 'L's' overpass as protection from the elements and used its proximity to the crowds around Wrigley Field to panhandle.

The Forensics Bureau technicians thoroughly processed Tony's makeshift home. Between layers of discarded cardboard boxes and plastic bags, the techs found news clippings about The Bricklayer, latex surgical gloves, an unopened package containing a blue tarp, and a pair of rusted bolt cutters—bits and pieces of essential features of the killer's modus operandi.

Fox Sports was televising the Cubs game the night of the shooting, and one of its many mobile camera crews rushed to the scene in the alley as word of the shooting spread through the crowd. The Chicago Fox

News affiliate almost immediately reported that The Bricklayer had been shot and killed. On-camera interviews with witnesses in the crowded alley added to the confusion of the night. Six witnesses told Fox they, too, thought Tony had a gun and that the police officer had fired in self defense; two other witnesses claimed Tony was shot in the back.

Sean was put on administrative leave pending an Internal Affairs investigation of the shooting. I made no effort to communicate with him. Whether the shooting was justified or not, Sean's sudden rush toward Tony and subsequent pursuit had been neither explained nor justified to my satisfaction. I would talk to him again if and when Internal Affairs cleared him and restored him to active duty.

As for me, in the hours and days following the shooting of Prottetore, I tended to the more immediate issue of Francis's fragile condition and his troubled mind.

Early Morning - Tuesday, May 26

I had been out late Memorial Day when Sean shot and killed Francis's childhood friend. I had heard the news on my car radio: The Bricklayer had been killed. I arrived home around 2:00 a.m., and found Francis sitting on the stairs leading down to my front door. I was tired and had not counted on a visitor at that hour, but I greeted him anyway. "Francis," I said, "I am glad to see you."

He said nothing as I held the door open for him. Obvioiusly disoriented and agitated, he stood in my hallway, dressed in jeans, a T-shirt, and sneakers. He looked past me into the apartment, looked back to the street, and finally asked, "Are you alone?"

"Of course."

He stepped past me in my small hallway and stood silent momentarily. Without looking back to me, and in a barely audible voice, he said, "I'm not really sure why I came here."

I closed the door and replied, "Because you are safe here."

We sat together in my living room in silence, his hands trembling. He scanned the room with furtive glances, and after a few minutes, stood suddenly and began to pace, going to the front door several times and securing the lock for the second and third time. Finally, he began to talk, mostly in a frenetic manner, hardly giving me the opportunity to ask any questions. He spoke of his suspicion that Beth had reverted to cocaine use, his indifference to the death of his father, and the horror of the Carlton murders—all of which I had heard before. When he paused, I started to question him about Tony and the shooting. He didn't remember the shooting; indeed, he could not recall the events of the past several days. The last thing he remembered with any clarity was seeing Tony standing across the street from the Grand Grill, staring at him.

His rambling stream of disjointed thoughts continued until 5:00 a.m. when, exhausted, he simply nodded off in mid-sentence and fell asleep where he sat. Forty minutes later, he woke screaming. I gave him some of my insomnia medication, and as he fell back to sleep on my couch, he muttered indiscernible words and phrases—none of it made sense.

Francis was still asleep several hours later when my cell phone vibrated. The caller ID displayed 'Dunbar, E.' From the outset, Eddie was irritated and a little more abrupt with me than usual, not that it was unwarranted considering the circumstances of the past twenty-four hours.

"Tommy, we've got a problem. Frank didn't remain at the scene of last night's shooting—he just walked away. I've left half a dozen messages on his cell instructing him to appear this morning at the Internal Affairs offices for a post-incident debriefing, but he failed to show. The IA guys are pissed, and he's still not answering his phone. Keisha went to his house, but he wasn't there. Do you have any idea where he is?"

"Yes. He's here with me. Francis showed up here around 2:00 a.m. and has been here the whole time."

There was a momentary silence before Eddie reacted. "You should have called and talked to me about it."

"We are talking about it now. I recommend that you either grant him a leave or put him on the medical roll. I do not care what you call it or how you do it, but in his current condition he is not fit for duty."

Angrily, Eddie shot back: "Tommy, you know the requirements of the department directives covering post-incident procedures when an officer discharges his weapon. He's breached protocol."

"I know the procedures, Eddie, but IA has plenty of witnesses from the crowd to interview, and they still have to process Sean, Alvarez, and M'Bala before they need to interview Francis. I've talked to Keisha. She told me about the arrangements you made for the meet at Wrigley. IA should be asking Sean why he rushed Tony before Francis gave the 'go' signal."

"Wait, where the hell was Frank between the time of the shooting and when he showed at your place?"

"He can't remember. Actually, he has no recollection of the past several days."

"You're telling me he has amnesia?"

"I'm telling you what I have observed since he arrived. He needs time to straighten out whatever is going on in his head. He's not himself."

Eddie took some time answering. "If he wants a leave or to be placed on the medical roll, he has to submit a written request."

"It is not a question of what Francis wants; it's what he needs. He may be suffering from PTSD. Temporary amnesia is a typical symptom."

Eddie went silent. I said nothing.

Finally, Eddie regained his focus. "He needs to be evaluated."

"I have arranged for that. Dr. Micah Feldman of the Stone Psychiatric Institute at Northwestern has agreed, as a favor to me, to stop by this afternoon and talk to him."

"Tommy, he should be seen by a department shrink."

"Yes, but not right now. I want to know what's going on in that talented, but troubled head of his before I put his career at risk."

Eddie came back at me with increased agitation. "That's not your decision to make!"

"Really? Excuse me, but Francis has no one else to turn to. He never really had family. Beth has filed for divorce and had him removed from his home, and he feels betrayed by Sean. No, Commander, Francis stays here where I can keep on eye on him and determine an appropriate course of treatment. He needs family right now, and I am all the family he has." This time I did not wait for a response. "Eddie, you have an officer down and you don't even know it!"

Eddie let out a long, loud sigh. "You've got twenty-four hours. Keep me advised."

Noon - Tuesday, May 26

Micah Feldman M.D., had been a good friend to my parents and me for many years. I often shared a meal with him in a private dining room at the Standard Club on South Plymouth where, as a psychiatrist, he provided me with valuable insights during those times when I was compiling psychological profiles and could not make sense of psychiatric research materials. I now turned to him once again for assistance.

He arrived around noon and spent two hours alone with Francis. As we sat in my small living room drinking coffee from my grandmother's fine china, he shared his concern over Francis's condition. "Tommy, he needs to be admitted as an inpatient."

"Not now. It will ruin his career."

"He has no recollection of the past three days and only bits and pieces of the past two weeks. He refuses to eat. He's sullen. He's anxious. His hands tremble, he was cleverly evasive when answering my questions about his childhood, and he tried to distract me by talking about his wife's history of substance abuse."

I shifted in my chair. "Look, Micah, I've seen plenty of homicide detectives lose it temporarily. Over the past six months, I have watched Francis struggle with one stressful situation after another, the death of his father, a painful divorce, the horror of a serial killer who mutilates his victims, and now he has witnessed the killing of his childhood friend."

"I assume he is the lead detective on this Bricklayer matter?"

"Yes, but I am convinced that case is closed. I'm certain now that his friend, Tony, was the serial killer Francis has been pursuing since November. Perhaps the realization that his childhood friend was a psychopathic killer was part of the shock he's experiencing."

"And you think that when he is able to cope with that realization, he'll regain his memory? Playing psychiatrist again, Tommy?"

"Look, the press has been reporting only half of the savagery of the torture and killings, and those horrific images are stuck in Francis's head day and night. Trust me. I've seen it happen to some very good cops. Given time, he will come out of it."

Micah stared into his coffee. "It's a lot more than this Bricklayer business, Tommy. Your amateur diagnosis of PTSD was a good guess, but it's only the tip of the iceberg."

"What is it then?"

Micah shook his head. "Certainly he is suffering from depression and has been for some time, and based on what you've told me about him and the time I spent with him, this isn't the first time Francis has experienced memory loss. I need to know more about him."

I had known for years that Francis experienced periods of time for which he could not account. He had spoken to me about it on several occasions. I thought it was simply his way of blocking the horror of the murders he was called on to solve, or the result of too much Bushmills.

"Isn't amnesia a symptom of PTSD?"

"Certainly it's a symptom of PTSD, but it may be more than that. I need to spend more time with him. I wish you'd reconsider and let me admit him as an inpatient."

"First of all, he'd never agree to it. Besides, I know a heck of a lot about that boy; it would take you months to get him to tell you what I already know. Let me have a few days with him here. If he is not better by the weekend, I'll check him into Northwestern myself."

Micah paused and leaned forward in his chair. "Then I want to come back tomorrow morning and have another session with him."

"That's very generous of you, but—"

"No 'buts'. I'll clear my morning schedule and be here first thing."

He placed his coffee cup and saucer on the side table, reached for his medical bag, and as he opened it, said, "I administered a strong sedative that should help him sleep for several hours." He retrieved three pill bottles and intructions written on a piece of paper from his script pad. "I anticipated his condition, and I have brought some medication—don't worry it is all properly signed out from the hospital pharmacy. Two of the meds will help him relax and sleep, and the third will begin to address the depression, although it will take a few days to be effective."

Micah rose from the leather couch, walked around the room, and, pretending to be looking at my collection of nineteenth century law reporters, casually remarked, "Tommy are you telling me the whole story?"

"What do you mean?"

Micah turned and faced me. "I take it he wasn't really close to this Tony fellow—hadn't seen him in years. It would be unusual that the death of such a distant friend should trigger these symptoms."

"It's more than just Tony's death, Micah. For God's sake, he saw his partner shoot and kill a man who he believed to be innocent. He probably blames himself for the murders of Anderson, Mathias, and Cervantes after not taking Protettore seriously last December when he tried to get help from him. Seems to me that's more than a simple shock brought on by just the death."

Morning - Wednesday, May 27

The sedative Micah administered was effective. Francis appeared to sleep soundly for the remainder of Tuesday afternoon and into the evening. Around 10:00 p.m., I gave him three mg of lorazepam, an additional dose of prazosin, and a small dose of ketamine per Micah's instructions. As Micah predicted, Francis slept through the night.

I was sitting in my father's old upholstered rocking chair at the foot of the bed when Francis opened his eyes, looked over to me, and said in a barely audible whisper, "Foster?"

I clicked on the floor lamp next to my chair. "I'm here. How do you feel?"

"I'm not sure. A little groggy, I guess. What time is it?"

I checked my watch. "It's five o'clock Wednesday morning. Do you know where you are?"

He sat up in bed, looked around the room, and then back at me. "Yeah, you told me. I'm at your apartment. This is your bed, right?"

"That's right." I prodded, "What do you remember about the last few days?"

He ran his fingers through his hair and said, "Well, I recall Sean and Keisha putting together a team to follow a suspect . . . wait, what do you mean what I remember about the last few days?"

"You showed up at my door around 2:00 a.m. yesterday. When we talked then, you couldn't recall anything about the weekend. You've been seen by a doctor, a friend of mine who—"

"You mean the shrink that was here . . . yesterday?"

"A psychiatrist. Dr. Micah Feldman. He concluded, as I did, that you are experiencing short-term memory loss, a common symptom of post traumatic stress disorder."

"Did you tell me this before?"

"I didn't, but Dr. Feldman did."

"I don't remember him telling me that, but, of course, I know what PTSD is. It follows a life-threatening or other type of traumatic event. What traumatic event?" Francis's voice trailed off, as he seemed to be searching his memory.

"The fatal shooting of Tony Protettore. The police believe that Tony was the killer the press called The Bricklayer."

"But I haven't seen Tony since—" A blank stare overtook his face, and we sat in silence for a few minutes. "I didn't think that Tony could possibly . . ." Finally, he laid down, rolled over, putting his back to me, and placed a pillow over his head. "Foster, I'm tired."

Without saying another word, I quietly left the room.

Good to his word, Micah arrived at 9:00 a.m. As he removed his tan Burberry raincoat and tossed it on my couch he asked, "How did he sleep?"

"Better than I expected."

"Have you spoken to him this morning?"

"Yes, but he did not have much to say. He still has a look of distrust and fear in his eyes, and he seemed to react defensively to trivial matters, but he is far more subdued than yesterday and his hand tremors have stopped."

After a ninety-minute session with Francis, Micah joined me at the kitchen table for coffee. As I poured him a cup, I asked, "Well?"

"He's moved from agitated and anxious to feeling emotionally numb and disconnected, but I got him to talk."

"And the depression?"

"There is a lot going on here, a lot that I'm unsure of."

Micah looked back toward the bedroom where Francis slept. "I'm confused about a couple of episodes he related to me."

"What did he tell you?"

Micah gave me a disapproving look. "You know I can't tell you anything he said to me in confidence. I want to discuss it with one of my colleagues, though."

Micah checked his watch, stood, and finished his coffee. "I've got to run. I'm going to be late for a luncheon engagement. I'll call you this afternoon."

About an hour after Micah left, Francis emerged from my bedroom and announced that he was hungry. He had been nibbling at peanut butter and jelly sandwiches for the last twenty-four hours, so I was encouraged by the return of his appetite. As we walked together to the kitchen in the rear of the apartment, I asked, "How did it go with Dr. Feldman?"

He ignored the question and eased himself into the kitchen chair that faced the small window above my sink and its view of the backyard and the garage. Without turning away from the window, he said, "I don't understand what's happening."

"We eat first. Then we talk."

Late Night - Wednesday, May 27

We talked well into the night. For all the years I had known Francis, and for all the secrets he had shared with me, he had never told me what he described that night, although I had always sensed that he had suffered a deep trauma that he had hidden from me. I was sure he was caught in a perpetual state of what he called "sadness," although more than once he had rejected my belief that it was severe depression and should seek counseling. I knew of the tragic death of his mother when he was four, and, although he spoke to no one else of it, he had come to learn that the fatal car accident that took her from him was caused by his father's drunk driving. He had finally admitted that he was trapped in an unhappy marriage born of a futile attempt by Beth to marry someone below her so-called social status solely to spite her Santa Barbara socialite mother. He had no answer for the loveless marriage. Beth found her answer in a string of affairs and cocaine. He had acknowledged that he still drank too much, but thought he hid it well. And I had known for some time of his jealousy of the growing relationship between Sean and Keisha and shared his concerns about Sean's eagerness to tie Tony Protettore to the string of murders, claiming that Sean was looking for a scapegoat. He viewed himself as isolated and incapable of a lasting relationship. But his description of an event on a warm spring night when he was seven years old and its lifelong consequences still haunts me.

"Tony and I were playing in the alley behind our garage—Tony was my only friend. Anyway, it was getting late. The street light in the alley had come on a half-hour earlier. That was the signal that it was time to go in. Tony tried to talk me into staying out later, and I wanted to, but I knew that I'd feel my father's belt against my naked butt if I didn't head in. Tony called me a baby, and I watched him run into his yard and up the gray wooden stairs into his house.

"I closed the gate behind me and walked along the narrow sidewalk that ran next to the garage. There was only a space of twelve feet or so between our garage and our neighbor's—it was dark and isolated there. It had rained that morning and I could still smell the odor of wet wood from the small pile of firewood that lined the side of the garage. Suddenly, my father appeared from the side door of the garage, grabbed me by the back of my neck, and pushed me against the side of the garage in the shadows. He yanked my pants down around my ankles and bent me over the pile of firewood, pushing my face hard against the brick wall of the garage.

"And then he raped me. At the time I was too young to understand what was happening. But, I knew it hurt. It hurt a lot."

Francis paused, touched the side of his face, running his finger across a faint scar that suddenly became more protuberant. "When I screamed in pain, he pushed my face hard against the rough bricks and the hardened mortar that had oozed from between the bricks when first laid in place. He pushed my face so hard against the bricks that it opened a gash on my cheek. Blood trickled down to my chin."

Neither of us spoke for several moments.

"When he was done, he went into the house. I slept in the garage that night on a blanket I pulled from his camping equipment. The next morning he said nothing about it or questioned where I had spent the night."

I didn't know how to respond. He must have sensed my feeling of helplessness.

"Foster, I buried that pain deep away. I have no idea how or why I remember it now, or why I told you."

When he finished, he simply got up from the couch, and, without saying another word, retreated to my bedroom, and closed the door.

Morning—Thursday, May 28

Francis was still asleep when, shortly after 8:00 a.m., Eddie and Sean came by. I had provided reports on Francis's condition to Eddie twice daily, keeping him at bay and facilitating Francis's extended medical leave. Eddie had called ahead and asked to talk to Francis, saying that there was a development of which Francis should be informed. He also advised me that Sean had been cleared to return to limited duty pending a final written report. According to Eddie, IA's investigation wrapped up quickly because more than a dozen witnesses in the alley that night supported Sean's account that Tony stopped, turned toward Sean in an aggressive manner, and retrieved a gun from his jacket pocket. Curious, I agreed to the visit.

They sat uncomfortably on my couch. I pulled up a dining room chair, placed it directly opposite them, and took a seat.

"How is he?" Sean asked.

I hesitated for a second and then explained his condition. I finished by saying, "I have filled most of the gaps in his memory, but not all. He doesn't recall all the details about Tony, but I told him that Tony was the so-called Bricklayer and that—" I hesitated again and looked at Sean, "—and that he had been shot and killed."

Dunbar looked to Sean and then back to me. "Tommy, that's why we're here. There's a strong possibility Tony wasn't The Bricklayer."

"What are you talking about?"

Dunbar leaned forward. "When I saw the photos of Tony's supposed home under the Addison 'L' tracks, I thought the cardboard boxes looked staged. It was all too neat. We ran prints on the bolt cutters and the tarp package—no prints."

"That's to be expected."

"Yeah, but my gut wouldn't let me buy it. I took a look at the bigger picture and reasoned that Tony would've required a van or pickup truck to transport his victims, and he'd need a very private place away from crowds where he could torture and kill his victims. I had teams of patrolmen canvass the neighborhood around Tony's street home—about two miles in each direction—in search of an abandoned van or pickup and I had them look for a shed, garage, or abandoned building, but they couldn't find any of those either. Besides, if he had a van or a garage, why wouldn't he have slept there instead of on the street?"

"Makes sense. Go on."

"After that search turned up nothing, we tracked down the homeless guy who had ID'd Tony for M'Bala and brought him in for additional questioning. Keisha finally got him to admit that late on the night of the shooting, a stranger wearing jeans and a gray hoodie had paid him $100 to feed us false information."

I threw a disapproving glance at Sean. He must have sensed my growing irritation with him.

"What about the .38 Protettore had on him?"

"The gun wasn't loaded. The cylinders, filthy. The forensics guys say it hasn't been fired in years. Besides, none of the victims had been shot, so in a way, the gun is irrelevant." Sean continued. "Look, Foster, I realize now that I was so convinced that Protettore was The Bricklayer that I ignored Frank's warnings about jumping to conclusions. Frank's instincts are usually right, but there were so many little things that pointed to Protettore. I thought Frank had lost his objectivity because of their childhood friendship."

I looked at Eddie. "So why did Tony stop running and confront Sean in the alley with a gun he knew couldn't fire a single shot?"

"I don't know. Perhaps suicide by cop? Frank told Sean that Tony's life had turned into a damn mess. Maybe he thought he had no future or maybe he couldn't tolerate the thought of going to jail."

Sean was still trying to justify his suspicions about Tony. "I'm not sure whether Frank ever told you, but when he moved back into his father's house, he discovered that a squatter had broken into the house and made himself at home. I was convinced the squatter was Protettore and was hiding out there between kills—the pieces fit. It all made sense at the time."

"Francis never mentioned anything about a squatter."

"We still can't completely rule out that Tony was The Bricklayer," Dunbar observed. "But it seems to me that the question for now is: who's the guy in the gray hoodie, who, three hours after Tony was killed, showed up and gave an old wino a hundred bucks to try to convince us of what we already believed, namely, that Tony was The Bricklayer?"

"Where does that leave your investigation?"

"For now, we're still taking a hard look at Protettore. The homeless guy's lie doesn't completely exonerate him, but we will shift our focus slightly and take a look at other possibilities. To start with, we need to re-canvass the area around Wrigley to track down the guy in the hoodie."

"But, you really don't have any other suspects, do you Eddie?"

Eddie paused and looked over to Sean. "There's one other possibility—the tech from the M.E.'s office, a guy named Allison. He had made a big deal out of the Anderson murder, asked a lot of questions, and threatened Frank and me. Out of the blue, he showed up at the morgue yesterday demanding to see Tony's body, but security wasn't able to detain him."

Eddie got up to leave. Sean looked over to me. "How will Frank take the news?"

I stood, looked over to Eddie and then back to Sean. "Perhaps relieved that Tony may have been innocent after all. I'm not sure. There's no telling how he'll react or what he might do."

After they left, I thought, Damn! How the hell did I miss all that? Did I just want the case to be closed to give Francis some modicum of peace no matter how short-lived? Was my judgment impaired by my fondness for Francis? A loss of objectivity—a detective's worst enemy. Or, was I just getting old?

Afternoon—Thursday, May 28

Francis woke shortly after Eddie and Sean left. His agitation had returned, and he was short-tempered. "Did you take the medication I laid out for you?" I asked.

"Yeah. Yeah. I'm only taking it because you told me to."

As I prepared breakfast, we exchanged terse small talk. While we ate, I avoided conversation about the events of the past few days; instead, I tested his memory by invoking recollections of his years as a student. Those memories remained. His amnesia seemed to be limited to the events of the past week or so.

As he rinsed off his plate, he asked, "Dunbar and Sean were here this morning, weren't they?"

"Yes, they were here. They wanted to talk to you. I said no."

Placing his plate and silverware in the dishwasher, he added, "Good. I'm glad you didn't come get me. I'm not ready to see Sean yet."

I sat at the kitchen table. Without getting up, I turned to Francis and said, "Pour yourself another cup of coffee and come sit down."

He did as I asked, and as he studied the cup of coffee on the table in front of him, he asked, "They had news?"

"They now believe Tony wasn't The Bricklayer."

I spent the next few minutes repeating the explanation that Eddie and Sean had provided. Francis sat silent and motionless for a moment after I finished and then, with a blank expression on his face, he looked over my left shoulder at the small basement window. "I said all along it couldn't be Tony, didn't I?"

"Yes."

Francis looked agitated and stood abruptly, pushing his chair to the side. "I've been thinking about it. It's all coming back to me. Clear images are returning. I've figured it out and need to get back on the street. I have a hunch I know how to find this guy. Can you get me my clothes?"

"No. You're in no condition to hit the streets again—hunch or no hunch."

He finished his coffee in one large gulp. Walking away toward the bedroom, he said, "You're wrong this time, Foster. I can handle this. It's all coming into focus now. You've gotta help me."

I called after him. "Look, take some time to think it through. If in a couple of hours you still want to act on your hunch, I'll go with you."

He came to a sudden halt, paused as if he was considering my admonition, and turned back to me. "OK. But only because it's you. Only because you're asking."

I trusted Francis. He'd think it through like I asked. He wouldn't be happy about it, but I knew he'd map out his plan and if he found fault with it, he'd reconsider. I had taught him the folly of impulsive behavior.

Only minutes after Francis disappeared into my bedroom, Sean called. His tone telegraphed that he was still upset about his missteps regarding Protettore, but I immediately deflected his concern.

"I think we found the killer's vehicle. You need to see it."

"Where?"

"O'Hare."

"No, I mean where is it now?"

"Central auto pound on Lower Wacker. I'm there now." Sean hurried an explanation that the vehicle had been found at O'Hare in one of the long-term parking lots. Judging by where it was parked, it had been there since the night of the shooting. It was a fifteen-year-old Toyota Tacoma pickup truck with a small homemade fiberglass camper top added to it. It had been set afire after the license plates had been removed and stripped of everything of value. The Chicago Fire Department had extinguished the fire before it consumed the vehicle; and it was subsequently towed to the city's auto pound.

"What causes you to believe that it's the killer's vehicle?"

"When the pound's civilian employees took custody of the truck, they inspected the interior of the camper. It wasn't badly damaged by the fire, and even though it's covered with a thin layer of soot, the supervisor recognized graffiti on the walls as relevant to our case. Foster, you need to get down here and see it for yourself."

"Wait a second." I checked on Francis. He seemed to have fallen asleep in my father's chair. I looked over to where I had laid out his medication and a glass of water. The pills were gone, the glass empty. Good. I'd rather he'd sleep on his idea of charging out and following his so-called hunch. "I can't leave Francis alone."

"I thought of that. Keisha and Alvarez are on their way to your place. She can babysit Frank for a little while and Alvarez can drive you back here."

I paused. Micah had called earlier and asked me to meet him at his office later that afternoon. He had shared his interview notes with a colleague and obtained a second opinion. I had told him that I couldn't leave Francis alone and said it would have to wait. Sean's proposal solved that problem. Micah's office was a little less than a mile from the auto pound.

"Alright. I'll wait for Keisha. I'll take a look at what you have."

Late Afternoon –Thursday, May 28

Alvarez and Keisha arrived in front of my building fifteen minutes later, around four o'clock. Keisha rushed into the lobby where I was waiting. I instructed her to look in on Francis in thirty minutes or so to make sure he was still asleep.

Alvarez used his siren and dash-mounted blue strobe to get us to the auto pound in less than ten minutes. Wacker Drive runs parallel to the Chicago River at two levels. Lower Wacker is located at the same level as the river. Enclosed by a ten-foot-high chain link fence topped with razor wire, the auto pound is located on "Sub Lower" Wacker near Columbus Drive, the only spot in its two-mile length where Wacker Drive has three levels. Dark, damp, and forever musty, the sub-level captures the odor of a river that flows backward.

Sean was waiting for me at the front gate near the mobile trailer that serves as the pound's office, and then led me through a maze of cars and trucks to the far side of the fenced area where several fire-damaged cars were stored.

"There," he pointed, "the green camper."

I went ahead of Sean, circled the vehicle and studied the exterior; the worst of the fire damage was limited to the cab of the truck. I turned and looked at Sean gesturing as if to say, "So?"

"It's what's inside the camper."

Sean joined me at the back of the camper, opened the rear door, and handed me a large Mag flashlight. The heavy odor of burnt plastic filled the small, dark compartment, but Sean was right: only a thin layer of soot covered the interior; it had suffered little fire damage. I took one step in, slowly directing the powerful flashlight beam from one side of the camper's interior to the other.

The walls were full of what, at first glance, appeared to be graffiti, but was really a journal of sorts—a crude record of the killer's plans, travels, and accomplishments—all intermixed with indecipherable ramblings. The walls were full of hand-drawn maps of Chicago streets: Keeler and Grove, Karlov and Kelso, Lawrence, other addresses in Albany Park and Lake View, and maps of Wisconsin, Iowa, and Indiana. Above the maps was a list of dates, perhaps a dozen in all. The scribbling included familiar words and phrases: "Whiet Shutrsr" written above the scrawled word "fag." There was also a list of construction sites and a napkin from a place called Murph's Borderline Pub taped above articles from the *Tribune* about The Bricklayer. A printout of the CPD's sex offenders registry was taped to the back of the door with three names circled. On the wall above the camper's bench, the letter "A" was repeatedly written in six neat columns and ten evenly spaced rows almost giving it the effect of a wallpaper pattern. Most disturbing of all, above a storage container, I found crudely drawn figures of a penis and a hand with out-stretched fingers. Written below the figures, in what appeared to be dried blood, were the words "heim.4."

I stepped out of the camper, overcome by the lingering odor of smoke, and struck by the pathetic need of the killer to chronicle his story. No need for Sean to see my reaction.

"What else do you have, Detective?"

Sean appeared disappointed that I did not comment on the so-called "graffiti," but answered anyway, "The VIN on the driver's door pillar has been ground off, even looks like someone may have used acid on it. I need to check, but this model may have a VIN on the engine block. We will get Forensics down here to pull it apart."

"Good luck with that, but let me know what you find."

I turned my head and took another look at the vehicle saying, "What about security cameras at O'Hare?"

"I already called the Chicago Department of Aviation. They're running their search programs now. As soon as they isolate the gate, entrance ramp, and time frame, they'll download the images directly to the department's forensics section."

"Any hits on the BOLO on Allison?"

"What? "

"Allison. Have you located him?"

"No and can't find out what happened to him after he left the morgue. He was living with his mother—that's the only address we have. She claims she hasn't seen him for months, although she admits that he calls her every couple of weeks."

I looked back at the camper. I needed some time to purge my head of the macabre images on the camper's walls. I turned and started to walk away. I stopped abruptly as I suddenly visualized a seemingly unrelated image and a random thought struck me. I walked quickly back toward the truck and opened the passenger side door.

Sean called to me. "I looked. No registration or proof of insurance or any other papers that weren't burnt in the fire."

"That's not what I'm looking for."

The visor above the windshield on the driver's side was badly burned, and all that remained was a metal rod. I tried the glove box, but it was damaged and wouldn't open.

"Sean, you got a knife on you?"

Sean pulled a flip knife from his pants pocket. As he handed it to me he said, "I always carry this."

I pried the glove box open using the knife. What I was looking for wasn't there, and it wasn't in the center console either. I hurried around the front of the truck, struggled to open the driver's door, and reached under the seat. I felt something on the floor near the rear of the seat. I reached farther back and grabbed the small square object that I was looking for. I held it up.

"A garage door remote?" asked Sean.

"Do you have an evidence bag?"

Somewhat confused he replied, "In my car."

"No time for that. How about an evidence glove?"

Sean pulled one from his jacket pocket and handed it to me. I quickly wrapped the garage door opener in the latex glove and stuffed it in my sport coat pocket.

As I walked away, Sean yelled to me, "Hey, where are you going? That should be bagged and marked as evidence!"

Late Afternoon—Thursday, May 28

I walked up two cement ramps into the bright afternoon sunlight at Columbus Drive where I crossed the Fahey Bridge that spans the Chicago River. Although I was in a hurry to meet Micah, I stopped in the middle of the bridge, lingered there, and looked out to Lake Michigan. It was a glistening blue with occasional streaks of deep green. It was calm. I was not.

I stood on the same spot nearly twenty years earlier when I lost Ellen, wondering how I would survive. Now I stood staring at the lake worried I might lose someone else I cared for, but not to a bullet. Instead I feared I could lose Francis to a childhood trauma that scarred both his face and his soul.

The wailing of an ambulance siren speeding behind me across the bridge brought me back to the problem at hand. I couldn't get the damn garage door remote out of my head, and I didn't know why. Sean was right, of course. It was evidence, and it should have been bagged, marked, and processed by evidence techs, but in the musty darkness of Lower Wacker I had suddenly been overcome by an ominous prescience that led me to believe that the remote was going to open more than a garage door. I had no other explanation for taking it with me.

Micah's office was on east Huron, about a mile north of the bridge. I grabbed a cab, and ten minutes later arrived at the hospital's highrise annex, which housed the offices of its physicians and staff. I took an empty elevator to his office on the twenty-sixth floor. His assistant had already left for the day, so I let myself into his inner office where he was sitting at his desk, on the phone. He looked up and gestured toward a small conference table in the corner of his office where I took a seat in a chair that was designed as a style statement, but not built for comfort. I waited patiently as he finished a telephone conversation that sounded like a discussion of Francis's symptoms.

After Micah concluded the call, he joined me at the table. "That was the colleague about whom I spoke this morning—a brilliant woman, Dr. Arlene Dougherty, who specializes in amnesia disorders. She needs to know more before we can concur on a diagnosis, so she would like to meet with Francis, perhaps as soon as this evening, but I wasn't sure how you or Francis would react to that."

I rubbed my brow, got up from the table, and walked over to his office window which had a view to the west across the city and beyond to the northwest suburbs. Typical Chicago weather: fifteen minutes earlier the sun had been shining brightly in a clear blue sky, now storm clouds were slowly moving in from the west. Without looking back at Micah, I said, "Before we get to that, I should share with you what Francis told me last night. It may help you and your colleague refine your thinking without talking to him again." I turned to face him, leaned back against the waist-high windowsill, and proceeded to recount Francis's story of his rape. I reluctantly repeated all that Francis had shared with me about his father's attack. I held nothing back.

I watched closely for Micah's reaction. He was visibly troubled. Certainly he must have known that somewhere in Francis's past lay a trauma with which he had struggled to cope, but he looked as if he had not imagined something so serious. He looked down at the notes that he had made during the phone call just concluded and pushed them aside. Appearing to be considering the significance of Francis's revelation, he tapped his Mont Blanc pen on the table.

"Tommy, an assault like that is the ultimate betrayal for a child—a violent sexual attack by a parent. My God! Compound that with the lack of the nurturing influence of a mother—well, it's amazing he's been able to function at all. Of course, we now know that his coping mechanisms have broken down."

"I take it that his story changes your diagnosis."

"No, it only serves to confirm it."

I returned to the table and sat directly opposite Micah. "Go on."

"The trauma of the rape was so horrible he surely tried to suppress it, likely with limited success. His conscious self willed that someone else carry the burden of the memory—probably an imaginary friend or an attachment to a person who he wouldn't have otherwise befriended."

I thought about it for a second and replied, "He never spoke of an imaginary friend, but he did become friends with his next door neighbor who was the same age."

"Are you certain this friend wasn't imaginary?"

"The friend was Tony Protettore, you know, the man Francis's partner shot and killed Monday night. He wasn't proud of that friendship. He told me that Tony was always in trouble, short-tempered, and he tormented other kids in the neighborhood, but Francis maintained the relationship because Tony protected him from class bullies. He said he was ashamed that he had to rely on Tony for protection."

"But Tommy, there were no class bullies. In Francis's mind Tony was protecting him from his father and the memories of the rape. And the shame he felt—probably still feels—was the blame he placed on himself for the attack. Victims of sexual assault usually assume it was their fault. When his imaginary friend was inadequate to shoulder the burden, he turned to Tony. He probably told Tony what had happened in the hope that if he could put the memory in someone else's head, it would somehow leave his consciousness."

"I'm sure Tony knew his secret," I interjected.

"Something must have happened to their relationship when they were kids."

I nodded. "When he was fifteen, Tony's family moved out of state."

Micah slowly shook his head. "Leaving Francis alone with the memory."

"And with his father."

Just then my phone rang. It was Keisha. "Foster, I'm sorry." Her voice was panicked. "I'm so sorry."

"Settle down, Detective. What is it?"

"He's gone. Frank is gone!"

Early Evening—Thursday, May 28

"He left a note." She read from a pad of paper I kept on my nightstand to scribble latenight thoughts on my cold cases. *'I've got this. I know where to find him, but first things first.'* Foster, what does it mean?"

"He thinks he knows who The Bricklayer is and wanted to set out to find him, but he's not ready. Damn it! He's not himself. He should have waited for me."

Keisha struggled to regain her composure and explained what happened. After I had left her in the lobby, she had entered the apartment and then quietly opened the bedroom door and determined that Francis was asleep. She then used the bathroom in the rear of the apartment just off the kitchen, returned to the living room, and paced the floor reviewing her case notes. An hour later, she looked in on Francis only to discover he was not there. She checked the bedroom's en suite bathroom and found Francis's meds in a wadded-up tissue on the bathroom floor.

"Stay there in case he comes back. I'll be there as soon as I finish up here."

Then I called Eddie. While I waited for him to answer his phone I summed up the situation for Micah. He was alarmed and cautioned that Francis should be considered dangerous. I disagreed. I was concerned, but not alarmed.

When I got through to Eddie, I asked for his help to find Francis. I reminded him that Francis and I often took walks around the North Pond or sat on a bench at Diversey Harbor. "If he is trying to plan his next steps to locate the damn Bricklayer, he may be venturing no farther than those spots. At least that's what I hope he's doing. I suggest you have a couple of patrolmen start there."

"What do you make of his note?"

"The note is his way of telling me not to worry about him," I lied. "That's all. I'm not concerned about the note, just where he is."

Eddie agreed and alerted the Mounted Patrol Unit to search the park and the lakefront, and dispatched a blue and white to patrol the Lincoln Park neighborhood. Eddie also called Sean and instructed him to join Keisha at my apartment and await further instructions.

Although I wanted to return to the apartment immediately, Micah implored me to stay and hear him out. "Tommy, in his present state of mind, he may be dangerous to himself. Look, Dr. Dougherty's preliminary diagnosis may explain a lot. It may help you find him and keep him safe until we can admit him—"

"That again?"

"Just listen, will you?"

I sighed and nodded, and Micah laid it out for me.

I found his diagnosis hard to swallow. I peppered him with questions. "It may take some time to digest that."

"Arlene Dougherty is highly respected in this area."

"All the same . . ."

"I understand your skepticism. I'll admit without spending more time with him, there's a good deal of speculation baked into the diagnosis."

He tried to elaborate, but I cut him off. "I gotta go. I need to get Francis off the street. If you're right, for his own good."

There was a slight, distant rumble of thunder from the west as I stood at Michigan and Huron, attempting the near impossible—looking for a cab during rush hour with an impending storm brewing. I finally waved one down and fifteen minutes later was back in my apartment, where Eddie, Keisha, and Sean were debating strategies for locating Francis. I wasn't listening. I couldn't get Micah's diagnosis out of my head. I checked the time and calculated that Francis had been gone for more than two hours.

Frustrated, I got to my feet. "This is a waste of time! You're focusing on how to locate him. Figure out why he left—that's more likely to lead you to him."

Annoyed with my impatience, Eddie barked, "And I suppose you think he has set out alone to find The Bricklayer. Is that it?"

"After I told him this morning that you weren't convinced Tony was the killer, he said he had a hunch and was adamant I permit him to get dressed and follow his instincts."

"I assume you said no."

"Of course I said no. He wasn't ready to go anywhere, let alone go looking for a killer. But, if he decided to set out on his own anyway, then the first place he'd go would be his home—if for no other reason than for a change of clothes and his service revolver."

Eddie shot back. "I thought you already eliminated that as a possibility."

"That was an hour ago! Come on, given his state of mind and that note, the last thing either of us wants is for Francis roaming the streets with a weapon in his hand. Do me a favor. Send Keisha and Alvarez to Francis's house on Newland."

Eddie looked over at Sean and Keisha. "Yeah. OK. M'Bala, grab Alvarez and get going."

Keisha stood and started putting her jacket on, but I asked her to wait a moment.

I went to the kitchen, returned with a key. "This is the key to Francis's front door. He gave it to me when he moved there in case of an emergency. Enter through the front and proceed carefully. Francis may not be himself right now. He may be dangerous. Clear the house, be careful, and then," I looked over to Eddie, and he nodded, "and then call me."

Evening—Thursday, May 28

It took Alvarez and Keisha thirty minutes to arrive at Francis's home, and another fifteen to clear the house and for Keisha to call me. It was almost dark by the time they got there. "No luck, but it looks like he's been here. There's a half-eaten fresh sandwich with a couple of bites out of it and a cold Coke on the kitchen counter next to the sink."

I pictured Francis eating over the sink, looking out the window at his backyard. I had seen him do it before. Maybe he saw something in his backyard or in the garage and went to investigate.

Keisha added, "Foster, it looks like Frank uncovered some additional victims but didn't tell us. I was looking at the maps and other stuff he has taped to his dining room wall. There are pushpins on his maps that weren't there before and photos of victims I don't recognize. Why wouldn't he share this with us?"

I had assumed for some time that Francis was holding back information, maybe because he was losing confidence in Sean or to protect Tony. "Francis is like me. Sometimes he prefers to work alone. Those additional victims are probably what caused him to believe he knew where to find the guy. What are the locations of the new pushpins? They could lead us to Francis."

"Wait a second, let me get closer. There are red pins near LaSalle-Peru, near St. Charles, Des Moines, and two more in the Crown Point area in Indiana."

When I did not respond immediately, Keisha became anxious. "Hello? Hello? Foster are you still there?"

"Yes. I'm thinking."

Eddie had stepped into the hallway to take a call. I wasn't going to wait and clear it with him, so without asking, I gave Keisha further instructions. "You and Alvarez should get back in the car. Park down the block out of sight, but park in a place from where you can view the front door."

By the time I finished the call with Keisha, Eddie had returned and said, "I just got a call from the 21st District. A member of the Mounted Unit reported that someone matching Francis's description was sighted near Addison and the Lake. He may be headed toward Wrigley. Maybe he's returning to the alley where Tony was shot."

"That's possible. If it is Francis, we shouldn't let a stranger approach him. It should be someone he knows."

"Do you want to go?"

I paused. If Micah's analysis was correct, Francis was probably still blocking memories of the shooting. Odds were against the likelihood he would regain his memory and revisit the site, but I couldn't dismiss it. "No," I answered, "but maybe you should head up there. Based on what Keisha reported, I have a hunch I know where Francis might be."

"Are you sure?" Eddie asked.

"No. I'm not sure, dammit, but if my hunch proves to be right, I'm the person Francis needs to talk to."

"As distraught as Frank might be right now, is it possible that if he finds this guy, he won't even try to make an arrest? Would he just impose his own sense of justice?"

"You mean find him and kill him? That's exactly what worries me."

Eddie eyed me with a hint of suspicion, looked over to Sean. "Sean, you go with Foster. I'll call the 21st and let them know not to approach Frank—if it is him—until I get there."

I started for the door, but Eddie grabbed my arm. "Tommy, you're not telling me everything about what's going on with Frank, but as you always warned me, keep your emotions in check."

"Eddie, you really think you needed to tell me that?"

"Yeah. Yeah, when it concerns Frank, you bet your ass I do."

He was right, of course.

Late Night—Thursday, May 28

Driving an unmarked Ford Interceptor with the siren and blue strobe clearing our way, Sean weaved his way through the late night traffic west on Fullerton Avenue. A light rain began to fall, giving the asphalt a black sheen. In the distance to the west, a sudden flash of sheet lightning revealed a wide front of storm clouds heading our way. Seconds later, rolling thunder roared in the distance. Sean was clearly on edge, but not because of the weather.

As we approached the intersection of Grand and Newland, he pressed me for information that I wasn't willing to share. "Look, I don't understand what's going on, but you seem to. What did your psychiatrist friend say about Frank?"

"Not now."

"I need to know!"

"I said not now, Detective."

Without taking his eyes off the road, Sean snapped, "Why are we going to Frank's house? Keisha cleared it. It sounds like he was there, but left."

I didn't answer. Instead, I instructed Sean to drive two blocks west of Newland, take a right, and double back on the first side street to the alley behind Francis's house.

"The alley?"

Just then, a blinding bolt of lightning struck the ground no more than a hundred yards ahead of us, and a sharp loud clap of thunder followed immediately. Bright orange and yellow sparks exploded from what had to be a transformer. The neighborhood went dark. The sudden cloudburst sounded like the roof of the car was being pelted with ball bearings. The wipers couldn't keep up.

Over another clap of thunder, Sean shouted, "Foster! Why the alley?"

"I have Keisha and Alvarez covering the front. I want to check out the back of the house. Trust me on this, Detective!"

By the time Sean turned into the alley behind the 2500 block of Newland, the downpour had slowed to a steady rain shower. "Sean, turn your lights off and drive slowly toward the middle of the block." Using the car's side spotlight, I strained, looking for address plates on the garages.

Sean peered through the rain at the row of garages. "Which side of the alley?"

"My side." I read off the numbers that I spotted on the garages. "2531, 2535 . . . Stop here."

I pointed about twenty yards ahead. "There, that one." It was a brick garage with a small address plate hanging from a single nail, "2545." I snapped off the spotlight.

"I want you to pull the car in front of the garage door as if you were going to pull in. Wait for lightning. Use the thunder that follows to cover the sound of the car's engine, and be prepared to turn on your high beam headlights when I tell you."

"I wish to hell you'd tell me what we're doing!"

We waited only a few seconds before thunder roared again. Immediately, Sean pulled the car in front of the garage and killed the engine. I dug into my coat pocket and pulled out the garage door opener that I had removed from the pickup truck.

"Christ, Foster! What are you doing?"

I didn't respond. I depressed the remote switch—nothing happened.

"Foster! What the hell are you doing?"

While I removed the back cover of the remote and wiped a thin film of soot from the remote's copper contacts, I explained. "Look, you speculated that Tony was Francis's squatter. Maybe he was, maybe he wasn't. But someone took over Francis's house, and it may have been our killer. Francis may have figured that out, too. That's why we're here. I'm playing the same hunch as Francis."

"Why would The Bricklayer move into Frank's house?"

"Not sure that he has, but I told Francis … You were there, remember? It was the day Francis found Cervantes's body dumped at his front door. I told him then that this so-called Bricklayer must have some kind of connection to him. If he had some kind of connection, then maybe he took over Francis's house in his absence."

"And the remote?"

"If the squatter was our killer, he would have hidden his camper in the garage and helped himself to the remote. I think Francis left my apartment to follow his hunch that the killer had been using his house and may have returned while Francis was staying with me."

Pointing to the side of the garage, I said, "Look there, just below the roof line, the window, there's a light on in the garage. Someone's in there. Maybe Francis was checking out the garage and—"

"And, may have stumbled across our killer."

I finished cleaning the remote, replaced the back cover, and depressed the button again. Just as another flash of lightning filled the sky, the wood-panel garage door lurched up. "Now!" I yelled. "Hit your brights!"

Midnight—Thursday, May 28

The headlights' bright beam pierced the rain and silhouetted the stooped figure of a man wearing a gray hoodie, the edge of the hood hanging down over his forehead. He stood in the center of the garage and held a gun in his left hand and a camping lantern in the other. I couldn't see his face through the rain. The hooded figure straddled what appeared to be a man lying on the garage floor. I couldn't tell who that was either, but he was moving his head side to side—if it was Francis, at least he was still alive. I slowly opened the passenger door of our car and stood behind it.

The hooded figure placed the lantern on the ground, shaded his eyes from the car's high beams and yelled out in a high-pitched drawl, "Who's there? That you ol' man?"

Sean threw open his door and began to draw his weapon. Without turning my head toward Sean, I instructed him to holster it.

"But that has to be Frank on the ground!" Sean yelled over the din of the rain.

"Holster it, Sean. I know what I'm doing."

"It's me—Foster. Who are you?"

"Ah, it's the great Thomas Aquinas Foster, formerly of the fuckin' Chicago PD, come lookin' for his beloved Detective Francis Vincenti!"

I didn't want to play his game, but I had no choice if I were to protect Francis. "OK, you know my name. What's yours?"

"Names don't much matter to you, do they? Did you call him Frank like everyone else? Hell no, you insisted on that insultin' habit of calling him Francis! He hates being called Francis."

"Tell me what to call you."

"Anthony. My name is Anthony."

In a quiet voice, Sean said, "Foster, that could be the M.E. Tech—you know, that guy Allison. He was from Mississippi. That sure as hell sounds like a southern accent. Get him to tell you his last name!"

"I'm Frank's friend—a better friend than you, ol' man, and a better one than Frank's asshole partner, Kelly. He's out there with you right now, ain't he?"

Sean shouted back with enough desperation for the two of us, "Yeah, I'm here. Is that Frank on the ground? Is he alright?" Sean whispered to me, "That's got to be Frank on the ground. We have to go in!"

"Not yet, Sean!" I looked back into the garage. "Who's that on the floor?"

Looking down, the hooded figure gestured with his gun to the body under him and said, "Him? What do you care?"

"Let him go," I pleaded. "It's me that you want. Isn't that right?"

More thunder and a quick flash of lightning, but farther away now—I waited for an answer, the cold rain seeping down the back of my shirt collar, the only noise the pinging of the rain on the car's hood. Just then, the man on the floor moaned and tried to sit up. I struggled to see the man's face. Too dark. Too much rain. Anthony pointed the gun down at him, fired a single shot into the man's thigh and then pointed the gun at me. The man on the floor bellowed in pain. Anthony ignored him. Sean reached for his Sig. "Kelly, go for your fuckin' gun, and the ol' man's dead before you ever get your hand on the grip."

Sean shouted back. "Leave Foster out of this!"

"Leave him out of it? He's damn well in the center of it! He didn't have a son of his own, ya know, so he had to steal one. He snatched Frank out of one of his phony criminal justice classes. Just plucked him out of the blue. Trained him up to be just like him. Ain't that right ol' man?"

I said nothing.

"Yeah, you made him into a cop so he'd fulfill your dreams—not his! You knew you could manipulate him, mold him like a piece of school-kids' clay. He was goin' be super cop to make up for you getting kicked off the force! Ain't that right?"

"Anthony, who's on the floor? He may still be alive. Let me come get him." I moved from behind the car door and started toward the garage.

Sean, frustrated, ever so slowly went for his gun. Anthony saw him and fired a shot over my head.

"Don't do it, Kelly! Next one goes into the ol' man's heart!"

"I'm coming in, Anthony. We can talk through this—"

Anthony raised the gun to shoulder height still aiming at me, saying, "Stay where you are, I ain't gonna fall for one of your tricks."

Sean looked over to me and nervously asked, "What the fuck are you doing?"

"It's me that you want, Anthony. Let me come in. We can talk."

"Naw, stay where you are. You just want to play head games with me, just like you done played with Frank all these years. No, ol' man, no more games."

Keeping his gun trained on me, Anthony looked over to Sean. "Kelly you don't know the half of it. You wasn't a true friend to Frank, either. You're a disloyal bastard—you and that black bitch you're always hanging around with these days. And I tried to warn Frank—warn all of you—about that crazy cokehead, Beth. But no one would listen. No, Kelly, you can go fuck youself."

"Anthony, Frank once showed me a picture of you. I want to see if it really is you!" I shouted.

"Is that what you want? You so damn anxious to see my face—fine." Anthony pulled his hood back over his head just as another sudden flash of lightning filled the sky behind us, piercing the rain, and like a flash bulb from a different era, illuminated Anthony's face.

At that moment, my worst fear was realized and Micah's diagnosis was confirmed. Detective Francis Vincenti stood there in the garage, staring back at us, with a gun in his hand pointed at me. Sean was shouting. At first, I couldn't hear him. I wasn't sure if his shouts were muffled by the rain or I simply didn't want to hear what he was saying.

"Holy shit, Foster. It's Frank!"

I regained my senses, looked over at Sean. "Feldman warned me to expect this, but I didn't believe him. I'll explain later, once we have him safe."

I yelled back into the garage, "Francis?"

"Dammit, ol' man, I told you—your precious Francis ain't here—and he ain't never comin' back."

"OK. OK. Anthony, tell me who's on the floor—maybe he's still alive. Let me come get him." I moved from behind the car door and started toward the garage. "Anthony, I'm coming in. I want you to give me the gun, and then you and I will go to a safe place and talk."

He answered my plea by firing twice more into the man on the floor.

"Stay where you are, Foster. And Kelly, you too. I got nothin' to lose now!" Looking down at the man whose life he had just ended, he paused and lamented, "I got nothin' to lose now."

"Who is he? Let me come in and get him some help."

"He told me his name's Dominguez and lives down the block. I saw the light on in the garage and caught him snooping around. After I slapped him 'round a little and showed him my bolt cutters, I got him to admit he likes to touch little boys."

Sean was able to draw his weapon without Anthony seeing it until Sean held it waist high. "Don't do it, Kelly! I warned you. Next one goes into the ol' man's heart!"

"I'm coming in, Anthony. We can talk through this. No one else has to die."

"We all have to die—some sooner than others. This is all your fault. I could've took care of Frank, but you had to interfere."

"I'm coming in, Anthony—for Francis's sake! I won't take no for an answer."

Francis raised the gun to shoulder height still aiming at me, saying, "Stay where you are, I ain't going nowhere ever again."

"I'm coming in—"

The bullet slammed into my chest, and I was knocked backward. The pain was excruciating, burning, blinding. As I collapsed, I heard a second and third shot from the garage and the shattering of the car's windshield, immediately followed by three quick shots coming from Sean's side of the car. From where I lay on the rain-soaked ground, I saw Francis crumple to the garage floor. Sean ran into the garage and kicked Francis's gun away from where it fell. He checked for a pulse and then ran back over to me.

Coughing and wheezing, I struggled to speak, spitting up a fine spray of blood. "Francis?"

"For God's sake, don't talk." Sean pulled a handkerchief from his pocket, covered the wound in my chest, and pressed hard. Moving my hand to the wound, he replaced his hand with mine. "Here, keep pressure on it."

I tried to sit up. Sean laid me back down, took off his sport coat, crumpled it into a ball, and placed it under my feet. As I strained to breathe and spat up more blood, I heard Sean call for an ambulance, yelling into the radio, "Officer down! Officer down!"

I heard movement, and realized Sean had removed an emergency metallized blanket from the car's trunk. He covered me to help retain my rapidly declining body heat and protect me from the rain.

"Hang in there, Foster. You're too fucking tough to let a single bullet kill you."

Sean knelt on one knee and leaned over me. Rain dripped from his face onto mine. He talked to me for what seemed like a long time, mostly small talk about his son, none of which I recall now. Sheet lightning bounced off the wet pavement and lit Sean's face, exposing his fear. My breathing became more labored and my eyes wouldn't focus. I saw Sean's lips move, but could no longer make out the words. With the wailing of sirens in my ears, I passed out.

Friday Morning to Saturday Night, May 29 – 30

A Chicago Fire Department EMT-Paramedic saved my life. Recognizing that the single bullet from Francis's gun had produced a sucking chest wound that penetrated my right lung, she applied a gauze dressing, made a small incision below the bottom rib on my right side, and inserted a tube into my chest's pleural cavity to drain the gushing blood. She strapped an oxygen mask on my face and instructed Sean to hold the small canister while I was lifted into the ambulance. They transported me to the closest approved Trauma 1 center at Loyola Medical Center in Maywood Park, about fifteen minutes away.

After a three-hour operation during which the thoracic surgeon removed the .45 caliber slug from the lower lobe of my right lung, I was moved to the ICU. I woke up briefly Friday morning, connected to a ventilator. I painfully turned my head looking for a familiar face, but saw only a confusing mass of tubes and wires. Then I passed out again. That night, the nurse took me off the ventilator, and I was able to take a few ice chips. I struggled to talk to the attending nurse, but she told me to save my energy for a few more hours, promising me that I'd be moved out of the ICU in the morning.

Saturday morning, less than thirty-six hours after I had been shot, I woke to find Sean and Eddie in my room. Eddie sat in the chair next to my bed reading emails on a new cell phone, and Sean paced near the foot of my bed. It was Eddie who saw me open my eyes and survey the room.

"Hey, look who's awake!"

Sean stopped mid-step and spun around to face me. "Foster! Welcome back!"

It took a few moments to find my voice. "I don't remember—"

Eddie tried to comfort me. "No need to talk right now. Save your voice. It will all come back soon enough."

"Francis?" I asked.

Eddie and Sean exchanged glances.

"Francis?" I asked again.

Eddie stood next to my bed, took my free hand in his, and said, "He's gone, Tommy."

I closed my eyes and willed myself back to sleep.

It was dark when I woke again. Eddie was there. I smelled food even before I opened my eyes, and saw that a food tray sat on a swivel table next to my bed. My throat was not quite as sore as it had been. In a gravely voice, I announced I was hungry. As I tried to sit up, Sean appeared at the door with Micah beside him.

Micah greeted me. "It's always a good sign when a patient's appetite returns."

I looked around the room and motioned to Eddie that I wanted to sit in the armchair next to the bed. Jostling with the IV pole and the tubes that ran from the pole's hooks to my wrist and the back of my hand, Eddie helped me out of bed and into the chair. He lowered the over-bed table and arranged my tray for me. As I drained the container of its weak chicken broth, I looked over to Micah. "Based on what I saw in that garage, I would say your diagnosis was accurate: Francis was indeed Anthony, and Anthony was Francis."

Eddie looked from me to Micah. "What? You two need to tell me everything you know, or even think you know."

I looked to Eddie and nodded at Micah. "When I met with Dr. Feldman … was that yesterday or two days ago?" Not waiting for an answer, I continued. "Dr. Feldman speculated that Francis was suffering from dissociative identity disorder—the existence of two or more distinct personalities sharing the same body."

Eddie, puzzled, looked to Micah. "Isn't that something fringe psychiatrists diagnosed on the basis of easily hypnotized patients?"

"It's no longer as misunderstood as it once was. Its source is usually traced to childhood sexual abuse and a general ambivalence in the child's household—the lack of a loving influence. The other night, Detective Vincenti revealed to Tommy that when he was seven years old, he had been raped—violently sodomized—by his father. Without the nurturing influence of a mother, he displaced the memory in order to cope. Francis had to move that memory and other memories of abuse to a separate compartment of his consciousness where they slowly seeped into his subconscious, eventually taking the form of an alter ego."

Sean was confused. "This 'Anthony' we encountered in Frank's garage looked different and spoke differently than Frank."

"As strange as it may seem, it's not unusual for an alter ego to take on differences in speech, affect, and, in some rare instances, even the demeanor of a different gender. During my two sessions with Detective Vincenti, he seemed to speak with a rural twang that almost sounded like a southern accent, and spoke of himself in the third person—that's what started me down the path of considering the identity disorder. Looking back, it may have been that the two identities had begun to unravel."

Now I interrupted. "Think back, gentlemen. There were many occasions when Francis could not account for blocks of time. He experienced blackouts and sometimes he went missing, for which he always seemed to have a hazy recollection. He may have invented credible cover stories for you, but he confided in me that these gaps in his recollection occurred regularly and frightened him. And although he always maintained that he had overcome chronic depression, his bouts of depression were obvious to all of us. All symptoms Dr. Feldman listed for me when he shared his diagnosis."

"During these gaps, his alter ego surfaced and took control," Micah added. "You need to understand that his primary identity, or personality, was, of course, Francis, the man you all admired and worked with. The brilliant detective. His alter ego was the person who identified himself as 'Anthony' to Tommy and Sean in the garage. Francis transferred his painful memories so deeply into his alter ego that he had no idea his alter ego even existed. Most likely, his alter ego assumed the persona of this Tony fellow, his childhood protector, thus the name 'Anthony'."

"I've been thinking about his speech patterns," I said. "His alter ego probably assimilated the rural twang of his uncle and aunt—farmers in western Illinois. People he hadn't seen in years, but who represented some modicum of safety and protection."

"Doctor," Eddie interjected, "Sean tells me that this 'Anthony' knew of Frank. He spoke of keeping him safe, talked about how everyone treated Frank or took advantage of him. So Anthony knew about Frank, but not the other way around?"

Micah nodded. "Correct. Francis's subconscious created Anthony in the first place as a repository for the painful memories. Anthony existed because Francis needed him, but Francis didn't need or want to know of Anthony's existence. Later, Anthony acted on the memories he inherited from Francis to protect him from further attacks."

"And to seek revenge," I added.

Micah continued. "Yes, and the occurrence of certain disturbing episodes in his daily life triggered the reappearance of Anthony. For example, Tommy tells me that the killing of Monsignor Anderson closely followed the death of Francis's father. Dealing with his abuser's death is the kind of incident that could have given rise to voices or hallucinations that compelled Anthony to kill. There were likely other traumas—some significant, others of little consequence for a normal person—that triggered his other kills."

"The hole in Francis's soul created by his father's abuse might have been healed by a loving and caring influence," I said. "But he never had that. Look, Francis had only three women in his life. The mother he never knew; Aunt Anna, his surrogate mother who walked out on him when he was fifteen; and Beth, whose love for him was shallow and who married Francis to spite her mother. I'm sure that if you go back and create a timeline of the killings, they probably correspond to blow-ups he had with Beth. Consider this: Beth issued an ultimatum about his job Thanksgiving morning—two days later you found Edwards's body."

Sean exhaled. "Then Frank's alter ego, Anthony, was The Bricklayer?"

"Sadly, yes," I answered. "To seek retribution for Francis's childhood sexual assaults, Anthony undertook a mission to punish and kill Francis's father—over and over again. His victims were 'father surrogates', for lack of a better term. If you study each one, you'll see that they resemble Francis's father, both physically and by temperament. Each of Anthony's kills was for Francis—'for him', the message in blood on each victim's chest."

Sean looked over at me. "And you knew all this when we went to his garage. That's why you weren't surprised at what we found?"

"More or less. I didn't brief you because I had trouble believing it, and I hoped it wasn't true. I was wrong. I should have told you. I should have."

The room went quiet, broken by Micah's final piece of analysis. "Francis was a good cop, a detective intent on apprehending The Bricklayer. He was chasing himself—but never knew it."

Sean shot a quick glance over at Eddie.

"What? What aren't you telling me?"

Eddie gave Sean a nod. "Go ahead."

"Foster, after I got you in the ambulance and you were on your way here, I cleared the immediate scene in the garage, and I found the freezer that this 'Anthony' person used to store the body parts he took from his victims."

Sean looked back at Eddie, obviously holding back.

I snapped at him. "Continue, Detective!"

"When I opened the freezer, I found plastic bags containing severed hands."

"His trophies." I leaned my head back and drew in a breath, waiting.

Sean hesitated.

I looked up at him.

"There were eleven of them."

Sunday Morning, May 31

I wanted to go home. I wanted to sleep in my own bed again. Around nine o'clock Saturday night, the charge night nurse chased Micah, Eddie, and Sean out of my room. Eddie protested, but Micah confirmed the nurse's admonition that I had enough activity for the day. I must have been exhausted because I couldn't recall how I got from the reclining armchair to my bed or when I fell asleep. It was the first good night's sleep since Francis had shown up at my door after the shooting of Tony Protettore. In the morning when I rolled over and opened my eyes, I thought I was in the middle of a bad dream.

"Well, you old son of a bitch, you're still alive. I'm disappointed."

Beth sat in the guest chair next to my bed having made herself at home and apparently waiting anxiously for me to wake.

I struggled to sit up. "What do you want, Beth?" I had no intention of being polite. She had tormented Francis. I wasn't about to let her torment me.

"When I heard the news of the shooting I had expected—no, I had hoped—to see you in the morgue, white as a sheet, all cut open, blood drained and lying next to your beloved Francis."

"You're not welcome here, Beth."

Beth was usually impeccably dressed and perfectly groomed. Not today. She probably did no more than run a comb through her hair; her expensive pantsuit looked like she had slept in it; and she wore no makeup. I studied her face. Her eyes were bloodshot, pupils dilated, and her nostrils were red and inflamed. Cocaine.

"You're not well, Beth." My emergency call button was on the TV remote under my pillow. I slowly reached behind me as I talked and squeezed the button.

"You know, Foster, you did everything you could to turn Frank against me. I always thought that sooner or later, he'd come to his senses and go back to school—become a lawyer or something more than just a cop. But, you didn't let him, did you? You kept pulling him back into your world. You convinced him—"

"No, Beth. Your marriage was doomed the moment you said 'I do.' He thought you loved him. I tried to tell him that you only loved what he might become and—"

"Oh, that's right. The high and mighty Thomas Aquinas Foster disapproved of the marriage, or was it just me you disapproved of?"

"Is this something you really want to talk about right now?"

"I'll talk about whatever I damn well please. Right now it's you and Frank." She stood and began pacing at the foot of my bed, head hung low and looking only at the floor. "You always thought I had an ulterior motive in marrying Frank. Oh yeah, Frank told me! *She married you to get even with her bitch of a mother.* Regular Sigmund fucking Freud, aren't you? Must've been the only time Frank didn't take your advice."

"Beth, you need help. The cocaine is only making it worse." I depressed the call button several more times like someone who thinks an elevator car will come sooner if you keep pressing the button.

"I once told Frank that I wished the damn Bricklayer would cut off his dick. Now, Commander Dunbar tells me that Frank was actually The Bricklayer, some theoretical psychiatric gibberish. Doesn't really matter now, but isn't that a kick in the head! Turns out I was wishing that he'd cut off his own dick. Now that's irony, Thomas Aquinas Foster, that's irony."

She abruptly stopped pacing and turned to face me. "I should have cut it off. It never did me any good."

"Beth, listen to me. Francis was sick—a product of his father's sexual abuse. He couldn't have helped himself even if he wanted."

"Sick? Bullshit! I had my own problems when I was a kid, and I turned out—" She began pacing again without finishing the statement she knew wasn't true.

"You're not making any sense."

"Sense? I lived with a homicidal monster all that time. I slept with him, ate meals with him, and—"

The floor nurse finally arrived. "Your door shouldn't be closed Mr. Foster. You buzzed and . . ." She looked over to Beth. "Ma'am, you're not suppose to be here now. Visiting hours don't start until one o'clock."

"She's not a visitor. She's an intruder."

The nurse's affable demeanor changed immediately. She took two steps toward Beth. "You'll have to leave. You'll have to leave now."

"Go to hell."

"Very well." The nurse walked over to the side of bed, picked up the phone, and punched a series of numbers. "I'll call security and have you physically removed—if that's what you want."

She glared at the nurse. "Don't bother. I've said what I came to say." Looking back at me, she added, "I hope you burn in hell!"

She didn't know it, but I had already earned my place in hell several times over.

With that, Beth turned on her heels and headed out of the room without saying another word. But she was right. My warning about the perils of marrying her was the only piece of advice Francis failed to heed.

Back Home

While I was still hospitalized, Beth claimed Francis's body. She had gone from a bitter petitioner in a divorce proceeding to a vindictive widow. She instructed the funeral director to conduct a direct burial— no visitation, no funeral, and no graveside service; and, as a final act of contempt, she arranged for his remains to be buried next to his father. She had a private viewing of the body. I was told she spent almost a half-hour alone with Francis and then closed the casket herself, as if by doing so she closed the book on a bad business deal.

I was discharged from the hospital after a four-day stay. Eddie Dunbar drove me home and helped me settle back into my basement apartment, where I spent peaceful days, but restless nights regaining my health. During that time, I found it therapeutic to expand my journal notations to prepare this narrative. As summer turned into autumn, I finally learned to be at peace with Francis's fate.

For years I had guarded the family secret of the true ownership of the building on West Fullerton Parkway where I had occupied the basement apartment. Only a few of the family's closest friends knew the entire history of the building. Fewer still knew of the Galt Family Trust Fund, of which I had become the sole beneficiary. In 1994, my father had persuaded her to use trust fund monies to purchase and restore the 100-year-old, three-story brownstone, and he had used his influence to have the building designated a Chicago Landmark by the City Council Commission on Landmarks. It took him more than a year to complete the restoration of the once-celebrated residence of a British aristocrat.

Within a few short weeks after I was released from the hospital, I had no choice but to move my father into a nearby skilled nursing facility. His health had declined rapidly, and I was in no position to be his caregiver. His first-floor apartment had remained unoccupied. Just as autumn began, I invited volunteers from the Margaret Ann Galt Foundation for the Homeless—a charitable foundation my father established to honor my mother—to remove most of the furnishings from my father's spacious three-bedroom apartment, and instructed that they be sold, with the proceeds to be donated to the Foundation's shelters. The same volunteers, at my request, moved my simple furnishings upstairs as I finally felt comfortable taking my father's place.

Sean called on New Year's Day expressing his hope that the new year would be better than the last. He told me that Beth had taken a leave from her firm and had again retreated to Santa Barbara where her brother checked her into a drug rehab center after a cocaine overdose.

Over the months that followed, Sean and Keisha paid frequent visits, initially on a social basis, during which they disclosed that they had been seeing each other. I was not surprised. Even before Francis's death, I had suspected that they had become romantically involved. Sean and I became close and collaborated on a couple of homicide cases, each of which Sean would have solved on his own anyway. I never asked him why he rushed Tony that night behind Wrigley, and we never talked about his shooting Francis. I figured that if he wanted to talk about it, he would tell me. That is a lesson I learned from Francis.

On a bright but cold Saturday afternoon in February, Sean and Keisha visited me and brought along seven-year-old James, Sean's son. James explored the apartment and found, on the nightstand next to my bed, a photograph in a simple black frame. Running from the room with the picture in his hands, he held it up for me to see and asked, "Is this your son, Mr. Foster?"

As I stood, I looked over at Sean and Keisha. They exchanged glances. They both recognized the black and white photograph. They knew too that the small holes in the corners of the picture were from the pushpins that had held it in place on the wall of Francis's cubicle.

"No, James . . ." I paused, looking at the black and white photo, repeating, "No, James." I took the photo from the child's small hands, walked slowly to my bedroom, and closed the door.

EPILOGUE
Thomas Aquinas Foster

A year after the death of Detective Francis Vincenti, Dr. Micah Feldman published a scholarly paper on his diagnosis of Detective Vincenti's dissociative identity disorder, commonly referred to as DID. His paper sparked anew the controversy regarding the disorder. Many psychiatrists continue to question whether the disorder actually exits, notwithstanding that DID is included in the Diagnostic and Statistical Manual of Mental Disorders, Fifth Edition, the reference guide that clinicians and researchers use to diagnose and classify mental disorders. That widely accepted reference manual states, on pages 294-295, in part, as follows:

> Interpersonal physical and sexual abuse is associated with an increased risk of dissociative identity disorder. Prevalence of child abuse and neglect in the United States, Canada and Europe among those with the disorder is about 90 percent.[1]

Dr. Feldman's paper attributed Detective Vincenti's disorder, and the related violence, solely to the developmental influences of early childhood sexual abuse and absence of a nurturing influence in the home. The paper dismissed any biological basis for the disorder although there had been a number of scientific studies employing neuroimaging that had found a connection between DID and certain segments of the

1   American Psychiatric Association: *Diagnostic and Statistical Manual of Mental Disorders*, Fifth Edition, Arlington, VA, American Psychiatric Publishing, 2013.

human brain.

Dr. Feldman's work discounted a 2006 study, reported in *The American Journal of Psychiatry* that same year, that made use of magnetic resonance imaging of the brains of patients diagnosed with DID to measure the volume of the hippocampus, which involves memory, and the amygdala, which deals with rage, to determine the relation between the volume of those two brain structures and the disorder. The study concluded that patients suffering from DID had lower volumes of their hippocampuses and amygdalas.[2]

Dr. Feldman's paper and his controversial contention that there is no biological basis for DID came to the attention of members of the Behavioral Research and Instruction Unit of the FBI, the specialized unit charged with responsibility for developing investigative strategies based on applied behavioral sciences and research on violent and aberrant behavior. On behalf of the FBI, the Justice Department sought a court order to exhume Detective Vincenti's body to examine his brain and extract samples of his DNA. The Court granted Justice's request and entered an exhumation order.

Detective Vincenti's casket was removed from its resting place at St. Joseph Cemetery in River Grove. It was taken to the facilities of the Cook County medical examiner on Harrison Street—the same place where Detective Vincenti had viewed the victims of his alter ego, The Bricklayer. The medical examiner of Cook County and an assistant medical examiner from the FBI were present when Cook County clinical pathology technicians opened the casket. Upon examination by the Cook County M.E., it was determined that the corpse of Detective Francis Angelo Vincenti was missing its right hand and genitals.

---

2   Eric Vermetten, M.D., Ph.D.; Christian Schmal, M.D. "Hippocampal and Amygdalar Volumes in Dissociative Identity Disorder." *The American Journal of Psychiatry*, April, 2006, volume 163, number 4, pp. 630-636

ACKNOWLEDGMENTS

I am very grateful for all those good and generous people who, for over eighteen months, provided support and encouragement, talked things over, read, wrote, offered comments, and stayed up late debating characters and plot. Without them Bricklayer would be just another Word document sitting in my trash begging to be permanently deleted. My heartfelt thanks to: Susan Balmert, Mary Joe Benedetti, Theresa Buchanan, Chris Chappel, Jen Chiaramonte, Mary Jo Coughlin, Sandy Garifo, Philippe Joncas, Mary Kennedy, Mary A. Kompare-Cross, Nancy Konrath, Mary Kay Kluge, Jack Kreismer, Greg Murray, Karen Murray, Alix Perrault, Mary Hutchins Reed, and Ira Rosenberg.

Special thanks to the people of Amphorae Publishing Group: Donna Essner, Kristina Blank Makansi, and Lisa Miller; my agent, Steve Shwartz; and my high school English Teacher, Vincent J. D'Agostino.

And my wife, Cathy, who forced herself to read a genre not of her choosing. And to Amanda Trost Malik, my personal editor and mother of my grandchildren, who taught me more than she knows.

ABOUT THE AUTHOR
TERRY JOHN MALIK

A Chicagoan to the core, Terry John Malik was and raised in the city he loves, son of a Chicago fireman, he now explores the dark back streets and alleys of the city's imagination. Mr. Malik is a graduate of the University of Notre Dame where he majored in English, and an alumnus of Loyola University School of Law. Terry brings to his work a wide variety of life experiences. He taught English for several years in the archdiocese of Chicago School System; designed computer systems for an international accounting firm; worked with distressed borrowers as a banker for the largest bank in Chicago; practiced law for twenty-eight years appearing in federal courts across the nation; became the president of a financially troubled high school; administered a foundation that provided scholarship funds for disadvantaged inner city girls; and created websites for local merchants and non-profits. Throughout his many careers, he has continued to hone his writing skills and never lost his passion for a story well told.

Prior to *The Bricklayer of Albany Park*, Terry hadn't written a word of fiction, although some federal judges mistakenly claimed he did. Terry now has two other thrillers in the works, weaving stories of killers and cops while sitting on a beach on Sanibel Island.

CPSIA information can be obtained
at www.ICGtesting.com
Printed in the USA
LVOW03s1615090817
544372LV00001B/1/P

9 781943 075348